'[An] author completely at h...

The S...

'Nick Brown has the craft of storytell...
The Siege is a fast-paced and s...
Russell Whitfield, author of ...

'*The Imperial Banner* is Roman adventure at its ...
brutal action leavened by a cynical brand of military humour,
history, mystery, romance and an almost tangible sense of
cohesion and camaraderie amongst Cassius and his cohorts.
It's a formula that works well in Brown's capable hands . . .'
Lancaster Evening Post

'If you love Scarrow, adore Iggulden and of course admire
Scott, then make sure you add Brown to your list. Great
stuff.' *Falcata Times*

'Brown has given this Roman military/adventure story a great
twist in having Cassius hail from the secret service ranks . . .
The Siege is also a character study and offers a rare glimpse
into 3rd century Rome and her occupation of Syria.'
Historical Novels Review

'[Nick Brown's] writing is always top-notch, his plots seam-
less and his narrative excellent . . . [*The Black Stone* has]
well-written and plotted and thoroughly realistic character
progression . . . Go get this series and read them through. You
will not be disappointed.'
S.I.A Turney, author of the *Marius' Mules* series

NICK BROWN

Agent of Rome
The Emperor's Silver

HODDER

First published in Great Britain in 2015 by Hodder & Stoughton
An Hachette UK company

First published in paperback in 2016

1

A CIP catalogue record for this title is available from the British Library

ISBN 978 1 444 77916 5

Typeset in Plantin Light by Palimpsest Book Production Limited,
Falkirk, Stirlingshire

Printed and bound by CPI Group (UK) Ltd, Croydon, CR0 4YY

Hodder & Stoughton policy is to use papers that are natural, renewable
and recyclable products and made from wood grown in sustainable forests.
The logging and manufacturing processes are expected to conform to the
environmental regulations of the country of origin.

Hodder & Stoughton Ltd
Carmelite House
50 Victoria Embankment
London EC4Y 0DZ

www.hodder.co.uk

For Joff, Emma and Rufus

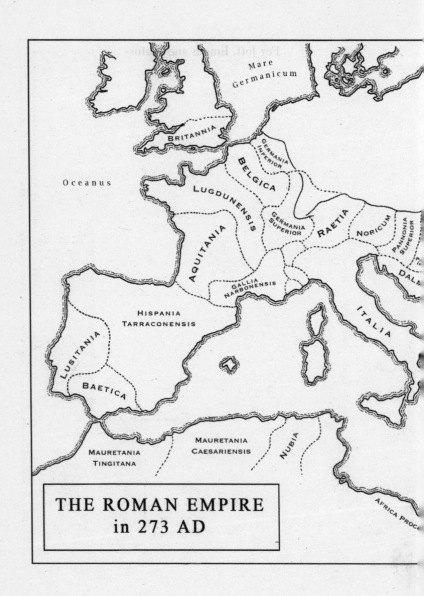

THE ROMAN EMPIRE
in 273 AD

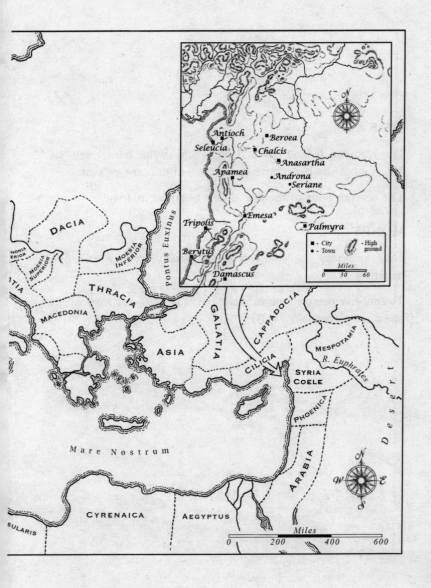

TIME

The Romans divided day and night into twelve hours each, so the length of an hour varied according to the time of year.

The seventh hour of the day always began at midday.

MONEY

Four sesterces (a coin made of brass) were worth one denarius.

Twenty-five denarii (a coin made partially of silver) were worth one aureus (partially gold).

Bostra, capital of the Roman province of Arabia. July, AD 273

Though he had been saying prayers for much of the last three hours, Simo whispered another one as he strode away from the church-house. Bostra was a comparatively safe city but the fourth hour of night had passed and he knew from recent experience to be careful.

It had been after the second of his meetings with Elder Maluch that the two thieves had sprung from the shadows, spitting threats in barely comprehensible Latin. Despite his fear, Simo had employed a trick suggested by his master: he took out a silver denarius, held it up for them to see, then flung it away. The thieves fought over the coin as he made his escape.

The memory quickened his pace as he reached Theatre Street and turned left towards the Via Petra. A pair of watchmen appeared, one holding a lantern.

Simo spoke loudly to avoid suspicion. 'Greetings to you.'

'Who goes there?'

'Simo, attendant to Officer Cassius Corbulo of the Imperial Army – on my master's business.' He held up his arms to show that he carried no weapons.

'On you go.' The watchman waved him past and led his compatriot away, imploring him to continue some story.

Simo picked an angular stone out of his right sandal then moved off. He didn't like to lie but the truth might easily provoke an unpleasant reaction. There were several hundred Christians in Bostra but the watchmen were often ex-soldiers, most of whom took a dim view of those who refused to worship the Emperor and the Roman gods.

As he glanced at the lights within the townhouses on either side of him, the night's prayers echoed through his head. The invocations concerned sin and temptation, and though Simo had recited them without error, Elder Maluch admonished him for not investing the words with sufficient weight and passion. Simo hoped he hadn't disappointed him; Maluch was an excellent teacher and it was good of him to make time at so late an hour. It had taken Simo several weeks to persuade Master Cassius to allow him to resume instruction and he hoped the lessons would continue.

Upon reaching the broad, colonnaded Via Petra, the Gaul jogged straight across to avoid three fast-moving horse-drawn carts. Once under the portico, he heard a roar of laughter from up ahead. He slowed, and saw half a dozen legionaries pass under a lamp. Several were weaving unsteadily and two had mugs in their hands.

Simo padded left and hid behind a column. If troubled by the soldiers he could always invoke his master's name again but it was better to avoid an encounter altogether. To his relief, the legionaries complained about the darkness and moved on to the moonlit street. One of them yelled a curse at the cart drivers but was silenced by a superior with a rather more refined voice.

Simo pressed on, thinking of his master. Cassius had decided that Simo had let him down during their last assignment and only kept him on after the intervention of Indavara – his body-guard and Simo's friend. Many times over the last few weeks the slave had thanked the Lord that he hadn't been sold. His relationship with his owner was improving but it was not what it used to be; Master Cassius rarely confided in him these days and was often sharp, though he had struck him only the once.

Any mention of sin brought him to mind. The young officer was drinking more than ever and now spent even more time in taverns and brothels. Cassius was resilient but he had been through a lot for a man of only twenty-three years. Simo knew his master wouldn't be truly happy until he finally escaped the army; he just hoped Cassius would get back on an even keel after the trials of recent months.

He turned left on to the Via Cappadocia. On the other side of the road was Bostra's largest sanctuary, where some nocturnal revellers were singing a local folk tune. Simo understood only a little Nabatean but it seemed like a happy song. Now back on familiar territory, he began to relax. The villa was at the far end of the street, just yards from the arched entrance to the city's fortress. As well as housing much of the Third Cyrenaican – Arabia's only standing legion – it now also accommodated the vanguard of the Emperor's army. Having put down the Palmyrans for the second time in as many years, Aurelian was journeying south to deal with a revolt in Egypt. He would pass through Bostra.

Simo and Elder Maluch had also spoken of war. They agreed that it often seemed as if the Empire was obsessed by violence and suffering and death. When there was no enemy to take on, the Romans killed animals for sacrifice and men for sport. Though he hadn't mentioned it to Maluch, Simo knew his master did not approve of the contests. He seemed to fear and detest violence almost as much as Simo, and fighting did not come naturally to him.

But during the last operation he had killed a man. Simo had refused to join in the violence and Master Cassius hated him for it. Simo suspected guilt was the real cause of his disquiet. The young Roman had never wanted this life for himself; he was a peaceful, intelligent man. Simo could not imagine what it must be like to have taken the life of another. He would rather die.

Nearing the villa, he spied the sentries at the fortress gate. Among the thousands of men sleeping in the buildings behind them was one whose presence always caused Simo concern. Officer Abascantius was Master Cassius's immediate superior in the Imperial Security Service and had a habit of dispatching the three of them on perilous assignments. The only one ever excited by such a prospect was Indavara, who seemed thoroughly bored by the two months of relative calm since they'd returned from the Arabian desert.

But from what Simo had gathered, Abascantius was simply

in Bostra to make arrangements for the Emperor; and Master Cassius was being rewarded for his recent successes with an extended period of administrative work. Simo longed for such stability; he was approaching his thirty-third year and wanted to be an elder himself by the time he was forty. If he continued to serve well, he felt sure he would be granted his freedom when Cassius's time in the army ended. The Gaul believed the Lord would give him this; surely he wanted him to be free to spread the word.

There was not a single light within the houses at the bottom of the Via Cappadocia. With a last glance at the fortress, Simo turned left down the alley that ran alongside the villa. He had a key for the front door but there was less chance of waking Cassius or Indavara if he came in through the kitchen. The bodyguard seldom stayed up late and his master had decided on an early night because of a morning meeting with Abascantius.

The humid summer air and his swift pace had left Simo sweating. He sighed with relief as he approached the rear corner of the property; he was glad to be home. He put his hand inside his tunic to retrieve his keys but his fingers never reached them.

He took one more step then froze.

Three dark figures had just scuttled across the street at the back of the villa. As they disappeared behind the rear wall, Simo took his hand from his tunic and walked carefully up to the corner. He could hear the men whispering to each other but he couldn't be sure of the language.

He peered around the corner in time to see one of the men spring upward. Grunting as he gripped the top of the wall, he then pulled himself on to it. The next man was given a leg up and, once he had joined his compatriot, they both reached down to help the third man.

Simo withdrew, his throat dry with fear.

The rear door is secure. I locked it myself before I left. The bedroom windows face the back but they're too small to fit through. But the kitchen window is big enough – and the shutters have been left open since the hot weather came.

They can get in. Whoever they are, they can get in.

4

Simo looked back around the corner. Only one man was still visible atop the wall. Then he too disappeared. They hadn't even tried the door to the yard; they must have known it was always locked.

Open it? No, they'll hear me.

Go round to the front? No time.

There was only one thing he could do.

■8►

Cassius Quintius Corbulo put the oil lamp down on the table and stared at the jug of wine. He was trying to cut down, especially since Abascantius had arrived. Three unwatered mugs a day was supposed to be his limit. This would be his fourth. He didn't want to break the new rule but he just couldn't sleep.

He was surprised Simo hadn't heard him get up. Perhaps the attendant was still at the church-house, doing whatever he did with his fellow believers.

Cassius picked up the jug.

'Indavara! Master Cassius!'

'Simo?' Having spilled the wine, Cassius put down the jug and walked around the table to the window.

'Wake up! There are men here.'

Definitely Simo, but what—

'At the back of the house. Wake up!'

'What—'

Cassius heard hissing voices, then feet scuffing the ground.

A man clad in a dark, hooded tunic vaulted through the kitchen window, shattering the amphora he landed on. Before Cassius could even move, a second man came through. He landed cleanly, hood dropping from his head. Cassius could see enough of his eyes to know he had spotted him.

'Indavara!'

Unarmed and wearing only his sleeping tunic, Cassius turned and ran. His left foot caught a chair leg. He lost his balance and came down on his knees, sliding on the smooth tiles. Hauling himself up, he half expected a blade to sink into his neck. He

5

was almost through the kitchen doorway when scrabbling fingers grabbed the back of his tunic. He tried to pull free but the hand swung him to the right.

Cassius bounced off the side of the doorway and spun into the atrium. Tripping over his own feet he landed on his back in the ghostly pale blue rectangle below the skylight.

The intruder came through the doorway. Because of his black clothing, his head appeared disembodied and the long wooden club seemed to be floating in the air. He lifted it with both hands, ready to swing down.

A fast-moving shape appeared from Cassius's right. Something cracked as the shape hit the intruder, catapulting him across the atrium and into a wall.

'Uff!'

The shape shook itself then straightened up. Cassius found himself looking at Indavara's broad, naked backside; the body-guard's bulky frame seemed white under the moonlight.

'How many?'

'Two at least.' Cassius scrambled to his feet and backed towards the window that faced on to the Via Cappadocia. Somewhere near there was a candelabra. He was relieved but not surprised to see Indavara had his dagger, which he slept with.

The second intruder leapt into the light, swinging his club at the bodyguard. Indavara retreated; there wasn't a lot he could do with the little knife.

Cassius reached the wall. The window shutters were closed so there was hardly any light coming through but he found the candelabra. He grabbed the iron shaft with both hands.

A third man ran under the skylight and cut off their path to the other rooms.

'Here.' Cassius put the candelabra in front of Indavara so he wouldn't have to turn. The bodyguard clamped the knife between his teeth and grabbed the five foot length of metal. Cassius had struggled to lift it but Indavara wielded it as easily as a sword.

From outside came a shout; Simo calling to the sentries for help.

The first man was back on his feet. He ordered the others forward in Greek.

As the pair prepared to strike, Indavara swung. He narrowly missed the head of the man to his left but struck the second warrior's club, knocking it out of his hands. Before they could counter, Indavara heaved the candelabra at them. It caught both men by surprise and sent them tottering back into the light.

Cassius didn't see the bodyguard take the blade from his mouth but he saw him dart forward and stab the closest man in the chest. The intruder gasped as he went down. The second warrior tripped over him but managed to roll away as the third man took up the attack.

He jabbed his club at Indavara and stepped over his dying compatriot, who was clawing at his wound, mouth fixed in a silent scream.

Indavara threw the knife into the intruder's face. It was not a throwing blade and bounced off his brow, but the moment's distraction was all the bodyguard needed. He leaped forward and launched his right foot straight into his foe's groin, connecting with a heavy slap. As the intruder crumpled, the man who had tripped flew back into the fray.

He drove an elbow at Indavara's face, striking his jaw with a shuddering crack. Cassius thought the prodigious blow might fell even the bodyguard. Though dazed, Indavara somehow stayed upright, grabbing his foe's tunic and holding him so he at least knew where he was. They struggled on for a moment, then stumbled over the candelabra and fell in a heap below the skylight.

Cassius circled them, peering at the ground, looking for a club or Indavara's knife.

Just as the naked bodyguard got one brawny arm around his foe's neck, his second victim found enough strength to give him some of his own treatment: he scrambled across the floor and punched Indavara's unprotected groin.

Cassius had never heard him shriek before.

The sheer shock of it propelled him into action. He grabbed the club he had just located and heaved it down at the intruder, catching him between the shoulder blades. Breath flew out of the man as he pitched forward on to Indavara's legs.

The bodyguard was panting like a dog, spitting indecipherable curses. His arm was tight under his victim's chin. Cassius almost felt pity for the poor bastard as his eyes bulged and his head spasmed.

'Yaaaaaahhhhh!'

The neck bones crunched like twigs underfoot. Indavara head-butted him for good measure then pushed the broken body away. Without a moment's hesitation, he kicked the last man alive off his legs, then crawled after him. He pulled the intruder's hood off and gripped the back of his head, hair springing up between his fingers.

'No, wait,' said Cassius. 'We need—'

Indavara drove the head down into the tiles. The noise of the skull cracking made Cassius gag. He staggered backwards and reached for the wall. Holding himself up, he stupidly looked back and saw dark blood seeping from under the crushed head. Cassius put a hand to his mouth but somehow stopped himself vomiting.

The key turned in the door. Lamplight flickered across the room as half a dozen legionaries piled in. They stood over Indavara, who was lying on his back, top half in the light, sucking in breath.

'It's all right,' said Cassius. 'We're all right.'

'Speak for yourself,' said Indavara.

One of the soldiers cursed as he slipped in a pool of blood.

'Excuse me.' Simo pushed his way through.

Cassius pointed at the bodyguard.

Simo knelt beside him and examined his damaged jaw.

'Forget that,' said Indavara. He nodded at his groin. 'Check there.'

One of the legionaries came forward: Leddicus, a friendly veteran who Cassius knew quite well. The soldier pulled back all the assailants' hoods and examined their various wounds. Cassius had recovered sufficiently to note that all three were between twenty-five and thirty years of age and wearing similarly dark clothing. Judging by their features, they could have been from anywhere from Thrace to Arabia.

'All dead,' said Leddicus.

'See what they have on them, would you?'

Indavara was on his side, eyes screwed shut. 'Sweet Fortuna, please help me. Simo?'

'It's . . . well, it's very red. But everything's where it should be.'

Cassius put a hand on the bodyguard's shoulder. 'Thank you. A shame you had to kill them, but thank you.'

'If that whoreson's done any permanent damage I'll kill him again.'

Simo took off his cloak and covered Indavara. 'I'll get you some wine.'

'Strongest we have. By the gods it hurts.'

Leddicus walked over to Cassius. He had searched the assailants and was holding several lengths of rope, a hood and a gag. Cassius realised why the trio had been armed with clubs instead of swords.

'Clear what they were here for, sir. Any idea who might want to capture you?'

'No.' Cassius stared down at the rope. 'Or why.'

I

'You must be Corbulo.'

Cassius belatedly realised there was a man sitting at a desk on the other side of the office. He was partially obscured by a stack of wooden chests.

'Indeed.' When he went to greet him, Cassius noted the narrow purple stripe running from the shoulder of his tunic to the waist. 'Sir.'

The tribune didn't get up but they shook forearms.

'Vitalian, Fifteenth Legion. And you're Abascantius's man.'

'Yes,' said Cassius, though he didn't much care for the description. 'Do you know where he is?'

'Getting some lunch, I believe.'

The raised eyebrow was enough; it was in neither of their interests to say much more about the infamous agent known throughout the East as 'Pitface'.

Vitalian was about Cassius's age, possibly a bit older; a slender, thoughtful-looking fellow who was already losing his hair.

'The Fifteenth,' said Cassius, who'd been taught the dispositions of Rome's legions by his father before his sixth birthday. 'Cappadocia. Did you come all that way with the Emperor?'

Vitalian was sitting on a stool, back against the wall. 'Every mile.'

'How long before the grand army arrives?'

'Less than a week, they reckon.' Vitalian nodded down at the papers in front of him. 'Trying to rustle up some extra horses from the local estates – we're running very low. Grain too.' He grinned. 'Isn't that supposed to be your job?'

Agents of the Imperial Security Service were commonly known as 'grain men' because the original function of the organisation had been to find provisions for the legions. Being so widely spread and well informed about the provinces, the Service had gradually transformed itself into an intelligence-gathering organisation and expanded the repertoire of missions it carried out for Empire and Emperor. As Cassius had discovered in the last year, they were seldom of the safe variety.

'I wish. Don't suppose you'd like to swap posts?'

'No thank you,' said Vitalian. 'I heard about how you only just got out of that scrape with the tribesmen down south.'

'It will all have been for nothing if a decision isn't reached soon.'

'The negotiations, you mean?'

'The Tanukh – that's the tribesmen – have come to the table but they're not getting what they want. I would hate for it all to—'

'Ah, Corbulo, there you are.' Abascantius hurried in with a well-stocked plate in one hand and a scroll in the other. He dumped both on his desk by the window, seemingly unconcerned by the half-dozen grapes that rolled on to the floor.

He walked over to Cassius and gripped his shoulder. 'Are you all right, then, lad?'

'I was . . . rather shaken last night, sir, but I'm fine now.'

'Indavara?'

'He took a blow on the jaw and another one to . . . to a more sensitive area.'

'Ah, well, I'm sure his sausage and beans are as tough as the rest of him.' Abascantius looked at Vitalian. 'Give us half an hour, would you, Tribune?'

'Very well.' Vitalian stood and picked up the pile of papers.

'Plenty of grub in the kitchen,' added Abascantius. 'You need feeding up, after all.'

Vitalian frowned at this but nodded politely to Cassius as he left.

'Officer.'

'Tribune.'

Abascantius kicked the door shut behind him and returned to his desk. 'Cannot believe I have to share an office. And there's some other snivelling wretch arriving tomorrow. Sit down, Corbulo.'

There was no seat on the opposite side of Abascantius's desk and the only one Cassius could find was Vitalian's. By the time he'd sat down on the stool, the agent had unrolled the scroll and spread it across the desk. It was a very new-looking map and – even examining it upside down – Cassius could see that it showed the south-east corner of the Empire, including Arabia and Egypt.

'You'll be staying with the grand army, sir?'

'Looks like it.' Abascantius studied the map. 'The route is yet to be finalised and trying to get the general staff to agree is like trying to balance small marbles on a big marble.'

When he took his hands off, the scroll rolled itself up. 'Anyway, that can wait.' The agent lowered his heavy frame on to a chair nothing like big enough for him. 'I'm more concerned with what happened last night.'

Cassius was about to suggest that he be relocated as swiftly as possible but Abascantius hadn't finished.

'This morning I checked the bodies and their gear as you requested. I agree that there's nothing there to help us, presumably as intended. Did you say they spoke Greek?'

'Yes, sir. Which doesn't tell us much. No discernible accent either.'

'So, any ideas?'

'Dozens, sir. They kept me awake all night. That and the atrium. Despite Simo's best efforts it still smells of blood.'

Abascantius grabbed the plate, then picked a corner off a wedge of cheese and popped it in his mouth. 'Can't be because of the business with the Persian flag, or that rogue centurion you took care of in Africa: I can't see who would be left alive to bother with you, and even if there were they'd want you dead, not captured.' He noted Cassius's expression. 'You don't agree?'

'If it was someone seeking revenge, they might have wanted to hurt me . . . torture me.'

'Possible, I suppose, but surely it's more likely to be connected to this Tanukh business.'

'Yes, sir. Given the timing, that is the logical conclusion.'

'Specifically?' Abascantius scratched a nasty-looking rash on his forearm then picked up a roll.

'I see two alternatives, sir. The person behind this could be someone left over from Ilaha's forces. Perhaps even the German mercenary or Ethnarch Kalderon – seeking revenge for my role in foiling their plans. Or it could be some faction within the Tanukh – I promised them a permanent deal on the import tax and now the talks have stalled. I presented myself as an envoy of Rome. I gave my word.'

Abascantius deployed a cynical look. 'You said what you needed to at the time – to get yourself out of there and stop that deluded charlatan Ilaha. The Tanukh are realists. They know as well as we do that they're not going to revolt. Especially with the Emperor and four legions coming their way.'

'Sir, once order has been restored in Egypt the Emperor will return to Rome and the legions will leave. This province and Governor Calvinus will still be stuck with the same old problems. Men gave their lives to create this opportunity. There is a chance for a real solution, one that will—'

Abascantius – now devouring the roll – held up a hand. 'Not your problem, young man. Especially as you're not going to be around much longer. I'm sure you concur that it's best to get you away from here for the time being.'

Cassius's commitment to a peaceful Arabia did not extend to risking his life again. 'Absolutely, sir.'

'And I can't think of a more secure posting than with the grand army.'

Cassius's stomach quivered. 'Sir?'

Abascantius pointed at the map. 'I have a couple of men in Egypt already but another intelligence officer wouldn't go amiss.'

Cassius folded his hands across his stomach but it didn't reduce the quivering. 'Egypt?'

The revolt there had already claimed the lives of hundreds of legionaries. Taking on the rebellious tribes and their charismatic leader Firmus would be a far bloodier affair than cleaning up the last death throes of resistance in Palmyra. Cassius knew he might well be safe there from whoever had tried to capture him, but it wasn't exactly what he'd had in mind.

'You've done your share of investigative work,' said Abascantius. 'It would be good for you to get some varied experience.'

'But that would be in the field, sir. You promised me six months sitting behind a desk.'

Abascantius frowned. 'Sitting? As in a sitting duck? With the army you'll be on the move. Safe.'

'With respect, sir, I've heard that before.'

The door flew open and Vitalian burst in.

'He's here,' said the tribune, hurrying over to his desk.

'Who's here?' snapped Abascantius.

'The marshal.'

'What? He wasn't due until tomorrow.'

'He's here. Just coming through the gate, apparently.' Vitalian took his sword belt off a hook and examined it.

'Ah, shit.' Abascantius got up so quickly that he kneed the desk, tipping his plate on to the floor.

'Double shit.' The agent marched over to another row of hooks where his scarlet cloak and black-crested helmet hung.

Cassius had put his own helmet on a barrel by the door. Fortunately Simo polished it every few days but he checked it anyway; his sword belt, scarlet tunic and boots too.

'Corbulo.' Abascantius waved him over and spoke in a low voice. 'The marshal knows your name – because of the black stone. He might talk to you. If he does, answer directly. But do not say any more than you need to – about the Service, or about me. Marcellinus is no enemy of ours but he likes to stick his nose in, sometimes where it's not needed or wanted. Keep it simple, understood?'

'Understood.'

The officers hastily gathered outside the headquarters. A legionary dispatched by Chief Nerva returned at a run. 'Coming across the parade ground now, sir.'

'Everyone get in line,' ordered Nerva. As chief centurion of the fortress, the portly veteran was currently the senior officer in Bostra. He stood in front of the entrance, below the two flags hanging limply in the enervating heat. One was red and bore the familiar pair of eagles and the SPQR legend. Until a few minutes earlier, the other had been the emblem of the third Cyrenaican (a lion), but after a frantic search a clerk had located the personal standard of Marshal Gaius Marcellinus, Protector of the East and one of Aurelian's most trusted men.

Lined up to Chief Nerva's right were five centurions, four tribunes (including Vitalian) and assorted junior officers, with Cassius and Abascantius stuck on the end. Cassius reckoned the arrangement offered a good metaphor for the position of the Service – out on a limb and well away from those who saw themselves as real soldiers. In fact, they were only there because it had taken Abascantius so long to brush all the dirt off his cloak.

The agent offered Cassius his canteen.

'No thank you.' Though they were standing in the full glare of the midday Arabian sun, Cassius wasn't about to share drinking equipment with his unhygienic superior. He checked his helmet was straight then put his arms by his side, trying to ignore the chilly streams of sweat running down his flanks.

They heard the horses coming along the avenue and watched the marshal lead the way around the hospital building and towards them. His entourage was small: eight Praetorian Guardsmen and a dozen clerks and assistants. The Praetorians carried large rectangular shields, each decorated with three white scorpions, the image assigned to the Guard upon its formation under Tiberius.

The marshal wore a lustrous purple cloak – triple dyed by the looks of it – and, as he rode closer, Cassius noted the same strong, compact frame he'd observed the previous year when Marcellinus had overseen the return of the Persian Banner. His fair hair was cropped short, his skin a deep brown. The golden muscle cuirass looked spectacular but his physique needed little embellishment; the bulky limbs and solid neck showed him to be every inch a military man. Marcellinus held up a hand, halting the Praetorians and the others. He let his horse take a few more steps until he was level with the flags, then stopped.

A servant ran up with the box.

'Keep it, boy,' said the marshal, his voice an intimidating rumble. 'I'm short but I'm not that short.'

The lad retreated as Marcellinus dropped to the ground. The men assembled in front of him had been saluting ever since he'd appeared.

'At ease, all of you.' He stretched out his arms and yawned, then shook forearms with Nerva. 'Sorry if I caught you out, Chief. Entirely unintentional, I assure you. An unexpectedly swift trip – the roads down here are far less busy than in Syria.'

'We are honoured by your presence, Marshal.' Nerva bowed low.

'Everything looks in order. We'll be ready for the Emperor?'

'Absolutely, sir.'

'Good, good. Well, have some lunch put out for me, would you? Some hot water too – bloody blisters are playing up again. All these tours and inspections take their toll.'

Nerva pointed at an elderly servant who bowed and hurried inside.

Marcellinus looked along the line and exchanged some light-hearted banter with a couple of the centurions. His gaze eventually reached Abascantius. 'And there's Aulus – still wearing his black crest. Thinks it makes him mysterious, you know.'

Nerva and the centurions chuckled.

'How are you?' asked Marcellinus. 'All this riding hasn't taken much weight off.'

'Unfortunately not, sir,' said Abascantius.

Cassius was surprised by how relaxed the agent sounded.

'And who's that with you there? Not Corbulo, is it?'

Cassius could hardly believe what was happening. The Protector of the East had just spoken his name!

'It is, sir.'

At a nudge from Abascantius, Cassius stepped forward and bowed.

'Ah, I was hoping to meet you, young man. You shall join me inside. You may as well bring Aulus along too.'

With that, the marshal strode between the flagpoles and through the doorway.

Cassius stood there, eyes wide.

'Well, come on, then,' said Abascantius irritably. 'And remember – say no more than you have to.'

There were six of them in the parlour. One was a Praetorian Guardsman; a towering grey-bearded giant who stood in a corner with his hands tucked into his belt, face impassive. Marcellinus was sitting on a chair turned away from the table so that he could dunk his feet into a bowl of water. According to Abascantius, the older, toga-clad man also sitting was named Glycia – the marshal's chief adviser. He seemed tired from the journey and was sipping wine from a glass. There was also a servant, on hand to provide the marshal with whatever he needed from the food and drink laid out on the table. Cassius and Abascantius stood together by the door, helmets under their arms, waiting. They had been called in after the marshal had spoken to Chief Nerva.

'Ah. There are few better feelings in the world than that.' Flexing his toes beneath the water, Marcellinus closed his eyes for a moment. When he opened them, he was looking at Cassius. 'Yours is a name attracting some attention, young man. The Emperor was very angry when he heard of the theft of the black stone. To have it returned to its rightful place with such speed was a great relief to him. Is it true, this tale of you raising your spearhead among a crowd of rebels and exposing this Ilaha character?'

'It is, sir,' said Cassius, trying to sound magnanimous. 'Though there were allies as well as enemies within that crowd. We received a good deal of help from some of the local tribesmen.'

'Troublesome lot, these nomads. Another breed, really. And what about this bodyguard of yours? This ex-gladiator? Apparently he played his part too. I'm told he's quite a specimen. Is he here?'

'He is recovering, sir,' said Cassius. 'There was an . . . incident last night.'

Abascantius took up the tale. 'Three intruders attacked Corbulo in his home. He and the bodyguard fought them off but all three were killed and we've little to go on.'

'By Mars. You all right, Corbulo?'

'Yes, sir. Thank you.'

Marcellinus waved a hand at them. 'Put your helmets down you two – parade's over.'

Abascantius and Cassius carefully placed them on a nearby chair.

'Well, Aulus, what are we going to do about this? We can't have valued officers fearing for their lives in their own homes. Presumably you're investigating?'

'Of course, sir. But as I mentioned, there's not a great deal of evidence to help us. The attack may be connected to Corbulo's dealings with the Tanukh so it might be advisable to get him out of the province for the moment. I think it would be best for him to accompany the . . .'

Marcellinus wasn't listening. Glycia had leaned across the corner of the table and whispered something to him.

'That's a thought,' said the marshal, before addressing the two agents. 'We have a rather troubling situation developing. It involves counterfeit currency. An alarming number of high-quality fake denarii have turned up across the eastern provinces, particularly Syria. We've always had a problem in the West but the Emperor doesn't want the same thing here and is keen to nip it in the bud. The treasury don't seem to be making much progress – a fresh pair of eyes might be useful. Obviously, you've got a bit about you, Corbulo. How's his investigative work, Aulus?'

'Fair, sir. But to be honest I think he would serve the Emperor best in Egypt. That is where we face the greatest danger, after all.'

Marcellinus flexed his toes again. 'Mmm. I suppose counterfeiting's not really within the Service's remit.'

Taking on fraudsters sounded a lot safer than hunting down rebels in far-away Egypt. Judging by what Marcellinus had said, he evidently wasn't aware of Cassius's involvement in the recovery of the Persian Banner. Cassius decided to take a calculated risk.

'I do enjoy investigative work, sir,' he volunteered. 'One operation last year was particularly satisfying.'

He could already feel Abascantius bristling.

'Go on,' said Marcellinus.

'I'm not sure I should—'

'You shouldn't,' said Abascantius sharply.

Marcellinus looked annoyed. 'Tell me.'

Abascantius walked over to the marshal, bent close to him and whispered. Marcellinus listened keenly and seemed impressed.

On his way back, Abascantius fixed Cassius with an irate glare.

'Well,' said the marshal. 'That was another outstanding piece of work. I had no idea, Corbulo. Aulus, you really must try not to hog all the glory for yourself in future. That settles it.'

Marcellinus turned to Glycia. 'Where would we send Corbulo to get started?'

Cassius didn't dare look at his superior but he was already wondering whether the negative consequences of his gambit might outweigh the positive.

'The imperial mint at Tripolis,' said Glycia. 'That's where the treasury have started the investigation. Not far, is it?'

'About a week away,' replied Abascantius, making a valiant attempt to hide his anger.

'Good,' said Marcellinus. 'Glycia can give you the details later, Corbulo. You should leave right away so I expect you'll want to make some preparations tonight.'

'Yes, sir. Thank you.'

'Right, then, we must discuss Egypt – Aulus, come and have a seat. I've an hour or two before I meet with Governor Calvinus.'

As Abascantius walked over, Cassius took a step towards the marshal; he knew he might never again get such an opportunity in his entire life. 'Sir.'

'What is it?'

'I have found that during such investigations it is most helpful to be armed with letters of reference. Such missives from Master Abascantius, Chief Pulcher and Prefect Venator have served me very well in the past and I wondered . . .'

'Of course. I'll jot something down for you later and send it over.'

Still sitting with his feet in the bowl of water, Marcellinus offered his forearm. Cassius didn't dare look at Abascantius as he shook it. How he wished his father and his family and his friends back home could be here to see such a moment.

'Watch your back, Corbulo,' said Marcellinus. 'An enemy that would dare strike at you here might not give up easily.'

'Yes, sir.'

Abascantius sat down.

'And don't worry about Aulus,' said Marcellinus with a grin. 'I'll make sure he doesn't punish you too harshly for your cheek. On your way.'

'What's up with Simo?' asked Indavara as Cassius walked into his bedroom.

'I just told him we're leaving. A disruption to his studies, I suppose. Gods, it's hot in here – humid too.'

Cassius elected not to mention the smell. He opened the shutters wider and leaned against the wall opposite Indavara's bed. The bodyguard was sitting up with a sheet covering his lower half. On the nearby table was an abacus – his preferred method of amusing himself when every last one of his weapons had been cleaned.

'So where are we off to, then?'

Cassius smiled. 'Tripolis. It's on the Syrian coast. A bit of breeze at last.'

'What's the job?'

'Counterfeiting.'

Indavara scratched his armpit. 'What's that?'

'Fake coins. Someone's making them and the Emperor wants them stopped.'

'Sounds dull.'

'I certainly hope so. If Abascantius had his way we'd be off to bloody Egypt but Marshal Marcellinus himself gave me the job.'

'Marcellinus. Protector of the East. He's a general or something, isn't he?'

'He's one up from a general. The only man who can give him orders is the Emperor. He knew me by name, because of getting the black stone back. You too.'

Indavara sat up. 'Really? Me?'

'Damned impressive character. Certainly told Abascantius what's what.'

Indavara seemed amused by the concept.

'And I managed to get a letter out of him,' added Cassius. 'There won't be many people – soldier or citizen – who'll dare say no to me now.'

He wandered over to the window and looked outside at the empty courtyard. Four guards had been assigned to the villa and he could hear the pair at the rear talking.

He turned round. 'Now – can you travel?'

Indavara let out a long breath and looked down at his groin.

Cassius said, 'How . . . er . . . how is . . . it?'

'It was red, now it's purple.'

'Ouch.'

'Hurts when I walk. Don't fancy sitting on a horse much.'

'What about a cart? We'll probably need one for our gear anyway.'

'That would be better. When are we leaving?'

'The morning. Before Abascantius or Governor Calvinus have a chance of changing the marshal's mind. Actually I'd better get going – lot to organise.'

'Corbulo – last night. You did all right. Better than usual anyway.'

Cassius came closer to the bed. 'Indavara – thank you again. I shudder to think what would have happened without you there.'

'We're lucky Simo was there to give a warning. Someone was looking out for us.'

Cassius noted the two figurines on the little table. One had been thrown to Indavara in the arena; a tiny, poorly made thing of low-quality stone. The other Cassius had bought for him; it was three times the size, copper covered with high-quality silver plate. He knew which one the bodyguard preferred.

'Your Fortuna?'

'Probably.'

'Personally, I have rather more confidence in you than the gods. How many times is that now?'

'I've lost count.' Indavara shrugged. 'Just doing my job, right?'

'Exceptionally well, I would say.'

Seeing Cassius was about to leave, Indavara held up a hand. 'Wait a moment.' He gestured at his groin. 'Simo thinks it's just bruising and it doesn't hurt too much when I piss but . . . well, I couldn't really ask him – you know what he's like about that sort of thing – but, well, how do I know if it's, er . . . you know . . .'

'Functional?'

'Exactly.'

'Well, I wouldn't advise getting a girl in here. I doubt you're ready for that yet. You'll have to try yourself.'

'You mean . . .'

'I don't think we need to spell it out.'

Indavara reached for his groin.

'By the gods, at least let me get out of the room, man.'

'I was just going to scratch it.'

Cassius walked out. 'Have fun.'

'Corbulo, I was just going to scratch it. Corbulo!'

Cassius was so keen to leave that he actually helped Simo pack and by the third hour of night they were just about ready. The morose attendant then departed to arrange the hire of the cart. Before he left, Cassius asked him to light a lamp in every room; despite the four sentries outside, he didn't want to be jumping at shadows all night.

Standing in the kitchen doorway, he stared down at the

rectangle of light where he and Indavara had fought for their lives just hours ago. Simo had scrubbed the tiles for over an hour but a few obstinate smears of blood remained.

Despite all the horrors Cassius had endured in the last three years, this was a different kind of fear. Someone out there wanted to capture him, almost certainly to do him harm. Even though he was leaving this place behind, Cassius knew he would not be able escape the two questions he had discussed with Leddicus in this very spot. *Who? And why?*

Thoughts of the legionary sent him back into the kitchen. The least he could do for the soldiers who would spend their night guarding him was take them some (well-watered) wine. He grabbed a jug and two mugs and made his way out to the rear door. The two men seemed appreciative though he could tell they didn't think much of their duty. To the average legionary, guarding a 'grain man' was not a particularly glorious task. As a long-standing rival of the regular army, the Service did not enjoy an enviable reputation among the ranks.

The legionaries stationed at the front of the villa were more talkative. They and Cassius were discussing the possible booty to be had from the Palmyran and Egyptian campaigns when a large, familiar figure ambled out of the fortress, closely followed by another large, familiar figure.

Knowing there was no escape, Cassius invited Abascantius in. Shostra – his thuggish and virtually mute Syrian attendant – was carrying a sack over one shoulder. Cassius led the way into the atrium, where he turned and faced his superior officer.

'I owe you an apology, sir.'

'Yes, but you wouldn't mean it. You are fortunate that I have bigger fish to fry, Corbulo, or I might be devoting more energy to being annoyed with you or giving you the smack you deserve.'

Cassius did not reply. From Indavara's room came the sound of snoring.

'I will, however, remind you of something. If Marshal Marcellinus was to learn of your two-year "holiday" in Cyzicus, he might not be quite so convinced that the sun shines out of your arsehole.'

24

'Point taken, sir.'

'I have seen Governor Calvinus. He wishes you well and agrees it's best you should go. He is also of the opinion that you've not been yourself since returning from the south. Apparently you have kept up appearances but neglected your duties. Other sources tell me you have been drinking too much and whoring too much.'

Cassius accepted all this with as much dignity as he could muster, though he wished the agent had dismissed his servant before discussing such a thing. 'Galanaq, sir.'

'You killed a man. I know. Not in battle. Not in a glorious charge or a heroic defence. But to save yourself. And if you hadn't, what state would the province be in now? You did what you had to.'

Cassius was looking at the darkened window beyond the agent.

Abascantius reached up and gripped his arm. The gesture was one of kindness; and so utterly out of character that Cassius didn't know how to respond.

'This work of ours takes us to some nasty places, lad.' Abascantius nodded over his shoulder at Shostra. 'He and I know them well. Sometimes there's just no way around them. Only through. You've got through; and you're stronger for it.'

'Yes, sir.'

'All things considered, this counterfeit job might be a good fit at the moment. And knowing you, you just might crack it. But be under no illusions that you will be in for an easy ride. The treasury are only a little more well inclined towards us than the army and you will face the usual problems getting the locals to cooperate. I want you to remember one thing more. You belong to me and Chief Pulcher the way that Gaul of yours belongs to you. Is that clear?'

'Yes, sir.'

'I expect to hear from you every ten days. Address your letters to the governor's office in Alexandria – they will be forwarded to me from there. Whether you receive replies or not, continue to write. If and when the investigation is concluded, either I or Chief Pulcher will notify you of your next assignment.'

Abascantius clicked his fingers. Shostra reached into the sack and pulled out three bulging bags of coins. He then retrieved a thin stick of charcoal and a small paper receipt. He offered them to Cassius, who signed for the money.

'Pay for the next two quarters,' said Abascantius. 'The two big bags are yours, the smaller is Indavara's. Believe it or not I've given you a raise.'

'Thank you, sir.'

'Don't thank me, thank the Palmyrans. I doubt there's a single pound of gold or silver left in the place.'

Cassius shook the hefty forearm offered to him.

'Marcellinus was right about being careful,' added the agent. 'Chances are you'll be safe once you're away from here but keep that one-man army of yours close.'

'Best of luck in Egypt, sir.'

Abascantius prodded him in the chest. 'Every ten days. Without fail.'

'Yes, sir.'

26

II

Alexon liked the villa but he liked the location even more. There wasn't another property within half a mile and the grounds were enclosed by stone walls and rows of closely packed conifers. Much of the surrounding forest was cedar; a favourite of his, with its refreshing aroma and sprawling, luxuriant foliage. And thanks to the hill on which the villa had been built, there was an excellent view down to the vineyards, the city and the coast beyond.

It was peaceful here. They had privacy, they had time and Alexon had done his best to ensure they were safe; he hoped they could stay for a while.

He alternated three different routes for his morning walk: today's took him alongside a lovely stream then past a farmhouse and oil press where the entire family were working hard. Alexon now made a habit of greeting them and often gave a few coins to the children. It was important to make a good impression. Once past the farmhouse, he met a shepherd driving a small flock up the hill. The white-bearded old man doffed his cloth cap and remarked that it was another fine day. Alexon agreed. He leaped nimbly over a stile and cut across the meadow towards the villa.

The owner had told them that it was exactly a hundred feet wide and fifty deep, a two-storey building bookended by modest but elegant towers with a fine terrace overlooking the drive. Ivy covered much of the brickwork, providing a home for dozens of pretty little birds. Above the front door was an old carving of some local god; a female figure reaching for the heavens.

His sister was already on the terrace, awaiting their visitor. Alexon glanced down at the main gate. Kallikres had just tethered his horse. He shut the gate behind him and started up the sloping drive, head bowed.

'A pleasant walk, brother?' asked Amathea.

'Very, thank you.'

Alexon sat next to her, under a parasol.

Skiron, their steward, looked on silently from the side of the terrace. He was fifty-something but had the upright stance and muscled physique of a man half that age. He had no hair upon his head and a pair of bulging, piercing, bright blue eyes. He had been with them for years.

'Oh, you've almost finished it,' said Alexon, looking at the sewing draped across Amathea's lap. She had been working on the tablecloth for some time and he was pleased she had persisted; it seemed to help her relax. She smiled and pushed the needle into the cotton once more.

Though they were not identical twins, the resemblance was obvious. Both were slim and tall, with less than an inch of difference in height and only four at the waist. They had the same flawless skin, green eyes and dark brown hair. In Alexon's experience, everyone found one of them attractive, many people both. It had often occurred to him that even naked their superior breeding and status would have been clear. In their clothes of Egyptian linen and Oriental silk, and with their jewellery of gold and silver, it was unmistakable.

'They're here,' said the steward. 'In case we need them.'

'Thank you, Skiron,' said Alexon.

Kallikres came up the steps warily. He was wearing a well-made tunic and a wide-brimmed hat which he now removed. He ran a hand through his curly black hair – which glistened with sweat – and offered a thin smile.

'Good day to you.'

Alexon nodded.

'Good day,' said Amathea.

Alexon gestured at the chair opposite them. Kallikres found himself facing the sun; he had to squint just to look at them.

'Wine?' asked Alexon.

'Thank you.'

Skiron came forward and poured it from a silver jug into a multicoloured glass. Kallikres drank half of it in one go.

'Well?' said Alexon. 'You wanted to see us?'

'Yes. One of your men was spotted at the market yesterday. By a Milanese clerk who remembered his face. The clerk told the procurator. The procurator told the magistrate.'

'We are aware of this situation,' replied Alexon calmly.

Kallikres leaned back and crossed his arms. 'I told you to be careful. And yet there he was, walking around in broad daylight without a care in the world.'

'Steps have been taken,' said Alexon. 'There won't be any more mistakes like that.'

'One is enough. I thought you people were professional.'

Alexon kept his tone conciliatory. 'Not everything can be foreseen. That's why we have you – to keep us informed. What action is being taken?'

'Nothing specific that I have heard about yet.'

'Hardly any need to panic then,' said Alexon. 'So the man was spotted. Taken alone, his presence here means little. They may well assume that he was simply passing through.'

'Perhaps you're right. Perhaps the magistrate will do nothing. But if there's another "mistake" then things could get very difficult very quickly. Sorry, but I've made my decision.'

Kallikres reached into his tunic, retrieved a bag of coins and put it on the table. 'I haven't taken a single one. Count them if you wish. Let's just pretend this never happened.'

Alexon glanced at his sister. She pushed her hair away from her face and discarded her sewing.

'I think we all know it's a little late for that,' said Alexon.

'You have my word. I'll say nothing. Here.' Kallikres pushed the bag across the table and got to his feet.

'Stay where you are.'

Alexon was sure Kallikres had never exchanged more than a greeting with his sister. Her words halted him.

Skiron walked around the terrace and stood behind their guest.

'With respect,' said Kallikres, 'I am a city sergeant. I can do as I please.'

Amathea gestured at the meadow below them. 'We're a long way from the city. This is not going well for you. Sit down, or I promise you it will get a good deal worse.'

Alexon kept quiet. He supposed other men might have felt ashamed. But not him; he loved and admired her too much.

Kallikres looked at him, then back at Amathea, who pointed at his chair. The sergeant smiled in disbelief. Alexon guessed he had never been told what to do by a woman before. But he sat down.

Amathea turned to Skiron. 'Bring them.'

The steward whistled and a lad ran out of the house. Skiron whispered to him and he hurried back inside.

Nothing more was said for a while.

Kallikres tried to appear calm by finishing off his wine. 'What are we waiting for?'

Amathea watched the three men file on to the terrace. 'Them.'

The trio were dressed in long green tunics with breeches cut of the same hardy material. They had thick, dark beards and unkempt hair. Each was carrying a long bow on his shoulder and a knife and quiver at his belt. They appeared unrelated but shared the same rangy physique, leathery skin and resolute gaze of those for whom violence is a way of life.

'Itureans,' explained Amathea with some relish. 'Hunters from the hills below the great mountain. We don't even have to pay them, would you believe? All they ask for is enough to eat and drink and a girl each. They all insisted on blondes, of course.'

One of the maids was dusting furniture just inside the door. A word from Amathea and an order from Skiron sent her running up to the table. She wasn't overly pretty but had a pleasant enough face and a fine head of straw-coloured hair. She and the other two were from Germania and had cost a small fortune; but they could at least double as domestic staff.

Amathea was still looking at the hunters. 'Every one of these fellows can skewer a pear at a fifty paces.'

Kallikres wiped his clammy face. 'You wish to intimidate me, is that it?'

Amathea said, 'It is one thing to hear of such skill, but another to see it. Girl, are you Lyra or Chloe? I always get you two mixed up.'

'Lyra, Mistress.'

'Take a pear from the bowl there.'

The girl did so.

'Amathea.' Alexon spoke softly. He expected to be ignored but felt he had to say something. Surely this would cause more problems than it would solve.

Amathea appeared not to have heard him. 'Lyra, walk down to the meadow beside the drive. Stop when you've taken thirty paces, then turn towards us and put the pear on your head.'

Kallikres put up both hands. 'This is not necessary. Why involve the girl?'

'Off you go,' said Amathea.

Lyra looked at Skiron, who cursed at her in Latin. Instead of obeying, she turned to one of the hunters, eyes pleading. The man spoke to Skiron in Aramaic. The steward translated.

'Mistress, he doesn't want his girl harmed.'

'Then he'd better shoot straight,' said Amathea.

The hunter understood that he had been given his orders. He took Lyra's arm and led her to the steps. She descended them shakily.

'Let's end this now,' said Kallikres, retrieving his money. 'You've made your point. I'll cooperate.'

Amathea ignored him too.

As Lyra continued down the slope, the hunter took his bow from his shoulder. He tested the string a couple of times then shook his head and spoke once more to Skiron.

'He says he was drinking last night, Mistress. His hands are shaking. He can't be sure of making the shot.'

Kallikres looked despairingly up at the sky.

'Let us all calm down,' said Amathea. 'If he hits her and she is disfigured we'll have her replaced.'

Upon hearing this, the hunter conceded. He moved up to the fringe of grass at the edge of the terrace and selected an arrow from his quiver. The other two moved aside and looked on.

Amathea stood up, then walked out from under the parasol

and positioned herself behind the hunter. 'You won't be able to see much facing that way,' she told Kallikres. 'Come here and join us.'

Skiron stood over him again, hand hovering by the broad dagger at his belt. Kallikres complied.

Lyra had stopped. 'I'm sorry. I lost count.'

'That's about twenty,' said Amathea. 'Keep going, girl.'

Girl. Alexon reckoned Lyra wasn't far off thirty, several years older than Amathea. He looked over at the walls and trees, to make sure no one was watching. His sister rarely considered such details.

'Skiron, my wine.' She took her glass from the steward.

'Don't do this,' said Kallikres.

'I wish we didn't have to.'

Alexon doubted whether anyone present believed her. Despite his determination to stand by his sister, he was suddenly struck by a vision of an arrow embedding itself in the maid's face. He walked over and whispered to Amathea. 'Sister . . .'

She held up a hand. 'That'll do, girl!'

Lyra stopped and turned.

'Back straight, head straight,' instructed Amathea. 'Then put the pear on top.'

The hunter was flexing his shoulders and wrists.

Lyra began to lift the pear then stopped. 'Mistress . . . Mistress, please . . .'

'Just put it on your head. I promise he won't harm you.'

'But . . .' The girl was crying.

Amathea tutted. 'Alexon, where are they from again?'

He knew she wouldn't stop now. 'Germania.'

'So they worship . . .'

'Aericura.'

Amathea raised her voice. 'Aericura will watch over you.'

'Mistress, how can you be sure?'

'Do you give offerings? Say your prayers?'

'I do.'

'Then he will watch over you.'

'She,' said Alexon.

32

'*She* will watch over you,' said Amathea. 'Be a good girl and just put the pear on your head. It will all be over soon and you can go back inside.'

'Do you promise I'll be all right, Mistress?'

Amathea was now struggling to sound pleasant. 'I promise!'

The hunter exhaled loudly, then checked the arrow and nocked it against the string. He turned side on and raised the bow.

Alexon watched Kallikres. The sergeant was wringing his hands like an old woman.

Lyra placed the pear on the top of her head. She held it there for a moment then put her arms by her side.

The bowstring groaned as the hunter drew it back. He closed one eye. The only noise was the ever-present buzz of crickets in the grass.

'By the gods, I can see his fingers shaking,' said Kallikres.

The hunter lowered the bow and glared at him.

Kallikres turned to Amathea. 'How can he make the shot if his hand is shaking? That poor girl . . .'

Without any prompting from his employers, Skiron walked over to Kallikres and stood beside him.

But now the hunter seemed unsure about continuing.

'Can he do it or not, Skiron?' snapped Amathea.

'Perhaps one of the others?' suggested Alexon.

After a brief consultation, Skiron answered. 'No, Mistress. If one of the others does it and . . . something goes wrong, it will cause a problem between them.'

Lyra reached for the pear. 'Should I . . .'

'Don't move!' yelled Amathea. 'I was told fifty paces.' She pointed at the hunter. 'This is thirty. Tell him to fire now.'

The hunter needed no translation. He raised the bow and drew the string back once more.

Lyra checked that the pear wouldn't fall then clasped her hands and closed her eyes.

Alexon and everyone else behind the Iturean was watching his fingers on the string. They *were* shaking, the tip of the arrow too.

The hunter let go.

The arrow flashed away and thumped into the turf well behind Lyra. It had missed the top of her head by at least a foot.

The hunter spoke.

'A sighter,' explained Skiron. 'Now the real shot.'

Kallikres looked away and ran a knuckle across his brow.

Lyra was already reaching for the pear. 'Is that it? Can I come back now?'

Skiron yelled at her to stand perfectly still.

Once more the bow was drawn. The hunter cocked his head to one side then lowered the weapon. This time nobody needed an explanation; a low-flying flock of noisy geese were flapping across the copse of conifers to the right. The only person who didn't watch them was Lyra, who didn't dare move.

Alexon peered at her. He couldn't see any tears now but her tunic was wet upon her thighs. He wanted this to be over.

Back came the string again. The hunter's fingers seemed to be steadier this time. He let go.

Alexon did not hear the arrow hit. All he saw was the girl's hand fly up towards her head. Then her legs went and she collapsed on to the grass.

Kallikres staggered over to the side of the terrace and threw up into a flower bed.

Alexon and his sister watched as the hunters and Skiron ran down the steps then across the meadow.

'Oh,' said Amathea.

'Is she moving?' asked Alexon.

'I think so.'

'By the great and honoured gods,' muttered Kallikres.

Skiron and the Itureans knelt in front of Lyra.

'Well?' asked Amathea. 'Did he hit it?'

Skiron turned. 'He did, Mistress.'

'Bring it to me,' instructed Amathea. 'I want to see it.'

One of the hunters slapped the girl and a moment later her head came up. Then two of the men lifted her, one taking her under the arms, one by the legs. While they carried her towards the terrace, Skiron recovered the pear.

Amathea and Alexon walked over as the hunters reached the

top of the steps. Lyra was looking at her mistress; everyone else was looking at her. Her face was so pale it appeared almost grey. The arrow tip had carved a thick line across the top of her head where her blonde hair parted. The flesh was horribly red.

'Is it bad?' asked Lyra.

'It will stitch up,' said Amathea.

The Iturean muttered a curse in his own language.

'You'll hardly be able to see it under all that hair,' added Amathea.

Skiron spoke to the hunters as he came up the steps. They took the girl inside and he handed Amathea the pear, or rather the two halves of it.

'A fine shot,' she said. 'Wouldn't you agree, Kallikres?'

The sergeant said nothing.

'Without a drink inside him, I'm sure he could do the same at fifty paces. Are you all right? You're almost as pale as the girl.'

Kallikres gripped his stomach. 'May I go?'

'Of course. As long as we can be assured that you've understood the point of all this. Once my brother and I begin something, we always see it through to the end. We expect the same from you.'

Kallikres nodded then walked away down the steps.

Suddenly Alexon and Amathea were alone. 'Sister, though I'm not sure that was entirely necessary, we seem to have made quite an impression on our guest.'

'You disappoint me, brother. I told you that we must always appear united when in the company of subordinates. You questioned me.'

'I'm sorry, Amathea. You're right.'

'I'm going to my room.'

He knew what that meant.

She was already on the balcony when he arrived. Alexon bolted the door and walked over to her. He had waited for an hour before coming up. Of their many routines this was the most established; it only increased the longing, the power of which amazed him every time.

Amathea was facing him but looking over the side of the balcony.

'Anyone there?' he asked.

'Only one of the girls. She won't see you.'

'You must try to be quiet, Amathea.'

'I shall do as I please.'

She stretched her arms out along the iron railing, fingers sliding on the metal. The diaphanous robe clung to her thighs, her form surrounded by the pink flowers and vivid green leaves that covered the balcony.

'Am I beautiful?'

'The blooms fade into insignificance beside you.'

Neither of them had ever touched anyone else. They found the very thought ridiculous.

'I am yours,' said Amathea.

'And I am yours.' Alexon dropped to his knees in front of her. He circled her ankles with his hands then slid them up, the robe bunching on his arms as he reached higher.

III

The coast road rarely strayed more than a hundred yards from the sea. It ran over countless rocky headlands and bridged ravines where water hissed and rumbled below. The only difficult section was north of Berytus, where the road steepened and twisted high above what was known colloquially as the Dog River. There they had passed the ancient statue of a wolf which was supposed to howl warnings to the locals if enemies approached. Some of the inscriptions on the rocks there were five hundred years old, dating back to when the Phoenicians had controlled the region.

The trio had been riding for seven days. It had taken four to reach the coast at Tyre, where they'd turned north, bound for Tripolis. Cassius was not in any great hurry; he'd sent a letter ahead to a man named Quentin, the treasury agent in charge of the counterfeiting investigation.

He never have imagined being glad to be back in Syria. Arabia – Bostra in particular – held dark associations for him now; he had left behind Abascantius, Governor Calvinus, the pressures of the troubling situation with the Tanukh and – most importantly of all – whomever had tried to capture him.

As suggested by Abascantius, Cassius had taken a series of precautions to remain undetected: they had left Bostra before first light, used a roundabout route out of the city, and been escorted by four cavalrymen for the first day. Though clearly bemused by such a duty, the soldiers had taken their responsibilities seriously, doubling back regularly to check the road behind them and leaving only when their charges found safe accommodation for the night.

Cassius was not in uniform and had used a false name at the

inns where they stayed. As the days passed, he had grown more relaxed and was looking forward to what would surely be a comparatively leisurely and safe assignment. It was now mid-afternoon and – according to the milestones – there were only five miles left to Tripolis. They would arrive well before dusk with plenty of time to meet Quentin and arrange their lodgings.

Indavara – who was riding to Cassius's left, closest to the sea – unleashed an almighty yawn. 'Hot again.'

'You ate too much lunch. Again.'

Indavara ignored him and pawed at an insect that had settled on his bulging right bicep. Though clearly happy to be on the move, the bodyguard never liked disruption to his conditioning regime and had to improvise exercises on the road. He'd spent half of the previous evening doing hundreds of push-ups and lifting a barrel above his head. His recovery had been remark-ably speedy and he'd spent only two days languishing in the cart. Even so, he was inflicting daily progress reports on his companions – apparently the pain was now negligible but the purple bruising had turned black.

Indavara looked over his shoulder. 'All right there, Simo?'

Cassius turned round. The attendant, who was driving the horse and cart, had set up a makeshift awning to protect himself from the sun.

'Yes, thank you.'

'Patch?'

'Seems fine.'

The hardy donkey who had been with them since their journey into the Arabian desert was tied to the rear of the cart. Indavara and Simo didn't even bother to pretend that they actually needed the beast for their luggage any more. Cassius allowed them this indulgence but was constantly amazed by how much care and attention they lavished on the creature.

'Can you think of any more?' asked Indavara. The game of 'guess the emperor' had been going on for some time.

'I believe we've exhausted our entire supply,' replied Simo. 'Perhaps another game?'

'I don't think you've heard this one,' said Cassius, looking down at the white sandy beach where four fishermen were bringing in a net.

'I once had a special collapsible boat constructed then used it to try and drown my mother.'

'Mmm.' Simo seemed perplexed.

'Let me,' said Indavara. 'Was it Caligula?'

'No,' said Cassius.

'Tiberius?'

'No. Last guess.'

'Nero.'

'Very good.'

'Ha.' Indavara slapped his thigh. 'Did it work?'

'The boat? Yes. But she managed to swim back to shore – that must have been an awkward conversation.'

Indavara shook his head. 'Emperors – mad buggers every one.'

Cassius pointed at him. 'Don't say that in company. And remember you've taken an oath to Aurelian. We should all consider ourselves lucky; we've not had such a capable character in the purple for quite a while.'

'Do you think he's seen the black stone yet?' asked Indavara.

'Probably.'

'Perhaps he'll see the god Elagabal like we did.'

Cassius didn't reply. He'd tried to forget the vision he'd had that day in the canyon and wished he'd never told Indavara about it.

'You saw him too,' said the bodyguard. 'I dream of it sometimes. I dream of him fighting with my Fortuna.'

'It was our minds playing tricks, that's all.'

'Of course,' said Indavara, rolling his eyes. 'You know everything. About everything.'

'As I said at the time: no – just more than you.'

'Very funny.'

'Move over.'

They were heading up a slight slope and Cassius had just spotted a cavalryman coming over the rise. The rider carried a scarlet and gold standard and was leading a squad of ten. They seemed to be well equipped for a long journey: the saddles were loaded with fodder, water skins and equipment which thumped and jangled as they trotted past. Each man also had a yellow oval shield with the same pattern of black swirls surrounding the bronze boss.

These were not the first soldiers they had seen; there had been two more units of cavalry and a century heading south. Cassius didn't like ignoring them; he enjoyed the camaraderie of greeting fellow soldiers on the road – seeing his crest, they generally assumed he was a centurion. But for the moment it seemed wise to draw as little attention as possible so he had forgone anything that identified him as a military man. He would have to wear his uniform in Tripolis while undertaking the investigation but (again at the suggestion of Abascantius) would continue to operate under an assumed name.

As the last of the cavalrymen passed them, they reached the top of the slope. Ahead, the road cut through thick scrub and olive groves, following the gentle curve of the coast before reaching Tripolis, most of which seemed to be crammed on to a promontory jutting out into the sea. It was a medium-sized city, not as large as some of those they had passed through like Sidon and Berytus. Cassius had no idea why the Emperor had decided to commission a new imperial mint there.

'Four to go,' said Indavara, spying another milestone. 'Hope there's some good eating round here. I'm starving.'

After obtaining some directions from a pair of legionaries patrolling the road, they headed straight for the nearest army way station. It was currently occupied by a party of surveyors, so while Simo went to find alternative accommodation, Cassius and Indavara were assigned a young lad to escort them to the mint. It was less than a mile away, on the eastern edge of the town in an area of factories and workshops. Unlike the other buildings, the mint was surrounded by a twelve-foot brick wall topped by spikes and guarded by a squad of legionaries. Confident he could find his way back, Cassius dismissed the lad and they waited outside the entrance for Quentin.

'Looks just like the one in Antioch,' said Indavara, examining the walls.

'Of course – you were with Abascantius when he thought Governor Gordio was mixed up in the theft of the Persian flag. Gods, what a mess he made of that. Fortunately, I was around to pick up the pieces.'

'By getting yourself captured?'

'All part of the plan,' said Cassius with a grin.

He let out a long breath and wished he'd brought his hat with him. He was wearing a thin, sleeveless tunic and his lightest boots but was still sweating. 'Hope Simo's found somewhere close to the coast, bit of sea air would be nice.'

One of the eight legionaries on duty opened the small iron gate next to the main entrance and a slight man of about forty appeared. Cassius's skin was on the fair side, but this fellow's was even paler and he grimaced as he was struck by the full power of the sun. His long-sleeved tunic was of good quality but the sleeves were marked with ink blots.

'Officer Crispian?'

'Yes,' lied Cassius.

'Lucius Gratus Quentin.' They shook forearms.

Quentin shielded his eyes as he inspected the other new arrival. Like Cassius, Indavara was armed with dagger and sword.

'May I see your documentation?'

'Of course.'

Cassius reached into the deer-hide satchel over his shoulder and took out the letter of introduction. Glycia had written it; Marshal Marcellinus had signed it. Only Abascantius had possessed the presence of mind to suggest that it identified Cassius as 'the bearer' instead of by name.

Quentin read the note and returned it. 'This is all rather irregular but we must of course do as we are bid. Please, follow me.'

Quentin went through the narrow archway first. As Cassius followed, one of the legionaries stepped in front of him. 'You'll have to leave the weapons here, sir.'

'I'm afraid it's policy,' said Quentin. 'You'll see that I carry no blade; only the soldiers of the garrison are allowed to do so.'

'You did see the name in that letter? Must I invoke it a second time?'

'Officer Crispian, this is an imperial mint. Security is of the utmost importance.'

Cassius considered a jibe about the counterfeiting investigation but decided against it.

He reckoned he could have got his way by scaring the soldiers with a bit more name-dropping but it seemed unlikely he would be at risk here. 'If you insist.'

Indavara – who never liked giving up his weapons – sneered as he removed his dagger sheath and sword belt. Cassius did the same and the soldiers took the four weapons.

Quentin led them across a strip of dusty ground towards the mint, which, like the wall, was constructed of red brick. All the small, circular windows were grilled with iron and well off the ground. Towards the rear were several chimneys, only one of which was issuing smoke. From inside the mint came the noise of clanging hammers and the occasional shout.

'Have you any experience of combating counterfeiting, Officer?' asked Quentin.

'None at all.'

Quentin made little attempt to conceal his dismay.

'I am hoping you will be able to educate me,' added Cassius.

Waiting outside the broad, arched entrance was a middle-aged man of about fifty in a light blue tunic decorated with yellow lozenges.

Quentin introduced him. 'Flavius Arruntius, chief of the mint.'

'Officer Crispian, Imperial Security.'

'Welcome, sir,' said Arruntius, a large character with rosy cheeks and an amenable face. 'My staff and I are at your disposal.'

'Many thanks.'

'I thought we might show you one of the workshops first,' said Quentin, 'so you can better understand what you are to investigate.'

'That sounds sensible.'

'It will have to be workshop two,' said Arruntius, 'the only one functioning at present.'

'Work has slowed down since the first issue,' explained Quentin.

42

'That was mainly for army pay. The rest will be introduced more slowly – payments for civic projects and wages for municipal workers.'

'These counterfeits,' said Cassius, 'are they just of the new denarius?'

'As far as we know,' replied Quentin. He produced a coin from a pocket and showed it to Cassius. 'You may not have seen many down in Arabia yet but these are being produced and distributed at Siscia, Cyzicus, Serdica, Antioch and here. The aim is for them to eventually become the primary currency for the entire Empire.'

'And now someone is making their own?'

Quentin exchanged an anxious look with Arruntius. 'We'll get to that. Let us first show you how they are made.'

Cassius gestured towards the arch. 'Please.'

Workshop two was divided into several sections. The first was a large room containing four ovens. Despite an open door that led out to a courtyard, the temperature reminded Cassius of a hot room at the baths. The rounded ovens were constructed of clay, each one with a chimney and an opening at the front. Only two were alight, burning bright orange inside. Half a dozen men were at work, wearing aprons over their tunics, skin glistening with sweat. They turned and nodded politely when they realised they had visitors.

Cassius noted some metal ingots stacked on a wooden pallet. Most were of bronze but there was also copper and silver. Arruntius led the other three to a central table and pointed at a rectangular lump of clay containing rows of hollows. 'This is the mould: made of what we call foundry sand – sand mixed with clay. We pour molten bronze into these then they go into the oven.'

He continued on and pointed down at two empty vats sunk into the ground. 'These would usually contain the liquid silver – when the bronzes come out of the ovens we apply the wash here.'

Guarding the arched doorway that led to the next section was a legionary who looked as if he was ready for another duty.

'Of course, security is crucial,' said Arruntius. 'We also inventory every last item at the end and beginning of the working day.'

He led them into the second section. In the middle of the room was a huge square table. On top of it was a wooden tray containing dozens of silver-coated coins. A worker was picking them out one by one, examining the surface and clipping off any excess metal around the edges.

'Once they've cooled, the "blanks" are checked in here,' said Arruntius.

Farther along the table was another worker by a set of scales. He was weighing every coin.

'Keeping a standardised weight is essential,' added the chief of the mint, 'and not easy to achieve.' He pointed at a bucket ·containing several coins. 'Anything not up to standard goes back for remoulding.'

Cassius looked at a tray containing approved 'blanks'. Having just been 'washed' these looked almost like silver, but he knew from experience that, after handling, most of the coins would end up looking like what they really were: bronze.

'So not much actual silver in a denarius these days.'

Arruntius gave an ironic smile and looked at Quentin, who answered.

'Should be five per cent.'

Arruntius took a single blank from the nearest tray and led them past another guard into the third section. No one was working but there was a circular table surrounded by four large anvils mounted on bases of brick. On the table were two cylinders of what looked to Cassius like lead, each about two inches wide and five high.

'These are the dies,' said Arruntius as they reached the table. 'See the images? One is the obverse, one the reverse.'

The obverse showed the head of the Emperor. He was wearing a crown and facing to the right. Written around the top half of the coin was his name.

'A good likeness,' said Quentin.

'You have seen the Emperor in the flesh?' asked Cassius.

'Yes, several times.'

'And?' said Cassius, unable to curtail his curiosity.

'*Very* impressive,' replied Quentin. Cassius supposed there wasn't really anything else one could say.

He looked at the next die and was surprised by what he saw. The design for the reverse showed a god-like figure standing over a captive. In one hand he held a globe, in the other a whip. The legend was clear: *SOL INVICTUS*.

'Oh. The sun god. I didn't realise . . .'

'Other solar symbols have been used on previous coinage,' said Quentin.

'Instead of Jupiter, though?' said Cassius. No one seemed keen to discuss the matter but it seemed obvious that the Emperor's interest in the solar deities of the East was developing at quite a rate.

'Sun god,' said Indavara. 'Not Elagabalus?'

Quentin answered quickly. 'The word from on high is that the design does not represent any single version of the sun god. It is to be considered an acknowledgement of what the Emperor sees as the importance of local deities in his reconquering of the East. Assurances have been made that it is in no way to suggest a supplanting of the great gods.'

'But these are being produced across the Empire?' said Cassius.

'Well, yes.'

'*His* coins,' said Arruntius with a shrug. '*His* design.'

He put the reverse die on the anvil and the blank coin on top. He then flipped the obverse die over and placed it on top of the blank. Holding the tower steady, he turned to the others.

Indavara looked confused. 'How do you get the . . .'

Arruntius gestured at the floor. Lying next to the table was a large hammer. 'Sheer brute force. We seem to be in need of a labourer, my friend.' He smiled at Indavara. 'The men who work in this section tend to look a bit like you.'

'You mean I can . . .'

'Please.'

Indavara picked up the hammer.

'Try and bring the head down as straight as you can,' said Arruntius. 'And preferably not on my fingers. You needn't try too hard. The weight will do the work.'

Despite this advice, Indavara couldn't resist giving it a good thump. After the impact, the tower fell on to the anvil with a clang.

Arruntius plucked the newly minted coin off the reverse die and handed it to the bodyguard. 'Here. It's yours.'

'Really?'

'Why not? You made it.'

Indavara looked down at the design now imprinted in the metal and grinned.

'Easy, eh?' said Cassius.

'Not if you have to do it all day,' said Arruntius. 'We expect an experienced pair to knock out a hundred an hour.'

Cassius looked around the room. Against the wall were racks of tools and amphoras of varying sizes and designs. 'So that's it?'

'Not quite.' Arruntius pointed past a guard towards another doorway. 'In the fourth section we weigh them again and give them a good polish. From there it's to the counting room, then the store at the rear.'

Quentin was looking impatient.

'Shall we move on to the issue at hand?' suggested Cassius.

'We can meet in my office – Arruntius has kindly put aside some space for me.'

'I'll have a maid come along with some refreshments,' said their host, hurrying away back through the workshop.

'Thank you,' said Quentin as he led Cassius in the opposite direction.

Indavara was still looking at his coin. 'I can really keep this?'

IV

The 'office' was in fact half of a large storeroom. It was considerably cooler than the rest of the mint, with air admitted through a dozen of the high circular windows and illumination via a square glassed skylight. The other half of the room was mostly shelves stacked with scroll-racks, waxed tablets and iron tools. Quentin had set himself up on a work table and was clearly a well-organised individual. Next to a framed map of the eastern provinces were several orderly piles of paper and a selection of labelled coins mounted on a board of cork.

As Cassius and Quentin sat on opposite sides of the table, Indavara took himself over to a nearby bench and lay down on his back. Quentin seemed bemused by this but said nothing.

'How long have you been in Tripolis?' asked Cassius.

'I was sent here originally in the spring to help set up the mint. The building was here but everything you see inside is new. When this . . . issue raised its head I was asked to stay on and coordinate an investigation.'

'Do you have anyone else to help you?'

'Two clerks. They're out gathering information as we speak.'

'Marshal Marcellinus seemed to suggest that not much progress has been made. Is that fair?'

Quentin sighed and rubbed the bridge of his nose. 'Perhaps if I start at the beginning?'

'Of course.'

Cassius had put his satchel on the desk. He reached inside and took out a stick of charcoal to make notes with. 'Do you have some paper?'

Quentin pointed at a pile of blank sheets. Just as Cassius took one, a maid hurried in with a tray. He was disappointed to see that she was middle aged and rather fat. Indavara sat up immediately, more interested in what she had brought.

'Afternoon, sirs.'

'Hello,' said Indavara, already on his feet.

The maid placed the tray on the corner of the table, prompting a tut from Quentin. She put down a jug and three mugs, a bowl of glistening red grapes and a plate of sweet-smelling pastries.

'Wine for everyone?'

'Not for me,' said Quentin. 'And don't spill any.'

With a practised smile, the maid poured wine for Cassius and Indavara, recovered the tray and departed as quickly as she'd arrived. 'Compliments of Master Arruntius. If you would like anything else, please ask.'

'Thanks a lot,' said Indavara. He slurped at his wine, eliciting another tut from Quentin.

'Why not go back to your bench?' said Cassius. 'Take the cakes.'

Indavara didn't need a second invitation.

'What he lacks in decorum he more than makes up for in other areas.'

'I don't doubt it.' Quentin put his arms on the table and interlocked his fingers. 'Do you know why this mint was commissioned?'

'So that the local and visiting legions can be paid; and the Emperor can introduce coins bearing his image – show his face, so to speak.'

'That's part of it, yes.'

'And also to restore confidence in the currency.' Finance was not Cassius's strong point but he knew inflation and debasement had worsened in recent years.

'Quite so. As I said in the workshop, we are aiming for a consistent five per cent silver in the new denarius. Under some of the Emperor's predecessors, it had dropped to as low as one per cent.'

'Strange, really,' said Cassius, 'when one considers that all coins were originally a hundred per cent gold or silver or bronze.'

'Unfortunately that is now impossible, but we are doing what we can.'

48

Quentin leaned across the desk and selected a coin from his collection. He handed it to Cassius. 'See the XX below the sun god? It guarantees the five per cent minimum – twenty coins would make one of pure silver. If all goes to plan, within a few months these denarii should be the dominant coin of exchange across the Empire. The XX mark is designed to breed confidence. Confidence is our best weapon against inflation.'

'But with all these coins being produced it's a perfect time to introduce and distribute false currency.'

'Precisely. And with counterfeits of such quality mixing with genuine coins, we will find it very difficult to identify the source.'

'So what about these fakes? Do you have one to show me?'

Quentin nodded at Cassius's hand.

'This?' He examined it. The detailing of the lettering and images was excellent.

Quentin passed him another denarius. 'This is genuine. It's actually slightly heavier – the fake is made with poor-quality bronze.'

Cassius held them in different hands. 'I can't tell.'

'Only a trained man can. If you look closely at the Emperor's crown and the lines of some of the letters, they are slightly different. This is how we know they are using the same initial die, though they must have produced copies because of the sheer number and spread.'

'I've seen the odd fake around,' said Cassius. 'Mostly bronzes. They're usually lighter, or smaller, or with ragged edges. It's obvious.'

'We see better counterfeiting in the northern provinces, Britain in particular, but these are the best I've come across east of Byzantium.'

'This gang has expert help, then?'

'Yes. And unfortunately there are a number of mint workers able to provide it. You are aware of the Felicissimus plot?'

'Not the details.'

'Felicissimus was Minister of Finance before Sabinus and was implicated in the fraudulent production of coins. He was making huge profits on the side, as were his accomplices at the mint.

There were quite a few senior men on his payroll and several escaped justice, taking dies like you saw just now with them. Unfortunately, the new coins had already been issued in large numbers; we had no choice but to persist with the double X design.'

Quentin leafed through another pile of papers.

Cassius glanced over his shoulder. Indavara was working through the pastries at quite a rate but at least keeping the noise to a minimum.

Quentin slid a sheet across the desk. It showed five names.

'These are the men with sufficient knowledge who are yet to be accounted for.'

'Any trace of them in this area?'

'Not that we know of.'

'Presumably it's also possible that an existing mint worker might be helping this gang.'

'Indeed. Which is one of the reasons why I started my investigations right here in Tripolis. As you saw, our labourers work only in a single section; few possess the knowledge or the skills to carry out the process from start to finish – certainly not to a high standard. We must focus on what we call "casters" – senior men who oversee the whole operation.'

'Anything so far?'

'My men are concluding their interviews today. Nothing particularly promising yet. I should add that Arruntius is convinced the fakes are not linked to this facility in any way. And to his credit, he seems to have vetted his staff and maintained security well.'

'How many casters are there here?'

'Eight currently employed, eight who still live in the local area and previously worked here. They wouldn't of course have had access to the new dies but they possess the necessary skills.'

'I see. Other lines of enquiry?'

'The second reason I based myself here is that – judging by the "sightings" of these fakes so far – the centre of production seems to be somewhere in Syria. The first report appeared several weeks ago – a fake spotted by an observant tax collector in

Emesa. Ten days ago, I wrote to the procurators in every town and city in Syria as well as the neighbouring provinces of Arabia, Palestine and Cilicia. I told them what to look for and asked them to conduct an urgent survey of coinage.'

Quentin tapped another stack of paper. 'Some of the replies are back; I'm expecting the rest soon.' He then pointed at the map. 'I hope to have collated the information within a day or two. That should allow us to narrow the search.'

Cassius made a few notes with the charcoal. 'So – our possible ways in: firstly, the casters; secondly, the coin locations. Tell me what this gang would need.'

'A smaller version of what you've seen here today.'

'The raw materials – the metals – is there any way of tracing their supply?'

'Possibly, but Syria has dozens of mines producing copper and silver, and both – like bronze – are used in a hundred different industries. This gang could easily lay their hands on enough without arousing suspicion.'

'And the other equipment? With a trained man could they produce it for themselves?'

'The most complicated piece is the die, the rest is comparatively easy.'

Cassius made a few more notes. 'Even though it would be a smaller operation, they would need somewhere secure to work. Plus sufficient transport to bring in the metals and take out the finished coins.'

'Somewhere remote perhaps,' suggested Quentin.

'More likely they'd locate themselves near other workshops or factories – places with smoking chimneys and artisans and carts coming and going.'

Quentin conceded the point with a shrug. 'We can start with the industrial areas of Tripolis, I suppose. But you must bear in mind that we cannot be too open about the scale of the counterfeiting. We must try to preserve confidence.'

'Understood.'

Indavara belched.

Cassius might have excused him, except that he was occupied

by another thought. 'Typically, what do these gangs do with the coins?'

'It varies. Sometimes they sell them to other criminals – at perhaps a fifth or a quarter of their "real" value. With fakes of this quality they could make legitimate purchases: precious metals, jewellery, gems. Ultimately, this is what will cause us the most problems – influential people who find out they have been given hundreds or thousands of fake coins. That kind of uncertainty can be catastrophic for an economy.'

Cassius gazed up at the skylight for a moment. 'The gang will assume that the treasury will eventually catch wind of what they're up to and investigate. So they will probably want to move the coins on quickly – turn them into something with genuine, long-lasting value.'

'Yes.'

'Apart from what you mentioned they might also purchase interests in shipping perhaps, or farming. Or land.'

'Possibly.'

'I should like to talk to your clerks – hear about these interviews, see their notes even.'

'As you wish.'

'And I'd very much like to see that map, when it's finished.'

'Of course.'

'Tomorrow morning I shall pay a visit to the basilica, establish what local records I can get my hands on – there may have been some unusually large purchases of late. And perhaps your clerks can think of a way to start checking over the factories and workshops. What do you think?'

Quentin was clearly surprised to be asked; it seemed obvious that he felt Cassius had been sent there to take over the investigation, not work alongside him.

'Again, that all sounds very sensible.'

'Thank you for bringing me up to speed, Quentin. At least we've made a start, eh?'

For the first time, the treasury agent offered a trace of a smile. 'I wish I had more men. Minister Sabinus demands weekly reports but has seen fit to give me only the two clerks.'

'I suppose I should feel fortunate. My master has told me I only need to write to him every ten days.' Cassius packed away his charcoal and the paper. 'Well, we must return to the city and get settled in.'

'You'll have to wake your friend up first.' Quentin nodded at Indavara. The bodyguard's head was hanging off the bench, his mouth wide open.

V

As usual, Simo had chosen well. Though rather hemmed in by apartment blocks, the inn's rear terrace offered a fine sea view. Dusk had fallen and only a handful of lights could be seen bobbing upon the black waves – the last few fishing boats returning with the day's catch. The water was less than a quarter-mile away, close enough to give a salty tang to the air. Night brought the same sounds to every city – parents calling in children, householders bolting their doors and shutters, watchmen shouting greetings as they did their rounds.

The terrace contained four tables, two of which were unoccupied. At one was a solitary merchant, copying something on to a waxed tablet by lamplight. Cassius sat at the other, glad that his fellow guest didn't seem keen to talk. He waved away a persistent fly and put his head back against the wall.

Arabia already seemed a long way away. He looked at the three sheets of paper by the lamp. Letters: one from his father, one from his mother, one from his eldest sister. They had arrived in a bundle a month ago. Around that time he'd been indulging himself with fantasies of leaving – Bostra, the Service, the army, everything. He could easily have ridden to the coast and found a ship bound for Ravenna. Once there, it was a short walk from the port to the villa – straight through the gates and into his mother's arms.

A month ago he had not felt able to read the letters. He'd taken a cursory look at them then locked them in his hardwood box. But he was feeling better now: drinking less, sleeping more; and his habitual optimism was returning. He had already done three years in the army; only two left. Surely the worst was past. With assignments like this one, he was confident he could make it.

Half an hour later, the letters had been read and the merchant had gone inside. Simo came out to ask whether Cassius was ready for his dinner. After informing the proprietor that he was, the Gaul joined his master.

'Where's Indavara?'

'With Patch. The cook found some carrots for him.'

'I swear you two spend more time looking after that bloody mule than the other three horses put together.'

Simo fanned himself with his hand. Though the sun had set, it was humid and warm.

'We've got all the luggage upstairs, though, sir – very convenient what with the stables so close.'

'Good choice, this place,' said Cassius, holding up his glass. 'Wine's decent too.'

Simo glanced at the letters. In times past, Cassius reckoned he would have asked about them but the attendant was clearly wary of taking a risk with his master these days. Cassius didn't regret what had happened; he felt it had been justified. But he wanted no more reminders of Arabia. He wanted things the way they were.

'I read them properly at last.'

Simo turned to him, ready to listen. It seemed like an age since they'd last discussed each other's families.

'Father seems very excited about the Cyrenaica affair. He's had senators and magistrates coming up to him, asking how I tracked down the man who killed Memor.'

'He must be very proud, sir.'

'And rather surprised, I should imagine. I didn't tell him about it.' Cassius moved the jug towards Simo. 'I don't really tell them all that much.'

'To spare their feelings, sir?' The attendant poured himself a little wine.

'My mother's, especially. Mine too, in a way. I find I can't write it down. Just all seems too much. I suppose if I saw them face to face I might be able to speak of it.'

'You must be due some leave, sir. Do you never think of a brief trip home?'

'I couldn't do it, Simo. Once there, I don't think I could bring myself to leave.'

The Gaul brushed his thick black hair away from his eyes.

'You need a proper haircut. We'll start your allowance up again. Take your first month's from what we have.'

'Thank you, sir. How is your father?'

'Some trouble with his eyes – he seems to think he's going blind in one of them. But his estates are earning well; his other concerns too. My eldest sister has had her second child, after another miscarriage. A boy. Father's very happy about that, of course.'

'And your mother, sir?'

'She wrote of day-to-day things: the family, the house. Asking if I'm eating properly, if I have enough clothes, can she send me anything.'

Simo smiled.

'There was such an excess of trivialities that she clearly could not say what she really wished to. I don't know what she imagined I did before but I would guess this talk of Cyrenaica has reached her. I suppose she must be very worried. She wrote that the great gods were watching over me; she wrote it three times, actually.'

'Would you like me to take out your figurines, sir? We could display them in the room if we're to be here a while.'

'Yes, do that.'

Cassius looked out at the sea again. 'Sometimes I wish I had carvings of my family instead. I have forgotten their faces, Simo.' He turned back to the Gaul. 'The Christian "kingdom"; your place of happiness – where everyone you love can be found and all is well?'

'Sir?'

'Mine is close, just across the water. And only two years away. Do you think I'll get there?'

'You deserve to, sir. I know that.'

With his usual immaculate timing, Indavara arrived just as dinner was being served: grilled bream with lemon, followed by apricots in syrup.

'Nice place, this,' said the bodyguard as he plundered the remains of Cassius's dessert. A slimy apricot slipped out of his hand and dropped into the bread basket.

Cassius shook his head as he watched Indavara pluck it out and slurp it down. He gestured at the basket. 'You'd better check that again – I think you missed a few crumbs.'

'My first master could eat a lot,' said Simo. 'His sons too. But nothing compared to you.'

'I take that as a compliment,' said Indavara.

Cassius reflected on how their relationship had changed. Initially, Simo had insisted on calling Indavara 'sir' but neither Cassius nor the bodyguard had liked that. They now spent so much time together that they behaved very much like equals, even though one was a freedman, one a slave.

'What's better in life than food?' said Indavara, wiping his mouth with his hand.

Cassius picked up a napkin and threw it at him.

Indavara ignored it. 'Well, maybe one thing.'

Simo looked away. He disliked vulgar talk and Indavara usually didn't mention such things around him, but he was on to his third mug of wine. It was a continual source of amusement to Cassius that the teak-tough bodyguard could consume so much food yet remained a lightweight drinker. He was an amusing drunk, at least.

'See the maids?' said Cassius, nodding towards the inn. 'Sisters, you know.'

'Yes. Pretty, eh? Simo, you're thirty-three this year, aren't you?'

'Yes.'

'Ever think about getting married?'

Cassius had often wondered about that. 'What's the Church's view?'

Though visibly squirming, Simo answered. 'The Church puts great value on marriage and a stable family.'

'More members for the Faith,' said Cassius.

'So you want a wife?' asked Indavara.

'Perhaps. I am mainly concerned with my studies for now.'

'You do like women, though?' said the bodyguard. 'It's just I never hear you—'

'Simo likes women,' said Cassius. 'Though he hides it far better than you or I. He likes larger women.'

Indavara cupped his hands in front of his chest. 'You mean—'

Cassius sniggered. 'Exactly, though he's hardly alone in that.'

The Gaul started piling up their plates.

'Sorry, Simo,' said Cassius. 'We don't mean any harm. Indavara, it's the Christians' way to deny themselves the baser pleasures of life. They believe a greater happiness awaits. The likes of you and I and most right-thinking people know we need to grab what we can from the here and now. Speaking of which.'

One of the maids came on to the terrace, sandals slapping on the stone. 'All done here, gentlemen?'

She was a tall girl with a mass of curly black hair tied up high. Her summer tunic was cut above the knee, showing a pair of strong but shapely legs. And though the tunic had a high collar, there was no hiding the impressive dimensions of her breasts.

The girl thanked Simo as he passed her the plates. When she leant over to take the bread basket, Indavara pinched her bottom.

She gave a little squeal then waved the basket at him. 'Cheeky.'

'You're drunker than I thought,' said Cassius.

'Just grabbing what I can from the here and now.'

Simo sighed.

'Any more customers in there?' Cassius asked.

'No, sir,' said the maid.

'And the other girl's your sister, correct?'

'Yes, sir.'

'Why don't the two of you come and join us for a drink later?'

'Master Neokles wouldn't like that, sir.'

'Is he still here?'

'No, sir. He's gone to his friend's house for the evening.'

'So he wouldn't know?'

'We've still got to tidy the kitchen, sir.'

'But you could come along after?'

The girl was biting her lip.

'What's your name?'

'Kitra, sir.'

'You don't have to call me sir. I'm Cassius. Kitra – that's Aramaic. If I'm not mistaken it means crown.' He looked her up and down. 'And by Jupiter, you are worthy of one.'

Even in the dim lamplight, the blush was obvious.

'You and your sister will join us, won't you? I hate to go to bed disappointed.'

Kitra smiled coyly then hurried away, almost dropping the plates on her way up the steps.

Cassius looked at Indavara and winked.

'Every bloody time. I don't know how you do it.'

'A lifetime of practice. Listen, most serving girls are local – take a bit of time to learn the meanings of the names and off you go.'

'May I be excused, sir? I must prepare your bed.'

'Of course, Simo.'

As the Gaul left, Cassius pointed at Indavara. 'Best start thinking what you're going to say when they come. You need to work on your technique. I'm going to keep quiet.'

Indavara pointed at the wine jug. 'Pass me that. Quick.'

The girls took a long time to tidy up. By the time they meekly ventured out on to the terrace, Cassius's three-mug rule was long forgotten, though he'd at least managed to limit Indavara's intake. Much of the intervening period had been spent giving the bodyguard some hints and reminding him that women liked to talk, especially about themselves. Cassius knew from experience that lowly girls in particular appreciated a friendly ear and a pleasant respite from their labours.

Kitra was clearly the more forward of the two. She came out with a fresh jug of wine and two mugs for her and her sister, who seemed reluctant to sit down or make eye contact with the men. As she clearly represented more of a challenge, Cassius stood up and took her hand.

'And *your* name?'

'Hanina,' she said quietly.

'Ah yes, it means gracious. Surely one so named will accept our friendly invitation.'

A slight smile.

'Please.' Cassius sat down opposite Indavara. Hanina elegantly lifted her tunic as she sat beside him. Her curly black hair was identical to her sister's but she had rather more delicate features and a slimmer figure. Cassius would have classed neither girl as pretty but they were both pleasant enough, especially with all that hair and that smooth, dark Syrian skin.

Kitra was standing at the front of the terrace, peering up at the balcony of the house next door.

'Come and join us,' said Cassius.

'I'm just checking that old mother Adelphe is in bed. She loves to tell tales on us to Master Neokles. We must be quiet.'

Indavara began to look twitchy when Kitra sat beside him. As usual, he pressed down his hair over his disfigured left ear. Cassius had told him countless times that his other physical attributes more than compensated but he remained self-conscious about it. Kitra poured wine for herself and her sister and topped up the men's mugs.

'Thank you,' said Indavara.

'Kitchen all done, then?' asked Cassius.

'At last,' said Kitra.

'Is Neokles a good master, Hanina?'

'Yes, sir.'

'I told your sister, please call me Cassius.' He gestured across the table. 'And that is Indavara. Don't let all the scars put you off, he's just been in a few scraps.'

Indavara looked down at his wine.

'He was just telling me how much he enjoyed dinner,' added Cassius.

Kitra smiled.

Cassius stretched out a leg and tapped Indavara with his foot.

The bodyguard looked up at the girls. 'I did. It was lovely, thank you.'

'Hanina's the real cook,' said Kitra. 'She did the bream.'

'Very tasty it was too,' said Cassius. He then waited for Indavara to weigh in.

'It was,' said the bodyguard after an awkward pause. 'Very . . . lemony.'

Cassius rolled his eyes. 'Neokles is a lucky man. Personally I'd pay you girls just to brighten up the place.'

Kitra smiled again. Cassius reckoned the two of them could have quite a bit of fun together but as she was the friendlier of the two sisters he would leave her for Indavara. He turned to Hanina.

'Does Neokles give you much time off?'

'About an hour in the afternoon, sir, yes. When there's not so much to do.'

'Cassius, please. And what do you do when you're free?'

Hanina looked at her sister. 'Sometime we go to see our mother, sometimes we go to the temple.'

'Ah, which temple's that?'

Cassius had never met a girl he couldn't get talking and as Hanina began to warm up, the other two were left to make their own efforts. Cassius listened in.

'Where are you from?' asked Kitra.

'Pietas Julia,' said Indavara.

'Where's that?'

'A long way away.'

The maid drank her wine. 'So how did you get to Syria?'

'On a horse. Walked a bit too.'

'Do you like Tripolis?'

'Yes. It seems . . . nice.'

'It's not bad. I like being close to the sea.' Kitra drank more wine.

Cassius thought about intervening. Despite his earlier enthusiasm, Indavara had clammed up as usual. But he had to learn.

'What about you?' he asked suddenly. 'Were you born here?'

'No,' she said, 'a little village down the coast.'

And off they went. Cassius switched his full attention back to Hanina, who was now enthusing about all the different types of fish that were caught at Tripolis and which ones went with which herbs and how Master Neokles didn't mind her experiments because they always turned out well. Cassius found it all rather dull, and he now noticed the girl had thin lips (which he was not fond of), but the wine and the wait had made him keen to move things along.

He wouldn't go too far – they might be staying at Neokles's inn for a while – but he wanted at least a kiss before bed. After a few minutes he turned the talk around to Neokles's wine collection and persuaded Hanina to show him what they had behind the bar.

By this point, Indavara and Kitra were getting along well. The maid was trying – but failing – to stop herself touching both Indavara's marked, bulky forearm and his equally marked, bulky knee. When Cassius announced that he and Hanina were off to fetch more wine, the pair barely seemed to notice.

Hanina lit another lamp in the parlour then went behind the bar. Cassius sat on a stool as she showed him each and every barrel mounted on a large wooden rack. 'Here is the raisin wine, here is the sour wine, here is the honey wine. Then there's the Rhaetic and the Caecuban. And this unlabelled one is actually Alban. Master Neokles doesn't tell anyone; he keeps it for himself and his friends – never lets guests have it.'

Cassius knew she wouldn't take much persuading. Even if they weren't slaves, maids and servants generally enjoyed minor acts of sabotage against their employers. Apart from Simo, of course.

'I do love Alban,' he said. 'Have you ever tried it?'

She smiled guiltily. 'Just the odd drop.'

Cassius grabbed his glass and her mug and emptied the contents into a bowl.

With a squeak of delight she poured them both a generous measure.

'Wonderful,' Cassius said when they'd tried it.

'It is.'

Cassius put his glass down and leaned across the counter. 'May I kiss you, Hanina?'

She surrendered with a coy pout.

Realising she was not the type of girl to appreciate an aggressive approach, Cassius kissed her softly on the cheek. Noting that her eyes were shut, he reached across and gently gripped her neck. He was just closing in again when a door latch snapped open.

'Gods, he's back!'

Cassius could tell by the panic in her voice that discovery might well endanger her job. As Neokles announced his return, he downed his wine and pointed at the barrel. 'You'd better plug that.'

Cassius ran out to the terrace, where he found Indavara sitting sideways on the bench and Kitra sitting on him, one large, pale breast encircled by the bodyguard's hand.

'Sorry to interrupt but Neokles is back.'

'Gods help me!' In her haste to get off Indavara, Kitra fell to the floor, giving Cassius a flash of her wobbling thighs.

He laughed as Indavara helped her up. Kitra rearranged herself then hurried back inside.

Cassius heard something smash on the floor and Neokles telling Hanina off. He sat down opposite Indavara, who looked as if he'd just awoken from a dream.

'Bad timing, eh? You'd better not get too excited, not in your condition.'

Indavara looked down at his groin. 'At least I know everything's working.'

'Again – really didn't need to know that.'

Neokles popped his head outside. 'I do apologise for the noise, Master Crispian. I trust these wretched girls haven't disturbed you.'

'Oh, not at all. On the contrary, they were most compliant.'

VI

The mosaic that took up most of one wall was a simple geometric pattern: hundreds of red and white triangles. After a while, Cassius's eyes began to swim. He looked away and shook his head.

'Hangover, sir?' asked Simo, who was standing beside the only window.

'No.' He was angry with himself for breaking his three-mug rule – by some distance.

The servant standing outside the waiting room drew back the curtain and a new man walked in. Cassius had so far been through three of them and was starting to get annoyed. Even so, he stood and offered his hand; it usually paid to be polite at first – other tactics could be deployed if necessary.

'Good day.' This fellow was about thirty; well built but with the pasty, unmarked skin of a career bureaucrat.

They shook forearms; Cassius was purposefully forceful. 'Officer Crispian, Imperial Security.'

'Assistant Procurator Dominicus.' He looked down at the table. Lying across it was Cassius's ceremonial spearhead.

'At last, a man of standing. I do hope you can help me.'

'What is it exactly you need from us? My subordinates didn't seem entirely clear.'

'Good,' said Cassius. 'It is important that as few people know about this issue as possible.'

'I see.' Dominicus sat down and adjusted his toga until he was comfortable.

Knowing his uniform would get him a long way at the basilica, Cassius was in a scarlet tunic and wearing the widest and most martial of his belts. He also had his sword belt over his shoulder, though he had left the helmet at the inn – it was far too hot. He held up the sword as he sat to avoid scraping the floor.

'You are aware of the ongoing investigation into counterfeiting?'

'Isn't the treasury in charge of that?'

'It is. But Marshal Marcellinus has also asked the Service to get involved.'

Though he masked it reasonably well, the mere mention of Marcellinus caused a change in Dominicus' expression. Cassius held the equivalent rank of a centurion and the spearhead marked him out as a specialist officer but in normal circumstances a soldier wouldn't dare make demands of a senior city official. Being a 'grain man' wasn't all bad; especially when one was acting on behalf of the Emperor's second-in-command.

'I need some information regarding recent significant land purchases in Tripolis and the surrounding area. Would you have that type of information here?'

'Yes. Any change in ownership has to be reported. That information would appear on the land register, including the value – for tax purposes.'

'I'm interested in purchases from the last two months.'

Dominicus put a finger on his chin to check what looked like a shaving cut. 'What would you consider "significant"?'

'It depends. What's the going rate for a square mile of decent farmland around here?'

'Anything between one and two thousand denarii.'

'It would probably be a large plot.'

'If memory serves the register is divided up. The roll for the largest purchases deals with values of above ten thousand denarii.'

'Could you provide me with that immediately?'

'Certainly within an hour, I should say. I would need some sort of authorisation from the magistrate's office.'

'I don't have time for that. Marshal Marcellinus considers this an urgent matter.'

Cassius was prepared to take out his letter but the second mention of Marcellinus was enough to persuade Dominicus.

'Very well.' He stood. 'Will you wait here or should I have the information copied out and sent to you?'

'I shall go for lunch then return.'

Dominicus checked the shaving cut again then left.

Cassius put the spearhead in his satchel. It was two feet long and didn't quite fit so he put the sharp end (protected by a cork) in first, leaving the shaft sticking out of the top. He gave the satchel to Simo.

'Let's go and fetch Indavara; I expect he's ready for some lunch.'

Behind the basilica was a walled garden where the bodyguard had taken refuge from the heat beneath a tall pine. Spotting Cassius and Simo, he ambled over.

'Feeling better?' asked Simo.

'A bit.'

'Pitiful effort,' said Cassius. 'I doubt you had more than four or five mugs. I can do that and still recite a dozen different poems.'

One of the soldiers on duty opened the gate at the rear of the garden. Cassius nodded to the legionary and his compatriot as they walked out on to the street.

'Still a good night,' said Indavara.

'Maybe for you,' said Cassius. 'That bloody Neokles spoiled my fun. You didn't waste much time, though.'

Indavara blushed and smothered a grin.

'Lucky swine,' said Cassius. 'You're fortunate I let you have Kitra.'

'*Let* me? It's not my fault if she knows a real man when she sees one.'

Cassius unleashed a roar of laughter at that. He would allow the bodyguard this victory; relations with women were one of the areas where Cassius was so unquestionably superior that there was no real element of competition. Come to think of it, apart from perhaps running, there were very few areas where they were close enough to compete. All things considered, Cassius reckoned that was a good thing.

'Anyway,' he said, 'where are we going for lunch? We've got an hour to kill so we might as well sit down.'

'The soldiers said there's a decent place by the statue of Marcus Aurelius. Plenty of choice, apparently.' Indavara nodded along the broad avenue that ran west from the basilica towards the coast.

'Let's give it a try,' said Cassius, leading the way. The avenue was busy with folk of all kinds, and they also had to get past a line of six plush litters, the occupants of which remained completely hidden. Emerging from under a portico, the trio passed a series of street entertainers who had attracted quite a crowd. There was a troupe of mimes, a juggler (who they stopped to watch for a couple of minutes), a pair of adult acrobats no taller than four feet, and – least popular of all – an elderly woman playing a flute.

Seeing the impressive bronze statue of Marcus Aurelius high above the multitude ahead, Cassius began looking for the tavern.

'What was it called, this place?'

Receiving no answer, he turned round.

Only Simo was behind him. 'I don't know, sir.'

'Where's Indavara gone?'

He looked back through the endless stream of pedestrians. The bodyguard was standing in front of the flautist, staring at her.

Cassius tutted. 'Fetch him, would you, Simo.'

The Gaul navigated his way back through the crowd. Cassius moved closer to a nearby stall to avoid the worst of the foul-smelling throng. He watched Simo speak to Indavara but the bodyguard didn't move. Simo spoke again and gripped his arm but Indavara completely ignored him.

'By the gods.' Cassius hurried back, cursing at a pair of young girls who seemed unable or unwilling to get out of his way.

'What are you doing?'

The flautist seemed rather disturbed by Indavara's stare. She stopped playing, lowered her instrument and looked curiously back at him.

'Indavara.'

He was standing completely still, arms by his sides. 'That tune . . . I know it.'

'So what?'

'I know it,' he repeated, now staring at the ground.

Simo said, 'Do you mean . . .'

Cassius said, 'From before?'

'I . . . I think so.'

Cassius inspected the woman. Her clothes were thin and dirty, the flute roughly carved. The cloth hat between her bare feet contained only a few brass coins.

'Keep playing.'

The woman's only response was to adjust the headscarf that covered most of her grey hair. Cassius tried Greek but again got no reply. Simo spoke in Aramaic. The woman smiled and started playing again. It was a simple, repetitive tune, no more than a dozen notes in all.

Indavara gazed at her.

'You sure you haven't heard it somewhere else?' said Cassius. 'We've been through a lot of cities, heard a lot of tunes.'

Eyes now wet, Indavara whispered something to Simo.

'What?' asked the Gaul.

'Ask her to stop. Tell her to stop.'

Simo did so.

Cassius took a sesterce from his money bag and dropped it into the hat. The old woman bowed to him.

Indavara seemed frozen to the spot. He was still looking at her but had wiped his eyes before the tears fell.

'Do you remember something more?' asked Simo.

'I – I thought so, but . . .'

'Simo, ask her where the tune is from.'

The attendant had to think for a moment about his Aramaic. Despite his best efforts the woman couldn't help. 'Her mother taught it to her but she doesn't know where it comes from.'

'Damn it,' said Cassius. 'Tell her to keep playing. Loudly.' He turned to the passing crowd and spoke up. 'Anyone here know this tune? A denarius to anyone who knows it.'

At the mention of money, several people stopped and listened.

Indavara put up a hand. 'Corbulo, don't. There's no point.'

'Nonsense. We might learn something more. You need to know.'

He repeated his announcement and soon a dozen people had gathered. When the flautist stopped for a moment Cassius yelled at her to continue.

An old man with a walking stick came to the front and spoke in Latin. 'I don't remember the name but I know where it's from. My neighbour used to play it on *his* flute. He was a Gaul and he said his province had the best music in the world.'

'You're sure?' said Cassius.

The old man listened carefully. 'Certain. I always liked that tune.'

Cassius addressed the small crowd once more. 'Anyone know the name? Anyone?'

When there was no reply, he gave the old man his denarius and turned to Indavara. 'Gaul. Do you think you heard it there? Do you think that's where you might be from?'

'I – I don't know.'

'Let's get to that tavern. I reckon you could do with a drink.'

Indavara said little over a brief (but good) lunch and Cassius left him with Simo in the garden when they returned to the basilica. Dominicus was already in the waiting room and escorted him to a small office where he could work undisturbed. The assistant procurator gave him a papyrus roll: the land register showing the largest transactions for the year. Politely asking Cassius to look after it, Dominicus left, shutting the door behind him.

Upon the office's table were a bronze pen, a pot of freshly mixed ink and some blank paper. Holding the wooden roller with one hand, Cassius unravelled the paper with the other. Once he could see it all, the roll was almost a yard long. Unsurprisingly, the ink was brightest at the bottom. The land register listed the location of the plot, its size (plus a description of number and type of buildings), the buyer, the seller, the date of sale, the price and tax paid. There was also a reference number for a more detailed report.

Cassius found a sale from around two months earlier and rolled up the papyrus so he could focus on transactions after that date. There were nine sales in total, most of them to a single buyer, a few to partnerships. Cassius filled up the pen and started writing. Next to the buyer's name he noted the date and location. He began to wonder how much real use the information might be but he wanted to get started; and as Quentin hadn't considered this angle it might not be a complete waste of time. The treasury agent had sent a message to the inn that morning; one of his clerks would deliver a summary of their interviews with the casters later in the day.

Once the list was complete, Cassius rolled up the register and put the page of notes in his satchel. The servant waiting outside went to fetch Dominicus, who escorted him out. When they stopped at the rear door, Cassius thanked the assistant procurator, who cordially asked whether he could offer any more help.

'There might be one more thing – purchases of gems and precious metals. Would there be any record of those?'

'Not here. Such transactions are private – conducted between traders and private individuals. No tax is paid unless the valuables are moved through toll gates.'

'As I thought. Thank you again. Good day.'

'Good day.'

Three hours later, Cassius was awoken from a mid-afternoon nap by Simo, who had a mug of milk for him.

'Any good?' he asked as he sat up.

'Very, sir. Fresh this morning, according to Neokles. There is a man here waiting for you. On behalf of Master Quentin.'

'Ah.' Cassius was so thirsty that he drank the milk in one go. 'That *is* good.'

He had been sleeping only in a loincloth. As he stood and yawned, Simo picked up his tunic.

'How's Indavara?'

'Not saying much, sir.' Simo lowered the tunic over his master's head.

'And in the garden? When you were alone?'

Simo straightened the tunic, then handed Cassius his belt. 'He didn't say so but I think he remembered something more than the tune. Perhaps *someone*.'

'Gods, no wonder it upset him. I still find it hard to imagine what it must be like to remember nothing of the past.'

Simo shook his head. 'I have prayed many times for him, asked the Lord to give him a sign.'

Cassius buckled his belt. 'You believe that was it?'

'Maybe.'

'Well, at least we know more than we did. Perhaps he'll remember more over time. Where is he now?'

'He left about an hour ago. Barefoot.'

'Ah, a run – to clear his head. Probably not a bad idea. Right, let's see what Quentin's man has for me.'

The clerk was named Segestes, a young man of around twenty. Cassius found him laughing along with Kitra and gruffly ordered him to accompany him back to his room. Simo cleared a few things off the table and they sat down. Segestes was carrying a lightweight wooden box which he slid across to Cassius.

'We finished the interviews this morning, sir. Our notes are summarised here. Master Quentin said you needed them immediately so he had Arruntius's scribes copy them out for you.'

Cassius opened the box. Inside was a pile of papers with names at the top and notes written in two different hands.

'Good. Anything stand out?'

'Not particularly, sir.'

'How many men did you interview?'

'All sixteen we were asked to. Eight currently employed at the mint, eight who used to be.'

'What did you ask them?'

'Firstly, if they were involved in counterfeiting.' The clerk said this with a straight face.

'Oh, very subtle.'

'You know, sir – to test their reaction.'

'Mmm. Anybody seem particularly anxious?'

'Most, really. Especially the ones that still work there.'

'Understandable, I suppose. What else did you ask?'

'If they had ever passed on any information regarding the mint and the manufacture of currency; if anyone had ever approached them; if they had seen or heard anything about fake coins; if they had travelled much recently—'

'About being approached – any of them say they had?'

'Most. A few said they never had been, which we thought might be a bit suspicious.'

'Those that had – any names come out of that?'

'No, sir.'

'Hardly surprising. Anything else strike you? Gut reaction?'

Segestes looked down and realised that his amulet – a red stone rendering of Mars – was hanging outside his tunic. He tucked it back in before answering. 'One of the retired men had a very nice villa by the coast. These casters do quite well, but not *that* well, and he'd only left the mint a few years ago.'

'What does he do now?' asked Cassius.

'Property, he said.'

'I would be more inclined to suspect the man concealing his wealth than the man displaying it.'

'It's funny you should say that, sir. What was his name? Eryx – one of those who said he'd never been approached about counterfeiting. He wore *very* plain clothes – and not a single ring or bracelet.'

'Right.'

'And – I think it was him . . .' Segestes rifled through the pages until he found the right one. 'Yes. He insisted on coming to the mint as soon as we contacted him. Didn't want us to go to him.'

'Or see his house, perhaps?'

'Maybe, sir.'

'What are you doing now?'

'I was going to report back to Master Quentin.'

'Do you have an address for this Eryx character?'

72

Segestes consulted the sheet again. 'Yes, sir.'

'Go and have a look at his house. See what it's like and what else you can find out. My man Simo will give you some coin – throw a bit at the neighbours if you have to. You're interested in who he associates with, whether he's spent much money recently, visitors to the house and so on.'

'That will take time, sir.'

'Don't worry, I'll make sure Quentin knows where you are. You can take a couple of coins for yourself too.'

'Thank you, sir.' Segestes checked the address again. 'It's on the other side of the city. I'd better get going.'

Simo came over with the money. He gave the clerk two sesterces and a dozen more for the bribes.

'Send word to me later,' said Cassius.

'I can call in, sir, it's pretty much on my way back to the mint.' Segestes left.

'Simo, write a note on my behalf to Quentin and find a lad to run it up to the mint. Thank him for providing me with these transcripts and inform him that I have sent Segestes on an important task. I will call in at some point tomorrow to liaise with him once more.'

'Yes, sir.'

Cassius reached into the box, took out the first sheet and started reading.

Indavara returned an hour later. Cassius's door was open to get some air in and he looked on as the bodyguard asked Hanina for a jug of water. By the looks of him, he had been running for the entire time; sweat was pouring off his face and his feet were black. Kitra came along and tried to talk to him but Indavara took his water and hurried into his room.

Simo was sitting on his bed, polishing Cassius's riding boots with a brush. He looked at his master and shrugged.

'We'll leave him be for now,' said Cassius. 'I dare say he'll show his face for dinner.'

'How are you faring, sir?'

Cassius had just finished the last page. 'There are a few potential leads but Segestes and his colleague haven't exactly been thorough. If we don't make any progress elsewhere I may have to interview these men again.'

'Do you think we'll be in Tripolis for a while, sir?'

'Hard to say. I expect you're wondering if it's worth seeking out the nearest church-house?'

Simo continued with his work.

'You *can* talk about it. I think we both know my position on the matter but I don't intend to stop you.'

'Much appreciated, sir.'

'I suppose I should seek out the Temple of Jupiter – give thanks for this assignment.'

'It does seem less perilous than some, sir.'

'Let us hope it remains so.'

Hearing Neokles snapping orders at the girls, Cassius watched the owner stagger in with two amphoras which he dumped beside the bar. A pair of lads were trailing along behind him, both weighed down with baskets full of bread and fruit.

'Something happening tonight, Simo?'

'Master Neokles belongs to a guild of innkeepers, sir. I believe he is hosting a function.'

'Balls.'

'Are you worried about the noise, sir?'

'No, Simo. I'm worried about the girls. They'll be busy all bloody night.'

VII

Even though Neokles had set up a grill on the terrace and the smell of roasting lamb reached every corner of the inn, Indavara did not appear. As the first of the innkeeper's guests began to arrive, Cassius knocked on the bodyguard's door. There was no answer but he opened it.

Indavara was lying on his bed in the same sodden tunic he'd run in. The windowless room was stuffy and hot. Cassius left the door open.

'Shut it, please.'

'Gods, man, it's like a furnace in here.'

'Corbulo.'

'All right.' Cassius shut it, then moved the bodyguard's fighting stave out of his way and sat on a stool. Indavara was staring blankly up at the ceiling. Cassius noticed his tiny Fortuna figurine on the bedside table.

'Not hungry?'

Indavara shook his head.

'What about some sword practice – I'll have Neokles put up some lamps outside.'

'Too tired.'

'Where did you run to?'

'Up the coast. Some town. Zi . . . something.'

'Zigara. That's five miles away. You ran ten miles in this heat? On the road?'

'Mostly beach, actually.'

'You have to have some of that roast lamb. The crackling's delicious.'

Indavara turned his head towards him at last. 'It's fading.'

'The memory?'

Indavara reached up with one hand and held it above his head. 'It was so clear. Now . . .' The hand formed a fist, which he smacked down on to the bed.

'What was it?'

'A clearing in a forest. It was cold. Frost on the trees. There were many of us. Someone spoke to me. A woman.'

'Could it be—'

'Could be anyone.'

'Anything else?'

Indavara shook his head.

'Was that tune playing there? There might be some association.'

'I – I don't know.'

Cassius pulled the stool closer to the bed. 'Listen, I can see it's difficult for you. But this is a good thing.'

'How? What if I never remember anything more? It could be a thousand places, a million.'

'The old man said Gaul. Frost? You've told me before you think you're from the northern provinces.'

'Simo told me Gaul is huge, bigger even than Syria.'

'There is more we can do. Remember my idea – writing to the Service man in Pietas Julia? I did a little research; there's no officer there but Abascantius gave me a contact in Siscia, not far away at all. It's only two years since you were freed – he can find out about this Capito, the organiser of games.'

Indavara picked up the figurine.

Cassius knew the wiser option was to tell him to forget it all; that there really was no hope. Abascantius had warned him about encouraging the bodyguard along a path that might eventually lead him away. To counter such a possibility, the two agents had persuaded him to take an oath to join the army earlier in the year. But, once again, Indavara had saved Cassius's life. What he owed the man could not be expressed in words, only actions. If he could help him solve the riddle that was his past, he would do it.

'Perhaps this was Fortuna's doing,' he said, nodding at the figurine.

'You really think so?'

'This is how the gods work. They give us signs. We're in Syria, yet we heard a tune from Gaul. I don't think you should ignore it.'

'Could you send the letter tomorrow?'

'Yes, but don't get carried away. It will take weeks to hear anything and there may well be nothing to hear. But it's a start.'

Indavara sat up. 'Then please do it.'

'That's the spirit. I shall write it first thing.'

Indavara looked down at the figurine again.

'So, some dinner?' asked Cassius. 'A wash might be advisable too or Kitra won't come near you again.'

'I'll stay in here tonight.'

'I know this is unsettling but try not to let it gnaw away at you. Life has to go on. Shall I tell Simo to get a plate for you? And ask Neokles for some hot water?'

Indavara got up off the bed.

'Good.'

Having failed to get to the baths, Cassius needed a wash himself. Once Simo had finished drying him, he put on a clean tunic. It was a rather effeminate light blue – purchased originally for him to disguise himself as a merchant while on assignment in Arabia – but he now found he quite liked it.

Segestes returned at the second hour of night. Disappointingly, the villa of the ex-caster Eryx had turned out to be utterly average; and the most incriminating evidence gleaned from his neighbours was that he always needed reminding to trim his hedge. Cassius thanked the clerk for his efforts and dismissed him.

Indavara appeared for a while to eat some lamb and spoke briefly to the girls but went to bed early. With Simo studying one of his medical tomes, Cassius was left alone at the bar. The inn was now occupied by a dozen or so men from Neokles's guild. Once they'd all had their fill of lamb, bread and accompanying vegetables, they sat around two big tables pushed together. Cassius exchanged the odd remark with the girls but once the meal was over they had quite a pile of crockery to wash up.

He sat there sipping his wine, thoughts alternating between what he'd like to do with the voluptuous Kitra and the counterfeiting investigation. If the gang were as professional in other areas as they were with the production of the coins, progress might be slow. It might become a laborious, time-consuming slog, and he doubted either Marshal Marcellinus or Minister Sabinus would be particularly patient. Even so, he remained hopeful. Quentin seemed sure that such gangs were not well established in this part of the world and this complicated endeavour would require a lot of people. Like any human activity, the greater the complexity and the numbers involved, the greater the chance of a mistake.

The girls took so long in the kitchen that Cassius considered taking a walk; he knew there were other taverns close by. But even though they were now so far from Bostra, it didn't seem wise to wander the darkened streets alone.

Eventually, Kitra and Hanina returned to the parlour, their main duty now to keep the guildsmen's glasses full. The fussy Neokles would catch their eye whenever one of his compatriots was getting low and repeatedly prompted them to bring fresh bowls of nuts and dried fruit. The innkeepers were getting louder, telling jokes and funny tales – mostly about guests past and present.

Cassius continued his charm offensive with Kitra and Hanina, adapting his style according to whom he was talking to. Kitra seemed genuinely concerned about Indavara so Cassius told her an old injury was troubling him. Hanina seemed keen to talk and spent her spare moments asking about his travels.

But when a guildsman returned from the latrine to announce it was blocked, the unfortunate girls were dispatched to investigate. Cassius would have retired then but his wine had just been topped up. He felt quite proud of himself; his last mug of the day was his third.

Talk in the parlour had turned to local politics. Cassius listened in and heard mention of several notable figures, including the procurator and the magistrate. Someone made a hushed comment and there was a moment of silence. Cassius turned and saw that half the guildsmen were staring at him. In a way the timing was fortuitous; it had just occurred to him that Neokles's guests might be of use.

He got off the stool and walked over, smiling. 'Gentlemen, please do not censor yourselves on my account.'

'Apologies, Centurion Crispian,' said Neokles, 'I would not want you to feel uncomfortable.'

'Please. This is not my city. Continue as you would normally. I shall soon be retiring, though I did wonder if I might ask for a few minutes of your time.'

Neokles stood. 'Of course, what can I do for you?'

'I meant all of you.' Cassius looked around the group. 'What is the name of this distinguished association?'

'The Guild of East Tripolis Inn and Tavern Keepers.'

'Ah. Today I met with Assistant Procurator Dominicus and I dare say I'll be meeting him again. As a gesture of mutual cooperation, I could perhaps put in a word for the guild. Is there a particular matter you might wish me to mention?'

For a moment no one spoke. Then a corpulent character wearing a heavily embroidered tunic caught Cassius's eye. 'Excuse me, Centurion.' He spoke a few sentences in Aramaic. The others considered his point then gave their assent.

'We would be most appreciative if you could bring up the subject of military billeting. We have heard that several centuries will be passing through in the coming weeks and there has been an unfortunate tendency to favour the western side of the city because it is fractionally closer to the army compound. We would like to see this imbalance redressed.'

'I shall ensure that the assistant procurator knows of your concern.'

The large man walked over and they shook forearms. 'Theopropides, chief of the guild.' He grabbed a chair for Cassius while the others cleared a space.

'Many thanks. I shall be back in a moment.' Cassius went to

his room and retrieved the spearhead and the page of information from the land register.

'Need me, sir?' said Simo, getting up off his bed.

'Yes – to make notes.'

While Simo grabbed some writing materials, Cassius returned to the parlour. He doubted the innkeepers would know a lot about the casters, but they were clearly familiar with the great and the good of Tripolis. As he sat down, Neokles placed his wine on the table.

Cassius laid the spearhead next to it. 'It is best that you know who you are addressing. I am Centurion Cassius Oranius Crispian, currently attached to the governor's staff of Arabia.' He thought it best not to mention the Service – partly to protect his anonymity in Tripolis, partly to negate any unpleasant associations his audience might have with 'grain men'. He had used centurion with Neokles because 'officer' would confuse him.

'I am here on an assignment given to me by Marshal Marcellinus himself. I'm sure it goes without saying that this is all in confidence.'

'Of course,' said Theopropides, pushing silver bangles up his chubby arm.

'Now, if I may, I will read out some names. I am not looking for scandal or secrets, merely some background information. It occurred to me that you gentlemen might be extremely well informed.'

'Please,' said another of the guildsmen.

Cassius pushed his chair back a little so that they couldn't see the list. Simo grabbed himself a stool and sat behind him, ready with writing block, paper and pen.

'Scribonius Maursus.'

Theopropides took the lead. 'Local landowner, his main estate is south of the city. Interests in shipping and olive oil.'

'Three vineyards also,' said another man.

Simo scribbled the first of his notes.

'Not particularly concerned with politics,' added Neokles. 'His brother represents the family on the city council.'

Cassius nodded appreciatively. He would have liked to ask

about the man's reputation and the very scandals he'd claimed not to be interested in but the guildsmen would instantly clam up. Despite their enthusiasm, he was a visitor and had offered them only a comparatively small favour; the innkeepers would not be impolitic enough to impugn their betters in so open a way.

'Good, thank you.' And so it went on. Cassius considered all the information useful but there was nothing of real interest until the sixth name: an individual named Vesnius Isatis. Theopropides offered the basics on his business interests but said nothing more and no one else seemed keen to contribute.

Eventually, Neokles spoke up. 'You might mention his name to Assistant Procurator Dominicus. He would . . . know more, I'm sure.'

'Very well.'

Cassius continued down the list. The guildsmen passed on what they knew. Simo made his notes.

The penultimate name was that of one Numerius Afer. Upon hearing it, Theopropides hesitated, grimaced, then took a sip of wine. One man was about to speak but another held up his hand. Then an argument broke out in Aramaic. Neokles leant close to Cassius and apologised. After a short time, Theopropides silenced the others and continued in Greek.

'Brothers, it is a matter of public record. The centurion here will learn this and more besides as soon as he mentions the name to Dominicus or for that matter anyone else in Tripolis.' He turned to Cassius. 'Several months ago, Afer's business concerns were appropriated by the procurator and sold off. It later emerged that he had built up an enormous tax bill. He also had to sell off some land and relocate to a smaller property. The next name?'

Once they had finished, Cassius thanked the guildsmen effusively and reiterated his promise to speak to Dominicus about military billeting. Once back in his room, he sat down at the table.

'Here, sir.' Simo put the notes down in front of him.

Cassius was more interested in what he'd copied down at the

basilica. Despite his supposed financial difficulties, Numerius Afer had purchased no less than four hundred acres of land north of Tripolis. It was both the most recent purchase and the most costly; almost thirty thousand denarii.

'Anything useful, sir?' asked Simo as he prepared his master's bed.

'Maybe, Simo. Maybe.'

VIII

'Sir, sir, wake up. Sir!'

'Yes, yes.'

Cassius was in the middle of a very pleasant daydream about Kitra. In fact the object of his desire was a composite: Hanina's face and Kitra's body. In any case, it took him a moment to remember he was sitting on a bench in the basilica garden.

'There, sir,' said Simo, pointing at the path.

Deputy Procurator Dominicus was striding along, a dozen subordinates in his wake. Still dozy, Cassius staggered as he stood up, then jogged between two sprawling bushes towards the path.

'Deputy Procurator.'

Dominicus stopped and turned so abruptly that some of his men collided with each other. The administrator could not hide his annoyance that he was being dragged away from his daily work once more.

'Good day, Officer,' he said with a thin smile.

'Good day. I have a couple of questions for you.'

Dominicus barged his way through his men and led Cassius into the shade of the basilica wall. 'Yes?'

'There are two individuals I need to know more about. One is named Vesnius Isatis. I gather he has had some difficulties of late.'

Dominicus flicked away a fly that was circling his head. 'That's something of an understatement. He's a notorious womaniser. A few months ago, his long-suffering wife finally reached the end of her tether. She put a list of his conquests outside the forum for all to see. Apparently it was only the recent ones but it still filled a page. The scandal ruined his reputation in Berytus – he managed to offend just about everyone who mattered. I used to know him quite well – only socially, you understand. He doesn't have the initiative to be involved in some criminal scheme, nor the time for that matter.'

'I see. The other man is Numerius Afer.'

'I believe he's had his own difficulties,' said Dominicus, 'financial, that is.'

'Apparently. Him I am definitely interested in.'

'What do you need?'

'Anything really – business interests, property, family, employees.'

Dominicus pointed at the basilica. 'I'll lend you one of my clerks, Planta, for the morning. He's worked here for more than twenty years, knows everyone in Tripolis.'

'Thank you.'

They walked towards the entrance. 'Officer Crispian, on behalf of the procurator and the magistrate I must ask you to tread carefully. I asked the same of Quentin. You may be operating with the authority of Marshal Marcellinus himself but even the suggestion of involvement in a criminal plot could be very damaging for one of our citizens.'

'I understand.'

'Come, I'll have someone find Planta for you.'

Despite possessing only one arm, the clerk soon proved himself to be both enthusiastic and capable. Cassius spoke to him in the same office he'd been assigned the previous day and Planta immediately confirmed that Numerius Afer had indeed fallen on hard times. Afer did not hail from one of the local families; he was in fact Sicilian, though Planta reckoned he had been in Tripolis for more than a decade. The clerk then suggested finding out what he could from the local census completed the previous year. Cassius asked him to do so, then took a walk around the basilica. He belatedly realised he had failed to pass on the concerns of Neokles's guild about billeting. Then again, he'd only mentioned it to secure their cooperation and – judging by their clothing and jewellery – Theopropides and friends weren't exactly struggling.

He found the other two waiting in the garden. Simo was reading (a religious tract this time) while Indavara was sitting with his arms crossed, looking rather depressed.

'I'm starting to wish you'd taken that Egypt job instead.'

'Not me,' said Cassius as he sat down.

'Reading all that stuff, talking all bloody day. Don't you get bored?'

'This is proper investigative work. A cerebral exercise and – to be frank – something I seem to be rather good at. Let's hope that Service man in Siscia is good at it too; he might find out something more for you.'

Cassius had sent the letter to the army way station first thing that morning. There was no quicker way to get a message across the Empire. More than a thousand miles separated Tripolis and Serdica but, with a bit of luck, Abascantius's contact might be reading it within two weeks.

'And I'll tell you something else,' added Cassius. 'If I can find this gang I might even impress Marcellinus enough to free myself from Abascantius's grip.'

'What are we waiting for now?' asked Indavara.

Cassius was looking at the path. 'Him.'

Planta was a bulky man with a peculiar gait. The left side of his tunic was sewn up, presumably to hide some ugly wound or withered limb. Despite his disadvantages, he had a youthful face and a hearty manner. Cassius had also taken to him because – unlike many easterners – he used Latin, not Greek.

'There you are, sir.'

'What have you got for me?'

'The relevant pages.' Planta was carrying a writing block and some papers with holes in one side. Evidently he had physically removed them from the census.

Simo stood, allowing Planta to sit on Cassius's left, between him and Indavara. The clerk nodded politely to the others. 'Good day.'

'Good day,' said Simo.

'Good day,' said Indavara. 'What happened to your arm?'

Simo tutted but Planta didn't seem to mind answering. 'It happened when I was a lad. I was helping my father replace some tiles when I slipped and fell. The arm was so badly crushed it had to be removed.'

'Surgeon?' asked Indavara.

Planta gave an ironic smile. 'My father. He had been a soldier. He did it with a wood axe, then sealed the wound with pitch.'

'You were lucky,' said Indavara.

'Very,' said Planta. 'Though I didn't think so at the time.'

Cassius frowned at them. 'If you're quite finished.'

'Sorry, sir.' Planta put the writing block on his lap and showed Cassius several pages. 'As you can see, the census was conducted in June of last year. This first page lists the acreage of Afer's estate, land use, buildings and so on. This second page concerns financial dealings: interests, holdings, taxes. The final page concerns household staff and other employees.'

Cassius put the second page on top but it was hard to make out the words. 'Bloody sun. Simo, give us some shade.'

The Gaul walked around to the back of the bench to shield him.

'That's better. Some big numbers here. This time last year Afer was a very, very rich man.'

Simo's hand suddenly appeared over the writing block. 'May I, sir?'

'Yes.'

The attendant pulled the paper down so he could see the third page.

'Ah, I thought so.'

'What is it?'

'Here, sir.' Simo pointed to a name on the list of Afer's employees.

'C. Varius Micon,' said Cassius. 'One of the ex-casters from the mint.'

Simo already had the satchel open. He found the right page and handed it to his master. Cassius checked the notes; Segestes and his colleague had recorded nothing suspicious about the man. He checked the census report once more. Micon was listed as one of Afer's silversmiths.

'Well, well. Good spot, Simo.'

Cassius looked at the list of employees again. Another name caught his attention. 'S. Novius Gallus'. This man had also worked as a silversmith for Afer.

'Wasn't there . . .'

Cassius checked Segestes's list. Gallus was also one of the retired mint workers. 'Two! Two of them.'

He examined the notes again; both men had left their jobs at the Tripolis mint the previous year.

Cassius leant back. 'So, the casters Micon and Gallus leave to take jobs with a bankrupt master who then somehow makes enough money to buy a huge tract of land.'

'Why didn't Segestes realise they both work for Afer?' asked Simo.

'Maybe they don't any more. The census is a year old – perhaps they left his employ to cover up their connection. Or maybe Segestes just missed it. In any case, I think it's time I had a word with Numerius Afer.'

Cassius considered contacting Quentin but the thought of returning to the mint having already identified a solid suspect was just too appealing. The helpful Planta obtained Afer's current address, which turned out to be barely a quarter-mile from the basilica. The respectable but modest townhouse revealed little about its owner. The servant at the gate revealed even less until Cassius threatened him with arrest for obstructing an imperial agent. Unfortunately, Afer was not at home: he and his wife were attending a function hosted by a local dignitary at a villa south of Tripolis.

The trio called in at the stables by the inn to fetch their mounts then got some directions from the lads there and set off. A mile beyond the city's south gate, they were delayed by a mass of riders and pedestrians queuing for a horse fair. Cassius employed his most commanding voice to clear a path and they continued on through pastures where young herders and their dogs watched over sheep and goats.

The villa belonged to a man named Megakreon, and the well-paved road that led to his home was marked by a marble stone bearing the name in huge lettering.

'No chance of anyone missing that,' said Cassius as they guided the horses on to the road. He could see only a gatehouse about two hundred yards ahead; the rest of the property was replete with ancient oaks, some with trunks ten feet around.

'I've got a good feeling about this Afer character,' added Cassius. 'Gods, at this rate, I'll have this gang in chains by the end of the week.'

'Why not just watch him?' suggested Indavara. 'If he is up to no good you might be able to work out who else is involved.'

'Yes, but we might also end up watching him for a week and get nowhere. Better to go straight in and catch him out before he hears we're on to him. See how he reacts. If he's involved, I'll know it. And he'll give every last one of the others up to keep his head out of a noose.'

'Lucky – spotting those names.'

'Lucky? No – all that talking and reading you thought so pointless. Proper investigative work. I think it's my orator's training – that and my memory, of course. I've always been good at making connections, spotting details.'

'Good for you,' said Indavara, wincing as he checked his nether regions. 'But you'd better not wrap it up too quickly or Abascantius might send us off to Egypt after all.'

'Not if I have anything to do with it.'

Stretching out of sight on either side of the gatehouse was a six-foot stone wall. As they reined in, an armed man came up to the imposing iron gate and inspected them. Cassius dismounted, spearhead at the ready.

'Good day. This is the Megakreon residence?'

'It is.'

'I am Centurion Crispian. I need to speak with a man named Numerius Afer and I believe he's here.'

'There is a function today.'

'I know. He's attending it.'

A second, older man appeared from behind the right side of the arch. 'Sorry, sir. Master Megakreon gave strict instructions that no one other than guests was to be admitted today.'

'But you *will* admit me.'

'Not unless you have an invitation.'

Cassius held up the spearhead. 'You do know what this is?'

'You belong to the governor's staff.'

It wasn't necessary to mention that the governor in question ruled Arabia. 'That's right. And the Imperial Security Service.'

The older man stepped up close to the bars. 'Then I would have thought you would know that Master Megakreon has some very influential and powerful friends. And that he would not appreciate an unannounced visit. The function will be over by the seventh hour. You can visit Afer at his own home.'

'I want to see him now.'

Indavara had also dismounted. He ambled past Cassius and up to the gate. 'You heard the man. Open up.'

He didn't usually make a move without being prompted; Cassius reckoned he was still in a bad mood after the previous day.

Indavara stepped back and eyed the wall. 'Or you can leave it shut. But then I'll have to climb over, kick the shit out of you two and open it myself.'

Cassius could have stopped the ex-bodyguard but he sometimes enjoyed such moments. With anyone else the two guards might have laughed the threat off or countered with an insult; but a swift look at Indavara's remarkable frame, countless collection of scars (including his disfigured left ear) and selection of weapons (short sword, dagger and fighting stave) kept them quiet.

Cassius was reluctant to invoke Marshal Marcellinus yet again so tried another tactic. 'Be assured that what my colleague suggests remains an alternative but I am not here to cause trouble, nor to disturb your master's function. All I require is a quiet word with Numerius Afer. I'm sure that can be arranged without too much fuss.'

The older man mulled this over. 'You'll wait where I tell you to until I've consulted Master Megakreon?'

'By all means.'

The guard took a large key from his belt and opened one side of the gate.

Cassius told Simo to wait outside with the horses. Indavara gestured for him to go through first.

'Why, thank you.'

IX

Once past the oaks, they could see the full extent of the villa's grounds. Cassius was reminded of some of the places he'd visited outside Rome; miles of parkland dotted with numerous artificial ponds, undoubtedly containing an impressive variety of fish. As they walked along the broad drive, a peacock strutted past, displaying its plumage as if under instruction from Megakreon.

The villa itself was less remarkable; a sprawling building in the rustic style favoured by Romans who lived a long way from home. To the right of the colonnaded entrance was a broad terrace where dozens of guests had gathered between colourful flowers, gurgling fountains and gleaming statues. A nearby trio of ladies wearing silk gowns with their hair piled high watched the strangers stop outside the front door, which was slightly ajar.

Another guard stood there; a burly man armed with a sword. He and his compatriot spoke briefly in Aramaic.

'Please wait here,' said the older guard. As he went inside, the large man moved in front of the door. His hair was cut short and his wide, iron-ringed belt was that of an ex-soldier who wanted people to know he was an ex-soldier. His sword was very similar to Indavara's.

Cassius took a handkerchief from behind his own belt and mopped his brow. 'Lovely day.'

The guard just looked at him and sniffed.

Cassius exchanged a grin with Indavara then retreated a few steps and looked over the hedge that separated the drive from the terrace. Though the ladies were displaying nothing but decorum, a group of men were clinking glasses and roaring with laughter. During a break in the noise, Cassius realised he could hear a harp playing inside.

When the older guard returned he looked flushed and even more anxious than before. With him was a man of a similar age wearing a dark green tunic and expensive shoes.

'Good day. I am Dryas, steward of Master Megakreon's household.'

'Good day. Your man told you why I'm here?'

'He did, and I have spoken to Master Megakreon. Numerius Afer is a good friend of his. Master Megakreon asked me to suggest that you arrange a meeting for tomorrow. If you consider that unacceptable, you will have to take the matter up with Centurion Cethegus. Cethegus is a *lifelong* friend of my master and – as I'm sure you're aware – commander of the Tripolis garrison.'

Cassius was aware of that; the men at the way station had told him. He also knew that Cethegus was away supervising repairs to the coast road and he wasn't about to waste time chasing after him. If Afer was involved in the counterfeiting, he could warn his associates or flee.

'Not good enough, I'm afraid. Has to be now.'

'Officer, please.' Dryas came forward and lowered his voice to a whisper. 'My master and his friends have been drinking most of the afternoon. He is in an . . . exuberant mood. If you were to cause a scene it might not end well for anyone.'

'There will be no scene if he sends out Numerius Afer. I doubt I will need more than quarter of an hour.'

'Sir, I really . . .' The steward somehow whispered even more quietly. 'Officer, what can I do *for you*? If you could make an accommodation I'm sure we could come to some arrangement.'

Cassius was not averse to a bribe on the right occasion but this was not it; he was rapidly running out of patience and the stakes were too high. 'I'll pretend I didn't hear that. If Afer's not standing where you are in two minutes, my friend and I are going to find him.'

Dryas sighed, then hurried back through the door.

Cassius watched some gardeners watering a dry patch of turf. A pair of maids appeared from the side of the house, each carrying a candelabra. Cassius winked at the prettier of the two but she ignored him. The guards parted to let them through the door.

'I reckon that's about a minute,' said Cassius.

Indavara nodded.

After a while the big guard laughed and pointed at him. 'Gods, I can see his lips moving. Not mastered counting in your head yet, friend?'

Indavara coloured and looked away. The older guard chuckled.

'And you are a mathematical genius, I suppose?' said Cassius. 'Here's a number for you. Twenty.'

'What about it?'

'If you're lucky, I won't have to tell you.'

Something thumped into the door behind the guards and a man lurched out. Judging from his lined, saggy face, he was well over sixty but his hair had been dyed a ridiculous shade of auburn. He was dressed in an opulent toga striped with silver and gold thread. He looked rather drunk and rather unhappy.

'You – are you this army fellow?'

'Officer Crispian. Good day, sir.'

Dryas exited the villa behind his master.

'As you can see, I'm entertaining.' Megakreon gestured towards the terrace. 'Come back another time, there's a good chap.'

'Sir, I'm afraid that's not possible. All I need is a few minutes with Numerius Afer. Perhaps there's somewhere quieter where we—'

Megakreon stepped closer; very close. He was tall, almost as tall as Cassius, who tried to ignore the foul breath upon his face.

'You do know who I am?'

Cassius kept his hands clasped behind him and his tone conciliatory.

'I do, sir. But I am carrying out a criminal investigation for the Imperial Security Service. I have made a polite request and I would like to see Afer now. If you don't mind.'

Megakreon slapped a hand on Cassius's shoulder.

'I've known Afer for ten years. It's not possible that he could be involved in anything criminal. Take my word for it.'

Cassius stepped back and took the spearhead from his satchel. 'Sir, I hold the rank of centurion and a written authorisation from Marshal Marcellinus. I have the right to question whomever I please.'

Megakreon glared at him. 'Not here, son. Not today. I suggest you turn around and walk down my drive or you'll be out of the army by the end of the week. All it will take is the right letter to the right man.'

Cassius didn't appreciate being called 'son'. Not now; not after all he'd been through in the last three years. He didn't much appreciate being told what to do either, not by this drunken old prick anyway.

'And I suggest you tell Afer to come out immediately, or we'll go and get him.'

'By Jupiter you shall not.'

Cassius walked around Megakreon, past Dryas and up to the door. He knew Indavara would be right behind him. He spoke to the guards.

'I am an officer of the Imperial Army and I am going through this door. I advise you to get out of my way.'

'Don't move an inch,' said Megakreon. Cassius was aware that a good number of the guests had moved to the side of the terrace to watch.

'That number,' he said. 'Twenty – the number of fights my friend won. In the arena.'

The guards looked at Indavara then glanced at each other and stepped aside.

'Very wise,' said Cassius as he walked into the villa.

'By the gods . . . I have never . . . this . . .' Megakreon sounded as if he were about to expire.

The first room was quite small and contained three luxurious couches and a dozen guests, who were already backing away.

'Good day,' Cassius said brightly. 'Can anyone tell me where I might find Numerius Afer?'

A middle-aged woman pointed through a doorway.

'Thank you.' Cassius and Indavara walked on, past a thick damask curtain and into a large atrium. The skylight was a colossal glass square. Four white busts framed the room, each standing upon a plinth of pink marble.

Sitting below the skylight was a female harpist. She was surrounded by guests but had stopped playing as others came in from the terrace to see what all the fuss was about. Cassius felt rather sick as he saw just how many were present at the party. He wanted this over quickly.

'Numerius Afer?'

'I believe he's outside,' said an elderly gentleman leaning on a stick.

'Ah, thank you.'

'Get them out!'

Cassius and Indavara turned to find Megakreon shepherding the guards from outside plus another pair towards them. He slapped two of his employees on the back. 'Do it or you'll never see a single bloody coin from me again.'

'Now, there's no need for any unpleasantness,' said Cassius, retreating.

Indavara stood his ground and took the stave from his back. 'I'm guessing no blades, right?'

'Right.'

'Rush him,' yelled Megakreon. 'Now!'

The two new arrivals charged. Indavara kept his hands in the middle of the stave and waited. He waited so long that Cassius almost shouted at him to do something.

The bodyguard struck out with the right end of the weapon first, catching one guard on the chin. His victim's eyes shot up into his head and he fell straight on to his backside, spilling a few coins that rolled away. Indavara shifted his weight then used the left end, hitting the next man a glancing blow on the cheek. As his hands went up to his face and he staggered away, Indavara thumped the stave down on to the curve of his back, pummelling him into the floor.

The older guard from outside had clearly decided he would risk unemployment but the big ex-soldier bravely elected to have a go. He was already moving at a run when Indavara shifted his grip to one end of the stave and swung the other into his flank.

The guard lurched to one side and cried out but then reached for his sword.

'Oh no you don't.' Indavara closed in and jabbed the stave into his opponent's hand, cracking it against his body. 'Didn't you hear? No blades.'

Gritting his teeth, the guard stared down at his red, limp right hand, then reached for the sword again, this time with his left.

'Some people just don't learn.'

The third blow caught the guard on the side of the head, sending him careering across the room like a drunk.

The harpist was already leaping out of the way. 'Look out! Not my—'

The guard plunged head first into the harp, knocking the instrument over then landing on top of it, one arm entangled in the strings.

Wincing, Cassius looked at Megakreon, whose face was turning purple.

A woman of about fifty ran in, holding up the flowing hem of her stola. 'Darling, what's . . .'

She looked at the three men on the ground, then Cassius and Indavara, who was already putting the stave over his shoulder.

'Excuse me, I'm Numerius Afer.'

Cassius spun around.

Afer was a small, balding man clad in a beige tunic. 'I was told you wish to see me about something.'

With Megakreon still too incredulous to speak, Dryas found them a small study where they could talk. Cassius stood by a window, watching as the guests trooped towards the drive, where their carriages were now lining up. Though Megakreon had created much of the problem himself, Cassius now realised he should have backed off and waited; things had got out of hand.

'Well?' said Afer, who was sitting beside a desk. 'After all this fuss, it had better be something damned important.'

Indavara – leaning against the wall – looked on.

'I am investigating a criminal conspiracy. It has come to my attention that – despite your financial problems – you have recently made a significant purchase of land. I would like you to explain how.'

'Why should I?'

'This investigation was ordered by Marshal Marcellinus himself. Cooperation is advisable.'

'Centurion, you seem to have little regard for a man's privacy, or the rule of law. But in the interests of settling this matter, I will answer you. I have had financial problems, it's true, but I recently received an inheritance – my aunt passed away.'

Cassius wiped sweat from above his lip.

'The purchase of land was for my brother,' continued Afer. 'He has been supporting me during my recent difficulties and I wish to repay him. It is to be a birthday gift – next week.'

'You have the documentation to prove this, I assume?'

'Of course.'

Unless he was a remarkably accomplished liar, Afer seemed to be telling the truth. Cassius knew he had jumped to a hasty conclusion regarding the money. But what of the former casters? Surely that couldn't be a coincidence?

The door opened and in came a man wearing a purple-striped toga. He was about the same age as Megakreon but slim and athletic with a thick head of wavy grey hair. He carried himself with an unmistakable air of authority and pushed the door shut behind him with an angry flourish.

Cassius noted a slight grin from Afer. His stomach turned over.

'Good day,' said the interloper. 'You seem to have ruined my friend's party.'

'That could easily have been avoided,' replied Cassius. 'Might I ask to whom—'

The man pulled out a chair for himself and sat down. 'Barrius.'

A name every Roman knew well. An ancient family of the highest rank.

'*Senator* Amulius Barrius Columella.'

Cassius felt a chill wash over him. 'Ah. Good day, senator.'

'Two questions,' said Columella, smoothing down his hair. 'One, who in Hades are you? Two, what in Hades do you think you are doing?'

'Sir, I am Cassius Oranius Crispian.' He couldn't believe he'd just given a false name to a senator but he could hardly start using a different one now. 'I am an officer of the Imperial Security Service and I am conducting an investigation into counterfeiting on behalf of Marshal Marcellinus and Minister Sabinus.' Cassius pointed at his satchel, which was on the desk. 'I have letters here if you would like to see them.'

'Oh, I believe you, Officer,' said Columella. 'What I can't believe is that you thought barging your way into my friend's house, roughing up his staff and bullying his guests was the best way to carry out your investigation.'

'With respect, senator, I made a polite request to see this man but Master Megakreon refused.'

'Of course he refused. I would have refused. You would have refused. Could you not have chosen a different time, a different place?'

Columella spoke with the smooth confidence of a man who generally got his way.

'Sir, there is evidence.'

'Megakreon is an honest man of excellent repute. He tells me that Master Afer here is an honest man of excellent repute. This evidence had better be good, Officer.'

Cassius thought it best to get the money issue out of the way before Afer could say anything.

'Oh dear,' said Columella when he'd finished explaining what he'd found out. 'Weak, Crispian. Very weak. I hope you have something else rather more compelling.'

'I believe I do.' Cassius addressed Afer. 'There are only a few men with knowledge of how to create good-quality coinage. Two former mint workers with that knowledge were employed by you. Both were recorded on last year's census. I have the information here.'

Afer looked confused, then apprehensive.

'Well?' prompted Columella.

'I know of only one man from the mint – he was named Micon. He came highly recommended, worked for my building business – repairing statues, that type of thing. Of course, I had to let him go last year because of my financial . . . misfortune.'

Cassius reached into the satchel and took out the page of employees from the census. He pointed to the second name. 'And this man – S. Novius Gallus?'

Afer started laughing.

'What?' demanded Cassius.

'I know Gallus,' said Afer. 'Or rather I did. Old boy – could hardly lift his tools any more, that's why we hired Micon.'

'Old?' Cassius checked Segestes's page of detailed notes on Gallus. He had the man's age as thirty-eight. He had also listed the full name.

'Sextus Novius Gallus?'

Afer was no longer laughing. '*Servius* Novius Gallus.'

Cassius couldn't believe he had been so stupid – Novius and Gallus were both common names.

Afer stood up. 'And I can assure you that he is not involved in your counterfeiting plot. He dropped dead last winter. My youngest son found him on the floor of the forge.'

For a moment nothing was said. Cassius could feel his cheeks glowing as he stuffed the papers back into the satchel.

Columella stood. 'Is there any reason at all why we should detain Master Afer here any longer?'

Cassius shook his head.

'Speak when you are addressed by a senator of Rome!' thundered Columella.

'No, sir.'

As Afer left, Columella's attention turned to Indavara. 'And who might you be?'

'Bodyguard,' said Indavara, still slumped against the wall.

'Out.'

Indavara looked at Cassius.

'You don't need this idiot's permission,' snapped Columella. 'Do as you are told!'

'Quickly,' said Cassius.

Indavara shrugged and left.

'Disgraceful, young man. An appalling lapse of judgement. You have a number of apologies to make before you leave this house. Do we agree?'

Cassius found himself looking at the senator's tunic rather than his face. 'Yes, sir.'

'I am on holiday, Crispian. It took me two weeks to get to Syria and I wanted to enjoy myself. I wanted to spend my afternoon relaxing with my old friend and his guests. Now I must spend it tidying up your mess and writing letters. The first will be to Marshal Marcellinus, the second to your superior in the Service. His name?'

'Aulus Celatus Abascantius.'

'You said you were working with the treasury. Who is your contact?'

'Lucius Gratus Quentin.'

'I'll need both names written down and addresses where I can reach them.'

'Yes, sir.' Cassius finally managed to look at him. At least some of the rage had gone from his eyes.

The senator sighed. 'How old are you?'

'Twenty-two, sir.'

'You have a lot to learn.'

X

Though hideous, the events of the next hour weren't quite the most humiliating of Cassius's life. That honour went to the occasion when he had been discovered with his aunt's maid (by his aunt, at her house, during her fiftieth birthday party). To be precise, the worst moment had been when his father had dragged him past his mother, sisters and the assembled guests then shoved him out of the front gate, telling him to walk home and start packing his chest. A week later he had left to join the army.

But this was still hideous enough. After grovelling to Numerius Afer (plus his wife), Columella (plus his wife) and Megakreon (plus his wife and all the remaining guests), Cassius had been instructed by the senator to empty his money bag and give all he had to the harpist. Indavara had also apologised to the girl, commenting that he should really have hit the bodyguard again, thereby knocking him to the ground and preventing the damage to the harp.

'That didn't really go very well, did it?' said the bodyguard as they rode out to the mint. Correctly adjudging that Cassius was in no mood to talk, it was the first thing he'd said since they'd left the villa. Cassius glanced across at him as they overtook a pair of lads hauling a handcart stacked with firewood.

'I don't really see how it could have gone any worse.'

'That Columella was full of himself.'

'He is a senator. A senator says jump – you ask how high. Remember that in case we ever meet another one.'

'What do senators do anyway?'

'Frankly, I can't be bothered to explain.'

'Didn't you say that Marcellinus is just below the Emperor? If you're working for him why do you have to worry about a senator?'

'If I'd been in possession of anything one could consider actual evidence then I might not have had to. I thought I was so bloody clever finding those names I put two and two together and came up with seven and a half.'

'Eh?'

'Forget it.'

A rider galloped past, his steed kicking up dust.

'Er, Corbulo, I think that was one of the messengers from Megakreon's villa.'

Cassius looked up and realised he was right. 'So Quentin will know all about it. Well, at least it saves me going over the whole sorry episode again.'

When he arrived in the storeroom, the treasury agent was just finishing the letter. He put it down then peered up at him. 'Interesting morning?'

'You could say that.' Cassius slumped down on a stool. He was alone, having left Indavara outside with the horses.

'By the gods, Crispian. A senator?'

'Damned bad luck, really. He's on holiday – summer recess, I suppose.'

'Why Afer? What did you have on him?'

'Nothing as it turned out.' Cassius briefly went through what he'd discovered since they'd last met.

'I can see why you would want to question him but—'

'My mistake. Overconfidence combined with carelessness. It won't happen again.'

Quentin glanced at the letter. 'Marcellinus and Sabinus will not be impressed.'

'I am well aware of that. But at least they won't hear about it for a week or so. I shall do my best to ensure I have something more substantial to report in my reply.'

Cassius glanced at the map of Syria and the surrounding provinces. Dozens of red paper circles had now been stuck to it.

'Ah, the coin sightings.' He stood up and walked around the table for a better view.

'I just finished – two-thirds of the replies are in now.'

'Each one denotes a single sighting?'

'Correct.'

Cassius leaned over the map. Almost all the cities of central Syria had at least one dot (Tripolis included); some had several.

'Does it look how you expected it to?'

'No,' said Quentin. 'The spread and the amount are far greater than I had anticipated. Whoever they are, this gang are producing a lot of coins and moving them quickly.' He thumped his hand on the table. 'And we're getting nowhere. Absolutely nowhere.'

Cassius continued to study the map. Quentin began rubbing his brow.

After a while, Segestes trotted in. 'Some more post for you, sir.'

Quentin scraped away the seal, unfolded the letter and read it. 'Well, it appears the gods might have chosen to throw some good fortune our way at last.'

'Oh?'

'Remember I told you there were still five casters from the Felicissimus plot unaccounted for?'

'Yes,' said Cassius.

'One of them's been spotted right here in Syria.'

'Let me guess – Berytus.'

'Yes. How did you know?'

Cassius pointed at the map. 'It's the only major city within a hundred miles where none of the fakes have turned up. They wouldn't want to draw attention to their base of production.'

'And now this caster's been spotted. Unlikely to be a coincidence, surely?'

'After the events of today, I certainly hope not.'

Berytus was thirty miles to the south. They agreed that Cassius should journey there while Quentin continued to collate information in Tripolis. The treasury agent would be free to investigate any other leads and if Cassius made significant progress he could get to Berytus within a day. Quentin also agreed to contact the magistrate there, outlining the importance of the investigation and requesting that Cassius be afforded whatever help was necessary.

Once back at the inn, Cassius told Simo to start packing up; they would be leaving the following day. The attendant began work immediately, placing their saddlebags on the floor and folding up clothes. Cassius slumped on to the bed and looked at the box on the table. Inside were the twelve figurines of the great gods – by the looks of it Simo had given each of them a good polish. Cassius couldn't escape the feeling that at least some of them were staring at him with disapproving expressions.

'Not a good day, Simo. Not good at all.'

'Perhaps things will look up in Berytus, sir.'

'Entirely my fault. I suppose all the flattery from the marshal inflated my head. I was so convinced I was on the right path that all sense left me. I embarrassed myself in front of a senator, would you believe? I only hope word of it does not reach my father.'

'Everybody makes mistakes, sir.'

'True, but I can't afford another one.'

Cassius noted a book on Simo's bed. 'You've been studying?'

'Yes, sir.'

'Not enough time to find a church-house?'

'No.'

'Well, I don't know how long we'll be in Berytus but I'm sure there'll be some of your people there. I must say I'm quite looking forward to it; I would have liked to make a stop on the way through. If things had turned out differently I might have been studying there now.'

'At the university, sir?'

'It was all planned. My father had agreed to pay for it; I was supposed to go once I turned seventeen.'

Simo didn't ask what had happened.

Cassius leant back against a pillow, fingers intertwined around his head. 'My parents went away for the weekend so I ordered all the servants to leave and invited a few friends over. About fifty, actually. One fellow took my father's horse for a ride, my youngest sister vomited on my mother's favourite couch and my idiot cousin Gaius set fire to the beehives because he'd been stung on the bottom. So I never made it to Berytus. Excellent party, though.'

Simo stopped folding tunics for a moment. 'Have you heard of Gregory Thaumaturgus, sir?'

'I have. Contemporary of Origen's, wasn't he?'

'He was, sir. He studied at Berytus too, and later became a bishop.'

'I remember – he abandoned the law and embraced religion.'

'Yes, sir. They say that when he arrived in Caesarea there were only seventeen Christians. But when he left there were only seventeen who were not.'

Before Cassius could formulate a cynical reply, Indavara walked in. He was sweating heavily from another bout of barrel-lifting.

'Corbulo, there's a man outside wants to talk. Says he's got some information for us.'

Frowning, Cassius plucked his sword belt off the hook it was hanging from.

'Good idea,' said Indavara, taking it from him. He led the way back through the parlour and out to the front yard.

Neokles's lad was there, sweeping up and humming to himself. A man of around Cassius's age was lurking behind the innkeeper's cart, anxiously scratching his chin. Judging by his tunic, he was a working man.

When they walked over to him, the stranger nodded at the sword. 'No – no – no – no need for that.' As well as the stammer, he seemed to be afflicted by some eye disease: both were red and one was weeping.

Cassius also spoke in Greek. 'I was told you have some information for me. About what?'

'M – m – m – money first.'

'Money for what?'

The stranger kept glancing at the street, as if wary of being seen. 'Important – it – it's important.'

'How do I know if . . .' Cassius shrugged. 'Very well. A denarius.'

The stranger wiped his weeping eye and held up five fingers.

'We'll call it two.'

'Fi – five. Important, important.'

'The man said two.' Indavara took the coins from Cassius and walked behind the stranger, so that he was blocking his path to the street. 'Wouldn't even think about taking them and running, would you?'

The Syrian shook his head. Indavara gave him the coins. The man slipped them inside his tunic.

'Well?' said Cassius. 'You can start with your name.'

The man shook his head again. 'No – no – need. I work round here.'

'And – this information?'

'Yes – yes – yesterday night. A man was asking about you. Asking about a Roman ar – ar – army officer.'

Cassius felt that familiar nausea. 'Asking what?'

'Wh – wh – where—'

'Where I was staying? Did you tell him?'

'No, no. I – I like the army. Want – want – wanted to join. But he still paid me. To – to – to keep quiet.'

'Did he ask anything else?'

The stranger shook his head.

'What did he look like?'

'Av – av – average height, s – s – strong looking. Not much hair. Shor – short sword, like the old army.'

'Have you seen him around here since?'

'No.'

Cassius took a moment to absorb this. 'If you see him again, you'll tell us?'

'Yes.'

'All right. Thank you.'

Indavara moved aside. The Syrian wiped his eyes again then hurried away.

Cassius walked on to the street, where the low sun cast long shadows. He was less interested in the stranger than the apartment blocks and townhouses opposite the inn. There were dozens of windows and several alleyways from where the inn could be observed. He returned inside with Indavara.

'What are you thinking?' asked the bodyguard.

'He said yesterday. So it can't be anything to do with what happened today. It's possible that someone in the city knew I was coming: the counterfeiters even or—'

'Same bunch that went for you in Bostra?'

Cassius stopped and leant back against the wall. 'Gods. Could they really have tracked me this far?'

'It's good that we're leaving.'

'I'll get a note to Quentin – make sure he tells no one where we're going. And we can't tell Neokles or the girls either, got it?'

'Of course.'

Cassius was in desperate need of a drink. 'I don't suppose I'll sleep a bloody wink now.'

'Maybe we should stay up,' said Indavara, tapping the sheathed sword against his leg. 'They probably know you're in here by now. Probably watching the place. What about trying to get to them before they get to you?'

They decided to wait until the third hour of night. Cassius limited himself to two large mugs of unwatered wine and, despite Simo's protestations, was unable to swallow a single morsel. The thought of being hunted by this mysterious foe (or foes) had twisted his stomach into knots. But, like Indavara, he was not prepared to sit around and wait for the bastards to come and get him.

While Simo was dusting off Cassius's dark brown hooded cape, Indavara walked into the bedroom. 'I was thinking – might not be the lot from Bostra. You had already been to the mint and the basilica when this man was sniffing around.'

'It is possible, I agree. But it would have been damned quick work and Berytus is looking like a more probable base for the counterfeiters. I think it's the same group.' Cassius glanced at the figurines. 'By the great gods, what could they want with me?'

'At least we know they're here,' said Indavara, 'thanks to our nervous friend.'

'That was damned strange in itself.'

'You don't trust him?'

'On balance, I do – mainly *because* it was so strange.'

'Sword.' Cassius took it from Simo and hung the belt from his shoulder so that the hilt was over his left hip. The attendant then draped the cape over him and tied the clasp at the neck.

'So what's the plan?'

Indavara – whose only garment with a hood was a thick cloak – already looked hot. 'We can start a few hundred yards out then work our way inwards. See if anyone's watching this place.'

'Sounds sensible. We'll have to keep an eye out for watchmen but this will be enough to keep them off our backs.' Cassius had a badge pinned to his tunic – a two-inch silver replica of the spearhead. 'Simo, I doubt we'll be more than an hour or two. Keep an eye out.'

'Yes, sir.'

In the corridor they passed Neokles, who was coming in from the yard clutching laundry.

'Good evening, Centurion.'

'Evening,' said Cassius. 'Just off for a stroll.'

Once outside, they crossed the courtyard. As they approached the street, Cassius glanced back at the inn. Through the grille of one of the downstairs windows he could see Kitra and Hanina working by lamplight. Both were bending over washing tubs, the front of their tunics already wet. Indavara stood beside him and they watched Kitra work, her plump breasts quivering.

'By Jupiter, I've seldom seen better.'

'I've seldom kissed better,' said Indavara.

'Lucky sod.'

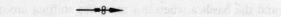

Having identified themselves to a pair of curious watchmen, they began the search, circling the inn and gradually getting closer. They stopped whenever they found what looked like a decent position but the large apartment block opposite obscured most views of the inn's courtyard and entrance. The first really feasible location was a strip of waste ground between two houses. It was on the opposite side of the road from the inn, fifty yards farther up the hill.

Cassius and Indavara reached the corner of a walled townhouse and inspected the waste ground. There was a little moonlight but not enough to illuminate anyone who might be lurking there. The ground was patched with rubble and bushes that might provide enough cover for a skilful spy.

'Let's just watch and wait,' Cassius whispered.

After ten minutes, he concluded that if anyone was there they were completely still and silent. 'We can't stand here all night.'

'Agreed.' Indavara put a hand on his sword then rounded the corner and walked straight across the strip of ground. Cassius stayed on his heels, paying particular attention to the bushes. They saw and heard nothing.

'We'll keep moving,' said Cassius. 'If they're anywhere they'll be round here.'

Next to the waste ground were two more walled townhouses, both with locked gates. A check of the alley that ran between them yielded nothing and the pair moved on again. Next came a trio of smaller houses, then the big apartment block.

Cassius looked at the two shadowy passageways beneath the building. 'If it were me, I'd be in one of those.'

'What about coming in from the back?' suggested Indavara.

'Let's try it.'

Separating the houses from the apartment block was another alley. They had to move slowly; barely any moonlight reached the ground and the flagstones were uneven. Once at the far end, Cassius briefly inspected the rear of the small houses. Each had a yard but all were secured by more locked gates and there was no space between them.

'Not very suitable,' he told Indavara.

'Unless they bribed someone to use their property.'

'Unlikely. Let's check the block.'

Cassius had already noted the basic layout. The building was large, probably containing thirty or forty apartments. The two broad passageways ran the width of the structure, providing access to the rear, the ground-floor dwellings and the steps leading up to the higher floors.

Beyond the pitch-black void of the closer passageway, Cassius could just make out the street and the wall beside Neokles's inn.

'Decent view,' whispered Indavara.

'Let's take a look. Slow and steady.'

Indavara carefully rounded a tree and crept towards the shadows. Cassius could see the odd light coming from the apartments above and hear someone singing in Greek. He stayed behind Indavara and almost walked into him when he abruptly stopped ten feet short of the passageway. Cassius then realised he could hear something else: snoring.

'Just some tramp probably. I'll see if anyone else is there. Wait here.'

Cassius did so, watching until Indavara disappeared into the murk. Then he listened; and soon heard the faint sound of the bodyguard's footsteps as he returned.

'A drunk – dead to the world. Let's check the second one.'

They took even more care this time; the second passageway offered a perfect view of the inn. Indavara waited until they were directly behind it before dropping down. Cassius knelt beside him.

'See there,' whispered the bodyguard. 'Left side.'

The street was far brighter than the passageway and Cassius could clearly see the shape pressed against the wall; he could even make out the head and shoulder. Still as a statue, the man was staring at the inn.

Cassius said, 'He must have seen us leave but he didn't follow.'

'Maybe he just has orders to watch the place. Well? Shall we grab him?'

'We have to try. Should I go around to the front?'

'That'll take too long. I'll come up behind him. You go along the right side in case he runs that way.'

Cassius generally acceded to Indavara in such matters. 'Very well.'

'Daggers. Swords will slow us down too much.'

They stood. Cassius held the sheath down and pulled out the

blade. It was the first time he had drawn it since Arabia. He pushed away thoughts of the man he had killed. He was getting better at doing so; he couldn't let it paralyse him for ever.

Indavara advanced slowly.

Cassius made for the right side of the passageway, treading softly. Not far away, two watchmen were conducting a shouted conversation, providing enough noise to cover the sound of their approach. Cassius kept clear of the wall, fearful of walking into a step or tripping over something. He could see neither Indavara nor the watcher; only the end of the passageway, dividing the inky black from the grey of the street.

Another shout from the watchmen. Then a cackle of laughter.

Indavara charged forward and slammed into the watcher, catapulting him across the pavement. The man slipped on the kerb and fell into the street. Indavara sprang after him, kicking him in the side before he'd stopped rolling. The watcher cried out.

Cassius heard fleeing footsteps. He ran out on to the pavement and turned to his right. The noise was coming from the side of the apartment block; the next alley along. He ran to it.

'Corbulo, where are you . . .'

Cassius skidded to a halt. The second man was making no attempt to stay quiet; he was sprinting away, boots thrumming on the ground. Cassius was almost tempted to follow but he couldn't know who else was out there. He heard Indavara swearing but his eyes were fixed on the street at the end of the alley. There was light there; a lantern above a door. The sound of the boots faded then he saw the dark figure reach the street, cut left and disappear.

Cassius jogged back towards the inn to find that a neighbour had opened his front door and was standing there with a lamp. As the Syrian enquired what was going on, Indavara dragged the watcher across the street by his cloak.

'Let's get a look at you,' said the bodyguard.

'What's going on?' asked the neighbour.

'Army business,' said Cassius. 'Bring your light forward.'

Indavara let go of the man once they reached the kerb, then planted a boot on his gut. The watcher was pleading for mercy in Greek.

Satisfied he couldn't move, Cassius placed the point of his dagger close to his face. The neighbour opened the lantern shutter wide and held it closer. The watcher was no more than fourteen or fifteen.

'Gods, Scrofa,' said the neighbour. 'Not again. I would have thought you'd learned your lesson by now.'

'You know him?' asked Cassius.

'He lives on the top floor of the apartments. I expect . . .' The neighbour peered around the corner of his house. 'Yes, I thought so. He likes to watch the girls – especially when they're doing the washing.'

Indavara took his foot off.

Cassius looked down at the youth. 'That true?'

'The watchmen caught him twice before,' continued the neighbour. 'He said he couldn't see enough from the third floor. What did Neokles tell you – you'll go cross eyed!'

Cassius withdrew. 'Get up. Go.'

Scrofa didn't need another invitation. He scrambled to his feet and ran back into the shadows of the passageway.

The neighbour muttered something then walked back inside and shut the door.

'Where'd you disappear to?' asked Indavara.

'There was a second man. When we broke cover he ran up the side of the alley and away. I saw him.'

'Shit. If that fool hadn't been there we might have grabbed him.'

'At least we know now. They're here and they're watching me. Well, they're not going to find me again. Let's go inside and get ready. I want to be on the coast road and away before dawn.'

XI

Unsettled by something, the tethered horses cracked twigs under their hooves and sniffed the air. Above, the branches swayed, moved by the same wind that had drawn a slight swell from the sea. The clearing was on the landward side of the road, a hundred yards away and twenty above, offering an excellent view in both directions.

Indavara and Simo were perched on the same outcrop of grey rock, finishing off their lunch. A few yards away, Patch crunched his way through some carrots. Cassius was leaning against a tree on the other side of the clearing, gazing down at the road. He had moved several times to ensure his position was completely shaded from the blistering rays of the midday sun. Three groups had passed since he'd begun his vigil; none so far concerned him.

Though he'd slept for no more than an hour, he felt surprisingly sharp and alert. Then again, he had to be. If his pursuers could find him in Tripolis, they were clearly capable of tracking him to Berytus, so he had to give them as little to work with as possible. Only Quentin knew where the trio were really headed. Cassius had decided to tell Neokles and the girls that their destination was Laodicea, a city eighty miles to the north.

They had left Tripolis with the streets still dark and encountered only watchmen. A mile beyond the city gates, Indavara had doubled back through an olive grove and checked behind them. He returned having seen nothing.

Cassius ran a hand through his hair and looked down at the carpet of pine needles beneath his feet.

Who? Why?

If they got hold of him, he'd find out soon enough. But for

now all he could do was hope he'd lost them and take every precaution possible. What of the days and weeks to come? Would he ever really be able to relax when he knew they were still hunting him?

At least they were fallible. The watcher had panicked, alerted them, drawn attention to himself. Cassius just had to stay one step ahead; until he escaped them for good or decided to pursue Indavara's tactic to its ultimate conclusion – hunter was an infinitely more favourable role than prey.

'We're clear,' said the bodyguard confidently. 'No way anyone followed us this far.'

'Shall I pack up, sir?' asked Simo.

Cassius looked back at the road. 'No. Take your time. We'll use the dark, enter Berytus after sundown.'

'Sir, you do remember the warning we were given when we passed through the city before? The thieves that operate from the coves?'

'Thieves do not concern me, Simo.'

Even so, he was just as relieved as the attendant when they reached the welcome glow of the torches at Berytus's northern gate. Standing beneath the high, ornate arch, they waited for one of the legionaries on duty to fetch his superior, a guard officer. When he appeared, Cassius showed him the spearhead, gave him a denarius and explained what he needed. The soldier fetched some keys, then escorted them along the walls to a small side gate. He agreed to tell no one of their arrival and let them into the city. Cassius asked for directions for a quiet inn nearby; within an hour the horses were stabled and the trio in bed.

As Simo drew back the shutters, sunlight flooded the room.

'Gods.' Cassius turned away and shut his eyes.

'Uh,' was all Indavara could manage.

'Sorry, sir, you did give me instructions to wake you at the second hour.'

'Yes, yes.' Cassius yawned and stretched, then hauled himself off the bed. 'Caesar's balls, this place looks even smaller in daylight.'

The two beds – Indavara and Simo had shared the double – were pushed up against the window and there was barely five feet between them and the door. Most of this space was now occupied by saddlebags.

'At least it's out of the way, sir.'

'True. I'd rather suffer this than be at some big, well-known place where we're easily found.'

Cassius glanced at a nearby pile of clothes. 'No uniform in public. We're going to keep our heads down while we're here, which will probably aid the investigation too. Got that?'

'Yes, sir.'

'Indavara?'

He was already snoring again.

'Shall I wake him, sir?'

'Ah, let him sleep – I'm not leaving here until I have my appointment with the magistrate. Fetch me my writing materials.'

While Simo dragged a saddlebag over and unbuckled it, Cassius lifted his sleeping tunic and relieved himself into the chamber pot.

'Urgh! What's that?'

Someone had already used the pot and there seemed to be as much blood as urine.

'From Indavara, sir. Less every day apparently.'

'Wonderful.'

'You would like a separate room, I suppose, sir?'

Having finished, Cassius lowered his tunic. 'I would. But for the moment I intend to keep as close to our big friend as possible – for obvious reasons.'

When Simo later returned from the basilica, Cassius was dismayed to learn that the magistrate could not offer an appointment until the ninth hour. They had a meal brought to the room around midday, after which Cassius and Indavara visited the nearest baths. While lounging in the warm room, Cassius spent half an hour considering what he had discussed of the case with Quentin and formulating his enquiries for the magistrate. Once they had finished bathing, both men put on clean tunics and returned to the inn.

Simo had tidied the room and was ready with Cassius's satchel, in which the spearhead was safely secured. Hoping he looked like a merchant accompanied by bodyguard and assistant, Cassius asked the innkeeper for directions and they set off for the magistrate's residence – a more private location for the meeting than the basilica.

It was now late afternoon, and even though most of the day's business would have been concluded, the streets of Berytus seemed unnaturally quiet. They passed a marketplace populated only by a few cleaners and at the Temple of Aphrodite saw only a handful of worshippers.

'Damned strange,' said Cassius. 'Innkeeper didn't mention any festivals today, did he?'

'No, sir. Might have been an outbreak of something.'

'Don't say things like that, Simo. Makes my skin crawl. By the way, you did give him the money?'

'Yes, sir. He won't be telling anyone about us.'

Their route skirted the north side of the city centre, towards the affluent residential district where the magistrate lived. Passing one end of a broad, colonnaded avenue, they found a dozen people staring south. Curious, Cassius stopped and joined them. What looked like a crowd of several hundred was marching towards the forum. He could also hear a chant and see sunlight sparking off the weapons and equipment of legionaries lining the avenue.

Cassius picked out a respectable-looking fellow accompanied by a servant holding a parasol over his head. 'Excuse me, what's going on there?'

The man looked him up and down before answering wearily.

'Another protest.'

'By whom?'

'Bloody weavers. Who else?'

A tall man standing in front of them turned round. 'Watch yourself – my brother's a weaver.'

'Why don't you go and join them, then?' said the gentleman.

'Don't much fancy catching a sword in the neck – got three children to provide for.'

A few others in the crowd were listening to the exchange.

'Nobody knows who killed that young man,' replied the gentleman. 'The weavers have been telling everyone it was a legionary because that's what they want you to believe.'

'Maybe that's what *Pomponianus* wants us to believe,' said the other citizen, 'to keep people away from the protests.'

Cassius was also listening: Pomponianus – the man he was on his way to meet.

The tall man nodded up the avenue. 'Not that brave bunch, though. Perhaps I will join them after all.' With a defiant scowl, he stalked away.

The Syrian rolled his eyes. 'What can you do? The ignorance of the lower classes never ceases to amaze me.'

'What's at issue?'

'It started with the corn dole, I suppose. It was withdrawn last month – the governor needs the food for the soldiers.'

'Same across Syria, though, isn't it?'

'Of course.' Even though the others were no longer paying much attention to him, the gentleman kept his voice down. 'But here we have over a thousand weavers employed in a dozen factories. When times are tough they take on other work outside hours. The old governor used to let it go but Pomponianus is fining anyone found to be doing extra.'

'Why bother?'

'A lot of people in Berytus – myself included – think the weavers are getting too big for their boots. Pomponianus has had trouble with them before and he wants to make sure they understand who's in charge. The factory owners are all friends of his and there's an election in September.'

'I see. And the young man that other fellow spoke of?'

'There was another protest last week. Usually there's a few speeches, a bit of chanting and everyone goes home. But on this occasion there was a scuffle. The weavers are saying a legionary stabbed the young man because he was a ringleader. The army are denying it.' The gentleman ran a finger along one of his bushy eyebrows. 'Frankly, I hope they grab a dozen of the bastards and burn them in the arena. That would put an end to all this nonsense. Good day.'

With that he strode away, his servant struggling to keep the parasol over his head.

Indavara cast a disparaging glance at him. 'This Pomp . . .'

'Pomponianus.'

'Yes, him – sounds like a bit of an arsehole.'

'Not necessarily,' said Cassius. 'Can't have a bunch of rowdy labourers running a city. People need to know their place.'

'People also need to feed their children.'

Simo was nodding. He desisted when he realised Cassius was watching him.

The magistrate's residence was an impressive townhouse surrounded by a substantial wall painted pale red. Cassius didn't want to draw attention to himself but there was no choice other than to approach the main entrance and the four city sergeants armed with hefty wooden clubs. Thankfully the guards were expecting him and opened the gate as soon as he gave his (false) name.

A servant was summoned who then escorted them to a side door, past shaped swards of grass and an elaborate fountain where – despite the season – water still flowed. Half a dozen gardeners were at work weeding and trimming the turf. The servant asked Cassius to wait under a cool portico, then trotted inside. While he drank from his flask, Simo told Indavara about the different varieties of flowers populating the beds between the townhouse and the wall. From within the house came the sound of giggling children.

After about five minutes the servant returned with a tall, brawny man dressed in a fine linen tunic. He looked to be about forty and sported several bracelets and an ostentatious belt-buckle. He was smiling and already had his arm outstretched.

'Officer Crispian, good day to you, and welcome to Berytus. No, I am not Magistrate Pomponianus.'

They shook forearms. 'Deputy Magistrate Diadromes. There are three deputies in Berytus. My area of responsibility is trade and commerce, which is why the magistrate asked me to speak with you. He is rather occupied today but I'm sure you'll meet at some point.'

'Ah,' said Cassius. 'Good day.'

Diadromes already struck him as unusual. Vulgar displays of wealth were rare among city bureaucrats and his accent and manner of speech were rather reminiscent of a street trader.

The deputy magistrate turned his attention to Indavara and Simo. 'Let me guess – bodyguard and attendant.'

'Quite right.'

'Good day.'

This, again, was unconventional, and caught the pair off guard. Even so, they both replied politely, Simo adding a bow.

'Shall we walk or sit?'

'I don't mind,' said Cassius.

Diadromes pointed at a long wooden bench shaded by the portico and facing the garden. 'I wouldn't mind taking the weight off – been traipsing round the cloth market all morning looking for fake silk, would you believe?'

Cassius followed him, noting the pronounced bald patch amid the deputy magistrate's fuzzy brown hair.

'So, counterfeiting?' said the Syrian once they'd sat down.

'We have good reason to believe a gang might be operating from Berytus. Firstly, none of their coins have – to our know-ledge – been sighted here, which suggests they don't want to draw attention to their centre of production. Secondly, the ex-caster that was spotted here last week.'

'Well, you're right about the coins. The letter from your man Quentin was passed to me a while back – I've had people checking but no, nothing so far. I must confess I didn't know about this caster until today – you have the name?'

'No.'

Diadromes reached into a pocket sewn into his tunic (again, not something most gentlemen would have) and pulled out a scrap of paper.

'Lucius Sepercius Florens. He was seen by a man from the procurator's staff who had worked with him back in Italy. There's a description here too.' Diadromes gave Cassius the note.

'Average height and build, cropped grey hair – not massively helpful. Have any enquiries been made?'

'Yes. No reference to him has emerged yet, though of course it's doubtful he would risk using his own name, even this far east.'

'It is essential that we find him. There are no other leads.'

'I must tell you that Berytus has never had a significant problem with counterfeiting. But we will of course assist your investigation.'

'Much appreciated. Apart from checking records, what else can be done?'

Diadromes grinned. 'As you may have gathered, I do not come from money. My father was a freedman and I worked up to this post from second assistant inspector of municipal drainage.'

Cassius couldn't stop himself chuckling.

'It's true – that really was my job. In any case, one of my later posts in the magistrate's office was chief of criminal investigations. If I and my staff can't help you, no one can.'

'Excellent. Can I ask – who else knows I'm here?'

'The magistrate and my two fellow deputies. That's all.'

'I would very much like it to stay that way.'

'Of course. I will use my most trusted man, Cosmas. He can put Florens' name out on the streets, see if anything turns up.'

'As you say, chances are he's not using it but we must still try.'

'Indeed. And of course he may have just been passing through.' Diadromes scratched his forehead. 'What if I have Cosmas ask about counterfeiting in general? Nobody need know that the enquiry came from you or the Service. As we've been checking for the fake coins there'll be some talk on the streets about it anyway. Cosmas is very discreet.'

'Very well.'

'He can also act as a liaison between us.'

'Good. Thank you.'

Diadromes stood. 'I'm afraid I must be going. My afternoon will be even busier than my morning.'

'I saw the weavers' protest,' said Cassius as he straightened up. 'A concern for the magistrate, I imagine.'

'A concern for us all,' said Diadromes gravely, causing Cassius to wonder how he might view the dispute. 'Where can I find you?'

'I'm staying at an inn over by the north gate – the Dolphin.'

'I know it.'

'It'll do for the moment but if we have to stay for a while I might need to rent. Somewhere secure.'

'Surely you're not that worried about this gang?'

Cassius chose his words carefully. 'Unfortunately, we in the Service occasionally make enemies. Enemies who sometimes seek revenge.'

Diadromes glanced along the portico. 'I see. Hence the need for your muscular friend.'

'Quite.'

'I own many properties. One in particular might suit your needs.'

'Ah.'

'I would be happy to provide it to you free of charge.' It sounded less a statement than a question.

'Yes?'

'The thing is, you may also be able to help me, Officer Crispian. A rather sensitive matter, but as a Service man I think you are exceptionally well placed to offer assistance.'

'If I can help, I will.'

Diadromes looked rather happy. 'This is neither the time nor the place to discuss it. Would you like to meet for dinner this evening? I know a nice place right next to the Temple of Aphrodite. Shall we say the eleventh hour?'

'Eleventh it is.'

XII

Cassius drove the sword straight at Indavara's face. The body-guard swatted it away and shifted his position with a single movement. As the pair circled each other, the horses at the other end of the stable snorted and puffed.

'Trying to get the sun in my eyes, eh?' said Cassius, careful with his footing on the slippery straw.

Indavara had moved in front of the wide doorway. 'I don't need any tricks to see you off but you should still be prepared for them.'

'Indeed. You are . . .'

Instead of finishing the sentence, Cassius leaped forward and jabbed the wooden sword towards Indavara's groin. The bodyguard stepped back and swung his own weapon down into a block. But Cassius had already flicked the sword upward. Even though Indavara threw his head back, the tip scratched his chin.

'Hah!' Cassius raised his arms in triumph. 'I got you! After all these bouts, all these hours, I finally got you. Simo, Simo . . .'

'He left, remember?' Indavara touched his chin; the contact hadn't drawn blood.

'Don't deny that I got you,' said Cassius, pointing at him with blade and finger. 'I got you.'

'The sun shines on every dog's arse sometimes. All you got was lucky.'

'Oh, come now, Indavara. Just admit it. I outfoxed you.'

'So what, that's it? You want to stop now to enjoy yourself?'

'No, let's fight on. I have a taste for it now.'

Indavara raised his sword.

'What's the focus?' asked Cassius. 'Speed? Recovery?'

'Do you think a real opponent will stop for a discussion first? Just fight.'

Cassius didn't particularly like the glint in the bodyguard's eye but he wasn't going to give him the satisfaction of stopping. Though they had been sparring for only a few minutes, it was baking hot inside the padded under-jackets they wore for protection.

Indavara started at a medium pace; a jab here, a sweep there. Cassius tried to forget his 'victory' and watched the sword and the hands as the bodyguard had taught him. After a minute or two, Indavara sped up. He crouched lower, came on more quickly, threw in some of the endless variety of combinations he could summon at will. He darted low, swept high; sidestepped, twisted and spun.

As stinging sweat ran into his eyes, Cassius parried and retreated until finally he found himself in a corner. The swords cracked together, sending tremors up his arm, weakening his grip. Another impact. Another. The fourth blow caught his thumb.

'Uh!' Cassius dropped the sword. 'All right, I get the point.'

He studied his thumb. The nail had split down the middle and blood was trickling across the skin. 'Look at that. Probably broken, you dolt.'

'Show me.' Indavara held the thumb then bent it at the knuckle.

'Ow! What in Hades are you doing?'

'Checking it's not broken.'

'Shit. It really hurts.'

'So you just give up because of a grazed thumb? Drop your sword and wait for the cut to your neck?'

'We're practising. It's not real.'

'And those men in Bostra? Real enough for you? It was for me.' Indavara dropped his sword then grabbed Cassius round the neck. 'And what if someone comes at you again? Like this?'

'Lesson's over. Get your hands off me.'

The bodyguard paused for a moment, then hooked his right leg around Cassius's ankle and shoved him in the chest.

Cassius felt himself fly backwards into a pile of straw. Before he could get up, Indavara pinned him with a boot on his chest.

'Get off me, you arsehole.'

Indavara glared down at him, pale green eyes unblinking. He dug the boot into Cassius's chest.

'It hurts. Get off!'

Cassius punched Indavara's bulging calf, to little effect.

'One leg against two arms?'

Cassius couldn't believe this was really happening. Had the bodyguard lost his feeble mind?

'Indavara, get off me right now or I will put you on a charge. You are in the army, remember, and I outrank you by some distance. Do it.'

He did not.

Cassius smashed his hand into the bodyguard's foot, then his shin, then his knee, but succeeded only in hurting his knuckles. He then clamped his left hand around Indavara's boot and pulled to the left. He continued to thump his right fist into the other side and at the third attempt dislodged it.

Indavara retreated. 'Better. There *is* a bit of fight in you.'

Cassius wiped dust off his chest. 'Cretin.'

'*Now* the lesson's over.'

'You're the one who's going to get the lesson, my man. About the real use of power.' Cassius dragged himself to his feet. 'Who do you think you are?'

'Your bodyguard. Dancing around with wooden swords only gets you so far. You need to know what it's like with someone in your face, someone who won't stop. Someone who wants you *dead*.'

Cassius's chest ached, though not as much as his thumb.

'Take ten deep breaths,' advised Indavara.

Despite himself, Cassius did it.

'If you still want to put me on a charge, go ahead.' The bodyguard stepped forward and pointed at his face. 'Or I'll give you a free punch if you like. Two? Three?'

Cassius let out another long breath. 'So I can break my hand on your caveman jaw? No thanks. All right, I see what you're trying to do but you could at least have warned me.'

'You think *they* will?'

'Just don't do that again.'

'I won't. Not for a while anyway.'

'I'm serious.'

'My job is to keep you alive, isn't it? I'm serious about *that*. What if there's five of them next time. Or ten?'

Cassius thought about that for a moment then walked past him and out into the sunlight.

The goddess stood upon a high, narrow plinth close to the bottom of the temple steps. She was wearing a crown and bearing standard and shield.

Indavara looked up at her. 'Aphrodite, goddess of . . .'

'Love, beauty, passion. Whatever.'

'Like Venus.'

'The Greek version, yes,' said Cassius.

'Looks more like a soldier. Nice jugs, though.'

Cassius ignored him and looked up the steps; Diadromes was not among the people waiting outside the temple.

'Still in a bad mood?' said Indavara.

Cassius knelt down to retie a troublesome bootlace.

'I'll take that as a yes.'

As he stood up, Cassius adjusted the small bandage Simo had wrapped around his aching thumb. The attendant was back at the inn, repairing his master's saddle.

'See all these people here, going about their daily business? They don't have to worry about fighting, or protecting themselves, or being hunted like a bloody animal. They just live their lives. Normal, everyday, safe lives. Look at these lucky bastards.'

He pointed at four cheery youths coming down the steps. They were wearing togas and carrying waxed tablets bound by twine. 'Students no doubt, with nothing more on their mind than the next lesson or the next tavern. Gods, what I wouldn't give to be back in Ravenna.'

'But you're not.'

'No. I'm here. With you.'

The bodyguard shrugged. 'I can leave any time you want.'

'That's not what I meant.'

Diadromes was late but the half-hour actually passed pleasantly enough. While the sky darkened, they sat on the steps and watched the world go by. Cassius found his mood improving and he embarked on one of his favourite activities: marking passing women out of ten. Indavara soon joined in and before long they were japing and conducting impassioned debates. Cassius pronounced Berytus 'better than average', and was especially taken by a young priestess who they – eventually – agreed was a solid eight.

'Good evening to you.' Diadromes came down the steps at quite a rate. He was dressed in a green tunic and had obviously applied a powerful – but not unpleasant – scent before leaving home.

Cassius stood up. 'Good evening.'

The Syrian looked at Indavara. 'What's your name?'

Indavara told him.

'Never heard that before. You look like you can take care of yourself. Ex-army?'

'Still serving,' interjected Cassius, 'though sometimes you wouldn't know it.'

Diadromes jutted his jaw towards the nearest avenue. 'There is an excellent eatery over there. Plenty of private rooms.'

'Please – lead on.'

They followed the Syrian across the well-scrubbed flagstones (a large crew of slaves were hard at work with brushes and pails).

'I must say I'm surprised to see you walking around on your own,' said Cassius. 'Not even a clerk?'

'When I started moving up the ladder, people would always tell me I needed a man or two. When I moved up again they said I needed four, then six, then eight. It's not uncommon to see my two fellow deputies touring the city with fifteen or even twenty. But I started out on my own and I like it that way. I have a clerk at the basilica, of course, and a select group to whom I assign certain tasks. But I'd rather have them out working than traipsing around after me.'

They waited for two carts to pass, then crossed the avenue.

'And no bodyguard?' asked Cassius. 'With respect, surely a man in your position must have made a few enemies here over the years?'

'Probably, but no one's ever tried anything yet. It's funny you should mention it actually; today the magistrate told us to be on our guard – he thinks some of the weavers might stage an attack.'

'Clearly you don't share his concern.'

'The workers just want what they think is fair. They'd never go that far.'

'You have some sympathy with their cause, then?'

Diadromes stopped as they reached the front of the eatery. It seemed a modest place; there was no doorman and the only advertising was a faded mosaic featuring a plate of food.

'Enough politics. Let's concentrate on dinner for now. It may not look much, but the cook here is one of the best in Berytus. Name a fish, and he will prepare it precisely to your liking.'

Diadromes noticed the beaming smile on Indavara's face. 'I see you like the sound of that, my friend.'

Though he found the 'man of the people' routine a tad unnecessary, Cassius had to admit Diadromes was excellent company. The Syrian insisted that they address no serious matters until later on and entertained his guests with tales gleaned from his long and varied career. The need for the private room was obvious; on their way through the dining room he had been approached by half a dozen individuals, most seeking a discussion of some issue or another. Diadromes handled them expertly; always appearing open and warm, never giving them a second to get started.

When the maid recited the menu, Indavara became so overwhelmed by his options that in the end Diadromes ordered a platter of 'catch of the day', which included five different varieties of fish plus crab, oysters and mussels. Cassius was still feeling a little sore from earlier and avoided the shellfish, but he sampled the trout and the bream; both were exceptional. Diadromes tried everything and gave his (mostly positive) views to the staff. Later, Cassius became so embarrassed by the sight of Indavara picking through bones and shells that he told the maid to remove the platter, even though Diadromes didn't seem concerned.

When the girl returned with more wine, the Syrian asked her to escort Indavara to the kitchen – to show him what was on offer for dessert. Guessing Diadromes wanted to keep this 'sensitive matter' between them, Cassius did not protest; surely he was safe enough here.

Diadromes let his belt out a notch and turned his chair towards Cassius. 'This will remain between the two of us, of course.'

'Of course.'

'My son is almost sixteen. He wants very much to study here at the university. I'm sure I don't have to tell you about its reputation and importance. He has the enthusiam, the ability and the necessary references. Unfortunately, they admit only fifty new students a year, and the intake for the autumn is already complete. I'm told nothing can be done.'

'They are very strict. I remember applying myself.'

'Really?'

'I trained for two years as an orator. An . . . unfortunate incident persuaded my father that I would be better off in the army. I entered the Service straight from training.'

'Unusual, is it not?'

'It is. I thought staying away from the legions might be a safer course.'

'Bearing in mind what you told me earlier, that doesn't seem to be working out very well.'

'Hazard of the occupation, I suppose. Your son – what about leaving it until next year? Seventeen or eighteen is a more typical age to start at such an institution.'

Diadromes grimaced and ran a hand through his thinning hair. For a politician, he had a remarkably expressive face. 'The lad wants to go now. He has always been one to change his mind quickly and I promised my wife I would get him enrolled before he changes it again.'

'I see. Surely you must have some leverage?'

Diadromes sneered. 'With those pompous prigs? The man in charge of admissions is named Sallustius – he comes from one of Berytus's founding families. The moment I open my mouth I can see the contempt in his eyes. He has refused me twice and now will not even see me.'

Cassius drank more wine; it was light and refreshing – a perfect accompaniment to the fish. 'The university is a most prestigious institution – they perhaps consider themselves above the world of favour and influence.'

'I'd say it depends on who is doing the favouring and influencing. But you, Crispian, are with the Service. Even Sallustius will know of Chief Pulcher, how close he is to the Emperor. He and the other professors make much of their close ties to the capital. There were rumours of a scandal involving Sallustius several years ago. Perhaps if I provide you with the details?'

Now it was Cassius's turn to grimace. 'To be honest, I think such a blunt approach unwise. I suppose my spearhead will get me a meeting at least. Then I can get a measure of the man and see what can be done. I wouldn't hold your breath, however.'

'All I ask is that you try,' said Diadromes. 'I have exhausted all other possibilities and my wife speaks of nothing else. The enrolment lists are published at the end of the month; time is running short. I will ask a third party to arrange a meeting for the morning.'

'Very well. I shall be interested to see the place at last. Now, this villa you spoke of . . .'

'There may be a small difficulty but if I can make it happen I shall. It is well located and *extremely* secure. You will be comfortable and safe there.'

They both drank their wine. Now there was the possibility of 'a small difficulty'. Cassius didn't need to be a soothsayer to predict that the small difficulty might become a major one if he didn't get anywhere with this Sallustius character.

Diadromes raised his glass. 'To the gods. May they favour us both.'

At first the cook seemed annoyed by the rough-looking man cluttering up his kitchen. But when the maid explained that Indavara was a guest of the deputy magistrate, he offered to prepare whatever he wanted. Indavara eventually settled on a large bowl of sweetened milk filled with roasted nuts and blanched fruit. As the eatery was extremely hot and the other two obviously wanted some privacy, he took his dessert out to the rear courtyard. It was a walled square lit by two lanterns, each one attracting a cloud of insects. Only when he had emptied the bowl and licked the spoon clean did he give any thought to the events of the day.

Indavara admitted to himself that Corbulo's 'victory' had riled him but he'd been planning the 'attack' for some time. The man had to realise that sometimes you just had to act. He was so confident of Indavara; too reliant on him. Indavara knew it would take only one mistake; he had seen it often enough in the arena. Even though he trained every day, worshipped his Fortuna and tried his best to stay sharp, his luck would run out some time.

He was about to return inside when he heard shouting. A young man came flying out of the kitchen then slipped and fell, groaning as he landed. An older man was right behind him, already pulling his belt from around his waist.

'You little turd. How dare you embarrass me in front of my friends. You speak only when you're spoken to.'

Indavara had seen such things many times. Before being recruited by Abascantius he had worked as a bodyguard for several rich men, which meant a lot of standing around at side doors and back doors. Most masters waited until they were away from their companions before confronting their servants.

The young man knew what was coming; he already had his hands up. Master was a squat individual in a bright orange tunic.

He lifted the belt high. Indavara was glad to see that at least he wasn't using the buckle end.

'What did he do?'

The Syrian was more surprised than alarmed. 'None of your bloody business.'

He spun around and lashed at Servant. Even though the belt striped his arm red, Servant kept his defences up. Master thrashed him three times more and – when the arms finally came down – struck a heavy blow across his head.

Whimpering, Servant scrambled back to the courtyard's rear wall.

'Please, sir. I – I apologise for my rudeness. It will never happen again.'

Master marched across the courtyard and lifted the belt once more.

'I reckon that's enough,' said Indavara.

'Who in Hades are you to tell me what to do? Why don't you piss off?'

Indavara put the bowl down on a nearby windowsill. He was about ready to walk over and strangle this arsehole with his own belt.

To begin with, seeing such things had not concerned him. He had endured far worse, after all, and spared not a thought for anyone else. During those six long years in the arena he had expended every last ounce of energy on his survival. Nothing else mattered.

But the world outside was a complicated place. A place of friends and enemies, powerful and powerless, masters and servants. Corbulo always said the world was cruel and there was no sense in trying to change it. He also said that Indavara and Simo should mind their own business; especially as they worked for him and the Service. But, as time passed, Indavara found it harder and harder to ignore things like this. It seemed to him that Corbulo wasn't quite right. Life was hard; but some men chose to be cruel.

And now, if he so wished, he could do something about it.

Master swung again, though the belt caught more stone than flesh.

'What's the rule, slave?'

'I must only speak when I am spoken to. I must only speak when I am spoken to.'

Master was breathing heavily. He turned round and put his belt back on, then looked across the courtyard.

Indavara stood below the lantern, glaring at him.

Master glared back; and Indavara wondered whether the man might have decided to take him on. But then the eyes dropped lower, taking in Indavara's body, and his scars, and the two blades at his belt.

Master summoned a final look of disdain then hurried inside.

Servant checked the welts on his arms then stood up.

'You all right?' asked Indavara.

Without a word or a glance, Servant followed Master.

XIII

Lying across the bed wearing only a loincloth, Cassius dictated a letter. He guessed Abascantius might still be in Bostra and it seemed advisable to report his arrival in Berytus, if only to reassure his superior that he was moving forward despite the difficulties in Tripolis. Cassius actually winced as he thought of the agent and Marcellinus reading about the disastrous trip to Megakreon's villa and the ensuing chaos. Most embarrassing of all was the amateurish way in which he had all but accused a law-abiding citizen of being a counterfeiter because of nothing more than uncorroborated, circumstantial evidence.

'Take that to the way station yourself, Simo,' he said as the attendant finished writing. 'And make sure the duty officer marks it correctly – most secret.'

'Yes, sir.'

Once he had rolled up the letter and sealed it with gum, Simo looked out of the inn window and began rubbing his neck.

'Spit it out,' said Cassius, who could always tell when the Gaul had something to confess. They were alone; Indavara was at the stables, visiting Patch.

'Sir, I spoke to one of the innkeeper's men yesterday. His father is active in the Faith and attends a church-house not far from here. If there is a meeting, might I be permitted to—'

'What do I always say, Simo? Of course you may, once all your duties are complete. But make absolutely no mention of my name whatsoever or what we are doing in Berytus.'

'Of course. Thank you, sir.'

Cassius sat up and pointed at a pile of clothes resting on one of the saddlebags. 'When I get back I'll need my best red tunic, my helmet and a freshly polished belt.'

'This trip to the university, sir?'

'Indeed. I'd prefer not to parade around with all that on but I need to make a strong impression.'

'Leave it to me, Master Cassius.'

'Before you go – where's my water?'

Simo pulled a bowl out from under the bed. 'Here, sir, probably only warm now. I can get—'

'It'll do.'

Simo carefully put the letter inside a cloth bag which he then hung from his shoulder. 'I suppose I should take one of the badges, sir.'

'Yes, you'll need that.'

Simo retrieved it from another saddlebag and pinned it to his tunic.

Cassius was about to dunk his hands in the water but found himself looking at the attendant. 'What's so special about these church-houses, Simo? I mean, I appreciate that it's your version of a temple but I remember that place in Antioch – just an average house, no finery, nothing to impress. It hardly glorifies your Christ, does it? There aren't even any statues or pictures of him – does anyone know what he looked like?'

'The church-house gives us a chance to be together, sir. To study, to pray, to sing. And to honour our Lord through good deeds. I have heard that much help is given to those in need here in Berytus.'

'And Christ?'

Simo smiled and put a hand against his chest. 'We do not need pictures or statues, sir. He is within all of us.'

The Gaul left, gently shutting the door behind him.

Cassius shrugged. As he began washing his hands, he noticed his hardwood box on another saddlebag. Simo hadn't had time to put the figurines out but the top was open and the gods seemed to be giving Cassius another reproachful stare.

'Just asking.'

'Ah, I should have joined the army,' said Diadromes. 'With your height as well – very impressive.'

'Can we get this over with?' replied Cassius as he buckled the helmet strap. 'I don't want to keep all this on any longer than I have to. You were going to give me some more information, I believe?'

They were standing behind one of the four vast columns at the front of the university, accompanied by Indavara, Simo and Diadromes's clerk.

'Yes, indeed.' The Syrian took a step closer and spoke quietly. 'If all else fails, it might be worth mentioning the scandal I spoke of. It involved Sallustius' brother – also a notable professor here – and a student who has now left. It was claimed that the young man received extra tuition, favourable reports and a good deal of . . . let us call it personal attention. There was much speculation at the time but Sallustius moved quickly to limit the damage and was able to keep his brother in his post. But rumour has it that this man now has another favourite. If such talk were to reach Rome . . .'

'Understood, but I'd like to avoid that kind of tactic if possible.'

Diadromes frowned. 'You're a grain man. I would have thought that was precisely your type of tactic.'

'I am an officer of the Imperial Army,' said Cassius as he straightened his sword belt. 'Putting the reputation of the Service aside for a moment, please credit me with some understanding of the concept of honour.'

Diadromes reddened slightly. 'Of course.'

His clerk subtly approached and whispered in his ear.

'We are very close to the fifth hour, Officer. Sallustius is not one to tolerate tardiness. Best of luck. My clerk will wait outside for you and let me know how it went. I'll send Cosmas over to you later.'

Cassius nodded and made a last adjustment to his chin strap. As Diadromes walked swiftly away across the forum, his clerk handed Cassius a piece of paper. It listed the time of his appointment and the room number for the meeting.

Cassius gestured to himself. 'Well?'

Simo tugged down on the middle of the scarlet tunic and made an adjustment to his left cuff. 'Perfect, sir.'

Indavara was leaning against the pillar, arms crossed. 'You remind me of that peacock we saw in Tripolis.'

'Oh, sorry, sir. I almost forgot.' Simo took the spearhead badge from his own tunic and carefully pinned it onto Cassius's.

'Careful, Simo, you know how much that linen cost. You two wait here.' Cassius couldn't imagine he'd be in any danger inside the university and wanted Sallustius' attention to be solely on him. He strode up to the entrance and received a polite greeting from the two city sergeants on duty. Inside was a high, broad corridor with a gleaming floor.

An elderly man sat at a desk with nothing on it. 'Good day, sir.'

'Good day. Room thirty-two?'

'Down to the end then right, sir. Third door on your left.'

Halfway along the corridor, he passed six students. They had been chattering but quietened as they passed him. Cassius felt a warm surge of manly confidence as the students cast concerned glances at his sword; a long blade with a bronze eagle at the base of the hilt. Most of the young men would arrive at the university in their late teens to embark on five years of study, so some would be Cassius's age or older. When he considered what he had seen and done since arriving in Syria three years ago, the thought of coming here seemed almost ridiculous. Sometimes – very occasionally – Cassius felt proud that he was a successful army officer instead of a fledgling orator.

He passed a room with the door ajar and heard a loud professor lustily outlining the intricacies of liability law as applied to offender and accomplice.

Cassius reached thirty-two and knocked on what looked like mahogany. Another elderly servant opened it and gestured for him to enter. The vice-chancellor certainly didn't stint on attendants; another man was standing by a table well stocked with food and drink while another was wafting a large fan.

Sallustius himself was at the far end of the chamber, behind a colossal, highly polished desk, also mahogany. He was facing away from the door, hands clasped behind him, looking out at a garden. Despite the folds of his toga, Cassius could tell he was quite fat.

Sallustius turned, hands still behind him. 'Good day, Officer Crispian.'

Greek, of course – the language of learning.

'Good day, Vice-Chancellor.'

Sallustius did not come forward to offer his arm; a first attempt to put off his guest perhaps. 'Please have a seat. My office is rather warm but Musa here is doing his best.'

The servant – almost certainly a slave – was employing a slow, long wafting motion that did seem to be cooling the room a little. Once he had removed his helmet, Cassius patted down his hair and gestured at the desk. 'May I?'

'Please.'

He put the helmet down very carefully.

'A drink?'

'No, thank you.' Cassius glanced at the two busts that framed the window. One he couldn't identify, the other was definitely Ulpianus, famed jurist and graduate of the university.

Sallustius had an unusual face. Clearly the fat didn't help, but it seemed to have no shape to it and even his greying hair was a curly, greasy mess. The eyes, however, were narrow and bright blue. Cassius doubted they missed much.

'I don't recall the last time an army officer requested an appointment with me. This is most unusual.'

'But not too unpleasant, I trust?'

'So far, no. However, I must press you to explain why you are here. As you will appreciate, I am a busy man.'

'As I understand it, one of your areas of responsibility is enrolment.'

'Ah. Let me guess – you are here on behalf of Aradates?'

'No.'

'Diadromes, then. I didn't know he had any friends in the army.'

'We are related.' This was Cassius's idea; the simplest way to explain his interest.

137

'I see.'

'As you will know, the university has not offered his son a place for the next academic year. This is causing a good deal of unhappiness in the household and the wider family.'

'That is regrettable but we turn away hundreds of prospective students every year. We can take only fifty.'

'I am aware of the numbers. I was once offered a place here myself.'

'Is that right?'

'In the end I chose the army instead.'

Sallustius glanced at the helmet. A fly was buzzing around the red horsehair crest.

'The lad is only sixteen,' Cassius continued. 'Yet he passed the entrance exam with ease and has excellent references. Surely another student can make way?'

'I do not see why another student – and another family – should be so disadvantaged. Young Master Diadromes can apply again next year.'

The fan stopped moving for a moment while the slave changed hands.

Cassius changed his approach. 'It may be the case that my cousin did not present his arguments in a manner befitting this institution. He is not a learned man, but he is exceptionally capable and hard working. His son has inherited these attributes and possesses a plethora of his own. Vice-Chancellor, I am sure you would concur that it is in the interests of the university to extend a warm welcome to the best and brightest, regardless of breeding or background. This institution is known as "the mother of law". No good mother favours one son over the other. Young Diadromes wishes to better himself; to serve this city, to serve Rome and – above all – to serve the law. Does he not deserve a chance?'

Sallustius put his elbows on the desk and interlocked his fingers. 'I must say you demonstrate a delicacy of expression not commonly found among the martial class, Officer Crispian. I'm sure you would have done well here. Sadly, as far as your cousin's son goes, my hands are tied.'

Cassius glanced at the bust. 'Domitius Ulpianus, is it not?'

'It is. A remarkable man. I had the great privilege of meeting him as a boy.'

'Remarkable indeed. I have always been fond of one maxim in particular: "to live honourably, to harm no one, *to give each his own*".'

'Once again, you have chosen your words well. It may be the case that some within the university make judgements based on what you term "breeding and background" but I am not one of them. My great-grandfather was a freedman. I and the rest of the admissions board reviewed young Diadromes's application along with the others and the decision has been made. This is not a fortress, nor a basilica, nor a court. This is the University of Berytus; we make law here. We do not bend rules.'

Cassius had rather enjoyed coming up with his little speech, even though he'd known it was probably a waste of time. At least now nobody could say he hadn't tried the honourable way.

'Diadromes is willing to make a substantial contribution to the university.'

'Is that right? Personally, I hate to talk about money, but I must always consider what's best for this institution.'

'I am reluctant to mention a specific number with your men present.'

'Please, they are all my personal slaves. The most sensitive of matters are discussed in this office every day.'

'Fifty aurei – for every year of the lad's study.'

'A sizeable sum.'

Clearly not sizeable enough.

Diadromes had already told Cassius his absolute maximum.

'One hundred, then.'

'Very generous.' Sallustius obviously had a number in mind too, and that wasn't it. 'But as I said earlier, my hands are tied. I'm afraid there's nothing more to be discussed today.'

Sallustius was about to get up but he stayed where he was when he realised his guest wasn't leaving.

Cassius sighed, his last hope of a gentlemanly discussion gone. He had learned quickly that the world often worked this way;

what was now his world at least. That didn't make it any less depressing.

'Unfortunately, you have left me no choice other than to bring up another matter. You still wish your slaves to remain?'

'Of course.'

'Very well. I believe it involved your brother and a young—'

Sallustius clapped his hands together. 'Leave us, you three. Immediately!'

— 8 —

Once outside, Cassius passed on the good news to Diadromes's clerk, who departed at a run. Cassius took off his helmet and gave it to Simo.

'So you got what you wanted?' asked Indavara, still leaning against the column.

'What I wanted? This wasn't about what I wanted. When is any bloody thing about what I want?'

'Only asked.'

Cassius took a light cloak from Simo to cover his tunic. 'Diadromes got what he wanted, yes. I've delivered – now it's his turn. This house had better be worth it.'

— 8 —

It wasn't a house; Cassius reckoned it would take him a while to decide whether it was worth it. The street was located in a quiet area of Berytus mostly occupied by townhouses, workshops and bakeries.

Indavara sniffed the air. 'I love the smell of bread.'

Simo dropped to the ground and gazed in dismay at the wall, though as there were more bricks on the ground than actually on top of each other, Cassius wondered if you could really call it a wall.

'Oh no,' said the Gaul. 'It's in a terrible state.'

'I like it,' said Indavara.

The tower looked rather like those Cassius had seen in the

140

deserts of Arabia and Syria, except it was circular. As Diadromes's clerk tied off his horse and walked towards it, Cassius used him for scale, estimating that the tower was no less than forty feet high and about fifteen wide. There seemed to be only one door; a reassuringly solid lump of wood banded with iron. There were many windows; all small, grilled and round. At the top, newer stone had been used to construct an open area beneath a pointed, tiled roof supported by three columns.

'Well, what do you think?' Having just arrived, Diadromes reined in beside Cassius. Once again, he could easily have passed for a mid-ranking citizen, though today he was wearing a chain of office around his neck. Hanging from it was a miniature silver club.

'Certainly looks secure,' said Cassius as he dismounted.

'Might need a bit of a tidy-up but I doubt there's a safer residence in all of Berytus.' Once on the ground, Diadromes called his clerk over and threw him his reins. He then retrieved a heavy ring of iron keys from a saddlebag and led the way towards the door.

Cassius followed him, inspecting the dusty, weed-strewn ground that surrounded the tower. 'Was there ever a path? Or a gate?'

'Not really,' said the Syrian cheerfully. 'I was never too bothered about the exterior, to be honest.'

He grinned as Indavara and Simo joined them by the door. 'Between you and me, this is where I used to play dice with my friends; brought the odd girl here too. Until my wife made an honest man out of me, that is. I was going to sell but I just couldn't do it. Must have had it fifteen years or so now.'

'It looks like a guard tower,' said Indavara as Diadromes brushed dirt off the rusty lock and slotted in the key.

'That's exactly what it was. Years ago this spot was beyond the city walls. There are a few inscriptions scratched inside by soldiers. The oldest one mentions Marcus Aurelius, would you believe?'

The key was refusing to turn. 'Always was a bit stiff. Ah, there you go.'

Hinges groaning, the big door opened. Diadromes pushed it all the way back and jerked out the key.

Cassius waved dust away from his face as he followed him inside.

'A tad smelly but that can be sorted out easily enough.'

'A tad dark, too,' said Cassius.

Diadromes pointed at the wooden stairway constructed against the wall opposite the door. 'That runs up to the bedroom, then there's another one up to the roof. I believe I left the table and chairs. Excellent view too.'

Indavara and Simo wandered around, peering into the shadows.

Diadromes grabbed Cassius's arm. 'Sorry, I forgot to thank you – must be the excitement. You can imagine what a happy house I left behind. My son and my wife are thrilled.'

'I told Sallustius that you knew nothing of my visit. I doubt he'll give you any more trouble.'

'I am in your debt, Officer Crispian. If this place isn't suitable I'm sure we can find something else. I suppose it all depends on which is more important: comfort or security.'

Cassius noted some furniture stacked up below the stairs; a bed, a cupboard, some small tables. Simo seemed more interested in the state of the floor, which was covered in patchy reed matting and hundreds of rodent droppings.

Indavara was already heading up the stairs. 'I like it. I really like it.'

Cassius turned to Diadromes. 'Security it is. Thank you.'

The Syrian gave him the keys. 'Have your man make a list of anything you need and give it to my clerk. I believe there's still a stables just over the road so that's the horses taken care of.'

'Latrine?' said Cassius.

'Good deep hole over there,' said Diadromes, pointing into the shadows. 'Ventilation bricks too.'

'You will put up a curtain, Simo.'

'Yes, sir. Master Diadromes, might I enquire – water?'

'There's a well at the back, covered with a big slab of granite. As long as you can get that off it should be fine. I'm afraid I have to be going. Tell you what, Crispian, I'll come over later with Cosmas around sundown. Oh, and thank you again, you have no idea how much easier you've made my life. I don't recall the last time I saw my wife with a smile upon her face.'

Diadromes marched out of the tower and back to his horse, already barking orders at his clerk.

Simo had located a broom. He started sweeping then stopped, as if there were no point even beginning such a huge task.

'Don't worry, we'll give you a hand,' said Cassius. 'And you heard what he said about the list.'

'Chuck me the keys,' yelled Indavara from the stairs. 'This door's locked too. I want to go up top.'

Cassius threw them to him then glanced around once more. 'Happy, sir?'

'*Happier*, Simo. Gods willing, I may even sleep tonight.'

XIV

For once, Cassius actually fulfilled his promise of helping out. Though there was seldom any need for him to involve himself in practical labours, he was not unused to them. He had grown up surrounded by servants but his father had always insisted he learn every skill associated with looking after his various horses and, as a boy, he'd spent countless hours helping the gardener in the villa grounds. Cassius had also dirtied his hands during training. He had cleaned and repaired kit, mucked out stables, cooked meals and heaved amphoras around; the legions made few concessions to status or prospective rank during the first few weeks of instruction. Generally, he found such work grindingly tedious, but he recognised that a few hours here and there was probably good for him. So while Indavara and Simo tidied the ground floor, he filled a bucket with water, grabbed a rag and climbed to the top of the tower.

He had already been up to check the view but resolved not to do so again until he'd finished his work. The timber floor was filthy; Simo could attend to that. The stone surround and the underside of the roof would also need attention – whichever birds had been occupying the place seemed to have discharged shit at every conceivable angle on to every surface.

Cassius decided to focus on the table and chairs. The birds hadn't done too much damage here but all the wood was covered in a thick layer of grime. Barefoot and clad in his oldest tunic, he soaked the rag and got started. Once the table was done, he decided he in fact deserved a break after all; he walked over to the surround and looked out at the city.

Like Tripolis, Berytus was built upon an angular promontory, the western corner of which pointed directly at Cyprus, some

144

hundred miles across the Great Green Sea. To the north was the harbour and the two long breakwaters that protected it. Dozens of high masts could be seen there, and Cassius counted thirteen large vessels at sea. Sails billowing, the ships seemed to be sliding effortlessly across the calm water. The sailing season was now in full flow; cargoes and passengers would be heading south towards Egypt and west towards the rest of the Empire.

The harbour was surrounded by dozens of large warehouses and Cassius also spied several tall cranes. Directly south was the centre and the open spaces of the forum. Here were three of Berytus's largest structures: the basilica, the theatre and the university.

Cassius moved across the tower and looked west. The city's sprawl hadn't yet reached the coast in this direction; there were several miles of golden sand dunes separating it from the sea. At the corner of the promontory was a slender lighthouse of pale stone. He could see smoke drifting from the top of it; the bronze mirror within would reflect the firelight outward, helping ships find their way.

Cassius threw the rag into the pail and looked east. Berytus was hemmed in by a spine of mountains, the low flanks of which were covered by dense, green forest. The highest of the peaks was Lebanon itself; said to reach almost two miles into the sky. For most of the year the mountain was capped by snow but now the summit was grey. Cassius could see at least three roads leading through steep passes, connecting the coastal plain to the fertile Bekaa valley, the rest of Syria and beyond. He wondered how many miles he was from Alauran, the desert fort he and the tiny garrison of legionaries and auxiliaries had defended against the Palmyrans three years earlier.

Despite the glare of the sun, faces appeared: Strabo, Secundus, Barates – the brave, resourceful veterans who had helped him. All gone. All dead because they fought under the flag of Rome. There had been others, too, since Alauran. Major, the bodyguard killed in Antioch; Eborius, the fellow officer killed by the rogue centurion Carnifex in Cyrenaica; and all the men lost in Arabia while fighting to recover the black stone.

Death had claimed them all. Death had been near so many times. Cassius had hoped this assignment would enable him to feel something close to safe, something close to normal. But not after Bostra, not after Tripolis. They were coming for him.

Who? Why?

'It's very quiet up there,' said Indavara from below. 'Haven't fallen asleep, have you?'

Cassius shook his head and dragged himself free of the reverie. He couldn't help the dead and they certainly couldn't help him. ''Course not.' He walked back to the pail and plucked the rag from the water.

———8———

With the possible exception of a few select soldiers and servants, Simo and Indavara were the two hardest-working men Cassius had ever met. Despite his bulk, Simo rarely stopped moving and was supremely efficient. Though far less organised, Indavara threw himself into virtually any physical task with a single-minded energy that at times seemed almost manic.

Descending to the first floor and calling Simo up the steps to collect the pail, Cassius saw that the pair had already tidied and swept the ground floor. The Gaul announced that he had completed and dispatched the list and that Diadromes's clerk would return with the supplies by the tenth hour. Once rid of the pail, Cassius walked over to one of the windows and looked outside. Indavara was bent over and walking away from the door, flinging rubble aside to create a path to the street. He had stripped down to his training kilt and was already attracting interest from a pair of girls hanging washing on a roof not far away.

Cassius examined his new bedroom; he had claimed it shortly after they arrived. There were a few holes in the timber but the flooring looked sound. The only contents were a large, strong-looking bed frame, another small cupboard and a chamber pot. Simo had already brought some of Cassius's ten saddlebags upstairs and laid them out on the bed. He employed a numbering system, and Cassius knew that number two contained his most prized belongings.

He took out the spearhead and put it in a corner. Then he found the hardwood box. In her letter, his mother had reminded him to display his figurines no matter how much he was travelling. This time he was determined to do it; he felt guilty for ignoring her request for much of the last three years. He took the box over to the largest window, beneath which was a niche of suitable size. After brushing some dust away, he opened the box and placed it on its side so that the figurines seemed to be standing up and watching over the room. Later, he would give the niche a proper clean and place some candles there; perhaps offer a libation.

Several months ago, back in Bostra, he had decided to make a consistent effort with his worship of Jupiter, hoping that the god of gods would hear his repeated pleas and keep him safe. He resolved to visit the local temple as soon as he could and pray to this little shrine every day. Despite the threat that hung over him like a black cloud, he was at last starting to feel a little better. He had secured a useful ally in Diadromes, this tower seemed ideal, and now he had the gods watching over him too. He had done all he could.

The deputy magistrate was once again late, which made Simo very happy; it gave him an extra hour to continue his efforts and prepare some food. While he worked on downstairs, Cassius sat at the newly clean table at the top of the tower with Indavara.

'Is that you?' he asked.

In the early days the bodyguard had given off quite a stench, but Simo had since civilised him and taught him the importance of daily washing.

'Probably,' said Indavara, munching his way through a handful of almonds. 'Some lazy swine didn't bother to clean off all the bird shit up here so I had to do it.'

'Fair point; but perhaps you should wash before our esteemed guest arrives? Plenty of water, isn't there?'

'There is – since I hauled ten buckets of it up from the well. What exactly were *you* doing all afternoon?'

'Cleaning my room.'

'And sleeping. I heard you snoring.'

'I'm not going through that again – I don't snore. You're the snorer, though to be fair we really need to invent a new word for the noise you make. I've never heard a rhinoceros in the wildest throes of passion but I can't imagine it's all that dissimilar.'

They had only a single candle alight so it was too dark for Cassius to see Indavara's reaction.

After a while the bodyguard sniffed. 'Actually, maybe you're right.'

'Of course I'm right. A fresh tunic too, perhaps?'

Indavara got up and started down the ladder. As he reached the bottom, a loud voice echoed through the tower.

'Evening, all! Is the new master at home?'

'Indeed he is,' answered Cassius.

Diadromes came up first, followed by a small man who Cassius assumed to be the sergeant Cosmas.

'Sorry about the gloom. Simo will be up in a minute with a lamp or two.'

'Here, a welcome gift.' Diadromes put a flask on the table.

'Thank you.'

'Ah, it's nice to be back up here.' The Syrian walked over to the surround. 'All the lights – I used to imagine the different scenes in all the different houses. Romans and foreigners, citizens and slaves, rich and poor.'

Cassius considered iterating that few of the poor would be able to afford to light their houses but he didn't want to spoil the moment.

'Good evening, sir,' said Cosmas, who had quietly moved round to stand opposite Cassius. He had a heavy Syrian accent and a slight lisp.

'Good evening. Please take a seat.'

Cassius shouted down through the trapdoor: 'Hurry it up with those lamps, Simo.'

'Yes, sir.'

148

Cosmas sat down but Cassius could see nothing of his face, which he found rather unnerving.

'Looks like you're settling in well,' said Diadromes as he sat beside the sergeant.

'I think we have all we need.'

'If you don't mind, Cosmas has some questions for you – about exactly how a counterfeiting gang might operate.'

'Of course.'

By the time Cassius finished answering, Simo had brought up two lamps, some glasses and more food. Indavara came up too. He greeted the visitors then set about lighting the lamps while Simo poured the wine.

'Finest Massic,' proclaimed Diadromes proudly. 'From my cousin's vineyard near Naples.'

'Ah.' Cassius hid his distaste. To him, 'finest Massic' was a contradiction in terms; it was a strong, unsubtle wine that his father refused to allow through the door.

As the orange glow of the oil lamps drew their faces from the darkness, Cassius looked across at Cosmas. The diminutive sergeant was a dark-skinned man with an angular nose and a striking face. His beard was as black as his hair and just as thick. Cosmas thanked his superior for the wine and drank, peering at Indavara over the rim of his glass.

He was clearly a bright fellow (certainly for a city sergeant) and had asked a dozen questions about the coins and the materials the gang would need. He planned to begin his enquiries the following day and report directly to Cassius if he made any progress. Diadromes had released him from his normal duties for as long as he was needed.

Cassius sipped a little of the Massic and swiftly ate a handful of raisins.

Simo gathered up a couple of empty bowls then spoke quietly to his master. 'Sir, might I be excused for the rest of the evening? There is a meeting at the third hour.'

'Now?'

'Sir, Indavara has offered to fulfil my duties if you need anything.'

'How long will you be?'

'No more than two hours.'

'And my bed is ready?'

'Yes, sir.'

'All your other work is done?'

Indavara tutted. 'When have you ever known Simo not do his work? He's barely stopped for breath today.'

Though annoyed by the bodyguard's interjection, Cassius ignored him and took his time. 'Very well. No more than two hours. Turn over my hourglass before you leave.'

'Yes, Master Cassius. Thank you.'

Simo set off down the ladder.

Diadromes said nothing but Cassius felt he should explain. 'He is a Christian – as soon as we stop anywhere for more than five minutes he goes looking for fellow believers.'

'There is a fairly large community here,' replied the magistrate, 'and growing steadily too. They do like to try and spread the word.'

'Indeed. Thankfully, Simo now knows to keep his ramblings to himself.' Cassius looked across at Cosmas. 'These informers of yours – you think they'll come up with something?'

'Hard to know. Honestly, sir, I think you may have the wrong city. It sounds like a big operation – materials, production, transportation. Would take a few bodies; hard to keep quiet and contained.'

'Officer Crispian has his reasons for thinking they're here,' said Diadromes. 'And we do have hundreds of factories and workshops. With all the traffic and material coming through the port—'

'Hiding in plain sight, perhaps?' said Cassius.

'Perhaps,' replied Diadromes. 'As deputy magistrate, I would like to tell you that Berytus is the safest, least corrupt place in Syria, but I'm afraid it is no different to any other city. It has its share of criminals, and secrets.'

Cosmas acceded with a nod.

'Not to mention several hundred unhappy weavers,' said Cassius. He was still interested to know of Diadromes's view.

'Thankfully yesterday's protest didn't last all that long. Maybe they have finally accepted that Pomponianus will not change his mind about their supplementary income.'

'You don't agree?' asked Cassius, noting the cynical expression on Cosmas's dark face. The sergeant glanced warily at his superior, who drank more wine then waved at his subordinate to answer.

'Without the corn dole, some are struggling to get food on the plate. Hungry men can get angry. Hungry men with hungry wives and hungry children can get *very* angry.'

'Why not just let them do the extra work?' asked Indavara. 'Who loses?'

Diadromes answered: 'Unfortunately, my friend, it is more a question of principle. For a long time, weaving was not considered a particularly worthy job for a man. Those who own the factories and occupy seats on the council come from families with land. Even though the weavers bring great wealth to the city, the rich look down upon them; they are certainly not about to give in to people they view as little better than slaves. If they know what's good for them, the weavers will stay in the factories and off the streets. Pomponianus will not hesitate to make examples of the leaders if he has to.'

'How would *you* handle it?' asked Cassius.

Cosmas also seemed interested in his superior's answer.

'Given my background, I am in a delicate position, Officer Crispian. Which means that I must always carefully consider my answers and my audience. To the weavers, I would say that I understand their grievances and will do what I can. To the factory owners and the council members – whose votes I depend on – I would say that I understand their grievances and will do what I can.'

'And to me?' asked Cassius.

Diadromes held up his glass. 'How do you like the Massic?'

XV

Cosmas did not return for three days; a quiet period which, to Cassius, passed pleasantly enough. Simo and Indavara continued their work and took turns to go out for provisions, while he spent the entire time inside the tower. Thoughts of his enemies were never far away and he often found himself examining the streets below for any sign of watchers skulking in the shadows.

On the third day, he threw himself into a long-neglected project: his translation of an obscure but compelling Greek tome on military strategy. He was on to his fourth page when a messenger arrived downstairs; Cosmas at last had some news and would be visiting around the twelfth hour.

By late evening, Cassius was bored with the translation and joined Indavara for a weightlifting session downstairs. The bodyguard had lashed two large stones to an old iron spear and was completing repetitions of twenty. After each set he would take a brief drink of water then start again. Simo was out; he had asked for two more hours to help the local congregation with what he'd described only as 'the Lord's work'.

'Can I have a go?' asked Cassius when Indavara finished his third set.

'Warm your muscles up first. Shoulders and back, especially.'

While the bodyguard completed his fourth set, Cassius did some push-ups, twists and jumps. Indavara was constantly lecturing him about how he had a good basic frame but needed to put weight and muscle on. Given his current predicament, Cassius could clearly see the benefits of being bigger and stronger.

'You sure about this?' asked the bodyguard when he walked over and examined the spear.

'Well, I can give it a go. How much does it weigh?'

'Simo reckoned about seventy pounds.'

'Seventy?'

'I can make up another one for you. There's a broom handle around here somewhere and some pebbles outside.'

'Very droll. At least let me have a go.'

'All right, but not above your head. Just try to get it off the floor.'

Cassius squatted and placed his hands at either end of the spear. He gripped hard and pulled upwards. The stones did not move.

'Caesar's balls.'

'Have you *ever* done weights before?'

Actually, the heaviest thing Cassius had lifted were the bodies of dead soldiers, but he didn't particularly want to think or talk about that.

He decided to try again. Just as he set his grip there was a knock at the door. While Indavara went to unbolt it, Cassius let go and moved away from the weights.

Indavara looked through the viewing hole in the door before opening up. 'Simo, that you?'

'Yes.'

Cassius tutted; he'd hoped it was Cosmas.

He shook his arms to loosen up, then returned to the weight and gripped the spear once more. Indavara had opened the door but Simo still hadn't come in. Cassius looked across at them.

'What happened to you?' said the bodyguard.

The Gaul came in slowly, head bowed.

Cassius let go of the pole again and hurried over. One side of Simo's tunic was dirty and he was holding up his hand to cover his face.

'Show me that,' said Indavara, pushing his arm down. The attendant's right cheek was discoloured and he had a cut just above his left eye. Dark blood had dried beneath it.

'Simo, what happened?' repeated Indavara.

'I – I—'

'Corbulo, get a stool for him.'

Cassius did so.

Simo slumped down on it then looked at his master. 'I am so sorry, sir. They wanted me to stay but I knew I needed to get back.'

'Gods, man, you're shaking. What happened?'

Indavara placed a hand on his cheek. 'Don't worry. Just checking.' He pressed against it with his fingers. 'That hurt?'

'Only a little.'

'Shape looks all right. I'll clean that eye up.'

Indavara grabbed a mug and filled it from an amphora of water, then went to look for a cloth.

Cassius's first thought was that it might have been his enemies, trying to get information out of the attendant. His second was that they might have followed him. He ran to the door and bolted it.

'Who attacked you, Simo?'

'I believe they are followers of a local cult opposed to the Faith. We were handing out bread to the poor in an area not far from their temple. The men said that we were trying to convert them but it is not true. We wished only to help.'

Cassius shook his head. 'Of course you did.'

Indavara brought the wet rag over and began cleaning the wound. 'They attacked you because of that?'

'We had women with us – they struck them too. One man has a broken finger, another a cut like me. And they took the bread. All of it.'

Cassius was still standing over him, any vestige of sympathy long gone. 'Four days we've been here. And off you go into a strange part of the city with people you've just met to make trouble.'

'Sounds to me like these cultists were the ones making trouble,' said Indavara.

Cassius pointed at Simo. 'You know full well that I cannot afford to draw attention to myself yet you get yourself mixed up in this. You lose all sense and judgement when it comes to your "faith". Well, it ends here and now. You will not visit this church-house or any other congregation while we are here in Berytus.'

'Sir, please, I—'

'Do not interrupt me. Did you hear what I said?'

'Yes, sir.'

Cassius looked over at the table; he was in dire need of some wine. But as Indavara took the bloodied rag away from Simo's cheek, he paused.

'Is it bad?'

'Nothing broken. I'd say he was wearing a ring. An inch lower and it would have been a lot worse.'

Cassius glared at his attendant. 'Idiotic. Absolutely idiotic.'

Simo and Indavara eventually decided that the cut needed stitches. Cassius told them to do it upstairs; he didn't want Cosmas asking any awkward questions about what had happened. The sergeant arrived half an hour later.

'Good evening, sir.'

'Evening,' said Cassius, securing the door behind him. 'You look rather tired.'

'Lot of walking today.'

'Come, have a seat.'

Cassius now realised that Cosmas was one of those men whose face and figure didn't quite fit together. Despite his compelling features, he was exceptionally short and slight for a city sergeant. He had of course forgone his club, and was dressed in an anonymous tunic.

They sat by the table, which was covered with the various foodstuffs and kitchen equipment Simo had acquired.

'Some progress, then?'

Cosmas ran a finger and a thumb down his beard. 'What we in the trade might call a definite possibility.'

'Ah, well, that's a start.'

'I've been around most of my tale-tellers now, though a couple are always hard to locate. Lot of talk as usual, much of it invented for the sake of a coin, much of it of no use. Nothing on Florens. Not a thing.'

'I expected as much. We don't even have an alias.'

'As far as counterfeiting goes, not a lot on that either. I've been down to the docks – nothing on illicit metals. I've been around the factories – nothing on new outfits needing premises with ovens and the rest of it. I've been round the cart drivers and the shipping agents – nothing on secret deliveries around the province.'

'That's a lot of nothing. What about this "definite possibility"?'

Cosmas leaned forward. 'A pair of brothers named Gorgos. One of my tale-tellers reckons they've been seen around town with some well-dressed fellow, possibly an Egyptian. Apparently they've been helping him out: buying a couple of small properties, introducing him to locals. One of those locals is a character named Hagnon – who owns two freighters and a cart-hire concern. Barely a year passes when the municipal court doesn't receive some accusation about him but so far none of the shit has stuck. Excuse the expression, sir.'

'Excused. All very interesting but please tell me you have something more.'

'The brothers. One is the muscle, the other an educated man – quite the scribe, in fact. Three years ago, he was charged with forgery. For a price he'd draw up false wills or other documents. I looked up the records at the basilica – he even tried his hand at creating false wax seals.'

'And the trial?'

'There were three witnesses. All retracted their testimony and refused to appear. The judicial prefect had to let it go.'

'I see. Well, taken together, that all sounds quite promising. What do you suggest?'

'If you don't mind, sir, give me another day. I'll watch these brothers, see what I can for myself. If I get no farther we can bring them in for questioning.'

'And this Egyptian?'

'Eyes and ears open for anything on him too, of course.'

'Good.'

'Can I . . .'

'Yes, of course. I expect you'd like to get home.'

Cassius led the way over to the door and opened it. Cosmas

had one foot outside when he stopped. 'Ah, sorry, sir, I forgot. Magistrate Diadromes wanted me to pass this on: the procurator's office have found one of the fake coins right here in the city. Apparently a clerk was going through his change from the market and spotted it.'

'Oh.'

'Goodnight, sir.'

Cassius quickly shut the door and bolted it. He stood there for a moment, gazing up at the windows facing west, where the last red rays of the sun speared the darkness.

It was all so damned tenuous; and once again he was basing the investigation on hunches and a few disparate threads that might add up to very little. Still, he was grateful for the help offered by Diadromes and Cosmas; staying off the streets was a definite advantage at the moment.

Indavara and Simo's beds had arrived the previous day. There seemed to be no end to Diadromes's generosity and the mattresses were well made and stuffed with straw. They had also been given two cushions each, and Indavara still wasn't quite used to such soft support for his head. He twisted and turned for a while, unable to get comfortable.

'Are you still awake?' asked Simo.

'Yes, unfortunately.'

'Do you think Master Cassius meant what he said?'

'Probably.'

Indavara adjusted the light blanket he used in the summer months. The tower was dark and silent. Outside, he could hear a cart bumping along the street.

'Simo, who were these people you were giving bread to?'

'Some were Palmyran refugees. Some were ill. Some were just poor. They gather near the docks, living off scraps. We'd only given out a few loaves when the men came. It has nothing to do with belief; just common thievery. They took the bread right out of the hands of the old and the young and the sick.'

Simo whispered a prayer to himself.

'What about the city sergeants – they're supposed to deal with crime, aren't they?'

'Not if it means helping Christians.'

'None of your lot will fight back, I suppose?'

'Actually one man tried to. He is a legionary – he follows the Faith but has to keep it a secret from his fellow soldiers.' The tone of Simo's voice changed. 'I fought too.'

Indavara turned on to his side, facing the Gaul. 'They'll try again, your friends – to feed these people?'

'I expect so. Without me, though.'

'Maybe not. What if I came to help next time?'

'Indavara—'

'Don't worry, I would leave my blades here. I just . . . I would like to help.'

'But what about Master Cassius?'

'Leave him to me.'

The following morning, Diadromes's clerk arrived with two letters (Cassius had asked the deputy magistrate to have his office collect any post that arrived for him at the basilica). The letters were bound together: one was from Abascantius, one from Marcellinus.

Cassius read them in his room after breakfast. Marcellinus had written only a few lines but had made it clear that – whatever the gravity of the investigation – he was to employ caution when dealing with men of rank. Abascantius seemed more upset by the wasting of time and overall lack of progress. Both of them concluded by reminding Cassius that he had to move quickly; Minister Sabinus had now brought the situation to Aurelian's attention and the Emperor was enraged by the thought of his likeness and new coinage being exploited by criminals. Abascantius reckoned Cassius had about two or three weeks to make a breakthrough. Once Sabinus's patience ran out he would send a senior treasury official to take charge.

Having read all that, Cassius felt somewhat guilty about the prospect of another unproductive day spent waiting around to see if Cosmas got anywhere.

The one material the gang would definitely need a lot of was bronze; and it would come in via either the roads or the port. Cassius called Simo up and dictated a letter to Diadromes; it was surely wise to capitalise on the Syrian's goodwill while the favour remained fresh in his mind. Cassius asked him to find out if the municipal tax collectors or anyone else maintained records on those outfits within Berytus that imported, stockpiled or made use of large quantities of bronze. He requested that any information be sent to him at the tower immediately.

When Simo finished writing and headed for the stairs, Cassius added a final instruction.

'You wouldn't dream of visiting your new friends on my time, would you? I am not going to change my mind about this. You deliver the note then come straight back.'

'Yes, sir.'

Cassius spent the morning up on the roof, working on the translation again. After completing another three pages, his pen ran dry. Unfortunately, Simo wasn't yet back from the basilica so – instead of going to prepare some fresh ink for himself – he sat there daydreaming, slumped on the table, head resting on his arm.

One of his uncles had a friend in Rome who published military texts. Cassius imagined returning home with his translation complete, then visiting bookshops with his mother and father, seeing his new work upon the shelf. *Cassius Quintius Corbulo, author.* He liked the sound of that.

'Corbulo!' shouted Indavara from below.

'What?'

'Want to do some sword work?'

Not particularly. 'I suppose so. Where? I'm not doing it outside with every bugger watching.'

'I've found somewhere quiet. Close by.'

Cassius sighed. 'Very well.'

'Somewhere' turned out to be a small sanctuary just down the street. Like the tower's, much of the wall had collapsed but the interior was shielded from prying eyes by overgrown trees and bushes, most of which had been dried to a crisp by the summer sun.

'Wonder which god or goddess it was for?' said Indavara, tapping his wooden sword against his knee as they made their way inside.

'No way to tell now,' said Cassius as he pushed a thorny branch out of his way. In the middle of the sanctuary was an open space and a dusty square where a large plinth had once stood.

'How could it get like this?' asked Indavara. 'Shouldn't the followers look after it?'

'Perhaps it was for a god who fell out of favour. It happens. Or it may have been built by people who no longer live here.'

'Do you know if there is a sanctuary or shrine for Fortuna in Berytus?'

'Probably somewhere, though it seems your friend Aphrodite is the local favourite. Ask Cosmas if you want to go and pay your respects.'

Indavara kicked a clump of weeds. 'How could they just abandon their god? I could never forget my Fortuna.'

'Only because you believe she has helped you. What if things took a turn for the worse? Everything went wrong and she seemed to have forsaken you? What then?'

'I would pray to her to help me. And I believe she would.'

Cassius began his warm-up, swinging his arms across his chest. 'Sometimes I envy you your conviction. It makes things rather simpler.'

'Well, you often tell me I am simple.'

'That is not what I meant, as well you know.'

Indavara stopped in the middle of his own exercises. 'I remember you once saying you liked the idea of Simo's "kingdom" – where everyone you've ever known and loved is together and happy for ever.'

'An appealing idea; but far too perfect to be something I could ever believe in.'

'Do you envy Simo? His con . . .'

'Conviction – a strongly held belief. No, I can't say I do. I think conviction can easily become delusion; and then we get incidents like last night.'

'He was just trying to help people.'

'All well and good. But he belongs to me; and his first priority is to help *me*. Clearly he needs regular reminders of that.'

'But . . .'

'But what?' Cassius looked up at the sky and wiped his already damp brow. 'By the gods, it's hot.'

'Nothing,' said Indavara. 'Let's fight.'

'Promise not to stand on me this time?'

'Yes. Promise not to catch my chin?'

'No.'

XVI

A dozen clucking quail bustled out of the trees. It was now mating season and two of the plumper males were pecking at the ground with their bright red beaks, trying to impress the females. Alexon was sick of the noise so clapped at the birds, driving them back into the greenery.

He looked over at Amathea, who was sitting at the edge of the meadow, which was growing drier and paler every day. Skiron was squatting by a bucket, washing his hands. He and the hunters had only just finished their work; digging up the ground on either side of the drive, ready for the flower beds Amathea wanted.

Alexon walked over to his sister, who narrowed her eyes when she saw the expression on his face.

'We don't have to show him. But I would like the option, that's all.'

Alexon nodded and sat down next to her.

Amathea continued with her sewing. 'Anything from Sidon?'

'Yes. They've moved all of it. They want double next time.'

'Excellent. How are they paying?'

'Sapphires, amethysts and ivory.'

'Ah, ivory. I might have another necklace made up.'

Alexon glanced sideways at his sister. Her mouth, to be precise. That perfect mouth. Even on the hottest, driest day, the plump, full lips glistened invitingly.

'He's here,' said Skiron. The hunters had walked over to the other side of the meadow to practise with their bows.

Alexon heard the gate bolt being opened, then shut. Kallikres appeared, again walking hesitantly up the drive.

'Over here,' said Alexon.

As he came closer, the sergeant looked at Skiron, who was

standing close to his mistress, sinewy arms folded across his chest.

'Good day,' said Amathea, putting her sewing to one side.

Kallikres did not reply.

'Well?' said Alexon. 'Your note mentioned a new problem.'

'I don't know the details but a man has arrived in the city. He seems to be working with Deputy Magistrate Diadromes – one of his sergeants has been out on the streets, questioning informers about two very specific things.'

Amathea brushed her glossy hair away from her eyes. 'Is this a guessing game? Continue.'

'Firstly, your friend Florens. Secondly, a gang that might be producing counterfeit coins.'

Alexon slumped back in his chair. He'd tried to control everything, predict everything; but it was always so difficult in their line of work. He looked up at the villa and hoped this wasn't the beginning of the end. Another end. He wanted to stay.

'Who is this man?' he asked.

'Possibly treasury,' said Kallikres. 'I don't know.'

'We need a name.'

Amathea shrugged. 'They were already asking about the coins – probably doing the same in every city. And we already knew that Florens had been spotted.'

'Sister, it is one thing for them to look for the coins, another for them to look for *us*.'

'Where is Florens now?' asked Kallikres.

'We'll get to that,' replied Amathea. 'My brother is right – we need a name plus whatever else you can get – who he works for, what he knows.'

Kallikres shook his head. 'Diadromes's department is entirely separate from mine. It's only because my superior happened to be at the magistrate's residence that I even knew this man was here. I had to call in a favour to find out what Diadromes's lackey was up to. Any more digging and someone will get suspicious. Everyone's jumpy enough as it is with all the protests.'

'We need a name,' repeated Amathea.

'I tried. This man doesn't want anyone to know he's here.'

'You need money, just ask.'

'It's not about money. I cannot expose myself further. If I am implicated at all—'

Amathea held up a hand. 'Perhaps I have misunderstood. I thought we were paying you for information; to tell us of any threat from the city.'

Kallikres was looking at Alexon. 'You said I would probably have nothing to do. You said I was simply to warn you if I heard anything. This is not my fault. It is your mistake that has brought this investigator to Berytus. If they find Florens, we're finished. Is he still here?'

Amathea smothered a little smile. 'Skiron.'

The attendant walked towards the drive, gesturing for Kallikres to follow.

'Go on,' said Amathea.

The sergeant did so; and soon found himself by one section of the prospective flower beds that was rather deeper than the others. When he looked down into it, his hand went to his mouth.

Amathea giggled.

Kallikres took three steps back. He bowed his head and ran both hands through his curly hair, pressing down on his skull.

'Apparently it will do wonders for my roses,' said Amathea. 'Come back here.'

Kallikres returned, his face clammy and pale.

'He had become more trouble than he was worth,' added Amathea. 'I do hope you will not make the same mistake. This investigator – get his name and whatever else you can.'

'Quickly,' said Alexon.

'I – I don't know how.'

'You'll find a way,' said Amathea.

Skiron was now using his shovel to fill in the hole. Kallikres was listening to the clumps of earth landing.

'I don't think there's any more to be discussed,' said Alexon. 'Contact us as soon as you have something.'

Kallikres turned away.

'Have a pleasant evening,' said Amathea quietly.

The sergeant stopped and looked back. 'What do you mean?'

'It's Thursday,' she said. 'Thursday is when you go to see your little friend, isn't it?'

Kallikres' jaw dropped.

'What's his name again?'

'Pedrix,' said Alexon.

After the last meeting, Amathea had tasked Skiron with finding ways of applying pressure to the reluctant Kallikres.

'In love with a slave boy, eh?' added Amathea. 'I never would have guessed it to look at you. I have always wondered, does one of you give and the other receive? Or do you take turns?'

Kallikres had not blinked for a long time.

'Please don't tell me a city sergeant takes it from a slave boy? Have you no shame? And I'm told it's been going on for years.'

'He must be very precious to you,' said Alexon. 'But I hear his master sends him all over the city on various errands at all times of the day and night. Clearly he doesn't value him as highly as you do. I mean, anything could happen.'

Kallikres screwed his eyes shut, then opened them. 'I will do as you ask. Leave the boy alone.'

'Quickly now,' said Amathea, 'no sense wasting more time.'

Kallikres hurried away.

Amathea watched Skiron for a moment, then picked up her sewing. 'I look forward to the time when we no longer need him. Disgusting creature.'

XVII

Cassius guided his horse out of the stable courtyard and on to the street. He rounded a pair of men struggling with a rebellious mule, waited for Indavara and Simo to catch up, then set off at a trot. Cosmas's directions were tucked into his belt but two readings had been enough for him to memorise them.

The sergeant's letter had arrived at dawn. Apparently, observing the Gorgos brothers had not been easy. They seemed to have no regular employment, took great care not to be followed and spent much of the day conducting clandestine meetings. Cosmas was convinced they were up to something and suggested a surprise morning arrest for questioning. Considering the previous charges, they would be under considerable pressure to cooperate. Cassius agreed; he could not afford to waste time.

The trio were to meet the sergeant and his men at a hamlet east of the city, then proceed to the Gorgos' house and hopefully catch them unawares. According to Cosmas, they were not early risers.

Cassius counted off the side streets to his left as he passed them; at the seventh they would pick up the main road leading out of Berytus towards the mountains. After so many hours in the tower, he felt rather exposed, even though he was wearing his mail shirt under his cloak. This could not be worn without a padded undershirt, which he was already sweating into.

Cassius saw potential threats everywhere: movement beyond a shadowy doorway; two ruffians lurking behind a cart; a high window shutter slapping against a wall.

After a while he realised his unease had spread to his horse and it was speeding up. He slowed and turned. Indavara and

Simo were quite a way back; they had stopped by the pavement and were looking down at something.

'That bloody pair.' Cassius wheeled his horse around and rode back to them.

'We had to stop,' said Indavara. 'Look.'

Sitting outside a crumbling, empty house were two women and six children. They were dark skinned, filthy and clad in little more than rags. Simo stuttered an apology; he was struggling to keep his horse still while opening the money bag attached to his belt. Three of the children were on their feet, dirt-streaked arms stretched up towards the Gaul. The rest were on their way.

'By the gods,' spat Cassius. 'Come away, you two.'

'Corbulo.' Indavara held up a hand.

'Simo, I'm warning you. Leave that bag shut and ride on.'

'But look at them, sir. They have nothing. I will take it out of my allowance, of course.'

'Ride on!' Cassius shouted so loudly that most of the young-sters retreated. One of the mothers came forward and dragged the last child away.

Simo looked at his master, mouth quivering. After several seconds of hesitation, he let go of the money bag and obeyed.

Indavara had taken out some sesterces of his own. Ignoring Cassius, he bent over the pavement and offered them to the mother. 'Here.'

After a brief hesitation she came forward and took the coins, thanking the bodyguard in a language Cassius didn't recognise.

'If you're quite finished.'

'Yes,' said Indavara. 'Are you?'

Cassius yanked his horse around once more, cursing as he passed Simo.

He kept up a swift pace until they were well beyond the city gates, then cantered on until he saw a bit of clear ground. Once off the road, he halted in the shade provided by a stand of cedars. He dismounted and looped his reins around a low branch.

'This isn't the place, is it?' asked Indavara.

'Just tether your horse.'

Despite a shake of the head, the bodyguard did so.

Simo stopped a little farther back and roped his mount to a milestone. Though he walked over to the others immediately it seemed to Cassius that he was dragging his feet.

'Hurry up, you useless sod.'

Soon the two of them were standing side by side; Simo with his eyes fixed on the ground, Indavara with his arms crossed.

'Can either of you explain to me why I was left alone in the middle of a crowded street?'

'Corbulo, it was only for a moment.'

'We've been over this before. What is your job?'

Indavara ran his tongue around his mouth and looked at the trees.

'I'll help you – bodyguard. How can you guard me if you're twenty yards back doling out coins to urchins?'

'Fair point.'

'And you?'

Simo was still looking at the ground.

'Sometimes I think you really do want me to let you go. And don't think I haven't noticed the little protests – stale bread for lunch, the creases in my tunic. Not very subtle. Well, nothing to say?'

'I apologise, Master Cassius. But the poor children.'

Cassius walked up to him. 'Look at me.'

Simo – who was only an inch shorter than his master – did so. Cassius knew that broad face better than any other and, though he tried, the Gaul could not quite conceal his anger and frustration.

'I think I have arrived at the conclusion that you will not remain in my employ beyond my time in the army. I will allow you to buy your freedom. Then you can do what you want; pledge your life to "good deeds" if you wish. But while you belong to me, you will do exactly as I tell you or you will be gone. Sold.' Cassius clicked his fingers. 'Like that.'

He pointed at Indavara. 'We all three of us know you are only here because of him. He will not persuade me a second time.'

Cassius put his hand on the Gaul's shoulder. 'Please do not force me into a decision I do not want to make.'

Simo's expression softened but he said nothing.

Cassius walked back to his horse. 'Quickly. We're already late.'

The hamlet lay at the bottom of a gorge; little more than a dozen dwellings and a water mill. The settlement was next to one of the few navigable sections of the river that ran from the coastal plain through the mountains and into the Bekaa valley, much of it underground. Today, the mill's wheel was still; there didn't seem to be much water flowing past.

'The Eleutherus,' said Cassius as they passed a few curious villagers. 'The proper name for the "Dog River".'

'Where we saw the statue on the way to Tripolis,' said Indavara.

'That's right.' Cassius pointed north-west. 'The mouth is only a few miles that way.'

'Think there's much water up there?'

'Probably not a lot at this time of year.'

Looming over the gorge was Berytus's main aqueduct; a huge three-layer structure built of the local pale limestone. The bottom two layers were similarly high, with broad arches spanning fifty feet. The top was much smaller and supported the water channel. Cassius estimated that it was at least a hundred and fifty feet above the river. Some kind of work was going on; labourers were walking along the top and dozens of rope ladders had been hung from the arches.

As promised, Cosmas was waiting by the mill. He had his own mount but the other five sergeants with him were on a cart: two at the front, three in the back. Every man was armed with sword and club. They seemed as curious as the villagers.

'Morning,' said Cosmas, a long piece of grass hanging out of his mouth.

'Good day,' replied Cassius. 'I see you're not taking any chances.'

'I found out that the brothers did six months' hard labour up in Sidon for horse-thieving a couple of years ago. Probably not an experience they're keen to repeat. I'll tell them we only want them for questioning but they may try and run.'

'Where's the house?'

Cosmas pointed at a narrow, winding road that led eastward up out of the gorge. 'Close to the top. Presumably you'd like to talk to them back at headquarters?'

'Yes.'

'Let's get up there, then.'

Ignoring an elderly local who'd come over to ask what was going on, Cosmas spat out the grass and set off up the road. Cassius waited for the cart to get some distance ahead, then followed.

'Why stay so far back?' asked Indavara.

'Look how steep the road is. Once when I was in Rome with my father, I saw two yoked mounts falter close to the top of a hill just like this. The cart was overloaded. The horses lost their footing and when the whole thing began to slide back the driver had no choice but to jump off. The cart tumbled all the way down the hill and fell apart. Both horses were killed and one unfortunate who couldn't get out of the way had his leg crushed. My father had kept us well back, so we had plenty of time to get clear.'

Indavara conceded with a nod. 'I don't like riding. And I think horses don't like us riding them.'

'The way you do it? Probably not.'

Indavara ignored him.

'The gods gave them to us for a reason,' added Cassius. 'And they're not good for much else.'

An attempt had been made to enclose the road but the stone blocks disappeared after a quarter of a mile. Towards the top of the gorge, some of the land had been terraced and various crops planted in the sandy soil. For a moment Cassius thought they were being watched until he realised the observer was in fact a scarecrow.

As the slope began to level out, Cosmas and the cart halted just before a ninety-degree bend in the road. While the driver got down and steadied the horses, Cosmas gathered the others and walked back to Cassius.

'Can your man stay and help with the mounts? I'd like to take four if I can.'

'Certainly.' Cassius waved Simo forward then dismounted and passed him his reins.

The sergeants' clubs were not as long or thick as Indavara's stave, but one end was reinforced by a bundle of thinner rods strapped together. For centuries a symbol of the magistrate's power to punish, what they lacked in subtlety they made up for with impact. Indavara also had his sword, as did Cassius, who noticed a couple of the sergeants eyeing the eagle head. He had instructed Cosmas to tell them he was an undercover army officer, nothing more.

The Syrian sergeant was both the smallest and the oldest of the six. He carried no club, just a short sword even more basic and roughly cast than Indavara's. Looped around his belt were some lengths of rope.

'A hundred yards beyond the bend is their property – to the left. It's their mother's place. We can come in along their front wall. If they're up and about, which I doubt, we'll just go straight for them. If they're inside, I'll take the front door with Cantaber and Arius. Vespilo and Gessius, you come in the back.'

'Any dogs?' asked one of the men.

Cosmas shook his head.

'Need us for anything?' asked Indavara keenly.

'Maybe just cover the road, in case they make a run for it.'

The bodyguard looked disappointed.

'I think we can manage that,' said Cassius. Holding the hilt of his sword, he jogged along with Indavara as they followed the sergeants up to and around the bend. Just before they ducked into the cover of the wall, Cassius glimpsed the dwelling; a low, shabby farmhouse with several tiles missing from the roof.

The only noise was the quiet slap of their boots as they approached the gateless entrance. Cosmas stopped and squatted down, then peered around the wall. Indavara moved up beside Cassius, stave in hand.

Cosmas pointed at two of his men. They ran through the entrance and around to the back of the dwelling, disturbing some hens that pranced away, squawking and shedding feathers. Cosmas and the two remaining men ran to the front.

Cassius and Indavara moved up to the entrance and watched as the sergeant rapped on the door. His compatriots were already looking through windows, brandishing their clubs.

'Open up. Magistrate's men. Come out unarmed.'

For a moment there was silence. Then Cassius heard a woman's voice.

'Open up!'

A bolt was withdrawn and the door opened a crack. Cosmas barged his way inside, hand on his sword hilt, closely followed by the other two. The woman shouted something, then boots thumped as the sergeants looked for the brothers.

'In here!'

'There he is.'

'Got the other one.'

The woman was now wailing, drowning out the men.

Cassius and Indavara walked up to the door, across compacted soil littered with straw and horse shit.

Cosmas was first out. 'Got them both.'

Cassius glanced at Indavara, who was tapping his stave against the ground. 'I know you'd rather be in there yourself but it's wise to delegate once in a while.'

Indavara replaced the stave on his back. 'Delegate?'

'Give the difficult jobs to other people.'

'You are very good at that.'

The mother kept up the voluble complaints as she pulled a shawl on over a tatty tunic. Next came one of her sons. He had his wrists tied behind his back and a sergeant's hand on each shoulder.

'Younger of the two,' said Cosmas. 'Known as "Knuckles".'

Indavara snorted.

He was a muscular, grim-looking man, barefoot and clad only in a sleeveless tunic. He reeked of wine.

'And here's Greyboy.'

Though less than thirty, like his brother, this man's hair was indeed entirely grey. He was also much smaller, with not an ounce of fat on him. He too smelled of wine, though he had summoned the energy to inspect Cassius and Indavara.

'Bring up the cart!' shouted Cosmas. 'Looks like these two had a jug too many last night. We had to pull them out of bed.'

Greyboy temporarily silenced his mother, then spoke to Cosmas. 'What's the charge?'

'No charge. Yet. I told you, we just want to talk.'

Greyboy looked again at Cassius. His brother moaned and shook his head. Staying on his feet was looking like a struggle.

The cart rattled along the road and the driver reined in by the entrance. Simo came along on foot, towing all four horses.

'Let's get them in there,' said Cosmas. As the sergeants pushed the Gorgos brothers across the yard, he did his best to calm the mother down, assuring her that her sons would be back by sundown.

Cassius and Indavara wandered back to the road and looked on as the sergeants manhandled the two captives into the cart. Once the pair were down, the magistrate's men sat on either side of them. Cosmas took charge of his horse and swung up into the saddle.

Indavara blew out his cheeks as Simo brought their horses around the cart.

'Should have gone to Egypt.'

'Really?' said Cassius. 'Considering what happened the last two times we tried to apprehend a suspect, I'm glad to see things go smoothly for once.'

As they mounted up, the tearful mother came over to the wall and spoke to Greyboy. Knuckles tried to speak too but instead vomited over the side of the cart. What splashed on to the road looked to be mostly meat and wine.

'Gods,' said one of the guards, 'what a stench.'

'Moving out.' Cosmas set off, closely followed by the cart.

As they rode back down the steep, twisting road, Cassius soon found himself alone. Indavara had dropped back to talk to Simo and – from the sound of it – was trying to raise his friend's spirits.

They were not the only ones talking. The Gorgos brothers seemed to have woken up and – despite the protestations of their captors – were insistent on continuing their discussion.

One of the sergeants shouted at them, then at the driver. As he halted the cart, Greyboy gave what sounded like an order. A moment later, his brother head-butted the man sitting to his right.

With a high-pitched yelp, the sergeant tipped over on to his side then fell out of the back of the cart.

Cassius yanked on his reins, pulling up only a few feet short of the man. The next thing he saw was the other three sergeants pounce on Knuckles.

Greyboy was not slow to take his chance. Showing considerable athleticism, he flipped his legs past the battling quartet, shunted himself to the back of the cart then dropped on to the road. Hands still bound, he bent down next to the fallen guard, then plucked his dagger from its sheath.

Without a second look at his brother, he ran up the bank to the right of the road and disappeared between two bushes.

Cosmas was already off his horse and haring after him.

As Cassius dismounted to help the guard, he heard something clatter on to the road. Indavara's stave rolled down the slope as the bodyguard bolted past and leapt up the bank.

'Uuuurgh.' The guard rolled on to his back, mouth open. The skin sliced open on his brow separated further and blood trickled out.

Cassius put a hand on him, not knowing what to do. 'Er . . .'

A heavy blow from one of the guards' clubs finally ended Knuckles' resistance. The sergeants pushed him on to his side and one began binding his ankles.

'Here, sir. Let me.'

As Simo arrived to help the stricken guard, Cassius ran to his mount and leapt up on to the saddle. Twenty yards back along the road was a track leading off to the right. He wheeled the horse and kicked down, urging it into a gallop.

──◆8◆──

Indavara kept his eyes on the ground. He was running across difficult terrain; sandy hillocks dotted with clumps of limestone.

He powered his way up another slope, arms pumping as his boots slipped on the dry soil. He reached the top and stopped.

Two hundred yards ahead was the aqueduct. Here – on the plateau at the top of the gorge – it was only three or four feet above the ground. A dozen or so of the labourers could be seen ferrying buckets back and forth. Greyboy was halfway there. Cosmas seemed to have disappeared.

'Who's that?' said a voice from below. 'I'm here.' The Syrian's arm appeared above a bush.

Indavara took the downward slope with a series of long leaps and landed beside the sergeant, who was examining his ankle.

'Did he cut you?'

'No, tripped me as I came down. Go get him!'

XVIII

Cassius had just startled a flock of birds. As they scattered, his mount slowed then shimmied sideways, tossing its head. He lashed a kick at its flank and pulled down hard on the reins but the horse was determined to flee.

'Bloody beast.' Cassius could have got it back under control but – as he'd just seen Greyboy reach the aqueduct – there was no time to spare. He let go of the reins, swung his left leg over the saddle and dropped adroitly to the ground.

Once free, the horse bolted back towards the road.

Just as Cassius reached the edge of the track, he spied Indavara leaping a low stone wall. He should have been watching his own footing: his left boot caught a root and he rolled down a short bank, ending up on his backside. As he wiped dirt off his face he was relieved to find nothing hurt.

'Caesar's length.' He dragged himself up and loped towards the aqueduct.

The labourers watched Greyboy splashing along the channel.

'Hey, you can't go in there,' shouted one man. 'That's drinking water.' He was so enraged that he dropped his bucket, splattering white paint across the ground.

Indavara vaulted over the wall of the channel and landed in three inches of water.

'Two of the buggers. What in Hades!'

Ahead, one of the labourer's compatriots had dropped into the channel to confront Greyboy. A threatening thrust of the suspect's knife sent him leaping straight back up on to the wall.

Greyboy wasn't slow but Indavara reckoned he was gaining. In the distance were the chalky walls on the far side of the gorge. He had no intention of letting the Syrian get that far.

———8———

'Army business!'

The labourers kept their distance as Cassius sprinted along the side of the aqueduct. When the ground began to drop away into the gorge, he had to clamber up on to the channel. Before continuing, he looked back towards the road; there was no sign of Cosmas or the other sergeants.

———8———

Greyboy looked back too; and what he saw evidently unnerved him, because he somehow tripped and fell. Arms flailing, he went down hard on his chest. Indavara was impressed by how swiftly he got back on his feet but the Syrian had lost valuable seconds and considerable momentum. Greyboy took only twenty paces more before realising he was about to be caught.

He stopped and turned, breeze ruffling his hair.

Indavara had been so intent on catching him that he hadn't noticed another labourer leaning over the wall beyond his opponent. The man straightened up, a paintbrush in his hand.

'Who are you two?'

'I'm army,' said Indavara, knowing that any mention of the legions usually had the desired effect. 'Clear out.'

The labourer looked over the left side of the channel. 'Arcus, come up. We've got to move. Just hurry!'

Greyboy wiped sweat out of his eyes as he sloshed backwards. The fall had done quite a bit of damage; his forearms had been scraped red and blood was dripping from his knee, colouring the water.

'You've got nowhere to go,' said Indavara.

'I'll go anywhere as long as it's not the quarries,' said Greyboy, blade sparkling.

'We just want to talk to you.'

'Heard that before.' Greyboy continued his retreat.

As he followed, Indavara made the mistake of looking over the side. They were directly above the gorge now; a few more steps would take him over the water. Shallow or deep, river or sea, the very thought of it sent icy tremors across his back.

He watched the second labourer clamber up the rope ladder and on to the wall. The man started questioning his friend then spied the knife in the stranger's hand. He put his pail and paint-brush down and the two of them jogged away along the channel.

Indavara didn't like the way Greyboy was glancing at the rope ladder. He gripped the hilt of his sword and drew it with a flourish; he had to convince this sly bastard to give up before he even thought about going over the side.

'No farther. Stay where you are.'

'You're not going to cut me. You want what we know. Or what you think we know.'

'Not another step.'

Greyboy glanced down at his bleeding knee. 'And I'm definitely not going to outrun you.'

The Syrian kept himself facing Indavara as he climbed on to the side of the channel. He put the knife between his teeth, lowered himself on to the rope ladder and climbed down.

'Ah, shit.' Indavara turned round; Corbulo would be there soon.

Having already let himself down once that week, he wasn't about to do so again. He sheathed his sword and leaped up on to the wall. The ladder was trembling but it must have been tethered lower down because Greyboy had already disappeared under the overhang. Indavara pushed his sword belt over his hip and followed him.

By the time Cassius arrived and looked over the edge, all he could see was the bodyguard's arms and the top of his head.

'Indavara, we've got the other one. It's not worth it.'

'Calm down, your voice is getting squeaky.'

'There's a thin line between brave and reckless.'

This was not the first time Indavara had crossed it.

Cassius waved at the labourers. 'Where does it lead?'

'Down,' said one.

'Where exactly?'

'Past the top level down the side of a pier,' said the other man. 'The bottom is at the base of the second level.'

'Is there another way down?'

One of the men gestured at the side of the gorge. 'Think there's a track there somewhere.'

Cassius ran back along the channel.

Hands and feet, hands and feet.

Indavara was making good progress down the pier – a ten-yard column of brick. Every time he looked down to check his boots were secure on the thin wooden slats, he glimpsed Greyboy, who was now close to the base of the pier, twenty feet below. There was only a yard of space between it and the edge.

Hands and feet, hands and feet. Don't look at the—

But it was impossible not to with the sun glinting off the river. Indavara had to stop and close his eyes for a moment. When he opened them he saw his white knuckles shaking on the thin, rough rope. In fact, now the whole ladder seemed to be shaking.

He looked down and saw Greyboy's face set in a sneer as he swung the ladder from side to side.

'You're going for a swim, friend! That's if you survive the fall.'

Indavara wrapped his right arm over one of the slats and clamped his fingers on another. Reaching down with his left hand, he flipped up the stud of his dagger sheath and pulled out the blade. Holding it by the hilt he aimed it at Greyboy.

'I've got a better chance of surviving that than you have a knife through your skull.'

With a final wrench that failed to dislodge his enemy, Greyboy ran nimbly along the edge of the aqueduct and around the corner of the pier.

Indavara sheathed the knife and continued downward.

Cassius had found the top of what looked like an animal trail. It cut steeply down through outcrops of lichen-covered limestone and small, spindly trees.

Cosmas arrived, limping. He looked at the aqueduct. 'Is that Indavara?'

'It is.'

'So where's . . . ah.'

Greyboy had reached the far side of the second level's widest arch. He glanced back briefly, then edged along the pier and disappeared behind it.

'He's gone,' said Cosmas.

They watched as Indavara reached the bottom of the ladder, then gave chase.

'Gods, he's like a man possessed,' said Cassius. 'What's the point? We've got the other one.'

Cosmas cupped his hands around his mouth. 'Indavara, leave him! Let it go!'

If he heard him, the bodyguard didn't show it.

Cassius sighed. 'Letting things go is not his speciality.'

Indavara checked his knife and sword were secure then ran along to the next pier. Slowing as he reached the gap between it and the edge, he leaned to his right and put a hand against the stone. Determined not to be distracted by the water again, he shuffled forward, eyes fixed on the corner.

Once there, he stopped and listened. He couldn't hear the bastard running; either he was too far ahead or he was waiting nearby. Indavara drew his sword and held it in his left hand.

He flew around the corner, ready to swing at anything that moved.

Apart from two stacks of pails, the broad stone platform beneath the next arch was empty. Hanging from both sides of the aqueduct were several more rope ladders. Indavara decided to keep his blade out. The next pier was forty feet ahead. He had taken only a few steps when he heard boots scrape on stone.

Greyboy had materialised between the pails, arm back, ready to throw.

Indavara had time only to bow his head and raise the sword.

The knife clanged against the middle of the blade and dropped to the floor.

By the time he looked up, Greyboy was on him.

The Syrian came in low under the sword, his shoulder catching Indavara in the ribs. Though by far the bigger man, the impact sent him tottering backwards. Too late he realised how close he was to the edge. His wet left boot slipped off the stone and he fell awkwardly on to his right knee.

Seeing another chance, Greyboy lined up a kick at his head.

Indavara had nowhere to go but down. He dropped his sword and let himself fall. As Greyboy's boot whistled past his ear, his hands came down hard on the edge, fingers already gripping tight. As he hung there, legs dangling, he was surprised to hear the sound of his sword splashing into the water. It had been a long time in the air.

Greyboy stood over him and gestured at his cut knee.

'Like I said, I wouldn't have stood a chance in a foot race.' He leaned forward and looked down at the river. 'I could just leave you hanging, I suppose, but something tells me you're not the type to give up easily. Sorry.'

The Syrian stamped on his left hand. If Indavara hadn't just gained a slight toehold on a knob of stone, he would have fallen. Doing his best to ignore the pain pulsing through the three fingers the boot had squashed, he forced the hand back on to the edge. That hurt too.

Cosmas yelled at one of the sergeants, who had just arrived on his horse. 'Get that bow from the cart. Hurry!'

Cassius started down the slope.

'Where are you going?' asked Cosmas.

'The river. He can't swim.'

'I don't think that'll be a problem. Look.'

Cassius dug his boots in and stopped. Two elderly fishermen were wading across the river, staring up at the scene unfolding above. The water was only slightly higher than their knees.

'Just get that bloody bow.' Cassius leaped down the slope.

'Ha,' said Greyboy with an approving grin.

The Syrian seemed to appreciate the strength and agility needed for what Indavara was doing: hauling himself along the edge by his hands, gaining two feet of distance from his foe with every swing. He had found no more footholds and was dependent on his ten digits, three of which felt like they were on fire.

'Where do you think you're going anyway? Ah.'

Teeth jammed together, arms aching, Indavara moved a few more inches towards the closest rope ladder.

Greyboy was following him. 'Again, sorry, but I don't have time to mess around.' He stomped down on the left hand.

But it – and the rest of Indavara – was already in mid-air. He had done his best to fling himself sideways but most of the movement was down.

As his right hand grabbed the ladder, his legs swung into it. The jolt of his full weight dragged his fingers off the rope but his leg had gone between two slats. He yelped as his tender groin took the impact but the pain from his left hand immediately reclaimed his attention.

'You obstinate bastard.'

The moment during which Greyboy disappeared gave Indavara hope. Unfortunately, the Syrian reappeared quickly, now holding his knife. He squatted at the edge of the platform,

grabbed one of the vertical ropes and began sawing through
it.

One dizzying look at the sparkling water was all Indavara
needed. He gripped the next rung and hauled himself up.

Cassius was moving so fast that he only just managed to stop
before reaching a treacherous patch of rocks carpeted with slimy
green weed. He looked up to see Indavara climbing the rope
ladder. Then he saw what the Syrian was doing.

'Gods.'

Now he was at ground level, the height looked even worse.
If Indavara fell, he would either die or suffer catastrophic injury.
And all for some bloody suspect they didn't really need and
who might not even know anything.

'Not like this. Please.'

The two fishermen were still standing in the middle of the
river, holding their rods, watching. Their boat was roped to a
rock only a few yards from Cassius.

Indavara was almost close enough to make a grab for the edge
when Greyboy severed one side of the ladder.

'Ha.'

Just as he sliced into the second rope, something hit the support
and fell past Indavara. Greyboy stopped, then ducked. Only
when a second object struck the platform – narrowly missing
the Syrian – did Indavara realise they were arrows. He looked
to his right and saw Cosmas drawing again.

He heard a curse from above, then fleeing footsteps.

'Nice one, Cosmas.' Indavara steadied himself and was about
to pull himself up when he spied the remaining rope. It had
partially unravelled, and was now held in place only by a few
threads.

He didn't dare move.

'Sweet Fortuna, please help me.'

The rope continued to unravel.

The fishermen were so entranced by the figure dangling above that Cassius was struggling to get their attention.

'Understand?' he said in Greek.

Finally, the pair dragged their eyes away and saw what he was holding.

'Is that mine?' asked one of them.

'Yes.'

'Understand what I want to do?'

The men nodded and each took hold of the circular fishing net.

Cassius looked up. The small figure seemed impossibly far away. There had to be a reason why he wasn't climbing back up.

'Indavara!'

He couldn't take his eyes off the rope. Though he was trying desperately not to move, the threads were still coming apart. He didn't have long.

Indavara looked down, past the wavering end of the ladder, to the river far below. One of the tiny figures waved. Corbulo's voice echoed along the gorge and up to him.

'If you fall we can catch you!'

Catch me? What is that? Is that a—

Falling.

Air rushed past him, rippling his hair and tunic. He could feel the ladder wrapping itself around his arms. The aqueduct seemed to be flying up, up and away.

'Pull it tight!' yelled Cassius just as Indavara thumped into the middle of the net.

The impact pulled one of the fisherman off his feet and he landed not far from the bodyguard, who was already thrashing about and trying to stand up. It took him a moment to realise he was sitting in two feet of water.

'Thank the gods,' said Cassius, who felt as if he'd just run a marathon.

Indavara sat there panting, hair over his eyes, arms now tangled in both the ladder and the net.

The fisherman stood up and clapped him on the shoulder. The other man looked on, mouth hanging open.

Hearing boots splashing through the water, Cassius turned to see Simo and Cosmas running towards them. Simo stopped and stared first at Indavara, then up at the aqueduct. Cosmas – still holding the bow and quiver – grinned.

Cassius walked across the net and offered a hand. 'You going to get up, then, or shall we take you to market as catch of the day?'

'Catch of the day?' said Cosmas. 'More like catch of the century.'

XIX

The headquarters of the magistrate's men was a converted townhouse just behind the basilica. Cassius, Indavara and Simo had been admitted via a side gate to avoid being seen with the sergeants and their captive. The headquarters was equipped with a small aid post, which Indavara used to dry off. Once Simo returned with a fresh tunic, he changed and drank the wine that had been brought for him by Cantaber, the youngest of the four sergeants.

While Simo examined the red, swollen fingers of Indavara's left hand, Cantaber looked on. 'Can't believe I missed what happened at the bridge. You're a lucky man.'

Indavara reached down to his belt, checking his Fortuna was there for at least the fifth time since the aqueduct.

'I know it. How's he doing?' Indavara glanced at Gessius, the man Knuckles had knocked out of the cart. A surgeon had been summoned and was talking to the sergeant. Simo had already cleaned and bandaged his wounded head.

'He's all right,' said the Gaul. 'You too. Nothing broken anyway. Better keep this on to reduce the swelling, though.' Simo gave him the small goatskin pouch he had filled with cold water; a technique gleaned from one of his medical manuals.

'At least it's my left,' said Indavara morosely. He turned to Cantaber again. 'Do you know how they're getting on with Knuckles?'

'I need a drink.' Cassius leaned against the wall outside the interrogation room. Opposite him, Cosmas looked thoughtfully at the black and white floor tiles.

They had been questioning the younger Gorgos brother for an hour. Whatever he was mixed up in, the Syrian was giving nothing away. He claimed that he and his brother did odd jobs for various people: labouring, construction, deliveries. Nothing outside the law, of course – he and his brother had turned over a new leaf. As for why Greyboy had fled? He was terrified of captivity. Their connection with Hagnon – the suspect character with all the ships and carts? Just did a bit of day work for him. And the mysterious Egyptian? Knuckles had no idea who they were talking about.

'There's no way of hurrying up the process?' asked Cassius. For striking Cantaber, Knuckles could be charged with assault of an officer of the law; an offence which would earn him some form of physical punishment or another term of hard labour.

'It will be several weeks before he attends court.'

'What about a special arrangement? In return for information we can put in a good word. Such things are done.'

'Yes, sir, they are. But again that will take time. Deputy Diadromes would have to consult the judicial prefect. And he will still be busy with those arrested during the protests.'

Cassius had seen some of these men; they were being kept in the building's holding cell.

'This man is a known criminal,' added Cosmas. 'A few friends in the city but no one who would care enough to trouble the courts. Might be time to apply a little more pressure.'

'You mean of the non-verbal variety?'

'He already has some bruises. No one will notice a few more.'

Cassius felt rather disturbed by the prospect of ordering such a thing but he doubted his conscience would trouble him for long; the Gorgos brothers had done plenty of damage themselves.

Cosmas said, 'You wouldn't have to be anywhere near it.' He gave a sheepish half-grin. 'I am rather small for such work but Arius and Cantaber can be quite effective when they need to be.'

Cassius wasn't convinced the sergeants would be quite 'effective' enough to worry the hulking Knuckles. He pushed himself off the wall. 'I think I know someone even better suited to such a role.'

━8━

With his fingers now bandaged, Indavara listened carefully as Cassius explained what he needed. They were walking back to the interrogation room having left Simo in the aid post, assisting the surgeon as he stitched Cantaber's cut.

'Cosmas and the other sergeants are in there now. They haven't touched him yet. It's important to make a big entrance: I suggest a couple of smacks then see what you can get out of him. The initial shock won't last long so make sure you ask the right questions. Remember, we are focusing on—'

'Leave it to me,' said Indavara as they reached the room.

Cassius watched him flex his shoulders and suck in some deep breaths. 'Building yourself up, I suppose? Making yourself angry?'

'Why would I need to *make* myself angry? The bastard's brother tried to kill me.' Indavara wrenched the door open and stalked inside.

Cassius hurried after him and shut it. Cosmas and the sergeants were standing opposite Knuckles. The seated captive had his bound hands resting on the table. His dismissive sneer vanished when he saw the new arrival.

'Out the way,' muttered Indavara, pushing Cosmas aside. With scant regard for his injured hand, he gripped the table (which was not small) and flung it sideways. Knuckles only just got out of the way as the table spun through the air and clattered into the wall. Indavara darted forward and swung his right boot.

As the stool flew away, Knuckles fell on to his side, heavy body slapping against the tiles. Eyes bulging, he watched as Indavara plucked Cosmas's dagger from its sheath.

'This won't take long.'

Cassius wasn't entirely sure what he was watching: reality or performance.

Knuckles tried to roll away but Indavara had already grabbed his tunic.

'Don't worry,' he hissed into the larger man's ear. 'The blade's for the rope. There's no fun in beating a fellow with his hands bound. I'll give you a chance.'

'No, no, please. Leave them bound.'

'What?' Indavara squatted in front of him, knife inches from his face.

'I – I – I'll tell you everything.'

Indavara kept the knife where it was. 'Everything?'

Knuckles nodded frantically, eyes almost crossing as they stared at the triangular tip of the blade. Indavara handed the dagger to a hesitant Cosmas, then helped the Syrian to his feet.

He had to reach up to tap his shoulder. 'Knuckles, you disappoint me. Now, you're going to have a nice long talk with these gentlemen and I'm going to get some grub. After chasing your bloody brother I've worked up quite an appetite so if I'm disturbed I'm going to take it out on you. So you answer all their questions, I'll have a quiet lunch and everyone's happy. Got it?'

The Syrian nodded, bottom lip quivering.

While the two sergeants retrieved the table, Indavara righted the stool and coaxed Knuckles down on to it. Cassius and Cosmas turned away from the captive and exchanged a grin.

The bodyguard was already through the door. 'All yours.'

The eatery was almost full but the maid recognised Indavara and found them a good seat.

'Nice, eh?' he said, doing his best to ignore the rather unpleasant smell drifting out of the sewers on the edge of the forum.

Simo was looking out of a diamond-shaped window at the basilica. 'Yes.'

'I told him I was taking you with me. Relax.'

Indavara often thought his friend didn't really know the

meaning of the word. When he was with his master he was desperate to please; when he was away from him he seemed unable to just be himself for an hour or two.

The Gaul wiped away crumbs left by a previous customer. 'I should not have stopped for those children.'

'He's all talk,' said Indavara. 'He'd never get rid of you. He needs you as much as he needs me. More, probably.'

'I don't think so.'

The maid brought them two mugs of the 'half and half' Indavara had ordered. 'What are we eating, then, gentlemen?'

'What's fresh?' asked Indavara.

'Oysters and mussels have just come in.'

'That sounds fine.'

'Both?'

'Yes, and some bread – bring that first, please.' Indavara inspected Simo's brow. 'How's the eye?'

'Sore. Though I must again compliment you on the quality of your stitching.' He peered at Indavara's bandaged hand. 'And that?'

'It's nothing. Lucky for me that the nastiest of the two Gorgos brothers is also the lightest.'

'I think you enjoy it. All this running and jumping, chasing and fighting.'

'Perhaps. Falling – not so much.'

'Quick thinking from Master Cassius – with the net.'

'He has his moments. The whole thing was my own stupid fault. Like Corbulo says, sometimes it's better to just stop and think.'

The bread arrived; four small rolls in a wicker basket. Indavara had the first one in his mouth before the maid had let go. 'Mmm. That is good. Crispy on the outside, soft in the middle.'

Simo was frowning, listening to something.

'What is it?'

'The music. Can you hear it?'

Somewhere within the hubbub outside was the noise of a flute.

'It's not—'

'No,' said Indavara. 'Different tune.'

Simo listened for a while longer then agreed he was right. He took a roll for himself, eating one modest mouthful at a time. 'Do you think Master Cassius will get anywhere with that letter to Pietas Julia?'

'I don't think so. I was told nobody knew anything about who I was or where I'd come from.'

Indavara didn't usually like speaking about his previous life, and while Corbulo occasionally pressed him for details, Simo had learned not to ask. But today, he found he wanted to go on. 'Someone said that I arrived at the arena in a caged cart with a load of others. Carts like that came in all the time. All slaves or condemned men.'

'What about the journey?' asked Simo. 'Do you remember any of that, or where you started?'

'Sometimes I think I can, but then I realise the memories are from other journeys since. I had taken a very bad blow to the head. Capito – he was the organiser of games – once told me I was drifting in and out and that he only took me because he got a good price and I looked strong. He gave the surgeon a week to revive me, which he did.'

'How?'

'Not sure exactly but I know he cleaned out the wound and restitched it. Waking with him looking down at me is the first thing I remember. His name was Asellio. He was the one who told me my name. The slavers had been given it by another man who'd been in the same cart but he was dead by the time I woke.'

'Asellio – was he kind?'

'No, but he knew his work. Two weeks later I was training; and Capito decided he would keep me.'

'Did you have any friends?'

'A fighter cannot have friends. I realised that soon enough.'

'Because you might have to face them.'

Indavara nodded. 'I suppose I had *one*.' He took out the figurine from behind his belt.

'Did you say a woman threw it to you?'

'After my tenth fight. Mostly they threw coins but I was too tired to pick them up and I couldn't spend them anyway.' Indavara examined the figurine, the tiny features of the face. 'I had to ask one of the trainers which goddess it was. When he told me I knew it had come to me for a reason.'

He looked across at Simo, noting the string around his neck; Corbulo made him keep the cross hidden.

'You've only known the Faith, I suppose? Because of your father.'

'Yes.'

Indavara glanced out of the window. 'We'd better change the subject.'

'Why?'

'He's coming.'

Corbulo was being escorted across the square by Cosmas, who came inside and thanked Indavara for his help with the interrogation before departing.

'Let me guess,' said Indavara as Corbulo sat beside Simo. 'Gorgos told you about something, but not the counterfeiting.'

'Precisely. How did you know?'

'Because Cosmas was smiling and you're not.'

'Well, your persuasive approach certainly worked. He did tell us everything: about the smuggling operation he, his brother and this Egyptian are running. You name it, they're bringing it in – best fortified wine hidden in cheap amphoras, luxury soap hidden in jars of fat. The list went on and on and on.'

'But nothing about fake coins?'

'Not a word.'

'And you believe him?'

'I do. Apart from the fact that you gave him the fright of his life, he is not bright enough to lie that convincingly. Cosmas is going to inform Diadromes now – at least we've done another favour for the magistrate.'

Corbulo took Simo's mug and drank from it.

Indavara turned to him. 'If I didn't say so before, thank you. For what you did at the aqueduct.'

'Think nothing of it. Just remember what I said about benefit versus risk. Girl!' Corbulo grabbed the maid's sleeve as she bustled past. 'Bring a jug of wine and a mug for me.'

'Yes, sir.'

Indavara could tell Corbulo was preoccupied: he didn't give a second look at the maid, who was young and pretty. He dropped a fist on the table. 'This damned investigation. Nothing but guesswork and dead ends. And I thought it was going to be easy.'

'There's time yet, sir.'

'Not a lot, Simo. Not a lot.'

Back at the tower, a sheet of paper had been slipped under the door and its contents raised Cassius's spirits a little. It was a list, at the bottom of which was a note from Diadromes. No one at the basilica had a reason to keep records on which concerns made use of bronze, but he knew a retired metal-smith who was able to compile the list from memory. The deputy magistrate couldn't guarantee that it was completely up to date, but to Cassius it seemed fairly comprehensive.

He could have done with a trip to the baths but didn't want to go out again, so he stripped down to his loincloth, lay on his bed and perused the list. The variety of industries and other outfits that dealt in bronze was remarkable: blacksmiths, metal-smiths, shipbuilders, cart-builders, window-makers, furniture-makers, lamp-makers, vessel-makers, statue-makers; and so it went on.

Cassius wiped sweat off his chin. Though the tower was comparatively cool, it was another hot day. He drank some water and forced himself to think about other avenues to explore; other ways to find the gang. A minute later he fell asleep.

When he awoke, the only light was the orange glow coming from beyond the windows. He heard feet on the stairs and the door opened.

'All right?' said Indavara, his face invisible in the gloom.

'Gods, it's dark. How long have I slept?'

'Didn't know you were sleeping – we thought you were up here working on some brilliant new plan.'

'I was, but I . . .'

'Listen, Patch isn't very well. Simo and I are going to take him out for a walk, see if a trot through a stream will rouse him. You'll be all right here, won't you?'

'Alone?'

'Just lock the door – no one can get to you in here.'

'I suppose you're right. Can't keep you with me every hour of the day.'

'Simo says he'll prepare some supper when we get back.'

'Very well.' Cassius got up and followed Indavara back down the stairs to the door.

'There are fresh jugs of wine and water, sir,' said Simo as the two of them walked out into the darkness.

'Yes, yes, as long as your bloody mule's all right – that's the important thing.'

Cassius pushed the heavy door shut then secured the bolts at the top and bottom. The tower suddenly seemed very quiet. He walked over to the table and poured himself a large mug of wine.

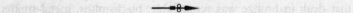

The structure ahead was almost unrecognisable as a building. Only half of one wall remained, a lonely stack of blocks that looked as if it might topple at any moment. The makeshift dwellings were alarmingly close: low, narrow shelters of reused brick with roofs of driftwood and branches. Outside one was a small fire, a beacon of warmth among all the emptiness and ruined stone.

Indavara and Simo followed Elder Cobon through the rubble. Faces turned from the fire. Two men stood, each holding iron spears. Cobon – who was carrying a torch – held up his other hand in greeting and spoke to one of the men, who swiftly lowered his weapon. Indavara listened and realised they were speaking in Aramaic (Simo knew a little but he did not). After a time, Cobon gestured to the sacks he and Simo were carrying. Indavara had only his stave.

The leader called out to his people. Men, women and children began to appear; some from the shelters, some from the shadows. By the time they were all gathered around the fire, Indavara had counted twenty-eight. Cobon and Simo handed over the sacks, then watched as the leader distributed the bread. He was scrupulously fair, giving larger loaves to adults, smaller ones to the children. His compatriot took the last few and began dividing them.

One of the women came forward. Indavara was surprised to see she was clad in a fine cloak, though it had clearly seen better days. She knelt in front of Elder Cobon and offered her hand. He took it and helped her back up. As she returned to her family, Indavara saw that she was weeping.

While Cobon continued speaking to the men, another family sent forth a child; a little girl of no more than three or four with some ribbons in her hair and a sweet smile. In her hand was a bracelet; colourful beads strung on thread. She offered it to Cobon, who put a kind hand on her head but refused the gift. Simo smiled to her and spoke to her in Aramaic but he wouldn't take the bracelet either.

Indavara thought the little girl would be scared of him but she offered it to him too. He didn't know what to do. The girl turned back towards her family; they seemed to be encouraging her to hand it over. Her face began to tremble. Indavara didn't want to upset her so he took it. The girl ran back to her parents.

'Why did you refuse it?' he asked Simo.

'We must not take anything in return. The food is a gift.'

'But—'

'You can take it,' said Simo. 'You're not of the Faith.'

He recovered the empty sacks. The children – except the little girl – were all eating. Most of the adults were proud enough to wait until the visitors had gone.

After a final word with the leader and a shake of hands, Cobon led them back to the street. He was a tiny man – barely five foot and with a rather crooked back but had marched down to the docks at quite a pace. He explained that two other groups had been delivering bread and that they would meet back at the church-house. Simo replied that he and Indavara would have to leave soon; they had already been out for an hour and a half.

As they walked back through an area where most of the ware-houses were still standing, Indavara asked Simo about those they'd helped.

'Palmyran refugees. Apparently they've been there for months. Before that they were in an apartment block but the other residents complained and the magistrates had them evicted.'

'Why?'

'Palmyra was the enemy of Rome for almost a decade. People don't want them here. But neither does anyone else in Syria and their city has been destroyed. They had money but most of it went on bribes to get jobs which they then lost anyway. Now they are barely able to survive.'

'The children are thin but with fat stomachs. It means they don't have enough to eat. I've seen it before.'

Somewhere a bell was tolling, marking the turn of the hour.

'We will be late,' said Simo.

'We could tell him,' replied Indavara. 'If we told him what you've just told me, he might understand.'

'No. No, he would not.'

The church-house was in fact no more than a large room at the rear of Cobon's dwelling. He was by trade a grocer and – according to Simo – spent his afternoons gathering spare food from sympathetic townspeople and other Christians. Indavara found it hard to think of it as a holy place – it looked like any other room and was equipped only with half a dozen chairs and a single table, on top of which were several scrolls and books. The other groups had returned first so Cobon apologised to them and let everyone in.

Indavara leaned against a wall, looking on as the Christians gathered to discuss their evening's work. All three groups had avoided the area where there had previously been trouble and – apart from some inquisitive city sergeants – met with no further problems.

Cobon announced that he would fetch everyone some wine, at which point Simo told him they had to leave. Farewells were exchanged; and Indavara was glad to hear the others address him by name. He had felt rather out of place, standing there with his scars and his stave among these quiet, peaceful folk.

There were as many women as men in the group and one of them came to the door with him and Simo. She was the youngest there but put her hood up so fast that Indavara saw little of her face.

'Will you be all right on the streets on your own?' asked Simo as he opened the door. The young woman offered the briefest of nods then hurried away. As she disappeared around a corner, the pair headed off in the opposite direction.

'That's not safe,' said Indavara.

'I know. But she cannot stay like the others. She does what she can then leaves.'

'I wonder why.'

'I expect she has to get back,' said Simo. 'I expect she is like me.'

XX

The courtyard was littered with them. Some were missing hands, arms, legs, even heads. The oldest cripples had been thrown on top of each other, limbs and bodies grotesquely intertwined. Closer to the building were the new ones; clean, polished and ready for mounting. The largest of them was ten feet tall; a bearded god holding a staff.

'They obviously do well,' said Cassius. 'I've already counted twenty workers.' He pointed at a broad chimney which was puffing out thick, black smoke. 'Forge over there.'

He ran his eyes across the rest of the statue-makers: one of the largest factories he'd seen. 'They've got everything the gang would need: a legitimate cover, transportation' – he gestured at the three large carts and the stables beside the courtyard – 'and inside the requisite ovens and metals. All it would take is a hidden room and a few men with dies and hammers. The trouble is, I could say the same for the other places we've seen this morning.'

Cosmas was tugging his beard, which he seemed to do whenever he was required to think. 'All told, I reckon there are only about forty outfits with ovens or full foundries like this. Why not just check them all? I'm sure we could come up with some excuse.'

'Forty? That would take a while.'

'It depends on how much help Master Diadromes could provide.'

'But if we don't strike lucky early on, word will get round quickly. Once they know we're here and looking they might halt production or move out.'

Indavara stepped forward. Like the others, he was standing

in the shadow cast by a temple wall. It was situated beside a road that wound up a hill overlooking the statue-makers.

'Might be two places. They might make the coins somewhere with an oven, then use the dies somewhere else.'

'Possibly, though that doubles the risk.' Cassius leaned back against the wall, tapping his boot against the stone. 'We need another way to come at this, a method that doesn't betray our real interest.'

A paunchy, middle-aged man strode around the corner of the temple.

'Excuse me, this is private property, you can't just—'

'City sergeants. Move along,' said Cosmas. This and a glance at Indavara persuaded the interloper to desist.

Cassius glanced up the hill, the top of which was largely undeveloped and covered by cedar trees. Coming down the road was a man with a bow over one shoulder and a pair of dead birds on the other. Kicking a stone along behind him were three lads each carrying sticks.

'Beaters,' said Cassius.

'Sir?'

'Do much hunting, Cosmas?'

'Only for law-breakers,' said the sergeant with a grin.

'The function of the beaters is to make a load of noise, panic the prey and drive it into the open for the hunter to pick off.'

'Sir?'

'I think I need to speak to Diadromes.'

The fourth hour was one of the busiest of the day. The markets were beginning to slow down but cityfolk of all types were pounding the streets, keen to conclude their day's tasks before the July heat reached its full intensity.

Cassius, Indavara and Simo let Cosmas lead the way; he had already proved himself highly adept at avoiding crowds, hold-ups and bottlenecks. Twice they passed someone who called out to the sergeant, but Cosmas pressed on. Cassius stayed close, with Indavara right behind him. It would have been pointless to bring the horses but he felt even more vulnerable down on the street. His eyes flitted from one individual or group to another until he almost made himself dizzy. Mopping his brow with his sleeve, he kept his hand close to his sword, ready to draw if need be.

Spying a long queue outside a temple up ahead, Cosmas cut left along a side street. Because of his merchant's outfit, Cassius attracted some interest from a line of hawkers with wicker baskets of assorted tat strapped to their chests. Cosmas waved them away but some were insistent and Indavara moved up to dissuade any who got too close.

Just as they passed the last of them, a young man sprinted by. He took a second glance at Cosmas then stopped. 'Sir?'

'Arpagius. You all right?'

'Thank the gods.' He pointed along an adjacent street. 'Sir, some men – I don't know who they are – they've cornered Norbanus Celer and his family. I'm not even on duty but I tried to warn them off.' He turned his palms skyward. 'They just laughed at me.'

Cosmas glanced back at Cassius, who realised this was not something the sergeant could simply ignore.

'Do what you have to.'

'There are a lot of them,' continued Arpagius. 'And they've been drinking.'

Cassius reckoned he might well regret this decision but it didn't seem fair to leave the helpful Cosmas to it. 'We'll come along too.'

'Thank you.'

With that they set off after Arpagius and soon saw the commotion up ahead. About a dozen men had gathered around a cart and were throwing stones at a smaller group cowering in front of a dwelling.

'Who's this Celer, anyway?' asked Cassius, holding his sword hilt as he ran.

'Owns one of the factories,' explained Cosmas. 'Not a particularly popular man.'

As the five of them slowed down, the men by the cart all turned.

Cassius almost laughed. Every one of them was wearing an identical actor's mask, each painted brown with an oversize nose and a surprised expression. Some were holding wineskins, others handfuls of stones which had obviously come from the wooden boxes in the cart.

On the other side of the street, a well-dressed gentleman, his wife and two young boys were huddled in a doorway. Each child was gripping one of their mother's legs. She was a good deal younger than her husband; an overweight fellow, whose eyes were wide with fear and rage. Slumped against the wall close by was a tall man nursing a bleeding nose; presumably the bodyguard.

One of the more inebriated 'actors' bellowed something indecipherable at the new arrivals.

'Oh, look, the young un's back with some help,' said another.

Cosmas walked straight up to the men. 'City sergeant. If you know what's good for you, you'll disperse.'

'I know what's good for me, thanks, shorty,' replied one of them, slurping down wine and earning a few laughs from his mates.

'They are very, very drunk,' said Simo.

'I know,' replied Cassius.

But not all of them. One man dropped his handful of stones and squared up to Cosmas. 'Don't tell me you're going to protect this arsehole? He's the most hated man in Berytus.'

Celer tried to move away from the doorway. A stone thrown by one of the men pinged off the plaster above him. One of the little boys squealed.

'Animals!' screeched the mother.

Celer retreated and pulled his family towards him.

The man who'd thrown the stone was still laughing when the end of Indavara's stave tapped the nose of his mask. He turned to look at the bodyguard, eyes bloodshot and glassy.

'Don't do that again.'

The man backed away but another wasn't so easily dissuaded.

He held the handle of his sheathed dagger and moved in front of his friend.

'Or what?'

'Or I'll give you such a beating you'll need that mask to hide your tears.'

'Easy,' said Cassius quietly, walking past Indavara to stand by Cosmas. As Arpagius joined them, he noticed that quite a crowd was gathering to their right.

'Fun's over, lads,' said Cosmas. 'Disperse now and we'll say no more about it. Don't make it worse for yourselves.'

The leader pointed at Celer. 'That greedy pig gets richer every day while our families starve. There's no justice to be had in Berytus. The sergeants and the courts and the likes of him are all in it together.'

'Starving, eh?' said Cassius. 'But clearly not thirsty.'

'Who are you?'

'A friend of the sergeant here. I suggest you move along or this matter will be in the hands of the magistrate before midday.'

'Twelve actors causing trouble?' said the leader. 'Magistrate's not going to get far with his investigation, is he?'

His compatriots chuckled.

'Actually there are thirteen of you,' said Cassius. 'And when I describe this incident I will replace "actors" with "suspects" and include the following description.'

Cassius kept his eyes on the leader as he recited what he had observed of the men, starting with Indavara's friend to the left. 'Suspect number one: height five feet, six inches, stocky build, wearing a pale brown tunic with a spear-symbol belt-buckle. Suspect number two: height five feet, eight inches, slim build, red tunic, trident tattoo on right calf. Suspect number three' – this was the leader himself – 'height five feet, eleven inches, slim build, brass ring on right hand, pale blue tunic, iron belt-buckle, a trace of the Roman slums in his accent. Demeanour: unpleasant.'

Two of the men had already sloped away. 'Come on, Ravilla.'

Cassius smiled. 'And name: Ravilla.'

Indavara laughed.

The leader threw a glare at his indiscreet associate. All the others were now on the move.

'Our day will come,' he said, making sure his mask still covered his face as he left.

'Not today,' said Cassius.

'Move along!' shouted Arpagius at the crowd, which was already breaking up.

Cassius and Cosmas walked across the street to Norbanus Celer. His wife was wiping her eyes, still watching the 'actors'. The younger of the two boys was snivelling; the older lad was offering his mother a handkerchief.

'My thanks,' said Celer, straightening up and trying to regain his composure.

Cosmas said, 'Sir, with respect, I'm not sure you and your family should be out on the streets at the moment. Tensions are running rather high.'

'So now I cannot visit the temple? I must skulk around as if *I* have done something wrong?'

'Those men will be dealt with, sir.'

'They damn well better be. I will be writing to Pomponianus immediately. The nerve of these gutter rats.'

'Perhaps if you paid your workers a little more.'

Cassius hadn't realised Indavara had joined them. When he caught his eye, the bodyguard simply shrugged.

Celer gritted his teeth. 'And who in Hades are you to tell a councillor of Berytus his business?'

'My bodyguard,' explained Cassius hastily. 'Please ignore him. Now, I suggest we escort you to a safe place immediately. Where is close?'

The young wife tugged on her husband's toga and whispered something.

Celer nodded. 'My uncle's townhouse is nearby. Let me be clear – I want those ruffians in chains by the end of the day.'

'We will do what we can, sir,' said Cosmas. 'Come now.'

Simo and Arpagius had helped the bodyguard to his feet and the wife had finally managed to prise the frightened boy off her leg. As they set off along the street, Cassius dropped back to walk alongside Indavara.

'Was that really necessary?'

'Is anyone else going to say it to him? Certainly not you.'

The lizard scampered ahead of the deputy magistrate and disappeared into a crack in the ground.

'At this rate, Officer, I shall have to ask Pomponianus to offer you a job.' Diadromes – arriving his customary half-hour late – strode up to Cassius and shook his forearm. The trio were waiting for him outside the sergeants' headquarters; a quiet spot where Cosmas had assured them they would not be disturbed. The sergeant was currently off dealing with both the Celer incident and the Gorgos investigation.

'Not an entirely unappealing prospect,' said Cassius.

'What about you, Indavara?' said Diadromes. 'I heard you helped your master put these thugs right.'

Again, the bodyguard shrugged.

'Anyway,' said Diadromes, joining Cassius in the shade. 'Cosmas tells me you have an idea.'

'Indeed. I can see no efficient way of searching premises that might be of interest to us without arousing suspicion and alerting this gang. But I may have a way of forcing them to break cover without knowing they are our real targets. That's if they are here, of course.'

'Go on.'

'You will be aware that there's been a lot of talk about Egyptian spies heading north to track the Emperor's forces.'

Diadromes scratched his bald spot as Cassius continued.

'What if you'd had word that one of these spies was masquerading as a metalworker here in Berytus? Might you not order your men to search the premises where such an individual could be working?'

'I might. And while they are there, my sergeants could also have a nose around, perhaps make a few arrests too?'

'Which might yield something of use; but the real aim is to flush out our quarry. If the raids could be carried out early and simultaneously, the gang might have no choice but to quickly shift the coins and equipment, possibly out of the city.'

'Right.'

'Which probably means the docks or one of the three gates. Cosmas tells me there is no other easy method for carts to come and go. With all the sergeants busy looking for this imaginary spy, the gates could be left guarded by only a token force, perhaps just a few legionaries. We could even leave one – let's say the eastern gate because it provides access to most other routes – guarded by only two; neither of them in fact local soldiers.' Cassius gestured to himself and Indavara.

'Ah. Yes, I see. A lot of manpower would be needed for the inspections. And I would have to obtain clearance from the magistrate, of course.'

'Of course.'

'He may not allow it. His primary concern is public order – incidents like today's cannot be allowed.'

'You will talk to him on my behalf, though?' Considering what he had done for Diadromes in the last few days, Cassius wasn't about to accept no for an answer. 'Forgive me, but it might also be worth mentioning that capturing these people is very much in the magistrate's interest. Marshal Marcellinus, Minister Sabinus and indeed the Emperor himself will be extremely grateful if we can put a stop to this counterfeiting.'

'Understood, but if I am yet to be convinced that the gang is really here, Magistrate Pomponianus is almost certain that it is not.'

'If we find nothing and make no further progress, at least the investigation might move on – away from Berytus. This outcome would also appeal to the magistrate, I imagine.'

'You make some forceful arguments, Officer Crispian.'

'I am dependent on your help, Deputy Magistrate, and time is very much of the essence.'

'If we are able to go ahead – what about the day after tomorrow?'

'That sounds fine.'

'Exactly which premises need to be inspected?'

'Anything with ovens or a full foundry. Two sergeants will be sufficient to carry out each check. Cosmas could then question them about anything suspicious without giving away the true reason for the search; it would be inadvisable for so many of the men to know where our real interest lies.'

'Agreed. What if the gang do clear out via the port? It's July – we have vessels coming and going all day.'

'We don't have the manpower to watch the docks and all the ships but I think if they do move out, it would be temporary. The gates are our best bet.'

'I shall consult with the magistrate and get an answer to you by tomorrow. Cosmas can handle the details.'

'Excellent. I thank you for your help.'

Diadromes came a little closer. 'If I am able to secure this assistance, it would seem clear that each of us will have fulfilled our debt to each other. Do you agree, Officer Crispian?'

'I do.'

Diadromes summoned Cosmas for a brief discussion about the plan then left. The usually cool sergeant seemed rather flustered; apparently the Gorgos investigation was progressing swiftly and though there had been no sightings of Greyboy, more arrests were imminent.

The outraged Norbanus Celer, meanwhile, had already communicated with Magistrate Pomponianus and now sergeants and legionaries were out on the streets hunting Ravilla and his band of 'actors'.

Cosmas escorted Cassius and the others to the rear of the headquarters and opened the gate.

'You there!' demanded a loud voice.

A tall grey horse was trotting up the street, ridden by a centurion in full uniform complete with scarlet cloak and crested helmet. Behind him were two legionaries on horses several hands shorter.

'Chief Centurion Nemetorius,' whispered Cosmas before hurrying over to the officer.

'Good day, sir.'

'This criminal who assaulted Master Celer – apparently some of your sergeants have found him. The magistrate has asked me to take personal charge.'

'Yes, Centurion.'

'They will bring him here, won't they?'

'They will, sir, yes.'

To Cassius, Nemetorius seemed like a man very keen to be regarded as a member of the city's elite. He certainly looked the part, what with the circular gold clasp for his cloak and the sleek horse, but there was a rather coarse edge to him, detectable not only in his voice.

'I shall wait,' he announced.

The two legionaries dismounted. One of them passed his reins to the other and ran over to steady Nemetorius' horse while his superior descended. Once on the pavement, the centurion removed his helmet. Though his face was craggy and lined, his hair was thick and (suspiciously) dark.

Without a single glance at Cassius or the other two, Nemetorius took a flask from the side of his saddle, removed the stopper and drank. 'Hope they won't be long.'

'Not sure, sir,' said Cosmas. 'I wasn't even aware he'd been apprehended.'

Nemetorius snorted, turned to his men and aimed a dismissive thumb over his shoulder. 'This lot.'

Cassius walked over to Cosmas. 'We'll be going.'

Cosmas matched his hushed tone. 'Sir, we will need the centurion's cooperation for the operation at the gates – especially if you two are to masquerade as legionaries. Diadromes will be contacting him of course but it might be wise to introduce yourself.'

Cassius didn't particularly relish the prospect but the sergeant was right; if not for the need for secrecy, he would have already presented himself to the city's senior military commander.

'Very well.' He pointed at his satchel, which Simo passed to him. Sticking out of one end was the spearhead.

Nemetorius had handed his helmet to the legionary watching his horse and was brushing something off his cloak. He looked up as Cosmas and Cassius approached.

'Centurion, this is Officer Crispian.'

Cassius offered his forearm. 'Imperial Security.'

Nemetorius waited a long time to reach out and greet him, which he did with unnecessary – but not unexpected – force. 'A grain man in Berytus, eh? I was not informed.'

'Apologies for not coming to see you sooner. I am working on a covert investigation for Marshal Marcellinus involving a counterfeiting gang. We believe they may be operating within the city.'

As Cosmas withdrew, Cassius pulled aside the top of his satchel so that the centurion could see the spearhead.

Nemetorius didn't seem interested. 'So how long have you been creeping around the city without my knowledge?'

Cassius decided not to use 'sir'. Technically, Nemetorius did outrank him, but the older man wasn't working directly on behalf of the Emperor's deputy. Also, Cassius didn't want to immediately give ground; he seemed like the type who would exploit it.

'Several days.'

A smile played across Nemetorius' face as he examined Cassius's outfit. 'What are you supposed to be?'

'A merchant. I do not wish to advertise my presence here.'

'Clearly. So I presume that you now need something from me?'

'I'm afraid so.'

Cassius briefly outlined the plan. 'I myself would like to pose as one of your officers and man the east gate.'

Nemetorius had been looking up at the cloudless sky while Cassius spoke. 'Counterfeiters in Berytus? I don't see it.' Now he stared at the younger man. 'Sure this isn't all an elaborate ruse so that you can pretend to be a real soldier for a day?'

Cassius held the gaze of the dark-eyed centurion, though it was not easy. 'I can assure you that Marshal Marcellinus and my superior Aulus Celatus Abascantius do not consider this a laughing matter.'

'Pitface, eh? I should have known you were one of his.'

Cassius was surprised at how he bristled at the insult. Had he not been dependent on the centurion's cooperation he might have reminded him of his place in the grand scheme of things. That was always the trouble with the leaders of these provincial cities – they forgot there was a world beyond their walls.

'I imagine Diadromes will communicate with you later. I simply thought it polite to introduce myself.'

'Play your games if you wish. But remember that the collection of tax at that gate is the army's responsibility. If the numbers don't add up at the end of the day, you will have me to deal with.'

Cassius wanted to end the conversation as rapidly as he could. 'If we do make any progress, and I remain here in Berytus, I may have to ask for your help again – a few men perhaps.'

They both knew that – armed with the spearhead – he was perfectly entitled to requisition any troops he needed; but Cassius doubted Nemetorius would make it that easy.

The chief centurion raised his chin, and again chose not to look at his fellow officer. 'To be frank, I have more urgent matters to concern me – law and order for one.' He pointed across the street at four city sergeants who were escorting a captive towards the headquarters. 'But if Marcellinus himself needs my assistance, I shall of course provide it.'

Nemetorius took his helmet from the legionary and put it on. 'Cosmas there knows how to contact me. What was the name again, grain man?'

'Officer Crispian.'

'Officer. Never understood that rank. Not really a proper title at all, is it?'

Nemetorius walked back to his horse and retrieved his whip, then set off across the road. Cassius returned to the others and looked on.

'This him?' asked Nemetorius.

The four sergeants seemed almost as taken aback by the sight of the advancing centurion as their prisoner.

'Yes, sir,' said one. 'Sestius Ravilla. He's a weaver.'

'Of course he is.' Nemetorius seemed oblivious to other road-users who had also stopped to see what was going on. 'Put him on his knees.'

'*Is* that him?' asked Indavara.

'Right build,' said Cassius. 'Yes, see the colour of the tunic. The dolt didn't even get changed.'

Nemetorius raised the whip back over his left shoulder and bellowed. 'Throw stones at a gentleman and his wife and children, would you? A friend of the magistrate's? A friend of mine?'

Ravilla knew what was coming. His hands were bound behind him so all he could do was dig his chin into his chest and close his eyes. Nemetorius cracked the whip across his head, then brought it straight back across his cheek. One of the sergeants winced and a woman cried out. Nemetorius stood over the weaver, crest ruffled by a breeze, tapping the whip on the ground, watching as blood dripped from torn skin on to the flagstones.

Indavara took a step towards the street.

Cassius put an arm out in front of him. 'Don't even think about it. Not our concern.'

Nemetorius circled around behind Ravilla and dragged him up by the rope, then led him across the street. 'Come now, master weaver, and we will see what you can tell us about your stone-throwing compatriots.'

Nemetorius handed the rope to his nearest man. Ravilla was trying to blink away the blood seeping down into his eyes.

Cassius approached Nemetorius. 'Centurion, we were there. I can give you details of the other men.'

'I have what I need.' Still holding the whip, Nemetorius mounted up and rode off, scattering onlookers.

Cassius handed his satchel back to Simo.

'What a prick,' said Indavara.

'You'll get no argument from me.'

XXI

She is wearing only metal: a thin chain at her neck and a thick one around her waist. The candlelight pools on her dark, smooth skin as she crosses the room. She pulls the ribbon from her hair, black tresses falling over her shoulders. She eases herself on to the bed and slides on to him, nipples hard against his chest. She kisses his neck then whispers to him.

'What do you want this night?'

'Master Cassius, Master Cassius.'

'What?' he snapped, rolling on to his side.

'A letter from Tripolis has arrived, sir. Also a note from Master Diadromes.'

Cassius yawned and stretched, irritated to be woken from such a delightful dream. In fact, it was more memory than dream. He thought often of Delkash. Surely the Persian bar girl was the only possible reason he might ever return to Bostra.

'What's the hour?' he asked as he got off the bed.

'Third, sir,' came the reply from downstairs.

He had told Simo to let him sleep. The factory inspections would go ahead the following day and he planned to remain at the tower; there was no sense taking unnecessary risks or getting mixed up in another incident like yesterday's.

Cassius pulled a tunic on over his head and glanced at his little shrine, where a candle and a libation now sat in front of the great gods. He'd spent almost half an hour at prayer the previous night. Some of his appeals to Jupiter had involved the investigation; most had concerned his survival. He opened the door and negotiated the stairs slowly, still half asleep.

'Good morning, Master Cassius.' Simo was already pouring him some milk. 'Fresh today. I've found a wonderful little farm shop just up the road. Some lovely rolls too – that's if Indavara hasn't eaten them all already.'

'Where is he?'

'Gone for a run.'

Simo pointed at the note and the letter on the corner of the table. Cassius sat down on a stool and drank some of his milk before investigating them.

'Cold water for your wash, sir?'

'In this temperature? Of course.'

'We're well shaded here at least.'

'You seem cheerful. And no more minor sabotage. You are sticking to what we agreed?'

Simo kept his back to him as he filled a jug from the water barrel and poured it into a bowl. 'Of course, sir.'

Cassius checked the note first – just a few lines from the deputy magistrate. Diadromes had obtained the appropriate authorisations from Pomponianus, Nemetorius and Berytus's procurator (who, like Nemetorius, was concerned that the daily functions of tax collection not be disrupted). Twenty-four sergeants were to carry out the search for the fictional Egyptian spy; each pair had been assigned three or four premises. Under Cosmas's supervision, they would aim to complete the operation by the fourth hour. Cassius was to contact Diadromes before the evening if he had any remaining queries. He did not.

Cassius drank the rest of the milk then looked across the tower and realised the door was open. 'Er, Simo.'

The Gaul turned round. Cassius pointed at the door.

'Sorry, sir, I wanted to get some air in.' He trotted over and bolted it.

'With no Indavara here? Gods' blood. Think, man.'

'Yes, Master Cassius. Apologies.'

Cassius looked again at Diadromes's letter: a black scrawl on fine paper.

He imagined the gang skulking in the corner of some factory; hearing of the sergeants' arrival, then hastily packing their tools and coins on to carts and speeding towards the eastern gate. He tapped his fingers against the table. It might work; a lot of effort for nothing if it didn't.

Having scraped the wax seal away with a spoon, he unrolled Quentin's letter. The treasury agent had continued collating his 'coin sightings' and now had the majority of replies. His findings confirmed that the fake denarii were now in widespread use across Syria and the adjacent provinces. Cassius thought about the coins themselves; could he somehow trace their origins, again without drawing too much attention? Quentin had little else to report and seemed more interested in Cassius's progress. (He too had received an impatient missive from Marcellinus – or his adviser Glycia, to be precise.)

'Something to eat, sir?'

'Roll. Any cheese?'

'Goat's.'

'That'll do. And a few of those pickled onions – I won't be breathing on any ladies today, more's the pity.'

Cassius watched Simo putting his breakfast together, his thoughts drifting back to Delkash. After he'd given him the plate, Simo poured more milk into his master's mug then leaned against the table.

'That weaver, sir – the one the centurion took away. What do you think happened to him?'

'Nothing pleasant.'

'Berytus does seem to have its share of problems.'

'We are interested only in one of them. I do wish you and Indavara would remember that.'

Cassius put down the onion in his hand and looked up at the Gaul. 'If you had the eyes of a god – any god – you would see arguments and fighting and cruelty and death in every part of the world. From the deserts of Arabia to the Pillars of Hercules. You two think only of what you see in front of you, as if to help one man is to help every man.'

'That is precisely what the Faith teaches us, sir.'

Cassius picked up the onion, then dropped it again. 'Do you or Indavara ever think about what *I* have done? In Arabia or here in Syria with the Persian flag – *I helped to avert a war.* What better way is there to prevent suffering and death? You could spend half a century throwing brass at beggars and you would never match that.'

Simo – though clearly surprised – nodded.

'I'm proud of it,' added Cassius. 'And considering how you both helped me, you should be proud too.'

'I suppose he has a point,' said Indavara. 'But you must always remember, Simo – Corbulo doesn't know what it is to go hungry, or be beaten, or imprisoned. He is not the worst of his kind, not by a long way. But he thinks only of himself.'

Simo stopped in the middle of the darkened street. 'I shouldn't be doing this. We shouldn't.'

'Come on. Corbulo is safe in that tower and we'll only be a couple of hours. Why would he suspect anything?'

Simo waited for a gang of labourers to pass. They were lugging huge amphoras full of something and muttering complaints and oaths with every step.

'It's the lying, the deceit. The Faith tells us we must respect our masters, do their bidding.'

'Well, you've already deceived him once, now twice. Might as well make the most of it.' Indavara put a hand on Simo's arm and coaxed him onward. 'What's happening tonight anyway?'

'Elder Cobon wants to get some food to those people in the area where we were attacked last time.'

'Stubborn old boy, isn't he?'

'Determined. We cannot simply give up in the face of adversity. Those people need our help.'

'And your people need a bit of security.'

'I expect that legionary will be there too. You did leave all the blades at the tower?'

Indavara was armed only with his stave. 'I did, though I can't say I'm happy about it.'

Once again, they met at the church-house, where Indavara counted fourteen people present. Elder Cobon first spoke to the women, who departed immediately, apparently with their own separate task.

While Simo and the others filled sacks with bread, Cobon took Indavara aside and introduced him to the legionary. A man of around thirty named Bromidus, he didn't seem particularly keen to be there. It took Cobon a while to persuade him to leave his dagger behind and take only a cudgel. The old man asked them both to use minimum force if the party was attacked. As he departed, the pair exchanged a cynical look.

Indavara asked the stocky legionary – who was wearing nothing to mark him out as a soldier – if he'd helped the group before.

'Few times,' Bromidus replied morosely, sipping from a small flask of wine.

'Why?'

'Family. We must all do our bit for the Faith.'

'You are part of the city garrison?'

'Last three years.'

Indavara knew there weren't that many Christians in the army. 'Is it difficult, with the other soldiers?'

'It might be if I told them.'

Bromidus left him in a corner, joining the other men as they formed a circle. They clasped their hands together and bowed their heads as Elder Cobon delivered a short prayer.

Indavara looked on and hoped there wouldn't be any trouble. He wanted to keep coming to this place and helping the Christians. There was a simplicity to it; people were hungry, you gave them food. He was sure Corbulo would consider it pointless but surely even he couldn't dispute that it was better than doing nothing.

Cobon sent the others outside while he locked up, then led them away. Even though it was another warm, humid night, Bromidus wore a cape with a hood which he immediately pulled up. Nobody spoke as they followed Cobon on what seemed to Indavara like a rather indirect route. Twice they waited in the shadows for city sergeants to pass, which elicited quiet curses from Bromidus. At one point they came close to the soaring walls of the theatre, from which muted cheers and laughter rang out.

Later, Indavara overheard the others talking; apparently their destination was an area known as 'back of the taverns'. They passed one brightly lit street where drunks lurched about and customers gathered at well-stocked counters and steaming grills. Indavara felt his stomach rumble at the smell of cooking meat.

Despite the roundabout route, Cobon clearly knew exactly where he was going. As the streets grew darker and the smells became far less pleasant, Indavara glanced at the surrounding buildings. Many were in disrepair, most seemed unoccupied. Cobon halted at a particularly gloomy corner and a message came back that they should watch their footing.

They turned left into a narrow alley. After only a few paces Indavara heard Bromidus trip and curse – loudly this time. Soon the harsh odour of burned wood overtook all others and they reached a more open area illuminated by the half-moon.

Here was another ruin, this one of timber. The warehouse was very long and would have been high too had the roof and a good portion of the walls not collapsed.

'Careful, all of you,' said Cobon.

One man with a lantern opened the shutter wide, casting a fuzzy glow over a patch of ground cluttered by foundation stones and planks painted black. There was no fire but Indavara could already hear people on the move. Cobon and the others looked towards an inky opening in the side of the warehouse. Four figures appeared, whispering to one another as they approached. Cobon took the lantern and held it up. The men blinked and turned away from the light. Their faces were as grimy as their clothes and two had livid lesions upon their skin. They were bearded and very dark, and looked to Indavara like Arabians.

Bromidus spoke into his ear. 'Stay well back. Might be lepers.'

Indavara hadn't thought of that and swiftly resolved to follow the legionary's advice.

Cobon was trying to speak to the paupers but they didn't seem to understand.

'Don't know that tongue,' said Bromidus. 'Could be—'

The legionary seemed to have heard something. 'Behind us?'

Indavara looked past him, back along the alley, but he could see nothing in the darkness. He heard Bromidus slip his cudgel from his belt and reached back to grab his stave.

The paupers advanced towards Cobon and the others with arms outstretched, desperate eyes fixed on the sacks of bread.

Then Indavara spied a light in the alleyway up ahead. It was faint, perhaps only a candle, but definitely coming towards them. 'Look, Bromidus. There.'

'I see it.'

By now Cobon had given one sack to the paupers but they were already fighting over it and more had come out of the warehouse. These men seemed to be older or weaker or both. One tripped in the melee, falling into the lantern's glow. He had lost all his hair and one entire side of his face was covered in thick, crusty scabs. The others were cursing and spitting at him.

Simo gave a large loaf to Elder Cobon, who handed it to the afflicted man. He nodded vigorously then scuttled away towards the warehouse with his prize.

'Indarus.'

'Indavara.'

'Behind us,' said Bromidus, 'they're getting closer. I can hear them.'

'This way too.' The light was perhaps only twenty feet away now; Indavara could see the fingers on the candle and the face above it.

Cobon and the others had retreated, unsure what to do. There were now at least a dozen of the paupers on the ground, tearing loaves from the sack and each other.

Indavara pulled Simo away. 'Get ready to move.'

Cobon and others heard him and turned.

'You go forward,' said Bromidus. 'I'll watch the rear.'

Indavara pulled the stave from his back and held it in both hands.

The candle had stopped. Above it was a narrow face and a fearful expression.

Indavara took three steps towards the man. 'Who are you?'

The stranger answered in Latin. 'Food. Do you have food?'

'Who are you?'

Bromidus moved up beside Indavara. 'Come forward. Show yourself.'

The man was not alone. As others appeared behind him his candle flickered and went out. Bromidus snatched the lantern from Cobon and held it up.

'Do you have food?' repeated the stranger.

With him were a woman and several children, each as grubby and emaciated as their parents.

'Please,' said the man. 'For them.'

Indavara moved aside as the Christians came forward with bread.

'I know that accent,' said Bromidus. 'Palmyrans.'

Indavara followed him to the rear, where the legionary held the lantern up once more. 'Who's there? Show yourselves.'

Indavara heard sniffing, then a confused whine. The two dogs padded out hesitantly from behind a pile of timber. They were tall, leggy things, with not a lot of meat on their bones.

'Gods,' said Bromidus. 'My nerves.'

Indavara looked around. The paupers seemed to have divided up their spoils and were now pleading with Cobon for the last sack. Indavara hurried over and took out two stale rolls then threw them to the dogs. They looked hungry too.

Back at the church-house, the women were busy with something inside. Indavara and Bromidus looked on as the men gathered in the yard, discussing what they had seen. Elder Cobon seemed keen to hear suggestions as to how else they might help the diseased paupers.

'It wasn't leprosy, Simo said so.'

'Expert, is he?' replied Bromidus with a sneer. 'I tell you one thing, you won't catch me round there again. Old Cobon's never satisfied with just helping out – I swear he'd prefer to be down in the dirt with them if he could. He's always telling us we must forget earthly trappings like food and clothes. Bloody ridiculous.'

'Why bother coming, then?'

'Told you – family. My mother's taken ill with something bad. She and my father reckon we need to atone for our sins, do good deeds so that the Lord helps us. Personally, I can think of better ways of spending my leave.'

The legionary glanced at Cobon, still addressing his earnest followers. 'Tell them I'll be back when I can.' Bromidus opened the courtyard door but then stopped. 'What about you? Why are you here?'

Indavara didn't have an answer for him.

The legionary left.

Indavara reckoned they should be getting back but Simo was still listening intently to Elder Cobon. He wandered along the side of the courtyard and up to the door to see what was going on – and to check if the young woman from before was there.

She wasn't. There were five women, all gathered close to the hearth. Four of them were middle aged, one was little more than a girl. Indavara wondered why they had a fire going; it was still very warm. At an instruction from one of the older women, the girl went to fetch something. Indavara now realised that they were all standing around a table. He moved closer. Upon the table was a wooden tub, and inside was a little pink baby, the tiniest he had ever seen. One of the women was holding its head up while two of the others washed its little legs.

'Beautiful, isn't she?' The woman on the the far side of the table had seen him watching. 'Come closer if you want.'

Indavara didn't move. He didn't feel right standing there, nor did he know what to say. The woman dried her hands, then left the others and walked over to him. She was wearing a scarf over her hair and had a friendly smile.

'Another one saved for the Lord.'

'Saved?'

'She is a foundling.'

'A what?'

'A baby left to die. We found her at the rubbish dump – that's where they leave the ones they don't want.'

'Why?'

'Sometimes because they don't have the money. Or because of some physical imperfection – but not this one, though. Probably just because she is a girl. Another was not so fortunate.'

The woman closed her eyes and turned away for a moment. 'What do you mean?'

'The dogs. They got to him before us. We can't be there all the time and the dump is so big. Sometimes we miss them. But at least we found her.'

As she walked back to the table the baby began to wail. Even though the little thing had been saved it sounded to Indavara like a cry of despair.

XXII

The eastern gate was a functional lump of dark grey stone adorned by some partially decorated columns and a lot of pigeon shit. The arch was on the narrow side but boasted a fearsome portcullis that could be raised and lowered by winch. There were two little rooms in the gatehouse, on either side of the road. One was used by the army, the other by staff from the procurator's office. The senior tax collector on duty was accompanied by three assistants and two scribes. On this particular day, the army could boast only half their numbers: Cassius, Indavara and a one-legged guard officer named Matho.

Standing in the doorway, Cassius looked on as one of the two Egyptian slaves also assigned to the gatehouse shovelled horse manure into an amphora. While waiting for loads to be checked, horses, donkeys and mules continually voided their bowels and bladders on to the hexagonal flagstones. The tax collector, Sellic, called over the other slave to mop up a yellow pool of urine.

'About average so far?' Cassius asked over his shoulder. Matho was inside, resting his good leg on a stool and polishing some belt-buckles.

'Let's see. What's come out? Er . . . about a dozen horses and mules, same number of carts? Yes, about average.'

Like Sellic, Matho had been told by Cosmas only that Cassius and Indavara were on special assignment for the army and the magistrate's office. The gatehouse staff were to continue as normal for the day but render any assistance required. Sellic – clearly as fastidious as most in his profession – had insisted on seeing the written authorisation.

Taking care not to tarry beneath the portcullis, Cassius walked towards the city and looked up at the hazy sun, now well above even the highest buildings.

'Must be in the second hour. Cosmas's men will have been into quite a few places already. You all right?'

Indavara was squatting in the shadow of the arch, seemingly unconcerned by what was being cleaned up a few yards away. He was staring blankly at the opposite wall.

'Indavara, you all right?'

The bodyguard gave a slight nod, then stood up and walked to the other side of the gatehouse. He looked out at the broad road that ran east, eventually reaching the lushly forested hills beneath the mountains.

'Get your rolls! Get your loaves!' bellowed a vendor. The gatehouse was a prime spot and the traders had set up outside well before dawn. A lot of their custom came from the farmers bringing in produce for the city's markets. Plenty had already come through but Cassius had left them to Sellic and his men; he was interested only in traffic *leaving* Berytus.

'Straight from the ovens of Baker Vetranio! Get your rolls! Get your loaves!'

'Must he yell like that?' said Cassius to no one in particular. 'I mean, really?'

Indavara had hardly spoken since they'd left the tower. The bodyguard walked past the bread and all the other food on offer, gazing morosely at the ground, thick fringe hanging over his eyes. Cassius reckoned he was worrying about Patch – apparently the mule was still ill.

Seeing a trio of riders approaching from the city side, Sellic directed one assistant and one scribe towards the chair and table situated on the pavement in front of the gate. The senior man then headed back into the shady room, barking at someone to hurry up with something.

Cassius walked out into the sunshine and took up his now customary position on the right side of the road. He ignored the pair of giggling teenage girls scrubbing the pavement in front of a clothier's and instead watched the new arrivals. Having decided that the helmet's crest would draw too much attention, he had nonetheless attired himself in his best scarlet tunic, most martial belt of ringed steel and, of course, the eagle-head sword. The appearance of a new officer might cause a stir but his accent and manners made him a rather unconvincing legionary and he felt he might need the rank to reinforce his authority with any suspects.

Matho had briefed him on the routine so he held up his hand and the riders came to a halt. They were clearly together; well dressed and riding fine horses – local landowners perhaps.

One of them wearily addressed Sellic's assistant; he obviously knew the routine too. 'Archestratidas and party, no trade goods purchased or sold, no taxable transactions made.'

Leaving the scribe sitting at the table, the junior tax collector wished the gentlemen good day then walked all the way around them, inspecting their saddles. The bags were not even full – perhaps just some clothes for an overnight stay. He returned to the front and gestured towards the arch. 'Thank you, sirs. Good day.'

Cassius wasn't interested in the trio either. As they rode on, he watched the next arrival; a long cart yoked to a pair of horses. Sitting next to the driver was a stocky man wearing a wide-brimmed hat. Cassius didn't need to see inside the barrels upon the cart to establish their contents; he could already smell the fish. As the driver reined in and the other man spoke to the assistant, Cassius peered over the side. The barrels were packed tightly together and secured by ropes. While he walked around to the other side, the assistant began counting the barrels. The merchant already had a money bag open, ready to pay his due.

Cassius pointed at the cart. 'I want to see to the bottom of one of those barrels. I'll climb up, you show me.'

'What?'

'Don't make me ask twice, citizen.'

The merchant got up and stepped into the back of the cart. Cassius clambered up quickly, conscious that there were more vehicles approaching.

'Any in particular?' asked the merchant sarcastically.

'Yes,' replied Cassius, pointing at one. The plump, grey-scaled fish were packed in salt and some type of leaf.

'You want me to take it all out?'

'Just enough so I can see the bottom.'

The merchant took his money bag and threw it on to the seat by the driver. 'Pay them, would you? Or they'll be fining us for holding up the line.'

Cassius let him unload two-thirds of the fish before accepting that there was nothing hidden underneath. He then jumped down and told the assistant to wave the merchant through. As the cart rumbled away, Indavara wandered out of the shadows.

'Ah, nice of you to join me at last.'

The next cart belonged to another merchant whose cart turned out to be empty – he had delivered a dozen amphoras of olive oil and was heading home. Cassius had a quick look under the cart then waved him through. Next came a husband and wife, each towing a mule laden with freshly dyed fleeces. They hadn't any space in which to secrete anything.

And so it went on. Over the next hour, they examined jars of stinking animal fat, rummaged under cowhides and cotton sheets, tipped dates and figs out of amphoras, opened endless saddlebags and found nothing illicit other than ten flasks of cinnamon wine that one unfortunate tried to smuggle out under a pile of rugs.

By the fifth hour, traffic was beginning to die down. Cassius paced around beneath the arch, wondering if he should visit the other gates or go in search of Cosmas. The sergeant was supposed to come straight to him after the inspections were concluded.

'Perhaps they found something,' he said to Indavara. 'Perhaps that's where he is.'

The bodyguard was still acting strangely. When unoccupied, he invariably located a rag and some water and started cleaning his sword or his dagger or his belt. But again he was just standing in the shadows, arms crossed, staring at the ground. Suddenly he spoke.

'Did you know that people take unwanted babies to dumps and leave them there?'

'What?'

Of all the things Cassius might have expected Indavara to concern himself with, this was not high on the list.

'Did you know – that people do that?'

'Here, you mean?'

'Yes.'

'Well, it is done, yes. Not as much as in the past, I believe.'

'Why would someone throw away a child? Their son or their daughter?'

'Er . . . why are you asking about this?'

'I – I didn't know about it. That it was done.'

Cassius looked towards the city; there was no one approaching.

'I imagine there are a number of reasons. Money – the woman or the parents can't afford it. Or if the child is ill – some disease or deformity. It is the father's right to decide if a child is to be accepted and raised by the family. If not . . .'

'But to throw such a helpless little thing away?'

'It can be for the best – if it would starve, or suffer, or grow up unwanted. Better a quick death.'

Indavara thought about this for a moment. 'Sometimes they are taken in by others.'

'As foundlings, yes. Though often not to their benefit.'

'What do you mean?'

'They are sometimes raised as slaves – to be worked or . . . you know.'

Indavara reached behind his belt and took out his figurine. He slumped back against the wall and shook his head.

'This troubles you.'

The bodyguard turned the figurine's face towards him.

Cassius added, 'They say the Carthaginians used to sacrifice their children to the gods.'

'Does that make you Romans better?'

'Still insisting *you're* not Roman, I note. Listen, disposing of these babies is not done out of malice; more often than not it is a simple practicality.'

'Life is cruel; there's nothing to be done about it.'

'You're spending too much time talking to Simo. Too much time worrying about others.'

'You'd prefer that I worry only about you.'

Cassius thought it wise to respond swiftly to that one. 'And yourself. Life is too short to bear the woes of the world upon your shoulders. You've had enough of your own to contend with.'

Indavara watched the two Egyptians. Sellic now had them cleaning furniture.

'In the arena I was used to entertain; just like a slave is used to serve. But if you have no use, you are left to starve in some filthy alley, or thrown away with the rest of the rubbish. You can say what you want about Simo, but he doesn't use others. He cares for them, tries to help.'

'And I . . .'

'You . . . are you.'

Cassius felt his throat tightening, his face reddening: he was getting angry. But he didn't want – and could not afford – to fall out with the man. These outbursts came now and again; Cassius put it down to his amnesia and the torment of his years as a fighter.

'Perhaps Simo *is* a better man than me. Perhaps you are too. I don't recall ever claiming anything to the contrary.'

This caught Indavara by surprise. 'I meant no insult.'

'I know. And I can see how such a thing would shock you; it is only two years that you have been . . . out in the world.'

Indavara came closer. 'You always tell Simo that it is not Satan or the demons who make men harm others. You say it is men themselves. Why?'

'I don't know. Gods, it's a bit early in the day for all this. Listen, look around you. Evil and suffering are not *everywhere*.' Cassius pointed across at Sellic's assistants; all three were examining a single waxed tablet. 'Look at this lot – not the most popular job but they've taken it to get on – decent lads trying to make their way.'

Cassius put a hand on Indavara's arm and took him out from under the arch towards the road.

'Look here.' He pointed at one of the vendors, who was showing his young son how to use a pair of scales.

'Or there.' Farther along the road, a girl was helping an elderly woman fill a bag with vegetables.

'People going about their business, looking out for themselves and others where they can. The world is not only death and destruction, though I concede we've observed our fair share.'

Indavara looked out across the fields, where the shadows of a few small clouds drifted across the swaying wheat. Cassius thought it rather beautiful.

'But behind us,' said Indavara. 'In every corner of this city . . .'

Cassius sighed. 'Even the gods cannot stop it. And it seems to me that they don't even try.'

Cosmas arrived around midday to report that the inspections were finished. He hadn't had time to hear from all the sergeants but they were convening at the ninth hour and he would pass on anything of use. So far, nothing notable had been discovered.

'What about the other gates?' asked Cassius.

'The legionaries are supposed to— ah, that might be them.'

Two soldiers had appeared from an alley and strode swiftly up to the gate. 'Officer Crispian, sir?'

'Yes.'

'We were told to report to you.'

'Yes. Anything from the northern and southern gates?'

'No, sir. Just a few bags of salt hidden in some hay.'

'Ah shit.' Cassius kicked the ground. Sellic peered out from the shadows, then disappeared back inside. An abacus rattled as his assistants continued totting up the morning's takings.

'Something might turn up later,' said Indavara.

'Optimism? From you?'

Cosmas walked over to a bucket one of the slaves had just brought out. He cupped water in his hands and threw it on his face, then wiped some on his neck to cool down.

The other slave trotted over to Cassius, mop in hand. 'Sir?'

'What?'

'You're looking for something in a cart, aren't you?'

'Yes. Why?'

The slave was an old fellow, whip thin with straggly, greying hair. He pointed towards the city. 'Two carts just turned on to the street from the right. When they saw you soldiers they went back.'

Cassius looked. There were no vehicles visible any more.

'Indavara! You two, come with me. Cosmas, watch the gate.'

Cassius set off up the middle of the road, as fast as he could with the heavy sword slapping around. Ahead, half a dozen water-carriers with amphoras balanced on their heads were crossing the street but they divided to let Cassius and the other three through.

Fifty or so paces took him to the corner. He stopped and peered around the stall of a spice-seller who insisted on quoting prices even when one of the legionaries told him to shut up. Cassius glimpsed the tail end of a cart turning left about thirty yards along the street.

'Come on.'

A group of craftsmen chipping away at stone blocks outside a townhouse stopped their work as they raced by. Cassius slowed a little to ensure the others were with him as he rounded the next corner. The street was narrow and the two cart drivers were drawing complaints from pedestrians having to squash themselves against walls and storefronts.

Cassius waved the legionaries past him. 'Get in front of them.'

He and Indavara waited until the soldiers had darted along one side and blocked the path of the first cart.

'Halt!' yelled Cassius.

The two legionaries put up their hands and the drivers reined in. Cassius peered over the top of the second cart; the cargo was large bundles of dried reeds. He went to check the first vehicle – also reeds. The driver of the second cart was trying to calm his horse.

'You – why did you turn round?'

The driver was a wiry little man, arms decorated with some badly rendered tattoos.

'Turn round, sir?' he said, avoiding Cassius's gaze.

'You approached the gate, then went back. Why?'

The driver of the first cart – a younger man – spoke up. 'We 'got a bit lost, sir, but we know where we're going now. Let us on our way, would you? We're already late.'

'Not until I've checked your cargo properly. Get down and steady your horses.'

'Very well.' The younger man climbed down. The older driver muttered an oath before obeying. Cassius indicated that Indavara should watch him, then hurried around to the rear of the cart and clambered on. The reed bundles were tightly packed but only two deep. He had only just picked one up when one of the legionaries gave a shout.

'You! I know you.'

Cassius let go of the bundle and watched as the little driver desperately sought an escape route. Unfortunately for him, he was trapped between the cart and Indavara. As he tried to dive under the vehicle, Indavara grabbed his tunic and hauled him up.

The vocal legionary said something to his compatriot, then ran alongside the cart. Indavara was so taken by surprise that, before he could react, the legionary had hurled the driver into the gutter. The soldier's sword rasped as he wrenched it from the scabbard.

'What are you doing?' demanded Indavara.

The startled horse was jolting the cart but Cassius made a safe landing and arrived in time to see the legionary raise his weapon.

'Just the flat of the blade,' he hissed. 'Which is half what he deserves.'

'Legionary, sheathe your weapon.'

When the soldier ignored him, Cassius turned immediately to Indavara.

The bodyguard chopped his hand into the legionary's shoulder; a light blow but aimed at a sensitive point. The soldier's blade clattered into a puddle beside the wide-eyed driver.

The soldier spun around, fists already clenched. He was a big man, with broad shoulders and thickly muscled arms.

'No,' warned Cassius. 'Don't.'

Too late. The legionary shoved Indavara in the chest, propelling

229

him back into the cart. As he bounced back towards him, the legionary swung an arcing punch into the bodyguard's head just above the ear. The thump was so loud that Cassius thought he might go down.

Indavara staggered, blinking, mouth open.

The soldier was still admiring his handiwork when the bodyguard rushed him.

He hit his midriff, knocking him back two yards and into a wall.

The driver caught a boot on his arm and yelped as he crawled away.

Before the soldier could strike back, Indavara had buried a heavy punch in his gut. The legionary would have doubled over were it not for the fact that Indavara's hands were now around his throat, pushing his head back against the bricks.

As his face turned from brown to red, the soldier waved at his friend. 'Wolfie, help!'

'Wolfie' didn't look all that keen on helping. Though also tall, he was as slender as Cassius. 'You shouldn't have hit him, Scato.'

Indavara was snarling, spit running down his chin as he tightened his grip.

'All right, that's enough,' said Cassius.

Scato bucked, trying to prise himself off the wall, which only made Indavara squeeze harder. The legionary's face was now almost purple. He tried to speak but all that came out was a strangled cry.

'Indavara!'

Cassius grabbed his right arm and tried to pull it away but the bodyguard had locked it in place.

Cassius moved close to his face, which was trembling as his teeth ground together. 'Indavara, you'll kill him!'

Scato's eyelids were fluttering.

'Stop him,' yelled the other soldier.

Cassius reached up and gripped one of Indavara's wrists with both hands. With this purchase he was able to take some of the pressure off.

The gasping breath that came from Scato seemed somehow

to snap Indavara out of the rage. He instantly let go; and Cassius had to hold Scato up as the legionary slumped against the wall.

Indavara backed away.

Wolfie finally came to aid his friend.

Chest heaving, fingers shaking, Indavara looked around for a moment, then walked back along the street.

Cassius had no intention of trying to stop him. 'By the gods.'

The little driver was still on the ground. As he picked himself up, Cassius put a hand on his sword. 'Don't even think about running.'

'I won't.'

Cassius nodded at Scato. 'Why did he go for you?'

'I . . . er . . . I know his sister, sir. If you know what I mean.'

'That's why you . . .'

'Yes,' admitted the Syrian.

Scato was making a strange sound as he breathed, as if something was catching in his throat. Cassius looked at his neck. Every one of Indavara's fingers had left its mark.

XXIII

Cassius had been through two canteens of water but still couldn't get rid of the headache. Cosmas stood beside him in the courtyard, tapping his thumbs impatiently against his belt.

'You have numerous other things you should be doing as well, I suppose?'

'Yes, sir.'

Having taken Indavara back to the tower and left him with Simo, Cassius had enlisted Cosmas to escort him to the basilica. Chief Centurion Nemetorius had heard about the incident with his soldier remarkably quickly and summoned Cassius for a meeting. Though it would be difficult to defend Indavara's actions, Scato was also to blame; and Cassius wanted to clear the matter up swiftly. Diadromes was also supposed to be attending but neither had yet arrived.

'May I go now, sir?' asked Cosmas. He pointed to the arch on the opposite side of the courtyard, where Nemetorius had just appeared, accompanied again by his two legionaries. Cassius would have preferred not to have been so outnumbered but there was little a man of Cosmas's rank could do.

'What about the deputy magistrate?'

'I'm sure he won't be too much longer. I will collate anything useful that came in from the inspections and come to the tower tomorrow.'

As the sergeant departed, Cassius turned his attention to Nemetorius. The chief centurion was marching towards him at a prodigious pace, the rhythmic tap of his boots echoing across the courtyard. Cassius wished he had his own uniform on but he'd changed into civilian attire to cross the city. With Cosmas gone, he now faced the prospect of braving the streets alone.

Gods, what a day. Where is bloody Diadromes?

Nemetorius held up a hand and his men halted some distance away. The centurion didn't come particularly close himself; perhaps because that would accentuate Cassius's considerable height advantage.

'Well, Crispian?'

'Chief Centurion?'

'I've seen him. The man's windpipe has been crushed. He can hardly speak.'

'I am sorry to hear that.'

'Where is he? Your man?'

'At the residence we are using.'

'I will speak with him.'

'I don't think that's necessary. Shall I describe to you what happened?'

'The poor bastard's already told me.'

'So he *can* speak?'

Nemetorius' glare instantly made Cassius regret his reply. He elected to deliver his version of events anyway. 'We had stopped these two cart drivers. I was questioning one of them when Legionary Scato grabbed him and threw him to the ground. He then pulled out his sword and was about to strike him. I instructed my bodyguard to disarm him, which he did without causing harm. Scato took exception to this and struck not only the first blow but the second. At which point my bodyguard retaliated.'

'By almost killing him. The other legionary told me that if you hadn't intervened he would have. Several witnesses attest to the same.'

'I agree. He went too far. But I gave Scato two orders: firstly not to attack the suspect; secondly not to react. He disobeyed both. He caused this incident.'

'Do you expect me to ignore an assault on a soldier under my command?'

'I have.'

'That brawling thug of yours is no soldier.'

'Actually he is. He has taken the oath and is on the books of the Fourth Legion under Prefect Venator, as am I.'

'Even better. I am the senior officer here. I have the right to punish a soldier committing an offence within my jurisdiction and I shall.'

'The question of jurisdiction is far from clear. My bodyguard and I are operating directly under orders from Marshal Marcellinus.'

'So you think yourself free to do as you please?'

Cassius was surprised by how calm Nemetorius was remaining. He wondered how his reaction might have differed without the fearsome influence of Marcellinus and the more shadowy presence of the Service to consider.

'Not at all. Refer this matter to higher authority if you wish, but that would mean the governor or the marshal himself.'

'The magistrate—'

'Is not of sufficient rank, as I think we both know.' Cassius held up both his hands. 'Chief Centurion . . .'

Nemetorius had advanced and it seemed as if his temper was finally about to get the better of him. 'You bloody grain men. What gives you treacherous double-dealing bastards the nerve to consider yourself equal to officers of the Imperial Army?'

Cassius swallowed hard but held his ground. 'Choice words, Centurion. I shall remember them.'

'How old are you?'

'I do not see that that is particularly relevant.'

Nemetorius gestured at himself. 'I took the oath twenty-eight years ago. I have served a dozen emperors in as many different provinces, led hundreds of men into battle and cut down the enemies of Rome. What have you ever done, you arrogant little shit stain?'

Cassius stepped backwards. 'This and that. Unfortunately, Chief Pulcher doesn't allow us to share the details of our work. I fancy I might share this conversation with him, though; Officer Abascantius too.'

'You dare to threaten me?'

'You are the one holding your sword hilt, Centurion.'

Nemetorius looked down; he hadn't even realised it. He straightened up and patted his hair, even though there didn't seem to be a single strand out of place.

Cassius's throat was dry. He had to cough several times before speaking. 'I – I am sorry for the suffering of Legionary Scato but he made a poor choice.'

Nemetorius aimed a thick finger at him. 'Despite my better judgement, I cooperated with you, Crispian. And this is how I am repaid?'

'Your cooperation is greatly appreciated.'

'Good, because there will be no more of it.'

'Gentlemen!'

Diadromes came in from the other entrance, to Cassius's left. With him was his clerk, who stayed well back, like the soldiers.

'Good afternoon to you both.'

'Good afteroon,' said Cassius.

Nemetorius cast a cynical glance at the deputy magistrate. 'I was just telling the officer here that after today's incident he can expect no more help from the garrison. Still, as you seem so keen to bend over backwards for him I'm sure he will continue to sneak about the place causing trouble, with no regard for rank or authority.'

Diadromes did not seem concerned by the slight. 'This incident at the eastern gate? I'm afraid I have not heard the details.'

'I do not intend to go over it again. Crispian, I expect payment – for Scato's medical costs.'

'I will consider that, of course,' said Cassius, anxious to salvage some vague semblance of goodwill if he could.

Nemetorius gave him a final scowl then turned away.

'Centurion,' said Diadromes, 'as you're here, I wanted to ask about this man Ravilla. My office has heard nothing since you took custody of him yesterday.'

'Rest assured we are working on that. Working on him, to be precise. We'll have the others soon enough.'

Now Diadromes did seem dismayed. 'Torture? Word will reach the people. It may enflame an already difficult situation.'

'I will remind you, Deputy Magistrate, that I am only involved in these matters because Pomponianus feels his subordinates have lost control of the streets. You are one of those subordinates. Like your young grain man friend here, perhaps you too should remember your place.'

Cloak flicking up behind him, Nemetorius spun on his heels and set off, the expressionless legionaries falling in five paces behind.

'A rather fiery character, our chief centurion,' said Cassius.

The deputy magistrate would not be drawn. 'This incident with Indavara was regrettable. A financial settlement is the best course of action.'

'Would Legionary Scato see a coin of it?'

'Yes. Nemetorius is impervious to such temptations. To his credit, he is concerned only with doing what he sees as his job; looking after his troops and assisting the magistrate.'

'Pomponianus may be the senior official in Berytus but Nemetorius is a chief centurion – he needn't answer to him.'

'Ordinarily perhaps,' said Diadromes, 'but Nemetorius covets a place with other veteran officers in Rome.'

'Ah, the urban cohort.'

'Yes. And to even be considered he will need excellent reports from both the magistrate and the governor.'

'Not to mention a reputation for being uncompromisingly strict and loyal.'

'Quite, as you yourself have observed. In any case, neither of us can afford to offend him.'

'I fear my very existence does that.'

'Let us walk, I have been sitting in meetings all day.'

As they set off across the courtyard, a small flock of pigeons in another corner fluttered upward then settled on the roof. A quartet of clerks walked past, each holding large bundles of waxed tablets. They started talking again only when they were well clear of Diadromes.

'Cosmas tells me your efforts at the gates were in vain.'

'It appears so, though the inspections may yet yield something. It is possible that we have done nothing more than alert the gang – if they see through the spy story. It is really not going well.'

'You are forgetting the contention that this "gang" was never here in the first place.'

'I haven't forgotten it. It is seeming more likely with every passing day.'

'But you will continue your enquiries?'

'For the moment, yes.'

'You may keep Cosmas for as long as you need him.'

'Thank you.'

Diadromes pushed his bracelets up his arm and grinned. 'Despite what I said yesterday, my well of gratitude is not yet completely dry. My wife's good mood shows no signs of abating.'

'Lucky for me.'

They reached the rear gate of the basilica, where a pair of legionaries stood guard.

'You are alone?' asked Diadromes.

'I thought it best to let Indavara calm down so Cosmas came with me. I left my horse at the stables.'

'This threat you spoke of when we first met – any indication that you are in danger here?'

'Not yet but—'

'Come, I shall escort you to the stables.'

Once beyond the looming shadows of the basilica, they walked in bright sunlight across one corner of the forum towards the giant stables used daily by hundreds of city officials. They hadn't gone far when a pair of elderly men each accompanied by a retinue of at least a dozen ceased their conversation to bid Diadromes a polite 'good day'. Diadromes returned the greeting but kept moving.

'Council members. If I were to engage them in conversation I'd be lucky to get away in time for dinner.'

'Busy day?'

'Oh yes. I doubt I shall get to the baths – again. By this evening I must sort out a dispute with a shipping agent about harbour fees, amend an urgent set of regulations about what is to be considered white bread and what is to be considered brown, and then there is the smuggling ring you uncovered. Plus tomorrow we have a trade delegation coming in from Hierapolis. They'll expect to see the weaving factories but Pomponianus isn't sure we should risk it – wouldn't want another incident to upset the visitors.'

'Gods. At least I only have one problem to deal with. Well, that and my impetuous bodyguard.'

'Ex-gladiator, I presume?'

'Indeed. Generally he's fairly biddable but when it comes to the rough stuff he . . . doesn't hold back.'

'Thoroughbreds are often highly strung. But please keep him under control. If your name comes to Pomponianus' attention again, he may decide to take more of a personal interest in your presence here.'

As it was now mid-afternoon, the stables were quiet. The younger lads were gathered outside, throwing walnuts into a clay pot. But one enterprising type was keeping a close eye out for potential tips and hurried over to Cassius.

'Fetch your mount for you, sir?'

'Certainly. Name's Crispian.'

'Won't be a minute, sir.' The lad sped away.

'Deputy Magistrate!' A young groom who had just emerged from the stalls ran up. He was wearing a long apron covered in horsehair.

'By Jupiter, here we go,' murmured Diadromes.

More grooms came out of the stables to see what was going on.

The young man bowed to Diadromes. 'Good day, sir.'

'Good day, Sorio.'

'Sir, what's to happen to Ravilla? Is Nemetorius going to have him flogged? Or worse?'

'I have no idea.'

'You won't let them kill him, will you, sir? Not for throwing a few stones.'

Cassius withdrew; he didn't need this much attention. Diadromes didn't particularly seem to be enjoying it either. More grooms had arrived and the boys had abandoned their game.

'That is a matter for the magistrate and the courts.'

Sorio wasn't the only one with questions:

'Why's the army got him, sir?'

'When will he be punished?'

'What does the magistrate think?'

'You know what that Celer's like, don't you, sir?'

The grooms had pressed in around the deputy magistrate quickly.

Diadromes remained calm. 'Now listen, lads. We can't have people assaulting women and children in the street. You all know that. The sergeants did their job and Centurion Nemetorius too. Back to the stables with you now.'

'It's you should be magistrate, sir,' said Sorio. Some of the others cheered.

'You're very kind but I'm too busy with my present post to stand for election.'

'Down with Pomponianus,' shouted someone.

'Now,' said Diadromes sternly. 'Let's have none of that. We all want what's best for Berytus.'

'Not Celer,' said another. 'He wants what's best for him. The rest of 'em aren't any better. There's only you what knows the life of a working man.'

'Look, lads, I don't have time for this now. But I'll ask you to stay away from these protests. I wouldn't want any of you getting into trouble.'

'It's the weavers you have to worry about there, sir,' said Sorio. 'Never known them so angry.'

'Everyone just needs to calm down,' said Diadromes. 'Besides, it's too bloody hot to get agitated. Oh, did I tell you this one – man goes to the surgeon. "Sir, sir, everyone keeps ignoring me." "Next, please!" "Sir, sir, have you got anything for a head-ache?" The surgeon gives him a hammer. "Try this." "Sir, sir, I keep thinking I'm a dog." "Sit on that chair and we'll talk about it." "I can't, I'm not allowed on the chair."'

Cassius thought this a rather desperate manoeuvre but by the time the Syrian had rattled off half a dozen more japes, the grooms were too busy laughing to pester him. With a wink at Cassius, Diadromes bade the young men farewell and headed back towards the basilica. Cassius heard a few complaints about how he hadn't really listened to them as he went to meet the lad with his horse. He gave a good tip, mounted up and rode for the nearest street; he didn't intend to stop for anything.

Simo's hands were slick with blood. As he continued to carve cuts from the slab of meat, Cassius lowered his aching body on to a stool and drank the wine he'd just poured himself. He had taken only one wrong turn on the return trip but even that had been enough to produce an anxious minute or two. While running back to the tower from the stables he'd passed Indavara, who was too busy pulling a pail up out of the well to notice him.

'How is he?'

'Keeping busy, sir. First it was weightlifting; then he cleared the rest of the rubble outside; now he's filling every spare container with water. He's barely said a word. What happened, sir?'

Cassius described the incident. 'He almost killed him, Simo.'

The attendant had stopped carving.

'And do you know what he has been talking about all morning?'

'No, sir.'

'Abandoned babies. How terrible it is. How terrible the world is – all the cruelty and suffering and death.'

Simo looked down at the meat.

'I wonder where he would have heard talk like that.' Cassius pointed at the Gaul and kept his voice low. 'Now you listen to me, and you'd better take it in this time. He is not like you or I. He does not have – or at least cannot recall – a good family or upbringing to see him through. Most of what life he remembers was spent in an existence that I don't even want to imagine. For all his physical strength, he is fragile. And the next time he loses control of himself who knows what he might do? Or to whom?'

'Sir, I have not tried to bring him into the Faith. But he is curious.'

'Perhaps. But do not weigh him down with these burdens – worrying about every waif and stray, agonising over every supposed injustice. It does no bloody good to anyone; and certainly not him. Now, tonight, you will cook a pleasant meal and we will drink together and we will talk only of the good parts of life. Is that clear?'

'Yes, Master Cassius.'

'I hope so, Simo. Because I will not allow you to drag him down.'

Cassius tried his best. After they had eaten what was indeed a fine dinner – peppered pork belly and green beans followed by nut cake – he tried to start up a game of 'guess the emperor'. Unfortunately it died a swift death and it became irrefutably evident that the evening would be a struggle when Indavara didn't finish his meal. The bodyguard spent most of his time staring out from the top of the tower at the dark sky.

Cassius then began reminiscing about good times the three of them had spent together; the drinking competition with the crew of the *Fortuna Redux*, touring the markets of Bostra where every imaginable food and good was available, seeing the remarkable King's Tomb of Petra. Simo played along but Indavara said little. When the Gaul cleared the plates away, Cassius recalled some of the more notable girls he and Indavara had encountered and suggested a trip to a brothel. The bodyguard shook his head emphatically, remarking that the girls there were 'just another type of slave'. Cassius was out of ideas.

They sat there in the darkness. From below came the sound of Simo quietly singing as he washed up the dinner things. Around them, the streets were quiet. A light breeze was coming in off the sea. The single lamp on the table flickered.

'How is he?' Indavara asked after a while, the first time he had mentioned the incident with Scato.

'He'll be all right.'

'His neck?'

'He'll be all right. Especially when he sees the money.'

'I'll give you all the coins.'

'No. We'll go halves, like I said.'

'I don't know . . . I don't know why.'

Cassius stood up. 'Well, he shouldn't have hit you. We all lose our temper sometimes.' He walked past Indavara to the edge of the tower, patting his shoulder as he passed him. 'Try not to worry about it, these things happen. Gods, I can't believe I missed the baths *again* today. What do you think about going along tomorrow? You can do your exercises, I can have a swim. Well?'

'If you like.'

XXIV

Amathea lay back, soapy water lapping against her skin. Her hair was tied up but the lower strands were dark and wet. Sweat glistened on her cheeks and neck.

'Leave us.'

The maid put down a bottle of oil and did so, closing the door behind her. Alexon could hardly breathe; it was a warm afternoon and the bath-house was clouded with steam and scent.

'Anything?' asked Amathea.

'Good news, I think.'

'You found him?'

'No, Skiron is still looking.'

Amathea shook her head.

'But I have cultivated another source,' added Alexon quickly. 'A legionary, or rather an ex-legionary.'

'You have leverage, I trust?'

'He is in debt. Heavily.'

'You used a go-between, of course.'

'I am not a complete fool, sister.' Alexon wished he hadn't said that.

'Go on.'

'All this business about an Egyptian spy – no one has heard anything about it before or since the factory raids, so in all likelihood it was a ruse. Apparently this man working with Diadromes was at the eastern gate. None of the legionaries know him – probably works for the treasury. But we have a name: Crispian. Usually with some big bodyguard.'

'Anything else?'

'Not yet. Kallikres may know more but until we—'

'There are a lot of people waiting for our coins, brother. Sidon,

Antioch, the Cappadocians. Is there really anything to concern us?'

'We cannot be sure yet. Crispian's not housed with the army or the sergeants so we can't track him. We don't know if he's still investigating or not.'

'And the work crew?'

'They left the facility secure and are lying low. They can continue production with an hour's notice. But I would prefer to hear from Kallikres first.'

Amathea reached for her glass, showing the swell of both breasts before sinking beneath the slick of white foam once more.

Alexon – who was still holding his riding cape – moved it in front of his groin. While he tried to think of something unarousing, Amathea sipped at her wine and gazed up at the steam swirling above the bath.

Alexon found he could not think of anything else. Perhaps she would relent this time. 'Amathea, I am rather dirty – from the ride. Could I—'

From outside came the noise of heavy footsteps then a rap on the door. 'Master Alexon. Are you there?'

'Wait, Skiron.'

Alexon met him outside. 'Any luck?'

The attendant hadn't even had time to take off his riding gloves. 'No. The tricky swine is clearly trying to avoid us.'

'You don't think he's gone? I mean permanently?'

'No, sir, not without the boy. Shall I keep searching?'

'Yes.' Alexon returned inside. 'Still no sign of Kallikres. Perhaps we can use the boy as bait.'

'I don't know why you haven't done so already, brother. Use whatever methods you must to bring that deviant under control. We cannot afford to delay delivery to our customers for much longer.'

'I know.' Alexon put his cape on a chair. 'So . . . may I join you?'

'If you wish, it is a large bath. I should tell you, though – it is that time of the month. There may be some blood in the water.'

Alexon knew full well it wasn't that time of the month. But what could one say to such a thing?

'Ah. I shall get on with this Kallikres business, then.'

'Do so, brother. Please do so.'

Cassius looked down at the clump of weed and driftwood entangled in a fishing net. There was a dead gull floating past too: a shapeless mess of grey feathers and bones identifiable only by the head and beak. A few yards away, two lads babbled in Aramaic as they lowered their crab lines from the top of the breakwater. Cassius was leaning against a squat stone tower from which a huge rusting chain ran into the water, emerging on the other side of the harbour entrance, where it was attached to an identical structure. Apparently it had been originally constructed for defence but the chain now rested on the bottom and the workings were so old that it could not be raised.

Indavara – who'd been inspecting the crabs in the boys' pail – came up beside him, eyes narrowed against the midday sun. 'Looks a bit like the *Fortuna*.'

The freighter entering the harbour was being towed by a dory manned by a dozen local oarsmen. The sea was calm and they were making easy work of pulling a vessel ten times the size of their own. Most of the freighter's crew were on deck rolling up a sail, weathered skin dark against their pale tunics. To the rear, an older man stood behind the helmsman, clutching the tiller bar that controlled the ship.

'Never hard to spot the captain,' said Cassius.

'Wonder where Asdribar and his mates are.'

'Could be just about anywhere at this time of year. It would be nice to get back to Rhodes some time, eh? You could say hello to Annia.'

'And you to Clara.'

'I'd do more than say hello.'

The ship was almost past them. Cassius used his hand to shield his eyes from the glare coming off the water. Unlike many vessels, the freighter had no metal plaque on the stern, just a name rendered in white paint.

'*Okeia*. That's her.' Cassius was already on his way back along the breakwater. 'Let's go.'

The report had arrived from Quentin the previous afternoon; the first good news in the five days since the factory inspections. Cassius had been on the verge of returning to Tripolis to liaise with the treasury man and look at the investigation afresh. Almost two weeks had elapsed since they'd first met and it was hard to avoid the conclusion that his efforts in Berytus had been utterly pointless. Diadromes had ensured that the men guarding the city gates remained vigilant but they had still found nothing; nor had the Gorgos case uncovered anything relevant.

But this lead seemed promising. A sharp-eyed assistant procurator up in Seleucia – the port that served Antioch – had noted a shipment of bronze sheeting bound for Berytus. This was not in itself unusual; as Cassius had already established, numerous industries made use of it in the city. But there were only three well-established freight businesses which specialised in transporting metals by ship along the Syrian coast. The *Okeia* – about which little was known – did not work for any of them. Cosmas had dug up another interesting fact: the vessel had visited Berytus only once before – two months ago, about the time when the counterfeiting gang might have started production.

The sergeant was waiting for them at the main wharf, looking on from behind a stack of barrels as the *Okeia* came alongside.

'That her?'

'That's her.' Cassius had grown impatient waiting around for the whole morning and had walked out on to the breakwater when they'd spied three vessels turning east towards the harbour. The *Okeia* was last in, having taken a maddeningly long time to lower her sails.

'So now what?' he asked.

'The captain will report to the harbour master to tell him what cargo he'll be unloading and when he intends to depart. Once the harbour master gives permission, he can unload.'

'Bronze should be easy to spot, right?'

'Yes. The sheets are usually quite large – thin but very heavy. Apparently they load them into carts separated by reed matting.'

'What if it goes to more than one location?'

Cosmas took his eyes off the ship for a moment and pointed at a nearby cart where a vendor was selling bags of nuts. Standing there talking to him were two of the men from the Gorgos raid.

'Ah, Vespilo and . . .'

'Gessius.'

Like Cosmas, they wore nothing to mark them out as sergeants and were armed only with daggers.

'Will they use *those* carts?' asked Indavara.

'Don't point,' said Cassius sharply.

Lined up on the wharf close to the road were half a dozen vehicles. The horses were clearly used to the work; they stood placidly despite all the noise from the sailors and loaders.

'Not sure,' said Cosmas. 'Sometimes they're just hired on the spot, sometimes they work for the outfits where the goods are headed. We'll see soon enough.'

'Not that soon,' said Cassius. The captain was still overseeing the tying of the mooring ropes and the gangplank hadn't even been lowered yet.

'We need somewhere better to observe from.' He looked along the seafront and saw a respectable-looking tavern where a 'merchant' like himself might eat lunch. 'That'll do.'

By the time the bronze sheeting was finally unloaded, Cassius could have ordered dinner. Gessius had dozed off twice and he'd had to limit Indavara and the legionaries to three mugs of well-watered wine.

Most of the *Okeia*'s cargo had already been taken away, including scores of amphoras, bales of cotton and baskets of iron implements. Once all this had been dispatched, the hands were called into the hold and up came the sheets, each one requiring four men to lift it. Three sturdy carts had been moved up to take delivery and – from what Cassius and Cosmas had observed – they seemed to be bound for three different destinations.

As the first cart set off, Cosmas sent Gessius and Vespilo to discreetly follow.

Cassius examined the other two vehicles and their drivers. 'Not much to choose between them.'

'Actually, there is,' replied Cosmas. 'See the one closest to us? Those markings on the side – it belongs to a man named Kimon. He runs a cart-hire and warehousing concern not unlike that friend of the Gorgos brothers.'

'Ah. As your sergeants checked all those factories and workshops with their own transportation, I'm inclined to think a hired vehicle might be of more interest.'

'I agree,' said Cosmas.

'We'll take it.'

Cassius turned to Indavara, who was slumped on the table and looked about ready to slit his wrists.

'Drink up.'

Following the cart was not easy. The driver clearly knew the city well and favoured only wider routes where he could avoid delays. Cassius and Indavara had to alternate between a swift walk and a jog, which attracted attention from a few cityfolk but thankfully not the driver and his compatriot.

'Thank the gods,' said Cassius, flicking sweat off his forehead as they finally got a break. The cart had reached a narrow side street and it took the pair a while to manoeuvre the horses and the vehicle around the corner without hitting the kerb. Once they were under way again, Cassius and Indavara sidled up to the corner and looked on. As the cart stopped about a hundred paces away, one of the men gave a shout. Another tight turn took them off the street.

Cassius and Indavara walked on, slowing as they neared the gate. It was a sturdy affair of iron bars and spikes set in the middle of a high wall. Beyond was a medium-sized townhouse similar to those adjacent. The two drivers were down on the ground and talking to some other men who had just exited a timber-built workshop attached to the rear of the dwelling.

'They make something in there,' said Cassius. 'So it may already have been checked by the sergeants. Let's take a look at the front.'

They passed a wall covered with graffiti.

'These names,' said Indavara. 'I've seen them all over the city.'

'Candidates for elections,' explained Cassius as they rounded a corner, 'advertisements of a sort, I suppose.'

'If all these weavers don't like the magistrate, why don't they just vote for someone else?'

'The likes of them can't vote for magistrates; that's decided by the council and the rest of the higher classes. Common people can vote only for the assembly, which is much less powerful, though it can influence the council to some extent. From what we've heard, I doubt Pomponianus pays it much attention.'

They took the next turn to the right and found themselves on a broad, porticoed avenue. Judging by the appearance of the citizens perusing the stores, this was clearly one of the more affluent areas of the city. A group of stonemasons were making some final modifications to a broad plinth in the middle of the avenue. Cassius noted from the plaque already mounted that it was to bear a statue of Aurelian himself.

'Fourth one along?' said Indavara.

'That's it,' said Cassius, relieved when they entered the cool shade beneath the portico. They passed a carpet-maker, a mosaic-maker and a clothier before reaching the front of the building. On one side of the door was a glassed window offering a display of fine jewellery. Above it was a silver plaque so well polished that they could see their faces. It bore the name of the jeweller: *Isagoras*.

Cassius inspected the goods on offer: necklaces, bracelets, brooches, clasps, many of them inlaid with gems.

'Not much bronze,' observed Indavara.

'True. But they may also make products for the cheaper end of the market.'

'Want to look inside? You fit in very well around here.'

Cassius was still wearing his merchant's outfit.

'Not sure there's much point. A jewellery-maker taking delivery of some bronze? Hardly unusual. Let's get back to the head-quarters, see if the others have got anywhere.'

Cosmas also had little to report. He'd arrived back before them and had trailed the last cart to a weapon-smiths. Like Isagoras the jewel-maker's, this building had already been checked by the sergeants.

Gessius had more promising news, having left Vespilo moni-toring the warehouse where their cart ended up. The driver had been admitted by a guard and departed half an hour later, the vehicle empty. A crew of five (presumably there for the unloading) had left shortly after, leaving only the guard. The warehouse was in an area close to the harbour and Gessius had found himself a decent observation point at a nearby inn.

'Well,' said Cassius, 'hardly conclusive proof of nefarious activity but we must watch that warehouse.'

'Unfortunately I can't leave Vespilo there,' said Cosmas. 'He and Gessius here have other duties. I was only able to borrow them for today.'

'In the absence of anything else even vaguely promising, we must find out where that bronze ends up.'

'I'll go now and watch the warehouse tonight,' offered the sergeant. 'If it's still there tomorrow, perhaps you could take over?'

'Oh, joy,' said Cassius with a sigh. 'Don't worry, Cosmas. We'll take our turn.'

XXV

They left the tower before dawn. As the city awoke, doors were opened, shutters latched, chamber pots emptied. Thin trails of smoke from scores of fires reached high into the pink sky.

Indavara had told Corbulo that Simo needed his help fetching some food before they went to meet Cosmas. Corbulo had listened to this with his eyes half open, then struggled out of bed and down the stairs to lock the tower door behind them.

Simo hardly spoke until they were nearing Berytus's largest statue of the Emperor Hadrian, where Elder Cobon and his group had already gathered. The Gaul stopped in the shadows of an awning. 'I should not be doing this. I should not have told you.'

Returning from the market the previous day, he'd confided to Indavara that he'd bumped into one of the Christians. Cobon had discovered another group of paupers living by a rubbish dump; the men would take provisions to them while the women again searched for abandoned babies.

Indavara wasn't entirely sure himself why he wanted to go. He didn't enjoy putting Simo through all this worry but it was something he felt he had to do. 'I told you – he's all talk.'

'You can't be certain of that.'

'So what, then? You will have no part of this "good work"?'

'I want to, but—'

'Simo, they are waiting for us and we haven't any time to waste. Come on.'

———8———

The dump was on the southern edge of Berytus, surrounded by a decrepit section of the old city walls, some ramshackle apartment buildings and two large encampments. Cobon had learned that one camp was occupied by more Palmyran refugees, the other by nomads from the Syrian desert. Bordering the dump was a dusty track and a shallow ditch filled with brown water. Several narrow paths led over earth bridges into the piles of refuse, which must have covered at least a square mile.

Elder Cobon stopped by one of the paths, where two lads with a handcart had just arrived to discard a mound of seashells. Cobon spoke to the men – all of whom were carrying sacks of food – and they set off towards the closest of the camps. Amongst the women was the one Indavara had spoken to at the church-house and the girl they'd met on the first visit.

Indavara tapped Simo's arm. 'I'm going to stay here.'

'But the men are going to the camp.'

'Shouldn't someone watch them? A place like this?'

'Do you want to come with us?' The older woman had remained behind while the others walked into the dump.

'They don't need me to hand out bread,' said Indavara. 'I could help you look.'

'Another pair of eyes would be useful but you should probably ask Elder Cobon.'

The dynamic leader was moving quickly and hadn't even noticed what was going on behind him.

Simo shook his head. 'I'll meet you here, then. We mustn't be too long.'

As he hurried after the others, Indavara followed the woman over the bridge.

'I'm Alfidia,' she said as they passed the two lads, who were already shovelling out the seashells. 'What's your name?'

'Indavara.'

'I've not heard that before.'

He never knew what to say to that.

'Why must you get back quickly?' she continued. 'An impatient master, I suppose?'

'Yes. Though he's not really my master.'

'Is it true that you do not follow the Faith, Indavara?'

'It is.'

He thought that might upset her but Alfidia just smiled kindly. 'Then can I ask why you are here?'

'I don't know really.'

They reached the others, who had stopped and formed a circle. Before anyone could speak, a little boy of about eight came running up to them. 'I saw one, I saw one. Give us a coin and I'll tell you where.'

'Or you'll just run off with it like you did last time,' said one of the women.

They tried to ignore him, even when he started pulling on their tunics. Alfidia shooed him away but he turned his attention to the young woman. 'Come on, just some food, then? Just a bit of food.'

She tried to move away but he was insistent.

One step forward from Indavara was enough to change his mind.

'Curse you all!' he yelled before running off.

The young woman nodded a shy thank-you.

'This is Indavara,' said Alfidia. 'He is going to help us this morning. Now, shall we divide up as usual?'

While they spoke, Indavara looked at the young woman. She was quite tall and very thin, so thin that her pale blue tunic hung straight from her bony shoulders. Indavara thought her quite pretty and didn't mind the faint brown birthmark on her right cheek. Her curly black hair was tied up messily with what looked like string. Aware that the others might notice his interest, he dragged his eyes away.

Alfidia had decided he would help her and, once the group split up, led the way. Indavara told himself that the girl wasn't important, that he should concentrate on what they were there for. Alfidia stayed on one side of the path and directed him to the other. 'They're often left in baskets or wrappings. We must listen carefully too.'

As they ventured farther into the dump, the smell worsened. It wasn't as bad as what came up out of the sewers, but there was clearly a lot of rotten food somewhere and in some places a fetid steam was rising. Some of the higher mounds of refuse were three times the height of a man. Indavara still found it almost impossible to believe that they might find a baby here. Aside from the stench and the dirt, the dump was strewn with dangers: shattered amphoras, broken tiles, fragments of glass.

They passed a group of lads dumping animal bones, apparently unconcerned that most of them ended up on the path. More boys appeared at the summit of another mound, wicker baskets strapped to their backs, hands wrapped in cloth. Alfidia spoke to them in Aramaic then continued looking. As the path bore around to the right, Indavara kept his eyes on the rubbish.

Broken red clay lamps. A mouldy rectangle of leather. Rotting apples. A block of pockmarked limestone. A sandal. The skin of a melon.

Movement. But it was just a big black-shelled insect, crawling across the handle of yet another broken amphora.

He realised Alfidia had stopped. Now that they were away from the boys, it was quieter. 'Listen. Your hearing will be better than mine.'

'Not in this ear.' He pointed at it, then stayed silent. They listened for more than a minute but heard nothing.

Continuing on, they came upon a little dog sniffing something by the path. Alfidia thanked the Lord when she discovered it was just some old animal hides.

'What do you do for work?' she asked as they set off again.
'Bodyguard.'

Alfidia glanced at the dagger upon his belt. 'Violence is a sin. The Lord tells us that we must not harm others.'

Indavara thought of the legionary. What was his name? Scato. He couldn't remember actually attacking him; just the look on his face when he let go. 'Sometimes it just happens.'

They kept searching for another half an hour then met up with the others in the centre of the dump. When he heard that no one had found anything, Indavara felt disappointed, then realised how stupid that was.

'A good thing, I suppose,' he said as they trudged towards the street.

'Yes,' replied Alfidia. 'Especially as we haven't found somewhere for the other little one yet.'

'Where do they go?' asked Indavara, remembering what Corbulo had told him.

'To good homes. Only good homes.'

Indavara glanced over his shoulder. The young woman was behind them, walking alone. Knowing he wouldn't get a better chance to talk to her, he dropped back.

'Another hot day.'

'Yes, sir.'

Indavara might have laughed had he not been so nervous. 'You don't have to call me sir. I'm Indavara. What's your name?'

'Mahalie.'

He wiped sweat off his top lip. 'Ah.'

She suddenly seemed keen to catch up with the others.

'Is that Greek?'

She still hadn't looked at him. 'No.'

'Aramaic?'

She nodded.

'What do you do for work, Mahalie?'

'Don't want to talk.' With that, she ran on after the others.

Indavara slowed down, face glowing. Once the women reached the edge of the dump, Mahalie spoke briefly to Alfidia then hurried away.

'That's why the men should stay with the men,' said one of the women. 'You leave her alone.'

His face grew even warmer. 'Sorry.' He walked past them, towards the camp.

'Indavara.'

Seeing Alfidia coming after him, he stopped. 'I'm sorry.'

'Don't be. There's no harm in talking to someone but Mahalie's very quiet. Especially with men.'

'I didn't . . . I wasn't trying to . . .'

'I know.'

They both watched as Mahalie disappeared around a corner.

'I do hope she doesn't get into trouble,' said Alfidia. 'She can't come very often.'

'She is a servant?'

'A house maid.'

'A slave?'

'Yes.'

'Are you?' asked Indavara.

'No. Some of the others are, though. What about you?'

'I was. Does she have any family?'

'Just a sister but they were split up when her master brought her here from Antioch. Poor thing, we found her at the Temple of Aphrodite, seeking sanctuary. She had run away but the priests wouldn't let her stay, so we took her to the church-house. Eventually, she decided to go back to her master. I think she enjoys being part of our group, though it's hard to tell – she's so quiet.'

'Why had she run away?'

Alfidia looked back at the others, who were all staring at her. 'I shouldn't gossip like this. Will you come to help us again, Indavara?'

'I'd like to. Do you come every day?'

'We try to send someone, yes. Sometimes the boys find a little one and bring it to the church-house. They know they'll get a coin or two from Elder Cobon.'

The Christian men had emerged from the camp.

'I should be going. Good day.'

'Good day, Indavara. And do not worry – you have done nothing wrong. The Lord knows it.'

'By the great gods, what a shit hole.'

The tavern was quite possibly the worst Cassius had ever seen. The proprietor had just left, having escorted them up to the second-floor room, where they found Cosmas sitting by the single window.

'Good view, though, sir,' said the sergeant. 'And that fellow didn't ask much to keep his mouth shut.'

'Probably his only source of income.'

There had been no customers down in the parlour, nor any sign that the other rooms were occupied. The walls were streaked with dirt of varying shades and visible collations of dust had gathered in the corners. The 'bed' was about a foot high, with straw leaking out of a holed mattress. While Indavara drank water from his flask, Cassius stepped over some rodent droppings and joined Cosmas.

'Over there, sir.'

The warehouse was about fifty yards down the road to the left but because of a collapsed apartment block they could see almost the entire building. It was brick-built, with a gently sloping tiled roof; perhaps forty yards long and half as wide. There were two gates: one across the broad entrance, one within the surrounding ten-foot wall. A sentry was sitting on a stool in the shade, picking at his toes.

'Just the one way in?' asked Cassius.

'Yes, and just the one guard. Swapped with his mate at dawn. It's odd – no other comings and goings.'

'Quiet round here,' said Indavara, joining Cassius by the window as Cosmas stood up and moved aside.

The sergeant yawned and inadvertently belched. 'Sorry. Long night.'

'Best go and get some sleep,' advised Cassius.

'I wish. Diadromes needs me on the Gorgos job. I might catch a couple of hours at headquarters later.'

Cassius looked around for somewhere clean to place his satchel and cape. There was nowhere, so he dumped them on the bed.

'How's that going, by the way?'

'More arrests and the court are writing up charges. Apparently Pomponianus is keen to hurry things along.'

'Successful prosecutions before the election?'

Cosmas nodded as he tightened his belt. 'I can be back by the ninth hour. That all right?'

'It'll have to be.'

'If we decide to keep this up, I can hire someone reliable to keep an eye on the place.'

'Good,' said Cassius.

Indavara had noticed the plate lying on the floor. 'How's the food?'

'Don't ask.'

'Tell the owner to bring in another chair,' said Cassius.

'Will do,' replied Cosmas as he left.

'Shall I take first watch?' offered Indavara.

'If you like.' Cassius looked around again and wrinkled his nose at the smell of mould. 'Ah, the glamour of life with Imperial Security.'

Indavara pulled the chair forward to improve his view. 'Still think the gang's here in Berytus?'

'No idea. But if I don't have something to report within the next few days, I doubt it will be my problem much longer.'

'So what then?'

'I hate to think. Probably something dangerous.'

'So we could be leaving soon?'

Cassius pointed at the window. 'I'd be grateful if you could try to master watching and talking at the same time.'

A knock on the door.

'Come.'

The elderly proprietor brought in a chair, which Cassius took from him.

'Some wine and two mugs. And make sure it's all spotless.'

The Syrian muttered something and withdrew.

Cassius sat beside Indavara. 'You seem a bit more yourself today.'

The bodyguard kept his eyes on the warehouse. 'Again, sorry about . . . what happened.'

'I told you – forget it.'

'What you said at the gate – about the good people do.'

Cassius brushed horsehair off his tunic. 'Yes?'

'You were right.'

'Well, there's plenty of evil too, I'll grant you. But it is worth trying to keep things in perspective. Do you remember our discussion about Marcus Aurelius?'

'Yes.'

'He said: "Dwell on the beauty of life. Watch the stars, and see yourself running with them."'

'I understand the first part. But the second?'

'I've never been entirely sure. But I like it.'

━8━

257

Indavara was out getting food when the two riders arrived. Cassius dragged the chair closer to the window and peered out as the men dismounted. They tied their horses to a ring set into the wall then each detached two bulging saddlebags. The guard unlocked the gate and escorted them into the warehouse. Cassius looked up and down the street. Apart from a woman emptying a tub of water down a drain, all was quiet. He glanced at the hourglass he had brought; it was half past the sixth hour. He picked up the sheet of paper and stick of charcoal on top of his satchel and made a note.

Heavy boots thumped on the staircase, then came a knock. 'It's me.'

'Well, come in then.'

'I thought you might be worried,' said Indavara as he entered.

Cassius realised his mistake. 'Sorry, you're right. I doubt anyone could ever find us here but I suppose I mustn't let my guard down.'

'Who was on the horses?'

'Two men. They took something inside. Still in there.'

Cassius frowned when he noticed Indavara was carrying a wicker basket.

'I had to buy it to carry everything. I've got fresh rolls, spiced sausage, goat's cheese, apples and raisin cake.'

'What about the water?'

'Found a fountain – very clear.'

'Well done.'

Cassius's stomach was growling but he kept his eyes on the warehouse. 'You eat first, I'll—'

Indavara already had a roll in his mouth.

The two visitors left half an hour later and before Cosmas returned to take over, Cassius had made two more notes: one concerned the new sentry who replaced his compatriot around the eighth hour, the other the cart that arrived with another delivery shortly after.

'Six amphoras and a barrel.'

'I'd love to know what's in them,' said the sergeant, now wearing a fresh tunic and smelling rather more pleasant than when he'd left.

'As would I,' replied Cassius. 'There's no way that they could hide an oven in that warehouse, is there?'

'I don't see how – where would the smoke and the fumes go?'

'Did you get anywhere with the building owner?'

'I've got a man working on it. We should know by tomorrow.'

'And locally?'

'I had Gessius make a few enquiries on the street but nothing of interest came up. We could try again, I suppose.'

'Perhaps if we don't get anywhere.' Cassius stood up and put his satchel over his shoulder. 'Now, when shall we take over again?'

'Third hour of night? If you can go through to the morning I'll get someone else along first thing.'

'Very well. By the way, I just about managed to stop Indavara consuming every last morsel so there's a bit of food left.'

The bodyguard shrugged as he sank his teeth into an apple.

'Thank you. See you later.' Cosmas sat down on the chair, already twisting his beard.

'Back to the tower?' enquired Indavara as they hurried down the stairs.

'Briefly. After hours in this pit and several more coming tonight there's only one place I wish to spend the afternoon.'

'The baths?'

'The baths.'

XXVI

Cassius was woken by Indavara's snoring. He cursed quietly but was grateful that he'd been spared the shame of the bodyguard finding him asleep during his shift. He sat up in the chair, rubbed his eyes and looked down at the warehouse. According to Cosmas, the guard had been on duty as night fell; presumably he was still there now but not bothering to keep a light. Of the building itself, Cassius could see nothing but the angular outline. There wouldn't have been much to observe except that a combination of moonlight and a few lanterns partly illuminated the street.

Indavara – slumped beside a little table where a candle burned – snored on.

Cassius checked his hourglass: the bottom half was almost full, which meant that midnight was close. Resting his elbows on his knees and his chin on his hands, he continued the vigil. After a while, he realised something was moving down on the street. He watched the shape until it revealed itself to be nothing more than a large rat nosing its way along the gutter.

He thought of all the other darkened streets and alleys; and all the buildings here and in the other cities of Syria and beyond. Where were his enemies? Still hunting him? Had they tracked him to Berytus?

Despite the warmth of the night, he shivered. Every day without incident should have brought him solace but he just felt as if he was waiting for the inevitable moment when they finally caught up with him. He couldn't live with this fear indefinitely, he knew that much. Once this job for Marcellinus was over, there were only two alternatives. He had to either get far, far away from Arabia and Syria or turn the tables on his pursuers and find out once and for all who they were.

At least the evening had brought a little respite. Floating in the pool of the warm room, he had closed his eyes and imagined he was at the baths nearest to his family home; a place he had visited almost every day for a decade. With the obvious exception of female company, there was everything a man could ask for: friendly faces, stimulating conversation, endless gossip, tales of adventures and exotic lands, jokes and japes aplenty. Even his father had been more relaxed there, proud to be out in public with his bright, handsome son; often challenging him to a swimming race until Cassius had finally become too good.

Indavara's chin dropped on to his chest and he ceased snoring.

Someone inside the tavern was coughing; presumably the owner – they still hadn't seen any other residents or staff. When the coughing finally stopped, Cassius heard the soft tap of footsteps below. He looked downward and saw three men arrive on foot by the warehouse gate, one of them holding a half-shuttered lantern. The other two had heavy packs over their shoulders. Soon the guard appeared from the shadows.

Cassius stuck out a boot and kicked Indavara gently on the leg. The bodyguard snorted then asked what was going on.

'See for yourself.'

Indavara got up on his knees and shuffled over to the window.

After a brief discussion, the new arrivals hurried inside and the guard locked the gate behind them. The lantern painted a moving yellow blotch that disappeared when they entered the warehouse.

'What do you reckon?' asked Indavara.

'Hard to believe they're on legitimate business at this time of night.'

'Want to take a look?'

'How?'

'We can get over that wall. And they didn't shut the warehouse door. And there's no dogs. And they're only armed with daggers.'

'I don't know,' said Cassius. 'If they are involved in the counterfeiting this can't be where they're doing it.'

'So then we're wasting time here. It would be good to know one way or the other.'

'Mmm.'

'I checked the wall this afternoon,' added Indavara. 'There's no glass, no spearheads. No problem.'

Cassius reminded himself not to be too easily swayed by the bodyguard. Indavara was a little more thoughtful these days but invariably favoured action over inaction. But he was right about the possibility of wasted time. It was better to know.

Cassius stood up and took his sword belt off the chair. As he hung it from his shoulder he heard Indavara glug down some wine.

'Now listen. You will stay calm, won't you? Whatever happens.'

'Just a bit of sneaking around, right?'

'Indavara. We don't know what—'

The bodyguard snuffed out the candle with two fingers. 'I think you're the one who needs to stay calm.'

The proprietor wasn't particularly happy about being woken but a couple of sesterces shut him up. This was clearly not an area where doors remained unbolted in the hours of darkness so Cassius told him to wait until they returned. He and Indavara walked fifty paces to the right before crossing the street, then approached carefully until they were between the ruined apartment block and the warehouse wall. Pausing for a moment, they agreed they could hear nothing from inside, then proceeded to the rear corner.

'How do we do this, then?' asked Cassius.

'You give me a leg up, then I pull you up after me. Tuck your sword into your main belt.'

'Why?'

'So it doesn't clang against the wall when you jump – that's why.'

'Ah.'

'Now – back against the wall. Link your hands together and give me a good boost.'

'Those boots of yours had better be clean, I—'

Indavara was already on his way. Cassius thought his grip might falter but he held on and heaved as best he could. The bodyguard's other boot thumped into the wall an inch from his ear and in an instant he was up. Cassius turned round and watched him scramble into a sitting position.

'Looks clear. Take a good run. One foot on the wall. One hand up to me.'

Cassius checked his sword and kicked some pebbles out of the way as he retreated. He reckoned this wasn't all that different from the high jump competitions he'd performed in as a youth and he took the same five quick steps. With a bit of purchase from his boot, he threw his arm upward. Indavara clamped a hand on his wrist and hauled him the rest of the way. Cassius found himself lying across the wall, staring down at the murky yard below.

'Checking the ground, eh? Good idea.'

'Most amusing.'

As Cassius righted himself, Indavara lowered himself, dropping the last two feet.

'Can't hear anything,' whispered the bodyguard. 'Come down.'

Cassius somehow scraped his chin as he hung from the wall but landed well.

Indavara was already moving. 'Watch your footing – bit of rubble and a few holes.'

Cassius followed him to the closest corner of the warehouse. The large, circular windows high above allowed them to hear the voices inside, though they could not make out what the men were saying.

'Up to the front?' whispered Indavara.

'We're not going to find out anything from here.'

On they went, staying close to the wall and moving as quietly as they could.

When they reached the other end of the building, Cassius put a hand on Indavara's shoulder. 'Careful, they might have left a sentry.'

They took it one step at a time, always stopping when there was a pause or a change in the muffled speech drifting out of the warehouse. Once at the gate, they peered inside. The lantern had been put on a low table and the men were gathered around it. Cassius couldn't see their faces so he counted legs.

'All four of them.'

'So we going in?'

Cassius grimaced as he received a faceful of Indavara's breath (the bodyguard had monopolised the goat's cheese). 'It'd be useful to hear what they're saying but what if they see us? Or hear us?'

'I'm guessing this is a "no blades" situation, right?'

'Right.'

'We run straight back to that corner, repeat the routine and get back over the wall. No way they'll catch us.'

Cassius couldn't really find fault with the escape plan. 'Fair enough. Lead on.'

The gate had been left slightly ajar. He turned side on, and squeezed through rather more easily than Indavara. They took ten more paces inside the warehouse then stood still in complete darkness, fifty feet from the four men.

'Close enough?' whispered Indavara.

'Yes.'

Though Cassius could make out some bulky shapes surrounding the foursome, it was impossible to see exactly what was being stored in the warehouse. They were speaking Greek.

'. . . can hide his stuff at his brother's. Don't see how they'll get to him.'

'What about Ibykos?'

'I'll talk to him tomorrow.'

'And his girl?'

'He ain't with her no more.'

'The new one – the baker's daughter.'

'I know – he ain't with her no more!'

'Macar?'

'Saw him this morning. He's stashed everything in his uncle's cellar out in that village. No problem there.'

'Who else? We have to think of everyone. Every little thing. Could be tomorrow they come knocking on our doors.'

'We sure this place is safe?'

'Gods, it better be, the stuff we've got in here—'

Cassius heard something smack against the exterior wall.

The four conspirators looked up. Two drew their daggers.

'Go,' hissed Cassius. 'Out!'

As he and Indavara cleared the gate, two men holding lanterns clambered up from the street side on to the wall.

'They're running for it!' shouted one of them.

Cassius and Indavara hared around the side of the warehouse and towards the far corner. Another light appeared above the wall to their right.

'Who are they?' asked Indavara.

'Quiet,' replied Cassius. 'Let's just get out of here. Oh, gods.'

Another man with a light had just appeared close to their corner.

'Other side,' said Indavara.

They cut left and ran past the rear of the warehouse. Cassius felt weeds thrash his legs then his left boot thumped into something. He at least managed to turn as he fell, protecting his face and striking the ground with his shoulder. He rolled to a halt then cried out as his hand was stung by some nettles.

'Corbulo, where are you?'

'Back here.'

Cassius couldn't even see Indavara. All he could see was yet another man with a lantern coming over another section of the wall.

'Where?'

'Here.'

At last Indavara emerged out of the darkness. He helped Cassius up.

'At the back!' came a shout. 'More of them at the back.'

Three lights and three men were converging on their position.

'We're not going to make it,' said Cassius.

'Sir, over here,' shouted one of the men as they closed in.

Cassius spied the club in his hand. 'City sergeants. I'll talk to them.'

He walked towards the nearest man. 'You there, I am an army officer. We are conducting a—'

'Of course you are.'

The sergeant's club thudded into his stomach. Gasping for breath, Cassius fell to his knees. He would have given in to the pain and rolled over were it not for the sight of Indavara marching past him. Cassius grabbed his belt.

'No!' he spluttered. 'Indavara, *do not fight*. We will sort this out.'

Cassius gripped his aching gut with one hand but kept hold of the bodyguard with the other. 'Promise me you'll not fight.'

'Drop the blades, big lad,' shouted one of the sergeants as more of them appeared from the gloom.

'Just listen to me,' yelled Cassius. 'We're—'

'I said drop them!'

Indavara pulled his sword belt from his shoulder. It landed on the ground next to Cassius. Next came the dagger.

Cassius gave in to the pain and fell forward.

By the time they'd been taken from the covered cart and shoved into the headquarters building, he had recovered enough to speak. To his immense relief, Indavara had stayed quiet and calm, even when their hands had been bound behind their backs.

However, he now found himself in a quandary. The four men from the factory were clearly confused about the two strangers also captured and Cassius didn't want to announce his real identity with them present. But as they were now being escorted by no less than eight sergeants towards the holding cell, he was left with little choice. He had hoped to spy a friendly face but recognised none of the magistrate's men.

'Excuse me. You there.' He addressed what he gathered was the senior sergeant.

'What?'

'Listen, I am an army officer. You need to talk to Cosmas or Deputy Magistrate Diadromes.'

Some of the guards laughed.

'Army officer? You look more like a student to me.'

'Just get Cosmas down here. At once.'

'Oh, don't worry, I'm sure he'll be here in the morning. There'll be plenty of people wanting to talk to you lot.'

They rounded a corner; at the end of the corridor was the cell. Two sergeants were on duty and on the other side of the reinforced gate behind them were about a dozen prisoners already inspecting the new arrivals. One of the guards poked his club at them and told them to move back. The other took a large ring of keys from his belt and eyed his prospective charges.

A couple of the prisoners shouted greetings; another man shouted an insult. Both were told to shut up by the senior man, who ordered the guard with the keys to open up. The sergeants began untying the men and escorting them inside one at a time.

Cassius and Indavara were at the back, having been last out of the cart.

'Listen to me,' insisted Cassius. 'This is a mistake. I'm telling you I'm an army officer.'

'Don't bother,' said one of the men from the warehouse. 'They've got us and that's it.'

His compatriots soon caught on to the game.

'They're not going to believe you, mate.'

'Don't embarrass yourself.'

Cassius shrugged off a guard who tried to shove him forward. 'Just listen to me!'

The senior sergeant grabbed him by his tunic. 'You need to calm down.'

'And you need to listen.'

The guard looked at Indavara. 'And I suppose he's an army officer too?'

'My bodyguard. By the great and honoured gods, I swear I am telling the truth.'

'Maybe. But I know all the army officers in Berytus and you're not one of them.'

Cassius lowered his voice. 'I'm with Imperial Security.'

'Prove it.'

Cassius didn't even have the badge with him. 'I can't but—'

'Listen. I was told to raid that warehouse and grab everyone and everything. Which I've done.'

'I know Diadromes personally,' countered Cassius. 'He will be very angry. Get him down here immediately.'

'At this time of night? Oh, he'll be angry all right – with me. If you're telling the truth then we can sort it out in the morning. In you go.'

Cassius looked at the faces of the prisoners. 'With *them*? You can't—'

One of the sergeants pushed Indavara past Cassius towards the cell. The bodyguard reacted; bucking backwards and knocking the guard into the wall.

'Corbulo, I'm not going in there. Not behind bars.'

One of the guards took his club and prodded Indavara's chest. 'You'll go where you're told to, sunshine.'

Cassius's hands were still bound but he walked up to Indavara and stood close. 'There's no need to get angry. We can just wait for Cosmas.'

Indavara was staring at the cell.

'It'll be all right,' said Cassius.

The senior sergeant intervened. 'You going to listen to your friend?'

Indavara took a deep breath then nodded.

'Then I'll untie you.'

The sergeant did so, with every one of the other guards watching. They all seemed very relieved when Indavara shook the stiffness out of his hands then walked into the cell. Once Cassius was free, he went in too, the door clanging shut behind him.

'You lot behave yourselves,' said the sergeant before departing with the others, leaving the two guards on duty.

There were about twenty prisoners in total, some of whom looked as if they had been there quite a while. The four from the warehouse stood together, eyeing Cassius and Indavara. Cassius thought it wise to take the initiative and strode straight

268

past them. The Syrians did not react and he and Indavara kept walking until they reached the far wall. They turned round and leant against the cold stone; at least now they could see any threat coming.

Unsurprisingly, the cell made the tavern seem the height of luxury. It was hexagonal in shape and constructed entirely of brick, including the roof and the four wide columns. Six splashes of light were provided by lanterns on hooks, leaving several areas cloaked in darkness. Close to the gate was a large amphora, presumably containing water. There was only one tiny window; above the latrine, which was a roughly hewn hole ringed with shit. Cassius could smell it.

'Let's just try and blend into the background,' he said, more in hope than expectation. It had often occurred to him that remaining unnoticed was not their strong point. He was six inches taller than most men and Indavara had his sturdy, battered body and disfigured ear to mark him out.

Some of the sleepy prisoners now retreated to the sides of the cell, where Cassius spied a few blankets, mugs and bowls. The men from the warehouse spoke quietly, occasionally glancing towards the rear of the cell.

'Brilliant move, by the way,' said Indavara, 'announcing to a bunch of prisoners that we're in the army.'

'They won't try anything. Not with the guards outside.'

'*They* might.'

Cassius had been so focused on the four that he'd only just noticed the two who'd emerged from behind one of the columns. One was tall and well built, the other much smaller, with one very distinctive feature.

'Well, well,' said Cassius. 'Knuckles and Greyboy.'

The Gorgos brothers looked at him and Indavara for a moment, then walked up to the other four.

'So they got you lot too, Trenico.'

'Ah,' said the leader. 'Thought you might be here.'

The six men greeted each other with weary nods and handshakes.

'Oh, gods,' said Cassius.

'Doesn't bother me,' said Indavara. 'I've got some unfinished business with that little bastard.'

'That's not what I mean. They all know each other – which means they're probably all part of this smuggling ring. That's what they were talking about back at the warehouse. I'll wager they don't know a thing about counterfeited bloody coins.'

Cassius pressed his fingers into his brow but it had no effect on his headache. 'When's our luck going to turn? It's just one disaster after another.'

Greyboy was still looking their way and doing a lot of talking – in Aramaic.

Indavara said, 'I can't believe I let you give up my weapons.'

'We had no choice. Anyway, like I said, they won't do anything. Not with the guards there.'

Cassius found himself rather less convinced when Greyboy marshalled his men and led them to the rear of the cell. 'So you're with the army, eh?'

Cassius couldn't see much point in denying it; in fact he reckoned it might discourage them from violence. 'That's right. Imperial Security.'

Greyboy aimed a thumb at his associates. 'We had a good thing going. A very good thing. Until you turned up.'

Cassius decided he would try to keep a good-natured tone to the conversation. 'Sorry about that. I suppose the magistrates might consider it a happy accident. How did they find you?'

'Thanks to your meddling they found all of us.'

Greyboy advanced another two paces, the others close behind him. This time his brother didn't seem quite so concerned about Indavara; then again, he did have five mates with him.

'I wouldn't even consider laying a hand on us,' said Cassius. 'We'll be out of here in hours. You assault an army officer and they'll flog you so hard you'll be lying on your front for the next year.'

Greyboy gave a grim smile. 'Flogging's the least of our worries. The magistrate and his friends are coming down hard on the likes of us. They'll take our hands.'

Trenico came up beside Greyboy. He was a broad man, barrel-chested and powerful with a yellow scar across his forehead. He thumped a fist into a palm. 'So maybe we should use them while we've still got them.'

Indavara pushed himself off the wall.

Cassius called out to the guards, who had just noticed the impending confrontation. 'You men need to stop this.'

'Army, eh?' Another prisoner had walked over to join the others; a tall, heavily bearded man with dirty skin and a sore upon his cheek. 'I hate the bloody army.'

He took something from inside his tunic and walked over to the door.

'What's going on in there?' asked one of the guards.

'Get more men down here,' yelled Cassius, his voice wavering. 'Now!'

The prisoner took whatever he had in his hand, bent over and stuffed it into the lock.

'What are you—' One of the guards reached through and tried to grab him but the prisoner was already walking away. The other guard tried to put the key in but the lock was jammed. His compatriot ran away along the corridor.

The tall prisoner came up beside the other six. Cassius looked around the cell; it didn't seem that anyone else was joining in but with seven they hardly needed them.

Indavara was rubbing his hands together.

'Last warning,' said Cassius. 'I am an officer of the Imperial Army and he is a soldier. You touch either of us and you will pay for it a thousandfold.'

Greyboy appeared unmoved. 'Unfortunately for you, Officer, we don't have a lot left to lose.'

Indavara stepped forward. 'You're going to wish your mate had left that door alone.'

'Oh,' said Greyboy. 'Why?'

'Because soon you'll be begging to be let out of here.'

Cassius felt himself shudder. His throat seemed to have frozen solid, his bowels quite the opposite. He wouldn't have doubted

Indavara's ability to deal with three or even four of them. But seven? He had to help somehow; provide a distraction at least. Greyboy was closest to him.

'They say that hair that colour in a young man is a sign of wisdom. Given your present situation, you seem to be the exception to the rule.'

'You—'

Indavara was on his way. It was obvious to all that he would go for the imposing Trenico but the lunge at him was a feint. The kick aimed at the tall opportunist, however, was not. The reinforced tip of his left boot caught the prisoner low in the gut. As his breath flew out of him and he tottered backwards, Indavara slid under Trenico's short, straight punch and hammered his own fist upward. It went between the Syrian's arms, missed his jaw but smashed into his nose. Trenico grabbed at thin air, then toppled sideways, striking the floor with a thudding slap.

Cassius had already tried to kick Greyboy but the smaller man had neatly evaded it. Fists raised, he backed Cassius into the wall and was about to strike when Indavara grabbed his left arm. He flung him like a rag doll, straight into the others. Greyboy tripped over the bleeding Trenico and would have fallen had his brother not caught him.

Cassius thought that was it but Indavara's first victim and another of the gang were not ready to give in yet. The tall man spat out a mouthful of phlegm and straightened up.

More sergeants ran into the corridor. The remaining guard was still fiddling with the lock.

The tall prisoner was holding something: a tiny dagger, the blade no more than three inches long.

'Full of surprises, eh?' said Indavara.

Still on the ground, Trenico had a bloodied hand over his bloodied nose. 'Stick him. Do it.'

As the pair advanced, Indavara unbuckled his belt and took it off. He held the end without the buckle and locked his eyes on the knife.

'Put it down,' Cassius told the tall prisoner. 'The guards will be inside any minute.'

'A fight with a soldier when I'm the one with the blade? You think I'm going to waste this chance?'

He pushed his mate to the left and came on in a crouch. Indavara held his position and whipped the belt at him. The buckle cracked into the prisoner's hand, sending the knife clattering into a corner. He looked down at his crushed fingers.

'Who in Hades are—?'

The next swing of the buckle caught him on the head. He shrieked and spun around, then fell to his knees. The iron had torn flesh from his brow. Blood was already dripping from the wound.

'All right, who's next?'

The second man was already retreating but Indavara swung the belt at him anyway. The prisoner ducked and managed to avoid it so Indavara chased him for five paces then launched a flying kick into his flank. The unfortunate was sent careering into one of the columns. He bounced off it and hit the floor.

Indavara wasn't finished. He walked back towards the gang, only two of whom were still on their feet.

'What about you, Knuckles? Grown a pair of balls yet?'

Knuckles, Trenico and the others ran or crawled away but Indavara's attention was now on Greyboy. He dropped the belt and punched him in the stomach. As the Syrian doubled over, Indavara dragged him towards the back of the cell.

The guards had cleared the lock. They were shouting at the others to move but – as Indavara had predicted – the gang were now desperate to get out.

Gripping Greyboy by the back of the neck, Indavara held him in front of Cassius. 'Here, take a turn. Whatever you like.'

'You've done what you needed to.'

The bodyguard ignored him. He spun Greyboy around and circled his throat with one big hand. 'Thought you could kill me, did you?'

Greyboy either couldn't speak or didn't want to.

'Never,' growled Indavara through gritted teeth. 'Not me. Not in this life.'

Cassius looked on as those thick, marked fingers dug into the smaller man's neck. 'Indavara. Enough.'

The bodyguard looked at him and grinned. 'Don't worry.'

He let go.

The Syrian dropped to the floor.

Indavara looked down at him. 'Now say sorry.'

'I am sorry.'

'Sir.'

'Sorry, sir. Sorry, sir. I'm sorry, I'm sorry.'

The senior sergeant arrived, club in hand. He glanced at each of the fallen criminals, then at Indavara, who had picked up his belt and was now calmly putting it back on.

'Can I make a suggestion?' said Cassius. 'I think it would be preferable for all concerned if we were accommodated elsewhere.'

XXVII

The look on Cosmas's face suggested that he was up to speed with the night's events. He dismissed the young sergeant who had unlocked the interrogation room door, then stepped inside. Cassius was sitting at the table. Indavara was lying in a corner, having just woken up.

The Syrian tugged anxiously at his beard. 'I don't know what to say, sir. Sorry.'

Cassius had managed about an hour of sleep by resting his head on the table. 'That's a good place to start but I would offer the observation that interdepartmental communications do not appear to be a strength of your organisation.'

'Pomponianus took personal command of the investigation last night and ordered the raids immediately. Even Diadromes didn't know.'

'We could have been killed in that cell.'

'The sergeants present will all act as witnesses. The court will add the assault charges to those relating to the smuggling ring.'

'Is it true – they will lose their hands?'

'Probably. They have defrauded the city of thousands.'

'Then I don't see the point of bothering with the charges. Especially as we probably won't even be here by the time it actually reaches the court.' Cassius stood. 'Except maybe that vicious bastard with the knife.'

'Idomeneus,' said Cosmas. 'A robber and rapist.'

'Gods.'

'You should have let me kill him,' said Indavara as he got to his feet. 'Where are our weapons?'

Cosmas turned to the door. 'Vespilo.'

The sergeant came in holding a bundle of belts, sheaths and blades. He also had Cassius's satchel over his shoulder.

'I had it fetched from the inn,' said Cosmas. He dismissed Vespilo then looked on as the pair armed themselves.

'I need some air,' said Cassius. 'I take it we're free to leave?'

'Of course, sir. Though I'm afraid it's inevitable that talk of this incident will reach the magistrate.'

'As things seem to be going from bad to worse with every passing day that seems highly likely.'

Out in the corridor, a group of sergeants watched them walk out. Unsurprisingly, they seemed most interested in Indavara.

Cassius straightened his sword belt. 'Cosmas, can we be sure that this smuggling ring has nothing to do with the counterfeiting? What about the bronze sheets?'

'The interrogations haven't begun yet but we'll know for certain soon enough. We've got most of the gang behind bars now and they'll get little mercy from the magistrate unless they can offer him the money men. They'll talk; and I'll be listening.'

As they reached the courtyard outside, another group of sergeants were bringing in yet more prisoners: a dozen youths, the youngest of them no more than twelve or thirteen. Beyond the gate, a larger group had followed the sergeants and their captives.

Cosmas questioned one of his compatriots and passed on what he'd heard to Cassius. 'They defaced a statue of the Emperor.'

'Cretins.'

'What will be done to them?' asked Indavara.

'Flogging at the very least,' said Cosmas.

'Even the young ones?'

'No more than they deserve,' said Cassius. 'Some things simply cannot be allowed.'

Indavara muttered an oath and stalked away towards the gate.

'I'll contact you if anything comes up, sir,' said Cosmas. 'And, again, sincere apologies.'

━8━

'Don't stop, Simo. I'm filthy.'

Cassius didn't have the energy for a trip to the baths so was standing naked in the middle of the tower while Simo cleaned him with a sponge.

'Sorry, sir, I'm just concerned about Indavara.'

'As am I. Even for him, it was quite a display. No wonder they loved him in the arena.'

The bodyguard was at the stables, having been encouraged by Cassius to go and see Patch. He had said little during the night and even less on the way back through the city. It seemed obvious that he was again in need of a calming influence.

'I suppose I should be grateful that he listened to me. But he had that look in his eyes again.'

Simo shook his head.

'I mean, he's always liked a good scrap – it's what he does. But . . . well, it was almost as if he was enjoying it.'

'Have you talked to him, sir? Arms up, please.'

Cassius complied, and tried to ignore the sponge tickling his armpits.

'Not directly. But I think I shall. I cannot afford for him to be . . . unstable.'

'Violence has always been a part of his life, sir.'

'The *main* part – of the life he knows, anyway. I wonder what more we can do for him.'

Simo squeezed the sponge out over the drain, then dipped it in the soapy water once more and ran it across Cassius's shoulders. 'Sir, I know your views on the Faith but I think he needs some kind of release. He likes to be active, to help others where he can. I believe it might help keep him on an even keel.'

'You would consider it a great triumph, of course, to turn him from the path of violence and sin.'

'No, Master Cassius. That is not what I meant.'

'Surely I don't have to remind you again of what we discussed?'

'No.'

'Gods, things were simpler when he just sulked around and thumped people when I needed him to.'

Cassius didn't add that he, Abascantius and the Service could not afford to blunt the bodyguard's edge. What was it Diadromes had said? *Thoroughbreds are highly strung.*

It now seemed this was more accurate than he'd previously realised. And if a man like Indavara became unbiddable, he would soon become a liability. Cassius could not let that happen – certainly not at the moment.

'But it is different now, sir, isn't it?' said Simo, as he cleaned his master's chest. 'Because he is your friend.'

'Yes. There is that to consider too.'

Cassius decided he could brave the two-minute walk to the stables alone but kept his hand on his sword all the way. He found Indavara helping one of the lads sweep out the stalls and heard a snatch of their conversation: they were talking about their favourite varieties of bread. Indavara didn't look particularly happy to see Cassius but stopped working and gave his brush to the lad.

'Need me?'

'A note just arrived. I am to meet with the governor at Diadromes's place. We can ride there.'

Indavara asked the lad to fetch their mounts. They were left alone, standing opposite three horses with their heads out of their stalls, solemnly looking on.

'Where's Patch?'

'In the field out the back.'

'Ah. Can we talk for a moment?'

Indavara had left his sword propped up against a stall. He picked it up and wiped something off the handle. 'If you like.'

'Busy couple of days,' said Cassius. 'I'm sorry that you've had to . . . well . . . some unpleasant situations.'

'What I get paid for, right?'

'Yes. I'm just saying . . . I appreciate that it takes its toll.'

'What do you mean?'

Being lost for words was not a familiar predicament for Cassius. 'I . . . er . . . I just . . . I hope you're all right. In yourself. I mean, there was the incident with the legionary, then last night.'

'You're unhappy with something? Just say so.'

'Not at all – you did exceptionally well, as always. It's just . . .'

Indavara put the sword belt on and stared at him.

'Ah . . . nothing,' said Cassius. 'I don't know what I'm on about really.'

To his relief, the lad returned with their horses.

'Right, well. We'd better be going.'

Indavara stayed where he was. 'You're worried that I might lose control of myself.'

Cassius could not think of a reply.

'I survived the arena for six years but I realised within six days that control was the most important thing I had to learn. No rushes of blood, no wild swings, no revenge. I know you think me ignorant but it was thought that got me through – the right decision at the right time. Just leave me to do my job. All right?'

'Right.' Cassius stood there for a moment, still absorbing what he'd heard.

Indavara took the reins for both horses and handed him his. 'We going, then?'

Diadromes and Magistrate Pomponianus were waiting in the garden, sitting under a solitary pine tree, the top of which looked to Cassius very much like a head of broccoli. Leaving his superior sitting on an ornate stone bench, the deputy magistrate hurried forward to shake Cassius's forearm.

'Careful,' he whispered before turning back, 'he's not in a good mood.'

Pomponianus was a rotund, dark-skinned man with a well-manicured beard. He sat hunched over on the bench, folds of his toga hanging between his legs, inspecting Cassius. Several yards away stood a legionary bodyguard and another man in a toga. Directly behind the magistrate was a young attendant holding a glass of wine.

'Officer Crispian of the Imperial Security Service.'

Diadromes then gestured towards the older man, who clearly had no intention of getting up. 'The honourable Placus Cipius Pomponianus, Magistrate of the City of Berytus.'

Cassius gave a slight bow. 'Good day to you, sir.'

Pomponianus nodded and stuck out a hand – not towards Cassius, but to his left. The attendant handed him his wine, which he sipped as Cassius and Diadromes sat on the bench opposite.

'A rather unpleasant night, I understand, Officer?'

'I've certainly had better, sir.'

'It could have been avoided, of course, had you and Deputy Diadromes here elected to keep my office fully apprised of your activities.'

'Indeed, sir,' said Cassius, reflecting that the reverse was also true.

'Fortunately no real harm was done – apart from to a few prisoners and we hardly need concern ourselves with them. But what of this legionary? Your man seems rather keen on dispensing violence – is that him?'

Pomponianus pointed across the lawn to the terrace at the rear of the villa, where Indavara was waiting.

'Yes, sir.'

'You need to keep him on a tighter leash, Officer Crispian. My chief centurion is very angry. I suspect he would like me to have you escorted to the city gates.'

Cassius said nothing; he would wait to hear what the magistrate intended.

'But that would be overly hasty, especially as you are here on the orders of Marcellinus himself. However, Diadromes has described to me the "evidence" used as the basis for your investigation here and the word is highly inappropriate. Is there some further information I am not aware of?'

'We were notified about a suspicious shipment of bronze, sir – which is why we were watching the warehouse.'

'But that is also connected to this smuggling ring, correct?'

'It seems so, sir.'

Diadromes intervened. 'Those investigations are at an early stage, sir. There may yet be some link.'

Pomponianus ignored him and examined his fingernails. 'But you would agree with me, would you not, Officer, that the reasons for your continuing presence here are weakening with every passing day?'

'That's probably fair, sir, yes.'

'Then let me explain how I think we should proceed from here. You will prepare a daily written report on your activities to be submitted to Diadromes and my office at the end of each day. If, after one week, you have made no further progress, you will leave voluntarily. I will then write to Marshal Marcellinus, politely explaining why I will no longer tolerate the baseless smearing of my city's good name. Does that seem fair?'

Cassius suspected he wouldn't get more than a week from Marcellinus and Abascantius anyway. 'It does, sir. Though I would respectfully suggest that you also write to Aulus Celatus Abascantius, my commander in the Service.'

'Mmm.' Pomponianus grinned. 'Is this the moment when I drop to my knees? Prostrate myself before the shadowy power of the "grain men"? Please, Officer, neither I nor Chief Centurion Nemetorius will be intimidated by the involvement of your organisation. We have both had dealings with Abascantius before. You will know that the governor of this province considers the man nothing less than an arrogant troublemaker and I can't claim to feel all that differently.'

Cassius briefly considered asking whether Pomponianus was also prepared to so readily dismiss Chief Pulcher, who was known to be one of Aurelian's most trusted aides.

'Merely an administrative point, sir.'

Pomponianus finished his wine and handed it to the attendant.

'One week, Officer. Make sure your daily reports arrive before the twelfth hour.'

The magistrate stood up and adjusted the thick silver chain around his neck. 'My sergeants and my soldiers are occupied with the well-being of this city. They do not need unnecessary distractions. You shall keep your investigations discreet.' Pomponianus jabbed a chubby finger towards the house. 'And you shall keep that thug of yours under control. Understood?'

Cassius and Diadromes had risen too. 'Yes, sir.'

'Good day,' added the magistrate smoothly. He set off towards the house, retinue close behind.

Diadromes looked at Cassius and shrugged. 'He's under a lot of pressure.'

'He's not the only one.'

Diadromes scratched his bald patch. 'Like I said, the smuggling investigation might turn something up.'

'The way things have gone so far, I very much doubt it. In fact, I'm inclined to return to Tripolis.'

Diadromes looked up at the pine, where some unseen bird was squawking. 'Sometimes I wish I could just leave.'

'More trouble? We saw a group of youths being brought in this morning. Something about a statue?'

'Young fools – just like Sorio and the other grooms. They share an inability to accept the world as it is.'

'A common affliction. But to attack an image of the Emperor?'

'I know. Nemetorius will push for the harshest sanctions, I'm certain.'

'And you?'

'As you will have noted, I am not currently the magistrate's favourite deputy but I will argue for clemency. The boys are young. That will help.'

'Pomponianus needs assistance from Antioch if he wants to keep a lid on this unrest. Another century perhaps. Or funds for the corn dole.'

'He will not ask. To do so would be to admit his own failure. Governor Gordio might even prevent him standing for re-election.' Diadromes led the way back towards the villa. 'I expect you're looking forward to a rather more comfortable night?'

'I am.'

Diadromes laughed. 'Cosmas told me those smugglers were begging to be let out of that cell. That bodyguard of yours would make a quite excellent sergeant but something tells me you would not let him go.'

'Indeed I would not.'

Indavara lay there in the dark, his hand upon his chest, the figurine clasped within it.

He thought of what he'd told Corbulo in the stable. He felt proud of his words, how he'd convinced him that he was all right. He just wished it were true.

At least he had stopped himself killing Greyboy. A thief deserved punishment but not death. A rapist did, though; and Indavara had killed three of them in the arena. Not that he'd really thought about who he was fighting. Criminal, prisoner, professional; it didn't matter. It was always either them or him.

But these men like the rapist. Men who cared nothing for others but simply took for themselves. Men like the centurion Carnifex in Africa or the slave trader Scaurus in Antioch. They were the demons Simo and his people spoke of; and if Indavara had a chance to rid the world of them he would do it.

The legionary Scato was not one of them and Indavara screwed his eyes shut as he thought of what he'd almost done to him. He thought again of Corbulo's awkward speech at the stable; he knew something was wrong and Indavara knew it too.

Why was it happening now? When he was free? When he had a place in the world and friends beside him?

If only he could remember something more; that would make everything better. The woman in the clearing? *Could* it have been his mother? There was no face, no voice, just a presence, something familiar. But the power of the memory faded with every day, like a feather drifting on the wind which he could never quite grasp. He almost wished he had never heard that accursed song.

Dear Fortuna, goddess most high, help me to be a good man. Help me to think, and be calm and to control myself. Help me be a good man.

Indavara wiped his eyes and pushed his blanket aside.

'You all right?' asked Simo in the darkness.

'I'm going.'

'Indavara, we've already pushed our luck too far. Master Cassius will be so angry.'

'He'll never know.'

'I can't.'

'Then I'll go alone.'

'What shall I tell him?' asked Simo.

'Whatever you want. I'm going.'

'Why?'

'Because I have to.'

XXVIII

It was still dark when he got there. He walked the paths between the mountains of rubbish, listening and looking. He was convinced he needed to be there, that he would find one of the abandoned babies. He hadn't actually heard Fortuna's voice say so, yet he was sure.

But the dump was quiet and as the hours passed and the light came he wondered if it was just the torment of the night that had led him there. The boys arrived, ready for another day's work, and he saw two dogs fighting over a bit of meat, snarling as they snatched the flesh from each other, neither able to eat it.

Indavara had completed at least three circuits of the dump when he saw a flicker of movement among a pile of shattered pots. He ran to the edge of the path and checked carefully but whatever it was had moved on.

Hearing someone run up behind him, he turned to see the lad from the previous day. The young Syrian had lost one of his sandals. He ran back and recovered it then blurted something in Aramaic.

'I don't understand,' replied Indavara in Greek.

The lad switched languages. 'Baby! You want baby? Come – got a good one.'

Indavara followed him to the side of the dump, close to a street where a few early risers had appeared. The lad stopped and held out his hand, palm upturned.

'Where is it?' asked Indavara.

'Very close. Very close. Give coin first.'

Indavara doubted the lad would risk tricking him so he took a sesterce from his money bag and handed it over.

The lad grinned, showing his sharp little teeth, and ran off again. 'Come, come. Look here.'

Lying close to the ditch were several broken stone columns. The lad pointed between two of them. Indavara leaned over one of the columns and saw a circular basket. A cloth cover had been put over the handle, covering the contents. The lad sprang between the columns and lifted the cloth. Lying inside the basket was a baby that, to Indavara, looked similar to the other one the women had found. The infant narrowed its eyes against the light and wrinkled its nose but didn't make a sound. The lad pulled back the tiny blanket covering it and pointed at its arms and legs.

'Good one, eh? Good one.'

He picked up the basket and handed it to Indavara, then ran off. Indavara looked down at the baby and realised two things. Firstly, it was a boy. Secondly, he had absolutely no idea what to do with it.

Thank you, Fortuna. Thank you, thank you, thank you.

The women came about an hour later, by which point Indavara was hiding in a nearby alley. He had initially sat waiting on the column with the basket on his lap but a local woman had come over, seen what was inside and started shouting at him in Aramaic. He guessed she thought he was taking it for himself so when she left he hurried across to the alley. The fuss had made the baby start crying. He had seen women moving them around to calm them so he swung the basket a bit and successfully sent the little boy off to sleep.

Alfidia was with five others, including Mahalie.

'Hello,' he said as they stopped beside the dump. 'I found one.'

The women looked at him suspiciously but Alfidia walked over and took the basket. Without even looking inside, she passed it back to one of the others.

'You came alone?' she asked.

'Yes.'

'Why?'

'I don't know.'

'The Lord called you here,' said one of the others.

Indavara shook his head.

'Or an angel,' said another.

'No,' said Alfidia. 'For this child, *you* are the angel.'

Indavara had heard Simo mention that word but he still wasn't quite sure what it meant.

After a lengthy discussion, it was decided that two of the women would take the baby to Elder Cobon. Even though Indavara had searched everywhere, the others decided they would split into two groups and have a look around. Indavara had hoped he would be with Mahalie but Alfidia took him with her. She said three times that it was the voice of her god that had drawn him there that morning.

After an hour they'd found nothing more so decided to leave. Indavara tried not to look at Mahalie but he wanted so much to speak to her. She just stood there, silent, as the others said farewells. Indavara watched them walk away.

They were halfway across the street when she turned and ran back to him. She reached into the cloth bag over her shoulder, took out an apple and gave it to him.

'Thank you.'

'My master has three trees and we can't use them all. I gave one to everyone.'

Indavara couldn't think of anything to say.

Mahalie ran back to the others.

Indavara continued watching them for as long as he could then set off around the edge of the dump. He smiled; he felt better than he had for days.

Just as he was about to cross the street and head back to the tower, a cart pulled up. The aged driver steadied the horses while a younger man climbed into the back and started flinging damaged amphoras on to the dump. He had barely started when a group of five lads – including Indavara's young friend – arrived.

'Look out, you little beggars,' cried the man. As soon as an amphora landed, they would grab it and check inside.

Indavara cleaned the apple on his sleeve. As he took his first bite, the man admonished the boys again.

'They're empty! They're always empty.' He caught Indavara's eye and shook his head.

'What are they after?'

'Who knows?' The man continued throwing the containers.

Another older boy arrived, watching as the younger ones persisted with their search.

'You speak Greek?' asked Indavara.

'I do.'

'What are they after?'

'Silvers.'

'Silver what?'

'Coins.'

'Why would there be coins in amphoras?'

'Don't know. But there was before. Not proper ones but good enough to sell.'

'"Proper ones"?' asked Indavara.

'They didn't look right. The Emperor's face was all squashed.' The lad pulled a face. 'We reckon that's why they chucked 'em away.'

'Denarii? The new ones? For Aurelian?'

'That's it.'

Cassius wiped gunk out of his eyes and blinked into the bright morning sun. He had been roused from his bed by Indavara, who seemed convinced he'd found out something about fake coins. By the time Cassius had washed and dressed, the body-guard was waiting outside with the horses and the three of them set off. Without Cosmas to guide them they got stuck several times amid traffic bound for the morning markets.

Indavara had revealed only that they were heading for the edge of the city and Cassius was surprised when they stopped at what was quite clearly a rubbish dump. As they dismounted, a lad of about twelve or thirteen came running up. He was a dirty-looking wretch with patchy hair and scabs under his nose.

'He's called Leo,' said Indavara.

'And?' said Cassius.

'Tell him about the coins.'

'They found 'em at the bottom of some amphoras.'

Leo's Greek was so bad that Cassius could barely understand. 'How many?' he asked.

'Not sure. I never got any because I was too late.'

'Where were they?'

Leo shrugged and gestured at the mass of refuse behind him. Cassius sighed. 'What did they look like?'

'Like normal except that the picture of the Emperor was all messy – you couldn't see his crown. The writing was messy too.'

Despite the obvious danger of disease, Cassius took a step closer to him. 'These were definitely denarii?'

'Silvers, yes.'

'Of the new kind?'

'Yes – for Aurelian.'

'The boys who found them – do they have any left?'

'Nah. Sold 'em.'

'To who?'

'Old Altes. He pays us for anything brass or bronze or silver.'

'Do you know where I can find him?'

The lad picked at his scabs. 'Don't know. He comes by every few days or so.'

'Could *you* find him?'

'Maybe.'

'And what about the boys who found the amphoras?'

'Myrto and his mates got most of 'em. They haven't been round here for a while. But I think Pallas got a couple too – he lives just over there.' Leo pointed at a ramshackle apartment block that faced the dump. 'His mother's keeping him in, though. He's ill.'

Cassius waved at Simo. 'Tie the horses up. Leo, you'll be going with my man there to get some information from Pallas. But I need to find this Altes too. There must be someone who knows where to find him.'

'I can ask around.'

'Good. Let's see what Pallas can tell us first.'

Simo had tethered the horses to a nearby tree that had been burned down to a blackened stump. 'Sir?'

'Young Leo is going to take you to see his friend, who found some denarii in amphoras. You need to find out firstly if he still has any, secondly *exactly* where they were found. Understood?'

'Yes, Master Cassius.'

'Off you go, then, you two.'

The lad turned to Indavara and put out his hand. 'What about my second—'

'Boy,' interjected Cassius. 'You help us find out where those coins came from and you'll be getting more than sesterces.'

Leo licked his lips in anticipation and hurried away with Simo.

'Why aren't we going?' asked Indavara. 'You don't want to get ill?'

'There's that. Plus Simo's very adept with the common sort. If a protective mother sees you and me there she's going to get anxious.'

'So what do you think?'

'Misshapen coins? There's no mint in Berytus. I suppose there could be some in circulation from other attempts at fakery, but it's promising, very promising. Well done.'

Indavara looked genuinely pleased with himself, which made Cassius wish he didn't have to ask the question. 'So tell me – what were you doing down here before dawn?'

'I was . . .'

'With the Christians?'

Eventually, Indavara nodded.

'But Simo was with me at the tower.'

'There's a girl.'

'Is there, now? Your interest becomes plain at last.'

Indavara looked away.

'Well, as you appeared to have uncovered our first decent lead you shall not hear me complain this time.' Cassius looked out at the expanse of refuse and showed his distaste at the sour smell drifting out of it. 'By the gods, this assignment becomes more prestigious by the day.'

Half an hour later, Leo led them to the other side of the dump, Simo following with the horses. The lad eventually stopped by the ditch and swept a hand at the refuse. 'Here. Pallas said somewhere in here. The amphoras were red.'

The closest pile of refuse was ten foot high and there must have been at least five hundred pieces of red clay in view.

'The *pale* red?' Cassius pointed at one fragment in particular. 'Not the red-brown?'

'Pale red.'

'Did the lads leave the amphoras or take them?'

'Not sure.'

Cassius stood there, thinking.

Indavara spoke to Simo. 'You're sure Pallas doesn't have any coins left?'

'I don't think he was lying. He traded them with this man Altes for food.'

'We'll never find the right amphoras in all that,' said Indavara. 'And how will we know them if the coins have gone anyway? Shouldn't we try and find Altes?'

Cassius was standing by the ditch. Noting all the wheel marks in the dirt, he beckoned Leo over. 'Carts often dump things here?'

'Yes – it's close to the street. But the sergeants will fine them if they see it.'

'Because they're supposed to drive into the middle?'

'Yes – to stop the ditch filling up.'

'When do the sergeants come?'

'Now and again.'

'Not every day?'

'No.'

'Do you know any of their names?'

'No.' Leo started picking his scabs again.

'Get me one of those fragments, would you?'

The lad leapt the ditch and grabbed one then returned and handed it to Cassius.

'Simo, you're going to stay with Leo. The two of you are to ask around and try and find Altes. If you do, questions to ask: firstly, what did they look like; secondly, what did he do with them; thirdly, does he have any idea where they came from? Got all that?'

'Yes, sir.'

'We'll meet you back at the tower. Take as long as you need.'

'Very well, sir.' Simo didn't look particularly enamoured with his new assignment.

Cassius grabbed his reins and mounted up.

'So where are we going?' asked Indavara.

'To find Cosmas.'

Neither of them particularly felt like hanging around at the headquarters – especially with all the curious sergeants watching – so they adjourned to the fish restaurant. Cosmas warned that it might take him a while to get the information Cassius had requested and it was almost midday when he joined them.

'Hot again,' he said, plucking his sticky tunic off his chest as he sat down beside Indavara.

Cassius examined the scrap of paper the sergeant had just given him.

'Those are the names of all the refuse collectors fined for improper use of a dump in the last year.'

'Nine. That's their business – refuse collection?'

'There's quite a demand for it, especially in the centre where space is limited. They have a fleet of carts and labourers – they take the rubbish, sort what they can to sell on, then get rid of the rest.'

'Why are three underlined?'

'The list didn't specify at which location the penalty was incurred but I did a bit more asking around and those three are the only fined outfits that use that dump.'

'Ah, well done. You can take us to them?'

'Certainly, though I need a drink first.' Cosmas waved at one of the maids and ordered some wine. Cassius refused on behalf of himself and Indavara – they'd already had two each.

'Anything more on the smugglers?'

'Up to a dozen arrests now, and half a warehouse of seized goods. The lead officers are reporting directly to Pomponianus but Diadromes has found out that the bronze was for selling on – to a furniture-maker in Ouzai. Nothing to interest us, I'm afraid. Oh, I'm also supposed to remind you about that daily report for the magistrate.'

'I haven't forgotten. Let's just hope there is something more to report.'

It took them an hour to reach the first place; largely on account of an altercation between a group of performers and a squad of legionaries. The dancers and actors (genuine actors this time) were performing an unsubtle play mocking both Nemetorius and Pomponianus. Fortunately, a senior city sergeant arrived and calmed the situation.

The refuse-collecting business was housed in a fenced yard with three large carts, one of which was being repaired. They found the owner – a surprisingly young Greek – inside a shack, doing his accounts. He looked alarmed when Cosmas mentioned the fines but cheered up when Cassius put a denarius on his desk and enquired about red amphoras. The Greek disclosed that his outfit had previously disposed of the broken vessels at the dump but for the last eight months had been selling them on to a builder who used them for foundation material.

The next outfit was only a few streets away. The yard was similar to the Greek's but silent and secured by a locked gate. Cosmas called out but no one appeared.

The third place was half a mile away but considerably closer to the dump. This outfit was the largest of the three, with half a dozen carts lined up and a crew of five labourers sorting through a pile of scrap metal and wood.

Cosmas questioned them and discovered that the owner was out. He showed the men the fragment of amphora and they laughed, replying that it could have come from anywhere. Having been buoyed by Indavara's discovery, Cassius felt a familiar sense of frustration returning.

As they had spoken in Greek, he took up the questioning. 'So all of you have unloaded similar amphoras at that dump?'

'Many times,' said one of the Syrians.

'And seen the children looking inside them?'

'When they're there,' said the man. 'But they usually just take the ones that aren't too badly damaged – someone can use them, I suppose.'

'None of you remember any of them ever finding coins? It would probably have been fairly recently.'

The man shook his head, as did two of the others.

Cassius noticed that the other two didn't seem to be responding. 'What about them?'

'They don't speak Greek.'

Cassius was about ready to slap the man. 'By the gods. Do they speak *Aramaic*?'

'Yes.'

'So ask them!'

The conversation went on for a while. Cassius didn't understand much of it but perked up when Cosmas said, 'Ah.'

'What?'

The sergeant pointed at the younger of the two workers. 'He remembers the children finding the coins. When he saw they were bad fakes he let them keep them.'

'Does he remember where the amphoras came from?'

Cosmas grinned.

The Baths of Marcus Aurelius were housed in a large, oval building ringed by a double layer of arches. The steam that rose from various points within and around it soon disappeared into the ether, unlike the smoke rising from several factories close by.

'Strange place to put it,' observed Cassius as they passed a row of litters. The passengers that emerged were all elderly gentlemen.

'I believe it's because there was no other space close to the main aqueduct channel,' said Cosmas. 'The factories need the water supply too, of course. And one of these as well.'

Having passed through the circle of conifers that surrounded the baths, they came to a patch of unsightly waste ground. The small pile of refuse in the middle of it was composed mainly of seashells, animal bones and some mouldy hides.

Cassius and Indavara listened as Cosmas spoke with the helpful labourer, who'd been given a denarius for his troubles. From where they stood, Cassius could see smoke rising from six different buildings. This was a busy location with good communications. Perfect, in fact, except that—

'These places would have been checked, right?' asked Indavara. 'The "inspections"?'

'Yes,' said Cassius. 'But they might have missed something. Those coins came from somewhere. Somewhere around here.'

Cosmas and the Syrian had finished talking.

'Here's how it works,' said the sergeant. 'This fellow's outfit has a contract with certain factories and workshops in this area. Usually the clients leave their refuse here for the carts to take to the main dump. But sometimes the refuse collectors go straight to the premises.'

'The red amphoras?'

'He's sure they came from this area because he's been on the route for several months. But he can't remember if they came directly from a factory or from here. However, he knows who dumps what and he reckons there's only four outfits around here who use amphoras.'

'Four, eh?'

'He can show me,' said the sergeant. 'Do you want to come?'

'Probably best for us not to show our faces.'

'Won't take me long.' Cosmas pointed back towards the trees. 'There's a nice little sanctuary behind the baths.'

'We'll be waiting.'

The sanctuary was indeed pleasant. Cassius and Indavara sat on a bench and watched as a priest and a group of young followers swept the paths and watered the flowers. The statue of the god was too far away for Cassius to identify.

He closed his eyes and told himself to calm down; there had been so many dashed hopes, after all. But he couldn't help feeling hopeful. Were the counterfeiters close? Perhaps even casting coins as they sat there?

He took a breath and resolved not to think about it until Cosmas returned.

'Simo hasn't been with you?'

'What?' replied Indavara.

'These visits to the Christians. Simo hasn't been with you?'

'No.'

'She pretty, this girl?'

'Yes.'

'I think it would be good for you, to have—'

'There's Cosmas.'

As he strode over to them, the sergeant took a handkerchief from behind his belt and mopped his face.

Cassius and Indavara stood.

'Three,' said Cosmas. 'Three with forges. I remember all of them from the inspections last week but I assume you'll want to check again?'

'What are they?'

'One is a glass factory, one makes iron railings and one makes sarcophagi.'

'Sar . . . what?' asked Indavara.

'Big stone coffins,' answered Cosmas. 'For rich people.'

'That's it,' said Cassius. 'It's that one.'

'How can you be sure?' asked the sergeant.

'Transportation. Sarchophagi are big and strong – think how many coins you could get inside. But even better than that . . .'

'No one will ever open them.'

'We have to get inside that factory,' said Cassius.

'It's almost the eighth hour. They'll be closing soon.'

'Tomorrow morning, then – catch them unawares.'

'After the inspections, though?' said Cosmas. 'We'll need a good excuse.'

'We'd better get thinking, then.'

Alexon knocked on the door, then waited.

'Come,' said his sister after an unnecessarily long time. He opened the door and found her sitting in front of her best oval mirror, the maid Lyra brushing her hair. Behind her, the sky glowed orange through the window.

'It worked,' said Alexon. 'He's on his way up the drive.'

She held up her hand and Lyra stopped. 'Well done, brother. I must admit I was beginning to doubt your methods. Shall we see him in the upstairs lounge? I think that would work best.'

'I agree.'

'Finish quickly, Lyra.'

Alexon paused in the doorway, watching.

He saw Amathea's face in the mirror; she was looking at the maid. 'Why do you still have that bandage on? It's been weeks.'

'Yes, Mistress, unfortunately—'

'You must get rid of it. It's so unsightly.'

'Yes, Mistress.'

Alexon closed the door. He hoped all would go well. He wanted – needed – her so badly.

Five minutes later, Skiron escorted Kallikres up the stairs and into the lounge. The attendant crossed his arms and looked on as Alexon beckoned the sergeant forward. He and Amathea were sitting on opposite ends of a couch just in front of the balcony, their necks warmed by the evening sun.

Alexon put down his wine. 'I'm glad you've seen sense at last.'

Kallikres stood there wringing his hands, eyes flitting between them. 'The boy. Where is he?'

'You simply can't bear to be without him,' said Amathea. 'What's so special? Does anything you ask him to, does he?'

'Nobody knows where he is,' answered the sergeant.

'We have a few things to discuss,' said Alexon.

'What about the boy?'

'First we talk. Skiron says you have something for us.'

'Only if you tell me about the boy.'

'We will,' said Alexon.

Kallikres blinked and ran a hand across the back of his head. 'The officer is named Crispian.'

'We know that.'

'He got the sergeants to inspect factories, looking for coins or equipment or . . .'

Amathea was shaking her head. Production had been suspended for several days now and she wasn't the only one becoming impatient.

'We know that too,' said Alexon. 'What about now?'

'Apparently the magistrate isn't happy about how this Crispian and his bodyguard have been throwing their weight about. Especially as they haven't found out anything – about your operation anyway. There's this smuggling ring—'

'We know. What about Crispian? Who is he?'

'Still not sure. Possibly—'

Amathea tutted.

Kallikres held up his hands. 'I haven't finished. The governor wants Crispian gone – he's sure there is no counterfeiting here and doesn't want any distractions, what with all the problems on the streets. They've got nothing on you. Nothing.'

'You're sure?' asked Alexon.

'As I can be. Please, where is Pedrix?'

Alexon turned to his sister. She smiled.

'Please,' begged Kallikres.

'It's a shame you didn't come to us sooner,' said Amathea.

'No.'

She stood up. 'But you left us no choice.' She walked around the couch and over to the balcony. 'Come.'

Kallikres' face crumpled; he covered it with his hands.

Alexon watched his sister trying not to laugh.

Skiron put a hand on Kallikres' shoulder. The sergeant walked to the balcony like a man facing the executioner's block. Amathea stood aside and gestured towards the ground.

Kallikres planted his hands on the rail and looked down.

'Oh . . . oh, thank the gods.'

Alexon joined them on the balcony. The slave boy was with one of the maids, who was singing quietly as they weeded the terrace.

'Pedrix will remain here for as long as we do,' said Amathea. 'And you will tell us the moment there are any developments we should be concerned about.' She reached out and tipped up Kallikres' chin. 'And when we are finished you can have your little toy back. How does that sound?'

Kallikres wiped his face and nodded.

'Now leave us.'

Skiron escorted the sergeant out of the room and down the stairs.

'We should restart production immediately.'

'Of course,' said Amathea. 'I congratulate you, brother. I must remind myself not to be so pessimistic in future. You do have some excellent ideas.'

Alexon couldn't have cared less about the platitudes. All he wanted was to be alone with her, for as long as she would let him.

Amathea walked up to the balcony and offered him her hand. When he took it, she led him up behind her.

'I am yours,' she said.

'And I am yours.'

He pushed himself into the exquisite softness, hardening instantly. His eyes closed and pleasure washed over him. *At last.*

XXIX

They had both tried to stop him: Simo because he thought Indavara shouldn't go to the church-house alone, Corbulo because he wanted him to concentrate on his job. Indavara had ignored them both. He wanted to find out about the baby and he wanted to see Mahalie.

But when he knocked on the door and Cobon opened it, the old Syrian wasn't exactly welcoming.

'You're on your own.'

'Simo couldn't come. I was wondering about the little one I found. Is he all right?'

Indavara waved a hand at the moths and flies drawn to the lantern hanging by the door.

Cobon stepped out on to the street. 'Son, there is something I must say to you. While we welcome all, this church-house is really for those who have accepted the Lord into their lives. We appreciate your help but it is not appropriate for you to come here unaccompanied. That is unless you wish to properly join our congregation. That would change things.'

Cobon reached out and took his hand. 'The Lord loves us all. He will help you lead a righteous life, steer you away from sin and towards eternal happiness in the Kingdom. Come, join us tonight and take your first steps along that path.'

Indavara shook off his hand. 'I worship the goddess Fortuna. She has always looked after me.'

'Then I am sorry to say you cannot come in.'

'The baby?'

'The child is healthy. We will find a good home for him.' Cobon backed towards the door.

'I would like to see Mahalie.'

'She is not here tonight.'

'Can you at least tell me where I can find her?'

'I'm afraid not. Mahalie is no longer part of this congregation.' Cobon withdrew behind the door. 'Goodnight.'

Indavara briefly considered pushing his way inside but he couldn't act like that here, not with these people. The latch rattled as Cobon closed the door. As he walked away, Indavara heard raised voices over the wall, talking in Aramaic. Then the door opened again. He stopped and saw Alfidia by the lantern.

'I thought it might be you.'

Indavara walked back. 'Where is she? Why isn't she here?'

'She was – earlier. I didn't hear all of it but something else must have happened at home. She was asking the others for advice but Elder Cobon told her she must do as she was bid; that it was a sin to disobey her master. I tried to stop her but she ran.'

'How can I find her?'

'I don't know. She would never tell anyone where she lived or who her master was.'

Indavara thought of what Simo and Corbulo had said. Perhaps they were right. Perhaps he should have stayed away.

'That poor girl,' said Alfidia. 'I wish we could do something.'

Indavara turned away.

'Wait. The market. She often talked about the fruit market by the Temple of Juno. She was sent there most mornings.'

'Allectus Carius Molacus, Department of Municipal Planning, Construction and Maintenance.'

Cassius took the forearm offered to him and shook it. 'Crispian.'

Molacus looked about forty. He ran a hand through his greasy hair and chewed his lip. 'I must say this is a very unusual situation. I could really do with another day or two to prepare.'

'No time for that, I'm afraid.' Cassius gestured at the waxed tablet Molacus was holding. 'That's for me, I assume?'

Molacus gave it to him and took a stylus from a leather case.

He was wearing a pale brown tunic with a ring of yellow circles at the sleeves.

'Have you been in this factory before?' asked Cassius.

'Yes, I believe it was last May – installations and plumbing.'

'You do have a story worked out?'

'We carry out regular checks on ovens and forges – anything within the city limits that carries risk of fire. The management might be a tad surprised but we never tell them about these inspections – for obvious reasons. I must say I am not comfortable with such deceit. May I see that note from Deputy Diadromes again?'

Cosmas handed it to Molacus, then looked at Cassius and rolled his eyes. Along with Indavara and Simo, they were standing in the same sanctuary they had used the previous day. Cassius was wearing his oldest, plainest tunic; he was to masquerade as Molacus' clerk.

'These bloody sandals of yours, Simo. How do you walk around in them all day?'

Cassius decided to pace up and down for a bit to get used to them. He walked over to Indavara, who was sitting on a bench nearby, staring down at a line of ants on the paving stones.

'Well – do I make for a convincing clerk?'

Indavara glanced up at him from beneath his fringe but said nothing.

'I see your mood hasn't improved. I take it things didn't go well last night?'

Cassius hadn't expected a reply and he didn't get it. He walked back to the other three. 'Well, Simo? Convincing?'

'Not bad, sir. May I?'

'Go ahead.'

Simo reached up and ruffled Cassius's hair, which he always kept short and well combed. The attendant then tugged at his master's tunic, leaving an unsightly swathe of cloth bulging over his belt.

'Really?'

'Sorry, sir.'

'Much better,' agreed Cosmas as he took the note back from Molacus. 'We should go, the gates will be open by now.'

Cassius pointed at Molacus. 'Please remember that I need to see as much of the premises as possible.'

'Very well,' said the Syrian. 'But a counterfeiting operation in Berytus? It hardly seems credible. And didn't I hear that the premises have already been inspected by city sergeants?'

'We have good reason to believe this is the right place,' said Cassius. 'You are looking for *anything* out of the ordinary and you're more likely to notice it than I am. Understood?'

Molacus sighed.

Despite his reluctance, the administrator proved himself a capable actor. He adopted what Cassius imagined was his usual brisk manner and led the way confidently through the gates and into the yard. A nervous young man who described himself as 'production supervisor' asked them to wait outside the factory while he fetched the manager.

Cassius looked around. The factory itself was brick-built and high roofed, with thin, arched windows. The only workers in view were gathered around a hoist which was obviously used to move the heavy sarchophagi on to and off carts. Eight vehicles were lined up neatly on one side of the yard.

'So where does their stone come from?'

'Most of it's Proconeesan marble,' said Molacus. 'It's shipped down to the port then brought here.'

'Blocks of it?'

'No, they shape the containers at the quarry before shipping. This place does the fine work; carving and so on – whatever the buyer has specified.'

'Why do they need a forge?'

'Some of the sarcophagi are given an interior lining, usually lead. They also use metal clamps to secure the lids. I believe this outfit manufacture their own.'

'Do you know anything about where they go from here?'

'Not specificially, but the marble is always popular with those that can afford it and it's an extremely widespread trade.'

'With a large potential market.'

'The dead? In Syria? Certainly.'

The manager arrived; a well-dressed fellow sporting several silver rings. He greeted Molacus politely and introduced himself as Bathyllos.

'Thank you for seeing me personally.'

'Not at all,' replied Bathyllos, without so much as a glance at Cassius. 'Always happy to help the city. I understand you need to carry out some sort of check?'

'We've had a few infractions regarding fire safety measures of late – I just need to ensure that you are keeping the risk to an absolute minimum. We have an excellent record in this area and my superiors are keen to maintain it.'

'Of course.'

'I will be checking all the other facilities in the area.'

Bathyllos smiled blandly. Cassius reckoned he didn't appear notably more anxious than any factory manager would when facing a surprise visit from the authorities.

'Where would you like to start?'

'Wherever's easiest for you,' said Molacus.

'Then follow me.'

Most of the building was taken up by one huge workshop where at least twenty artisans were gathered around sarcophagi mounted on sturdy wooden pallets. Many of the masons were working on the sides of the containers, which featured most of the artwork. Cassius could see why the marble was so popular; the handsome white stone was banded with grey and gleamed under the shafts of sunlight illuminating the factory. Using hammers and a remarkable variety of chisels, the men crafted the faces of gods, religious and solar symbols, and intricate garland and wreath designs. Cassius also noted that some were working from drawings and that most of the sarcophagi had names scrawled upon them in charcoal. The visitors attracted a few stares but again Cassius could deduce little from their reaction; there was certainly no sense of alarm.

Bathyllos showed them every corner of the workshop. Molacus made the odd comment and advised that all the window shutters be fully opened; the smell of an oil used to polish the marble hung heavily in the air.

The rear of the warehouse was accessed via a broad, high doorway. To the right was a storage area which opened out on to the yard beside the hoist. There were dozens of finished sarcophagi laid out in rows and Cassius spotted paperwork listing destinations as far afield as Bostra, Zeugma and Circesium, which was almost in Persia.

While Bathyllos and Molacus paused to discuss industrial accidents, he glanced down at the nearest coffin. It was lying open, with the lid propped against the side. Considering the weight, no one would notice a few hundred or even thousand coins stashed inside. Even better, an illicit cargo could be removed before reaching the eventual destination without the purchaser even knowing. As a cover, it was absolutely perfect; and yet he had seen nothing to indicate anything other than a well-run, legitimate business.

Bathyllos took them through a small office where a trio of clerks were at work, then to the rear left corner of the warehouse. This area was partitioned by an interior wall and contained the forge. A large oven was burning bright below a broad chimney and giving off a wave of heat that struck the moment they entered. The forge was also equipped with two broad anvils, clay moulds for the locking clamps and a stack of lead sheeting. The only two workers present were poring over a single sheet of lead, taking measurements with callipers and marking them with chalk.

Molacus pronounced himself unhappy with the proximity of some firewood to the oven and instructed Cassius to make a note. Bathyllos agreed to make the change at once; and looked on while Molacus swiftly surveyed the rest of the forge. The inspector knelt briefly to attend to an errant shoelace then straightened up and gave a formal nod to Bathyllos.

'Well, the small issue of firewood aside, everything seems to be in order. If you could make sure that it's attended to by the end of the week . . .'

'Of course,' said Bathyllos smoothly. 'Would you like to check outside also?'

'That won't be necessary,' replied Molacus. 'Exteriors are another inspector's responsibility and I have several more premises on my list for this morning.'

'Allow me to show you out.'

The manager took them back into the storage area then through a rear gate and around the side of the warehouse they hadn't seen. Here were more blocks of stone and a rubbish pit where Cassius observed a complete lack of pale red amphora. They also passed a broad gate that led through to some stables. Bathyllos explained that this was part of the business and Molacus was pleased to see that such a fire risk had been sited well away from the forge.

As the two then moved on to small talk and the 'disgraceful' defacing of the Emperor's statue, Cassius glumly considered his next move. Other than the suitablility of the sarchophagi for transportation, there was not a single reason to suspect the business was being used as a cover for counterfeiting. At least there were the two other factories to check.

Bathyllos escorted them as far as the gate and wished Molacus a good day. As they walked off, Cassius realised he'd gained a useful insight into the life of a lowly clerk. It was strange to be ignored; but he supposed that people of such status were simply accustomed to it.

'Well done, you were most convicing,' he told Molacus as they neared the sanctuary.

'As was Bathyllos, though he must know about it, of course.'

Cassius stopped. 'Know about what? You saw something?'

'Oh yes,' said Molacus. 'Two things, to be precise. You didn't notice the barrel just sitting there in the middle of the forge? I imagine it covers a trapdoor. A cellar is hardly a rarity, of course, but far more conclusive is the metal pipe behind the oven. I had to kneel down to get a good view – it comes from below and runs into the main chimney. For the counterfeiter's forge, I presume. Rather ingenious.'

'You mean . . . under the factory? It's hidden below the floor?'

'I can see no other logical explanation. Shall we get going? I suppose I must go through the charade of these other visits or we shall arouse suspicion.'

Molacus strode on towards the sanctuary. Cassius stood alone in the middle of the street, clutching the waxed tablet and staring back at the factory.

Diadromes leaned against the wall, listening as a flock of gulls wheeled and shrieked high above the tower. When Cassius had finished, the Syrian took another sip of wine then deposited his mug on the table.

'Gods, I can hardly believe it.'

'Neither did Molacus until he saw that pipe.'

'So what now?'

Cassius sat down beside Indavara. 'Clearly we need to find something conclusive but we're running out of reasons to check the place.'

Diadromes looked at Cosmas, who was standing on the other side of the tower. 'What's security like at night?'

'Not sure, sir. There will certainly be a guard or two on the main gate, perhaps more inside.'

'They might transport the coins after hours,' said Cassius, 'but I doubt they do any actual production. There's the noise for one, plus they can't use the chimney unless the forge is working upstairs.'

'What was the manager's name?' asked Diadromes.

'Bathyllos,' answered Cosmas.

'Don't know him. What about the owner?'

'I'm looking into it,' replied the sergeant.

'Subtly, please,' said Cassius. 'We can assume that Bathyllos is in on it and perhaps his employers too. If they hear of our interest—'

'We must be careful in any case,' said Diadromes. 'I agree it is all damned suspicious but we cannot be sure.'

'Don't worry,' said Cassius, 'if there's one thing I've learned over the last few weeks it's not to get ahead of myself.'

Diadromes said, 'As if there isn't enough going on at the moment. A criminal scheme between the gang and the factory, that's one thing. But if one or more of our notable citizens is also involved it will become quite the scandal.' He tapped a knuckle on the corner of the table.

'It's getting late,' said Cassius. 'I must compose my report for Pomponianus. Should I disclose everything?'

Diadromes considered this for a moment. 'You must. If he has an opinion he can offer it before you take any decisive action. Just observation for now, agreed?'

'Agreed.'

The deputy magistrate took his cape from a chair. 'Speaking of the magistrate, I now have the delightful prospect of a late dinner with him, my fellow deputies and the chief centurion.'

'Ah.' What Cassius had seen of Diadromes's role as deputy magistrate confirmed his long-standing theory that the burdens of such a post outweighed the benefits.

'Something tells me I won't have much of an appetite,' added the Syrian. 'I must persuade them not to kill five of the city's sons.'

'I'm sure I'm not alone in thinking that would be extremely counterproductive,' said Cassius.

Indavara spoke up. 'They wouldn't, would they?'

'Hopefully not,' said Diadromes. 'But the governor and the centurion have grown increasingly close, and increasingly convinced that there is only one method of response to unrest. But I have allies too. We will do what we can.'

'You can't allow it,' said Indavara. 'It's not right.'

'My friend, I wish it were that simple.'

Once Diadromes had left, Cassius told Simo to get started on dinner; Cosmas would eat with them, then they would get over to the factory and begin their second night-time vigil.

While Indavara helped the Gaul and the sergeant went to find a messenger, Cassius adjourned to his room to write a brief summation of the day's progress for Pomponianus. Once it was done, he rolled up the page and made a rough seal with some candlewax; just enough to prevent anyone at the magistrate's office getting curious. He was almost to the stairs when he paused and glanced back at his figurines.

Great and honoured gods, I thank you.

They were not so lucky with an observation point this time. The factory was surrounded by similarly large buildings and, like most of them, guarded by a pair of sentries. As they passed the gate, Cassius saw the two men squatting below a lamp playing dice.

They walked on – occasionally drawing suspicious glances from other guards – and eventually reached the square at the end of the street. They halted beside another looming statue not far from some beggars singing an indecipherable song. Cassius looked back. He had been so focused on his performance earlier in the day that he'd taken little notice of the surrounding area. 'No alleys or side streets close enough?'

'Not that would provide a decent view of the front,' said Cosmas.

'The rear?'

'It's right next to a warehouse, separated by an alley. No good for observation but there is a small gate – shall I go and check if it's guarded?'

'Please.'

As Cosmas jogged away, Cassius turned to Indavara, no more than a dark shape beside him. 'You're still quiet. What is it – this girl?'

The bodyguard sniffed.

'Come on, what have I told you before about bottling everything up? It might help you to talk about it, even with me. I promise to be pleasant.'

'She is a slave.'

'I see.'

'I think they mistreat her. She tried to run away.'

'And you will save her, I suppose?' Cassius instantly regretted his tone, if not the sentiment.

'Is that you being pleasant?'

'Sorry. Realistic. Look, I can understand it. You wouldn't be the first. Rushing to a poor maid's rescue, it's . . . attractive.'

'Attractive?'

'You know what I mean. But unless you have the money to pay off her owners – and we both know you don't – there is little you can do. And frankly, any suggestion that you could would give the girl false hope.'

'She has no one.'

'Isn't she with the Christians? Can't they help?'

'They say she should obey her master.'

'Well, I don't often agree with them but they are right. She must learn to make the best of it; she has no other choice.'

'She could run.'

'And what then? A girl, alone in the world? That is no solution.'

'So I can do nothing?'

'We will be moving on soon. There's no sense in getting caught up in all this.'

'You don't understand.'

Cassius reckoned he was probably right about that. Neither of them said anything more until Cosmas returned.

'No guard at the back. Strong gate and lock, though. Over the wall's probably the best way in.'

'Well, we have some experience in that field.'

'The warehouse?' asked the sergeant.

'The warehouse.'

'Dead quiet,' added Cosmas. 'Doesn't look like there's going to be much happening tonight.'

'Unfortunately, we still need to watch the place.'

Cosmas let out a long breath.

'You've done enough, these last few days,' said Cassius. 'Go and get some sleep.'

'Are you sure, sir?'

'Absolutely.'

'I won't deny I could use a bit of shut-eye. Goodnight.'

'Goodnight,' said Cassius as the sergeant set off across the square.

'Why don't you go too?' said Indavara.

'What?'

'It doesn't take two of us to watch the place. At least you can get some rest. I won't sleep anyway.'

Cassius appreciated the offer but he feared the prospect of journeying alone across the city.

Indavara said, 'If you hurry up, Cosmas can see you back to the tower.'

'You're sure?'

'I'm sure. Go.'

After their discussion, Cassius wasn't all that happy about leaving him but Indavara was a man of his word; if he said he'd stay and watch, he would.

'Very well. Thank you. But about this girl – you won't do anything silly, will you?'

'See you back at the tower in the morning.'

Cassius could no longer hear Cosmas's footsteps. He ran past the statue and across the square.

XXX

Dear Fortuna, goddess most high, help me. Please, please help me.

Indavara wandered through the fruit market, head lolling, eyes heavy.

The hours of night had passed slowly. He had ended up slumped against the bottom of the statue, watching the factory, his mind elsewhere. He'd decided to listen to Corbulo, to forget Mahalie. He'd reminded himself of who paid him, of the oath he'd taken to the army. He felt great pride about moving the investigation forward and was determined to see it through with Corbulo. That was more important.

But his resolve hadn't lasted long. He could not forget her. If he found her, he could help. He just knew it.

Sometimes, back in Pietas Julia, he had been put in a cell on the exterior of the arena. Capito – the organiser of games – often did this before a big fight. He called it 'advertising'. Indavara sat at the back, in the shadows, and spoke not a word to those who came to see him. There were children, women, gangs of youths, soldiers, gentlemen. They all looked at him, talked about him as if he wasn't there. The closest he'd ever got to speaking was when a young lad of no more than six walked up to the bars. He wanted to tell Indavara about his day.

'My father took me to the beach. I made a river in the sand and I watched the fishermen. The water was lovely and for lunch we had melon. You can go to the beach one day – when you get out. My father says you will win your freedom. My father is always right.'

Before Indavara could reply, the lad's mother had pulled him away. From the cell he could see nothing but the street. But the arena was on a hill; and almost every day he would look out through the arches at the glittering sea and the ships sailing by – free people going wherever they wanted. The ships gave him hope; just like the figurine thrown to him, just like the little boy who told him he'd win his freedom. Hope was all he'd had. Mahalie needed it too.

He wiped his sore eyes and plodded on. The sun had not yet risen above the city's buildings but the square was already filling up. Around him, carts were being unloaded and stalls stocked with produce. There were plenty of customers too; mostly women carrying baskets in their hands or on their heads. Indavara had been looking for so long that he'd seen some of the faces two or three times. He was starting to attract some strange looks from the stall-owners.

Suddenly feeling thirsty, he bought some watered wine from a stall, drank it, then handed the mug back to the vendor for a refill. As she dunked it into the amphora, he asked her if she knew Mahalie.

'Don't know the name.'

'She's a maid. Thin. Doesn't say much. About my age.'

'Sorry.'

He emptied the mug again, paid, then walked on. Looking at the nearby streets, he realised he didn't know the way back to the tower (he'd had to ask directions four times to get there). Perhaps this was Fortuna's way of telling him he shouldn't be doing this. Perhaps Mahalie would not come to the market today.

'Get your berries here!'

'Apples! Apples! Cheapest in Berytus. Apples here!'

'Fresh from the fields! Only the best from Pansa.'

Indavara thought about talking to the other stall-owners but most were now busy with customers. The fruit market filled half the square and was laid out around a crossroads and a stone kiosk, where a city official had just arrived. Indavara decided he would do one more circuit.

Three times he thought he'd seen her. With their pale tunics and sandals, dark skin and black hair, many of the Syrian girls looked alike. Indavara had checked two of the four paths and was walking back past the official's kiosk when he glimpsed someone abruptly change direction. He stopped and turned; she was already past him.

The woman was slight enough to be Mahalie but she was wearing a hooded cape. Despite the heavy basket of food in her hand, she was moving quickly. Indavara gave chase but his path was blocked by a quartet of burly men lugging amphoras full of dates. He dodged around them, then ran after her. Once he got in front he could see her face.

Mahalie stopped.

Indavara didn't know what to say.

'Why are you here?'

'I . . .'

'Leave me alone.'

She walked past him to another stall. He watched as she bought two red peppers. The female vendor seemed to know her and asked if she was all right. Indavara couldn't hear her reply. Once she had paid, Mahalie made straight for the edge of the market. Indavara followed her slowly, unsure what to do. The girl was so determined to get away that when she stepped down from the pavement she lost some of the contents of her overloaded basket.

Indavara sprinted forward and beat her to the pair of onions rolling across the street. 'Here.'

He put them in the basket, wedging them where they wouldn't fall out. 'Would you like me to carry that? Looks heavy.'

She put down the basket then covered her face with her hands and began to cry. A pair of women walked past, casting accusing looks at Indavara.

He looked around. On the other side of the street was a low wall shaded by a tree. Aside from an elderly man sweeping the pavement, there was no one else close by.

'Perhaps you'd like to sit down. Just over there?'

Mahalie kept her hands clamped over her eyes but nodded.

'I'll take this.' Indavara picked up the basket and walked across the street. He put the basket by the wall then sat down next to it.

Mahalie followed and sat with him, still sniffing. She took out

314

a handkerchief and dabbed at her eyes. Indavara looked at the slender, hunched figure beside him. He could see her shoulder blades sticking out even through the tunic and the cape. After a while, Mahalie stopped crying and pushed the handkerchief into her tunic sleeve.

Indavara said, 'I went to the church-house. Alfidia told me I might find you here. What's wrong?'

Mahalie adjusted her tunic so that it covered her knees.

'Is it your master?'

She picked at her bottom lip and gazed at the ground.

Indavara said, 'I was a slave. For six years.'

'You are free now?'

'Yes.'

'You have many scars.'

'Yes, I . . .'

'I too.' She suddenly pulled down the collar of her tunic. The area of her chest above where her breasts met was laced with thin but deep cuts. Face trembling, she tore the hood from her head. Her hair had been cut short but unevenly, with longer patches all over.

Mahalie pushed her tunic back up and raised the hood.

Indavara felt his throat tighten. 'Your master did this?'

'Yes.'

'Why?'

'It's her. Mistress. She thinks he wants me. So she told him to make me ugly. She held me while he did it.'

'What about running away?'

'I tried once. But they sent a man after me. I didn't even get out of the city. That's when they really started hurting me.'

'Your family? Alfidia said—'

'My sister is in Antioch but I don't know how to reach her. I don't even know where she is.'

Mahalie looked across the street then turned her head away.

'What is it?'

'One of my master's neighbours. I cannot be seen talking to you. I am not supposed to talk to anyone.'

'I'd like to help.'

'You cannot. If you try anything they will . . . they will hurt me again.'

Mahalie wiped her face, then stood and picked up the basket. 'I must go. What is your name? I don't remember.'

'Indavara.'

She looked down at him. 'Do you believe in the Kingdom? Where you can be with those you love and be for ever happy?'

'I don't know.'

'I wanted to. So much. Alfidia and the others, they believe they will go there. They really believe it. I tried to. I really did try.'

She walked away along the street.

Indavara watched her. As she struggled with the heavy basket, the hood slipped. She stopped and put it back then continued on.

Indavara took ten deep breaths as Corbulo sometimes told him to. At the end of it he felt less like following her, finding these people and hurting them. But only a little less.

An hour passed before they came out.

Indavara had let himself go with that soldier, and again in the cell; and it had felt good. The rage was like a fire burning within him.

But I control it. And I use it only against those that deserve it. With her master and mistress out of the way, Mahalie will be free.

The place where she worked was an average townhouse in an average street. He'd watched her go inside but seen and heard nothing more until now.

He was pressed up against the wall beside the gate. They were speaking in Greek. Their voices were soft and 'respectable' like Corbulo's. The woman was telling Mahalie to water the plants, to make sure lunch was ready when they returned. She told her she liked her hair more this way. The man hadn't said much.

The gate swung open and he came out first. He was very average looking; the type of man you wouldn't really notice.

'Come on, love, we'll be late.'

She was also pretty average looking, though a bit taller than her husband. While he locked the gate, she fiddled with her hair for a moment then realised she was being watched. She touched her husband on the back.

Indavara looked both ways along the street; there was no one around.

They seemed so harmless. But they were the devils. They were the ones who thought Mahalie was theirs – to do with as they pleased. Cut her hair. Cut her skin.

The woman snatched the keys from her husband and moved back towards the gate. Indavara came forward quickly, cutting her off. They retreated, shoes sliding across the stone. They held hands and the man muttered something. Indavara reached for his dagger but his fingers brushed against the smooth head of the figurine tucked behind his belt.

Fortuna.

He took it out and stared at it.

He heard them moving – walking, then running – but he couldn't take his eyes off the goddess's face. When he finally looked up they were gone.

Alexon was so far ahead that he had time to slow down as he approached the stream. He turned and saw Amathea galloping out of the trees, hair streaming behind her. A shame he hadn't been able to watch her but he'd always been the better rider and was determined to remain so. His mount splashed through the shallow water and leaped nimbly up the bank on to the track.

'Good boy,' he said, slapping the horse's neck.

Amathea had given up now and was trotting across the meadow. As she came closer he enjoyed the inevitable pout and bouncing breasts. He had still never seen a better figure on a woman anywhere; his sister combined athleticism and voluptuousness to truly devastating effect. Once across the stream and on the track, she drew up beside him.

'Well done, brother.'

'You don't mean that.'

'How well you know me. Where are those girls? They were supposed to meet us here with the picnic.'

'They'll be along presently. I have a blanket here. We could find a nice spot and . . . well . . .'

With production back under way at the factory, Amathea was in a good mood; he wanted to take advantage of it.

'Lunch first. I shall be your dessert.' She looked down and fingered drops of sweat off her cleavage. 'What would you like?'

Alexon wondered whether to risk it. How good a mood was she in? But once the idea had come to him, he couldn't resist. He tapped the object tucked into his saddle by his right leg.

'You want to take your whip to me, Alexon? It's been a while.'

Already hot from the ride, he now felt almost faint. He was about to dismount when he heard the thrumming of hooves behind him.

'Skiron?' said Amathea.

The old attendant was charging towards them, clods of earth flying up behind his horse. Alexon saw his heavenly afternoon drifting away from him.

Skiron reined in and took a moment to catch his breath. 'Mistress, Master.'

'What is it?' asked Amathea.

'Yesterday a municipal inspector carried out a safety check on the factory.'

'And?'

'They checked other sites too but the inspector had a clerk with him. I got a description from Bathyllos – tall, brown hair, very light skin.'

'Crispian,' hissed Alexon. If he hadn't been on his horse he would have punched something.

'Probably,' said Skiron. 'But Bathyllos is pretty sure they didn't see anything.'

'*Pretty* sure?' yelled Alexon. The outburst disturbed his horse, and it took a few vicious tugs on his reins to get it back under control.

'Calm down, brother,' said Amathea. 'They would have acted by now if they suspected something.'

'Not necessarily. They're probably watching the place.'

'You don't know that. Anything from Kallikres?'

Skiron shook his head.

Alexon couldn't believe that this accursed investigator was still pursuing them. 'We'll have to stop production again.'

'No,' said Amathea. 'The next shipment isn't going out for three days. Even if they are watching, the men can keep working.'

'Amathea, they could raid the factory at any moment. Bathyllos knows Skiron, he could lead them to us.'

'Surely this is why we hid the workshop.'

'We have to know more. Skiron, find Kallikres and tell him that if we don't find out what this Crispian bastard is up to he'll never see his little friend again.'

'Sir, Kallikres is not an easy person—'

'Now, Skiron.'

'Yes, Master.' The attendant spun his horse around and rode off.

Alexon spat on the ground. 'By the gods, I knew this day was going far too well.'

'So forthright, brother. You are at your best when we face a challenge. I do so like it when you show your teeth.'

'I thought we were safe,' he said as they dismounted.

'We don't know anything for certain yet. Even if this Crispian is getting too close we can take care of him.' Amathea let go of her reins, walked over to Alexon's horse and took out the whip. 'The girls still aren't here. Since you've suggested the idea, I must confess I now feel quite keen on it. Come, we must be quick.'

XXXI

'Where in Hades have you been?'

Cassius had already breakfasted and was drafting another letter to Abascantius and Marcellinus when Indavara returned.

The bodyguard shut the door behind him and mumbled something to Simo, who was brushing down Cassius's riding boots. The attendant fetched him some water.

'Well? Must be the fourth hour.'

Indavara's hair was even messier than usual and his eyes were puffy and bloodshot. 'Long night.'

'And? The factory?'

'At about the eighth hour some watchmen came past and the guards spoke to them for a minute or two. At about the eleventh hour a group arrived and was let inside.'

'A group? How many?'

'Maybe eight or ten.'

'Eleventh hour, eh? About right if you wanted to get people in without the rest of the workers or anyone else noticing. Well done. You should get some sleep. Tonight could be another long one.'

Indavara took the water from Simo and glugged it down then sat on his bed. He wrenched off his boots, laid back and closed his eyes.

Cassius considered the implications of what he'd heard. A quiet night at the factory – did that suggest all was continuing as normal? Even if the visit with Molacus hadn't aroused any suspicion, he couldn't afford to wait around: he had to see inside. With real evidence they could widen the investigation and involve Pomponianus; make sure they caught the whole gang and closed the counterfeiting operation down permanently. Cassius smiled as he thought of writing that letter.

But this one would give no indication of his belief that they were close; it would be a simple summary of how the investigation was progressing. He finished the first paragraph then realised it was better to stop. Cosmas was to spend the day investigating Bathyllos, the owners, and anything else he could find out about the factory. If he discovered anything useful, it would be best to include it. Cassius reread the paragraph – no mistakes – and left the ink to dry. He put his silver pen in the holder and got up from the table.

Indavara still had his eyes closed. Cassius considered asking about the girl but he reckoned the bodyguard might not want to talk about it in front of Simo. In any case, as long as it didn't affect his work, it wasn't of great importance. They would be leaving Berytus soon; he would simply have to forget her.

'That fresh tunic?'

'It's on your bed, sir.'

Indavara waited until he heard Corbulo's door shut.

'You all right?' asked Simo, who could always tell whether he was actually sleeping or not.

Indavara sat up. 'That girl. Mahalie.'

'Yes?'

'Her owners – they did things to her. Hurt her. She went to Cobon but he wouldn't help. He said she had to learn to live with her master and mistress. That was wrong, Simo. He was wrong.'

'You've seen her, then?'

'Yes. I . . . saw them too.'

Simo's face grew visibly paler. He sat on his bed, opposite Indavara.

'Don't worry. I didn't do anything. Perhaps I should have.'

'That is not the way. Violence is not the way.'

Indavara admired a lot about Simo and Cobon but he'd had just about enough of their stupid beliefs. A promise of paradise after death couldn't help Mahalie now.

He got up so quickly that the legs of the bed scraped across the floor. 'It's *their* way, Simo. It's their way. But if I did something to them, it's Mahalie that would suffer. Before we leave this city I am going to get her out of that house. By my Fortuna, I swear it.'

Cosmas didn't return until the eighth hour. After a shout from Simo, Cassius came downstairs and Indavara roused himself. It was another baking-hot day and the sergeant asked for a drink before disclosing what he'd discovered.

'Something's going on there. No question. The previous owner of the factory and the sarcophagus business was named Niarchos – local man, member of the city council, respected family. Three months ago, he sold the entire concern: the factory, the vehicles, the transport contracts, the clients all across Syria and beyond. The clerk at the basilica who dealt with the sale told me it raised a few eyebrows because Niarchos' family had been running it for more than a century and made good money out of it. But the new buyer paid well over the odds.'

'So who is he?' asked Cassius.

'That's where it gets interesting. The negotiations and the purchase were run through a third party.' Cosmas reached into a pocket and pulled out a scrap of paper. 'A man named Pylades who described himself as an independent broker. His name is on all the paperwork – the purchase was made in cash. Two thousand, eight hundred aurei. They really wanted that factory.'

'The transport and distribution network is just as important,' said Cassius. 'What about this Pylades?'

'No one I spoke to actually saw the man. His references all went through and Niarchos was happy to move swiftly with such a good offer on the table. The purchase dues were paid on time, as have all other taxes been since. As far as I can tell, the business has continued as normal, apart from one change.'

'Bathyllos – I bet these mysterious new owners brought him in.'

'Exactly right, sir.'

'What about tracking down Pylades?'

'According to the basilica, his offices are in Antioch.'

'Conveniently out of the way. Still, I can get Quentin on to it, Abascantius too.'

'That'll take time, though,' pointed out Indavara.

'It will.' Cassius turned to Cosmas. 'Excellent work. With what you've uncovered today I'm even more certain. We will try and get inside tonight. I'll inform Pomponianus that we're continuing to monitor the factory but not that we're going in.'

Cosmas grimaced.

'He is not favourably disposed towards myself or the Service,' explained Cassius. 'I need solid evidence before involving him.'

'I can't be part of it, sir – not without Pomponianus' authorisation. And what about Diadromes?'

'I don't want to put him in a bind. We'll say that we were watching the factory then heard noises and decided to investigate.'

Cosmas considered this.

'Please,' said Cassius, 'we have come so far.'

As usual, Cosmas needed a few tugs on his beard to make up his mind. 'Very well.'

'You'll help us? The Service will of course reward you appropriately for this and all your efforts so far.'

'"Appropriately" is a bit vague for me, sir.'

'Let us say four aurei if the investigation is brought to a satisfactory conclusion, two if it is not.'

'Fair enough, sir. Ah, there was one other thing – the factory was closed for two weeks – the first half of last month.'

'Essential construction work?'

'Could be.'

'And if we do find they're making the coins under there?' said Indavara. 'What then?'

'We grab whatever evidence we can, show it to Diadromes and Pomponianus, then raid the whole place tomorrow. Bathyllos will be the key – if we can turn him, we'll get this Pylades character and whoever else is pulling the strings.'

'What time do you want to try it?' asked Cosmas.

'Let's go over the details now,' said Cassius. 'We cannot afford to get this wrong. If Bathyllos gets spooked we might lose him and his masters. We have to get in and out without the guards ever knowing we were there.'

Cassius put the libation down then knelt before his makeshift shrine.

Jupiter, god of gods, I give this to you, a symbol of my lifelong and everlasting love and devotion. In return, I ask that you watch over us tonight. The Emperor himself has charged us with this noble mission; please help us succeed.

Clad only in his loincloth, Cassius stood. Lifelong and everlasting? Well, it was on and off, to be honest, but he had offered countless libations and prayers for the last year or so. And although he had prostrated himself in front of all twelve of the great gods, Cassius had recently decided to focus his efforts on Jupiter – it usually paid to go straight to the top.

He kicked off his sandals, then walked over to the bedside table and picked up his spearhead badge – it might be useful to have some form of identification with him. Other than that, everything else he would need was downstairs. He found Simo cleaning his mail shirt as instructed.

Indavara was clearly still not himself. Whenever there was any hint of prospective action he could usually be found checking and rechecking his equipment. But the bodyguard was sitting on his bed, looking down at the figurine in his hand.

Cassius took the old, short-sleeved tunic Simo had put out for him and pulled it on.

'A snack for you there, sir.'

Cassius eyed the plate of bread, goat's cheese and olives Simo had prepared for him. He reached for a chunk of bread, then decided his stomach was fluttering too much.

'You should have something, sir.' The attendant had laid the mail shirt out on a blanket and was polishing the rings.

'Pack it up and put it in my satchel for later, would you?'

'Yes, sir.'

Cassius wandered over to Indavara. 'Were I of a more sensitive disposition, I might take offence at the fact that I've never once seen you holding that very expensive silver-plate figurine of Fortuna I bought you in Antioch.'

'I have it,' said the bodyguard without looking up.

'Buried in a bag somewhere, I expect. May I see that one?'

After a long hesitation, Indavara gave it to him. Cassius noted that the folds of the goddess's tunic and the features of her face were even more worn than the last time he'd held it.

'You know you can get these repaired. A skilled craftsman could put the shape back into it – so it looks a bit more like who it's supposed to be.'

'I know who it is, that's all that matters.' Indavara put out his hand.

Cassius returned it to him. 'I suppose so. You all right?'

'Fine.'

'You didn't go and see her, did you? This girl?'

'Leave it, Corbulo.'

'Very well. Just make sure your mind is on the job tonight.'

From outside came the sound of shouting. Curious, Cassius walked over to the door; the tower was in a quiet neighbourhood and they rarely heard much noise. He peered through the viewing hole and saw a group of about twenty youths marching past. They began a vociferous chant in Aramaic.

'Wonder what that's all about.'

'They are celebrating, sir,' said Simo. 'I spoke to the water-carriers about it. The court must have decided on clemency for the youths who defaced the statue.'

'Probably a flogging, then. Looks like Diadromes got his way with the magistrate.' Cassius sat down next to the boots Simo had put out for him – a well-worn pair with a thick sole, comfortable and without the nails or studs that could be unreliable on a smooth surface – Cassius often referred to them as his 'running boots'. Once they were on, he stood up and walked over to the table. 'Right, I suppose I'd better get this crap on.'

He reached for the brown padded shirt that would go under his armour.

Indavara got up off the bed. 'You're really going to wear your mail all night? In this heat?'

'Indeed I am. You know how much I paid for the accursed thing and yet events have continuously conspired to ensure that I am usually found without it when I actually need it. What if there are more guards *under* that factory?'

Indavara drew his short sword from the sheath lying on his bed and ran a finger along the edge. The setting sun was still providing enough light to illuminate the tower.

'Might be tight down there.' He pointed at Cassius's sword, which was on the table beside the armour. 'Probably best if you keep that bloody great thing sheathed. Swinging it around in a small space you're as likely to cut me or yourself as anyone else.'

'Don't worry. As I've already caught you once this week, I shall do my best to spare you further injury.'

To avoid embarrassing himself in front of Indavara, Cassius had taught himself to put on the undershirt and the armour without Simo's assistance. Once the mail shirt was hanging straight, he put on a thick leather belt and buckled it. Next he lifted the sword belt and put it over his right shoulder. Indavara had made a good point; the blade was unwieldy and the ornate eagle head made it hard to draw quickly, but many officers favoured such weapons and Cassius was determined to get used to it.

'You've cleaned and oiled it, I hope,' said Indavara.

'Did it this morning. Just like you showed me.'

Indavara offered a grunt of approval.

Cassius took his dagger sheath and fitted it on to his main belt. 'Tell me what's in my satchel, Simo.'

'Lantern and the fire-starting kit, sir; your money bag, a flask of water, and the food.'

'Good. Put the spearhead badge in there too. I can hardly pin it on this.'

Cassius watched as the big Gaul did as instructed. In the old days he might have taken him with them. Simo was a peerless practitioner when it came to sparking a flame and knew a great deal about treating injuries, but his refusal to fight or even carry a weapon made him a liability; not to mention his lumbering frame and complete inability to run.

Simo was about to buckle the satchel but paused. 'If you're going underground might you need some rope? I believe we have a coil somewhere.'

'I don't think we'll be going far enough down to need a rope,' said Cassius.

'No, it's a good idea,' said Indavara, kneeling down to retie his bootlaces.

Simo waited for a nod from Cassius before delving under the table. He pulled the rope out of a sack and tied it to the strap of the satchel.

'You will be careful, sir,' he said as he put the bag over his master's shoulder.

'I will. Ready?'

Indavara sheathed his blade and followed Cassius to the door.

'Bolt it behind us and keep it locked.'

'Yes, sir,' said Simo as he opened it.

Outside, the streets and buildings were bathed in the orange glow that preceded dusk.

Cassius stopped just beyond the ruined wall. 'At the risk of repeating myself, I wanted to say – if we do run into trouble . . . you will stay calm?'

Indavara glared at him. 'I will do what I need to, when I need to.'

'Of course.' Cassius had felt he needed to say something but now wished he'd kept quiet. 'Sorry. I have every confidence in you.'

'Wish I could say the same.'

Alexon thumped a fist on to the iron rail of the balcony. 'How long have we been here? Not even a hundred days. I knew it. I knew it.'

He had seen the lantern at the gate and the two men hurry up the drive. Skiron had been gone for a long time and was now returning with Kallikres. Alexon was in no doubt that they were bringing the worst possible news.

Outside the lounge, the maids were packing up clothes and ornaments. Amathea had resisted to begin with but as the hours passed and darkness fell, she had acceded to his request that they at least be ready to leave if need be. She kissed him gently on the cheek and offered him his glass.

He returned the kiss but refused the wine. 'I must keep a clear head. So should you.'

He heard boots on the steps then hurried across to the landing, Amathea close behind. Skiron came up first. His tunic was soaked, his bald head wet with rain. Kallikres' hair was plastered to his brow.

'Well?' demanded Alexon.

Before Skiron could speak, Kallikres came forward, accidentally kicking a box of valuables.

'Sorry,' he spluttered. 'I wasn't hiding. I was out working – getting information for you.'

Alexon glanced at Skiron, who nodded. 'And?'

'Crispian is reporting to Pomponianus daily. I couldn't find out what he passed on today but Cosmas – the sergeant who's been working with Crispian – has been sniffing around the basilica, asking about the factory's owners and Bathyllos.'

Alexon felt as if he'd been struck. He scraped his fingers down his cheeks then rubbed his forehead.

'You're still not exposed, Master,' said Skiron. 'They know the name Pylades but not that it's you.'

Amathea put a hand on his arm. 'Skiron is right, brother, this is why you were so careful. You have protected us.'

'Gods, why can't you see it? Once they had the factory it was over. It's just a matter of time.'

'They may not know what's really there,' said Kallikres.

'You,' spat Amathea. 'You do not speak unless you are spoken to. If you'd done as you were supposed to we could have eliminated this threat immediately.'

Behind the two new arrivals, the maids were looking on.

'Get downstairs, you three!' shrieked Amathea. 'And send the men and the boy up.'

Alexon walked back into the lounge, past the candles and the couches into the dark centre of the room.

Amathea followed him. 'Alexon, this is not over yet. We can get rid of this Crispian, this sergeant too.'

'No, Amathea. It has gone too far now. We have made a good profit and we have the dies; we can start again somewhere new. We clear out the workshop and leave nothing behind. You and I will depart in the morning.'

He looked around the room. 'I'm just glad we didn't buy this place.'

Having expected resistance, Alexon was surprised by his sister's reply.

'You are right.' She walked back across the lounge.

Alexon had done his part. Now Amathea would do hers. He followed her back to the landing and watched the three Itureans come up the stairs.

They had been ordered not to drink and had already armed themselves. Their bows were strung and their quivers and long knives hung from their belts. The last of them also had a chain in his hand. Attached to the other end of it was an iron collar around the neck of the young slave Pedrix. The hunter pushed him forward.

Alexon watched Kallikres. The sergeant reached out and touched his lover on the arm. The young man looked up, eyes widening as recognition dawned. The sergeant gulped and opened his mouth but said nothing.

Amathea pointed at Skiron. 'Grab the workshop crew and a cart. You will empty the place of anything essential and bring it here.' She pointed at the hunters. 'Take these three with you in case of trouble.'

'Yes, Mistress.'

She moved on to Kallikres. 'Do you want Pedrix to see another day?'

'Yes.'

'Then you go with them. And if any of your sergeants or legionaries get in the way, you do what you have to. Because if our men and that cart don't make it back here, your sweet boy will not leave this place alive.'

Kallikres nodded, water still dripping from his hair.

'Go.'

Skiron barked a few instructions at the Itureans and followed them down the stairs. Kallikres tried to whisper something to Pedrix but Amathea pushed him away. 'Get out of here.'

When the noise of their boots had faded, Alexon picked up the chain and tied it around a banister. The young Syrian shuffled away from them and started snivelling.

'We must continue our preparations,' said Alexon. It wasn't the first time they'd had to halt an operation and move on. He doubted it would be the last.

Amathea was staring at a fresco on a nearby wall. The pastoral was her favourite in the house – she'd insisted the owner had it repainted before they moved in.

'Just as I was getting the place how I liked it.'

She darted forward, hair slicing through the air behind her, and slapped Pedrix hard in the face.

XXXII

They met Cosmas by the statue, arriving just as the last drops of rain fell. The sergeant was holding a short rope ladder, one end of which was equipped with metal hooks. He already had a lantern alight but shuttered it as they embarked upon a circuitous route to the rear of the sarcophagus factory. Having avoided the attentions of various nightwatchmen, they gathered by the gate.

'It's quieter if I secure the hooks by hand instead of throwing it over,' whispered Cosmas. 'Indavara, give me a leg up.'

Cassius took the lantern and watched as Indavara hoisted up the sergeant. The nimble Cosmas swiftly affixed the hooks then used the rope ladder to climb up. Cassius was next, then Indavara. Once they were all perched on the wall, Cosmas reversed the hooks and let the ladder down into the yard. When they were safely on the ground, they stood in silence for a while, listening for any sign of danger.

'Sounds clear,' said Cosmas eventually. 'But watch your step and keep quiet. Those sentries might be patrolling.'

With Indavara behind him, Cassius followed Cosmas towards the factory. Despite a few clouds there was sufficient moonlight for him to make out the building ahead and the surrounding walls. Once at the rear right corner, Cosmas headed left until they reached the broad gate through which Cassius had exited the previous day.

While the sergeant knelt by the lock and took out his picks, Cassius and Indavara dropped down on either side of him, facing outward in case the guards appeared. Cassius wiped sweat out of his eyes: it wasn't just the warmth and humidity of the night, the armour made every movement difficult and he was no longer used to hauling the sword around. Behind him, the picks scratched and scraped as Cosmas did his work. The Syrian seemed confident that he could open almost any lock; presumably another skill that had made him useful to Diadromes over the years.

After about a minute, the sergeant stopped.

'Problem?' whispered Cassius over his shoulder.

'Workings have been greased recently. I'll get it, though.'

'Maybe some light?'

'No, it's more about feeling than seeing.'

As Cosmas kept at it, Cassius's thoughts shifted to what they might find inside. There had been so many false dawns with the investigation that he wouldn't feel satisfied until he actually had a fake denarius in his hand. He shook his head as he reflected on how they'd got to this point. After all his theories and schemes and mistakes, the breakthrough had come because Indavara wanted to help Christians find abandoned babies, not to mention the pauper lads who'd retrieved the rejected coins from the dump. Surely some playful god somewhere was watching all this with a smile.

'Ah,' said Cosmas. 'Come on, you bugger, just a little . . .'

Something clicked. 'There we go.' The sergeant removed the picks then opened one side of the gate. Once they were several paces into the inky darkness, Cassius opened the shutter of the lantern an inch. Ahead were the angular outlines of the finished sarcophagi laid out in rows. As he was the only one who had been inside, he took the lead.

'Over to the right.'

Beyond the last of the coffins, they entered the forge. Cassius opened the shutter a little wider and located the barrel Molacus had noted. He held the lantern close to the top and found it contained hefty cuts of wood.

'Careful,' he said as Indavara and Cosmas each grabbed the rim of the barrel. 'We don't want it scraping on the floor.'

'Gods,' said Cosmas. 'Must weigh as much as a man.'

Indavara said, 'We need to tip it on its edge then turn it.'

He and Cosmas levered one side of the barrel off the ground. Once they had spun it out of the way, Cassius lowered the lantern towards the floor.

'Well, well. Thank the gods for observant factory inspectors.'

The wooden hatch was about two feet wide.

Cosmas knelt and put his ear against the timbers. 'Can't hear anything. Hopefully the workers are all tucked up in bed before their early shift.'

Indavara drew his blade and stood in front of the hatch. 'There's only one way to find out.'

Cosmas grabbed the knotted rope that functioned as a handle and lifted the hatch. Cassius stood by Indavara and felt a chill breath of air float up from below. He crouched down and lowered the lantern into the space, then pulled the shutter fully open. A sloping ladder led straight down about fifteen feet to an earthen floor. Also visible was the end of a table.

'Shall I?' asked Indavara.

'Please.'

'Keep that light there.'

Indavara descended facing forward, one hand on the ladder, sword at the ready. When he was halfway down, he looked up. 'No one here. Give me the lantern.'

Cassius did so then climbed down. As Cosmas followed, Indavara sheathed his sword and held the lantern up, spreading the misty yellow light. It was a small chamber, perhaps only six yards wide. The table had nothing on it and the high shelves lining all four walls housed only amphoras. Cassius felt his initial excitement fading.

Cosmas took the lantern from Indavara and held it close to the nearest shelf. 'They're all filled with some sort of white paint – maybe for upstairs. Perhaps they need to keep it cool.'

'Perhaps,' said Cassius. 'But if so, why hide the hatch? Looks to me like a handy excuse in case anyone found this place.' He glanced up at the roof, picturing where the oven was in relation to the hatch.

'Cosmas, some light here.' He walked to the right side of the chamber and inspected the shelving. Two sections were divided by a narrow gap. Cassius pressed his face close to the wall and saw that the shelf to his left hadn't been leant up against the brick but was actually attached to it.

'A fair attempt, but not entirely convincing.' He pushed his hand behind the shelf and soon located a hook. He took it out of the ring stuck to the back of the shelf then retreated.

'Hinge must be to the left.'

'Careful,' said Cosmas. 'The amphoras.'

'I wouldn't worry.' Cassius pulled on the shelf and the entire thing swung towards him. Behind it was a narrow doorway.

'By Jupiter.' Cosmas took a closer look at the amphoras on the shelf. 'Stuck to the back with glue.' He put his hand into one. 'It's not even liquid – just painted white to look like the others. Crafty bastards.'

'Luckily we have our own crafty bastard,' said Indavara as Cassius pushed the secret door all the way open.

Taking the lantern from Cosmas, he led the way into the second chamber, which was was so large that the light didn't reach the corners. Cassius was already grinning. Sitting on a wooden pallet in front of him were at least a dozen well-filled sacks. They weren't even tied at the top so he reached inside and pulled out a handful of denarii.

'Gods' blood,' said Cosmas as he and Indavara stared down at the coins. 'Must be thousands in each bag.'

Cassius dropped them back into the sack, keeping only one, which he held close to the lantern. The coin had smooth edges, precise lettering and a clear image of the Emperor's face. 'Looks like they're a long way past the experimental stage.' And when he looked more closely, he saw the two telltale marks Quentin had identified. 'This is it. This is the gang spreading these fakes all over the East.'

He dropped the coin into his satchel then walked to the left along the edge of the room. He passed several tables fitted with anvils and saw two hammers just like the one Indavara had wielded in the Tripolis mint.

'That's why it's so far down. Even when the factory's going, they need a few yards of earth to cover the noise.'

He reached another wall, then turned right. Close to the next corner was a small, shadowy tunnel.

'Wonder where that leads,' said Indavara.

'Might be for ventilation,' said Cassius. 'Or an escape route.'

334

'Could connect to the catacombs,' said Cosmas. 'There are thousands of tunnels under the city. Some lead to tombs, some to the water supply and the sewers. Shall I check it?'

'Yes, but be quick.'

As Cosmas lit a candle and set off, Cassius continued on around the edge of the room, pacing it out. The chamber measured twelve yards by eight; the gang must have worked quickly to construct it in only two weeks while the factory was closed. He also noticed a small vent at each corner, presumably running up to the surface.

Cassius stood over the oven, which was housed to the right of the door. Though it was on the small side, the only unusual feature was the chimney. Halfway up the wall, the clay pipe joined a metal cylinder that disappeared into the roof. Cassius bent over the oven and put his hand above the coals inside – they were still warm.

As he straightened up, Indavara joined him.

'Moulds here; bronze, iron and copper over there.'

'There's just one thing missing,' replied Cassius.

'The dies.'

'Yes. The sergeants can grab all this later but we can't risk losing the dies. They must be here somewhere.'

The workshop was very tidy and it didn't take them long to spot the strongbox. Cassius held the lantern while Indavara picked it up and dumped it on to a desk.

'Gods, that's heavy.'

It was a larger version of Cassius's, constructed of a thick hardwood and reinforced with iron bands. He was not surprised to find it locked.

'I doubt they keep the key here.'

'Use one of the hammers?' suggested Indavara.

'What about the noise?'

'It weighs a ton – you want to try getting it out of here and back over that wall without making a peep?'

'Maybe Cosmas can get it open with his picks.' Cassius turned towards the tunnel; the light from the sergeant's candle was faint. 'Hope that doesn't go too far.'

'Let's look for the key. You never know.'

While Indavara hunted through some small pots on a nearby shelf, Cassius checked the three drawers of the desk. He found only writing materials in the first and blank sheets of paper in the second. The third contained a large, leather-bound ledger which he took out. Flicking through the first few pages he found a remarkable level of detail, right down to how many pounds of metal had been used and how many coins had been produced each day. There had been a crew of eight labouring there under the supervision of a senior man who looked after the ledger. That very day they had minted over four thousand coins.

'By the gods.' He tapped the page. 'Got you, you criminal bastards. Got you.'

'It's not here,' said Indavara.

'No. We'll have to—'

The noise came from above.

They both looked up, heard boots crossing the factory floor. Cassius managed to put the ledger down silently even though his hands were shaking. They strode over to the doorway, looked up at the hatch.

Light; dim at first, then brighter. Voices; loud at first, then quieter.

They retreated into the workshop without a word. Cassius picked up his satchel and left only a half-inch of the lantern shutter open.

'The tunnel?' whispered Indavara.

'What if Cosmas didn't find a way out?'

'Isn't that why it's there?'

'We'd better hope so.'

As they passed the doorway, the first man was already coming down the ladder. Cassius hurried along the edge of the room, then ducked into the tunnel, which was barely five feet high. It was narrow too, cut from dark earth striped with sand and dotted with bits of rubble. Every few yards was a frame of timber covering the sides and the roof.

'They behind us?'

'Not yet, just keep going.'

336

Cassius had counted fifty paces when the lantern light caught something pale to his right. He stopped and heard Indavara mutter an oath. They were now standing at an intersection where a larger tunnel crossed the one they were in at an angle. To the left it was clear, to the right it had been walled off with limestone blocks after only a few feet.

'Corbulo, they're in the workshop.'

Cassius pressed on, head bent over, arms scraping the sides. After twenty-nine more paces, he came to what seemed like a dead end. Then he realised the the tunnel turned abruptly to the right.

'Quick,' said Indavara.

Cassius followed the turn and found the true end of the tunnel. Fortunately there was also a vertical shaft with a ladder attached to it. At the top of it he could see a square of starry sky.

'Cosmas?' Cassius didn't dare shout.

No reply.

'Where in Hades is he?'

'Just get up there,' hissed Indavara.

'You go first. It's difficult with the lantern.'

The bodyguard squeezed past. He put his foot on the bottom rung then looked up and froze. 'Cosmas, that you?'

No reply.

'Get ba—' Cassius didn't finish his warning.

Indavara threw himself backwards, knocking Cassius into the side of the tunnel.

Something thudded into the ground.

'What was that?'

'Arrow,' said Indavara.

'The other tunnel. Come on – we have to get back to it before they do.'

Cassius closed the lantern shutter completely and set off back around the corner. The lights in the workshop were now bright and he could see the silhouettes of men moving around.

Twenty-nine paces.

Twenty-five.

One of the men moved in front of the light. He was standing at the other end of the tunnel, looking into it.

Twenty paces. Fifteen.

The man moved. He wasn't coming forward but he was definitely doing something.

Five paces.

'Down!'

Cassius ignored Indavara; he was almost there. Just as he was about to dart into the other tunnel something punched his right shoulder. The impact spun him and he landed heavily on his back. The next thing he knew, Indavara had picked him up, dragged him into the blocked tunnel and propped him against the limestone wall.

An increasingly sharp pain was lancing into his shoulder. 'What happened?'

'Arrow.'

'Gods, it must have gone through. I can feel it.'

The lantern had smashed, leaving them in darkness so complete that Cassius couldn't see Indavara in front of him.

'Where did it hit?' asked the bodyguard.

'Shoulder.'

'Which?'

'Left, er, no, right.'

'Make up your mind.' Indavara ran his hand over the armour. 'It went through, didn't it? Just tell me the truth.'

'No. Few bent rings, that's all.'

'Don't give me that, I can feel it.'

'And I can feel the undershirt – not even a hole. You're fine. But next time I say get down – get down.'

Indavara moved away for a moment then returned. 'They're coming. Both directions. The men to the right will get here first. We need a light or we've had it. I'll stick the first man, you take his lantern.'

'Then what?'

'Go for that tunnel opposite.'

'We don't know where it goes. What do you think happened to—'

'Quiet. Get behind me.'

Cassius did so and heard Indavara's blade slide out of the

338

sheath. The lamplight coming from the right grew brighter. Then came a shout; and a conversation in a language Cassius couldn't identify.

'Use Greek!' yelled someone. 'Did you hit them?'

'Not sure.'

The light was close. Indavara pressed himself against the wall and moved forward.

'Keep coming,' said a voice from the left. It sounded like an older man. 'Quick, they might be in the other tunnel.'

'What other tunnel?'

Indavara was gone. Cassius leaped out behind him and saw the agonised terror on his victim's face as the blade pierced his neck.

'Lantern!'

Cassius reached around Indavara and pulled it from the dying man's grip. Once he had it, Indavara kicked his victim in the chest, sending him flying back into whoever was behind him.

Cassius was on his way. Hearing shouts from both sides, he sprang into the tunnel. Here at least he could stand up straight; the curved roof was a foot above him. Like the floor and walls it was brick: dank, mouldy and crumbling. Cassius couldn't run at full pace; apart from the armour and the uneven surface underfoot, he had to keep the lantern alight.

'Hurry!' bawled Indavara. 'If we don't find cover we're sitting ducks for those bows.'

In his efforts to speed up, the bodyguard lost his footing and nearly fell. Pausing to wait for him, Cassius glanced back along the tunnel. The two lanterns were bobbing, the dark figures moving quickly – no more than thirty feet away.

They ran on, side by side. An arrow flew past, so close to Cassius's ear that he flinched and almost stumbled. 'Gods!'

'Least you've got your armour,' said Indavara. 'Where's a bloody turn when we need one?'

Another bolt clattered into the wall just behind them.

'What's that?' said Indavara. 'On your side.'

They stopped by a narrow opening in the brickwork. Two rats that been running away from them scurried inside. Cassius looked back; their pursuers had stopped.

'Down,' snapped Indavara.

Just as they crouched, a third bolt shot past.

'No good,' said Cassius, reading the Greek on a plaque attached to the wall. 'A crypt. There'll be no way through.'

Indavara shuttered the lantern. 'We can still use it. You go on. I'll give them a surprise.'

'You sure?'

'Just go. But you must show them the light.'

'Right.' Cassius opened the shutter then got to his feet and pounded away along the tunnel, weaving from side to side as best he could.

Not now, please, Jupiter, not now. Not here. Not like this. Not like—

The arrow thumped into him. He stopped, waited for the pain.

But it didn't come. He looked down. The bolt had gone through one side of the satchel and stuck there.

Jupiter, thank you!

He ran on, even though no more arrows came.

After a few more paces he belatedly noticed that the colour of the bricks had changed. They were newer and in better condition. And he spied little channels in the walls dripping water on to the floor. Then he realised something else. The tunnel had begun to slope downwards.

XXXIII

Indavara had no plan other than to come out swinging. He was glad Corbulo was out of the way; this would be basic and bloody. The thrum of the footsteps came quickly, the grainy yellow light too. At the first glimpse he leapt out at them.

The first man was lucky. He tried to slow himself but slipped and was already falling when Indavara struck. The blade caught the bow in his hand, slicing the string but doing no other damage.

The others – three or four, he couldn't be sure – were almost past him when they realised they were under attack. One reacted far quicker than the others. Eyes glinting in a dark, bearded face, he dropped his bow and plucked a long knife from his belt.

Indavara sidestepped to his right; he had to protect his escape route.

The quick-thinking warrior charged past an older, bald-headed man, arm and knife outstretched.

Indavara swatted the knife away, rolled his wrists and sliced up at his face.

The warrior threw himself backwards, avoiding the blade by inches.

Indavara was about to strike again when a second wild-looking warrior came at him from the left. Knowing he couldn't get the sword around in time, he ducked low.

The knife edge scraped his skull. He threw an elbow up and caught the warrior on the wrist. As the blade clattered into the roof, Indavara drove up off his ankles and hacked two-handed into the warrior's side. The sword cut deep – like an axe into a tree. He only just kept hold of the blade as his victim groaned and fell.

The bald man took his turn. Calmly holding a lantern with one hand, he flicked his sword at Indavara's face, forcing him back against the wall.

With a bestial cry, the first knife-man rejoined the fray. Hair hanging over his face, he swung his blade in a wide arc. Indavara parried, then shuffled right again to stop the bald man cutting him off. He sensed movement to his left, a third man closing in. Two he could just about handle. Three?

Something flew out of the darkness and struck the bald man on the face. Shocked but apparently unharmed, he looked down at the ground. Lying on the tunnel floor was a hunk of bread.

'Indavara, there's a way out!'

He didn't need a second invitation and soon found himself running again beside Corbulo. 'Where?'

'We just have to keep going. This is a feeder channel, I think it runs down into the main aqueduct – remember how close to the baths we are.'

'Here?' Indavara slowed as they passed an intersecting tunnel of similar dimensions.

'No, straight on.'

Indavara snatched a look over his shoulder. Their pursuers were already on the move again. When he turned back he realised that the floor underfoot was now smooth and that they were splashing through several inches of water.

'Careful,' said Corbulo. 'It suddenly gets very steep up—'

He fell first, fractionally ahead of Indavara. The stolen lantern smashed, leaving them in utter darkness once again.

Indavara came down on his backside. His right arm hit a moment later, knocking the sword out of his hand. He slid down the slope, stone scraping his skin. Just as he spied a little light up ahead his legs plunged into cold water. Then it was up to his chest, then his head went under.

The shock of it froze him.

He couldn't think, couldn't tell himself what to do. His boots slid, unable to find purchase. His arms flailed around, trapped in the horrible nothingness he feared above all else. He felt it in his nose, his mouth, forcing its way inside. The water was trying to kill him again.

Something pulled his belt up, then fingers circled his arm.

Cassius hauled him out of the water. 'Just stand up, man! Stand up straight – it's only three feet deep.'

Coughing and panting, the bodyguard put out his hands and finally steadied himself.

'Gods. Calm yourself.'

Indavara sucked in some breaths, then crashed a fist into the water.

'Where in Hades are we?'

'I told you. The main channel.'

'We were better off up there! You should have left me to it.'

Ignoring this idiocy, Cassius looked around. The channel was about five yards across with a high, curved roof. Directly above them was a circular grille providing a bit of light from the streets above. The water was waist deep and flowing past them at some rate. Cassius had already taken his hands out to avoid the weed and other detritus. Unlike in the dank, musty tunnels, here there was a sweet tang to the air that somehow seemed even more unpleasant.

'There'll be maintenance access somewhere. We just have to work out which way.' As he checked he still had his sword and the satchel, he realised the cold water was already making him shiver.

From the feeder channel came the sound of voices.

'Help me find my sword,' said Indavara.

'I will but don't worry, we've got time. They won't follow us down here.'

'Corbulo, I just killed two of them.'

'There's no way they're going to follow u—'

The two shapes hit the water almost simultaneously. It took Cassius a while to absorb the fact that they were men.

Indavara waded forward, dagger already drawn. The first of them came up quickly. Indavara looked all set to stick him when

343

the warrior launched himself across the tunnel and clamped his hands around his wrists. They struggled on, twisting through the water, fighting to control the blade.

Cassius was reaching for his sword. By the time he realised his dagger would be more use to him, the second warrior was close. Cassius tried to back away but his right foot slipped and flew up. Before he could regain his balance the man was on him.

Cassius snatched a breath then went under. With one hand gripping his hair and another on his chest the warrior had him pinned.

He doesn't need a blade. He's going to drown me.

The bastard was strong. Cassius lashed out at the hand on his chest but couldn't shift it. He reached down to try to push himself back up but his right arm was weighed down by the satchel.

Satchel. The arrow's still stuck in it.

He gripped the shaft, wrenched it free.

Indavara turned the warrior towards the tunnel wall and pushed him into it. The man's fingers pulled and scratched at his, trying to loosen his grip on the dagger. Their heads were close; the Syrian's long, wet hair was tickling Indavara's nose. He felt breath on his neck, then teeth on his ear. His good ear.

Oh no you don't.

Indavara smashed his forehead into the warrior, catching him just above the eye. The bones could be broken there, he knew.

The second butt was harder. Pain pulsed through his skull but he'd heard the crack; with the eye socket broken, his enemy would be hurting more.

The grip on his wrists went slack. He knocked the warrior aside with his elbows. The man went under for a moment and came up spluttering.

Gripping the man's shoulder to help him aim, Indavara stuck the dagger deep into his throat. When he pulled it back out, the gurgling told him he'd done enough. As warm blood streamed down his fingers, he turned, ready to help Corbulo. All he could see was the warrior's back.

Cassius stabbed the point of the arrow into the hand. Instantly the weight came off his chest and his hair was freed. He pivoted forward, planted his feet and came up out of the water. The warrior was standing right in front of him, holding his wounded hand.

A broad shape loomed behind him then something thumped into the warrior's back. Breath rushed out of him. Head sagging, he gave a final whimper and pitched forward into the water.

'All right?' grunted Indavara.

'I am now,' said Cassius between breaths.

The flow of the water washed the dead warrior down on to him.

'Uh.' He pushed the corpse away.

Indavara grabbed the other dead man and sent him after his compatriot. 'Corbulo, tell me you can get us out of here.'

Still breathing hard, Cassius grabbed the wall to steady himself. 'I think so. Judging by the noise there's some kind of drop behind me so we should probably go the other way. Oh.'

There was light in the tunnel and the noise of someone sloshing towards them. Cassius moved up beside Indavara. The two figures could be seen quite clearly.

'Ah, shit,' said Indavara. 'That bald bastard and the other man. Probably only them left.'

'They must have found another way down. There's probably dozens of feeder channels.'

The bald man was carrying a bow, the other man a lantern.

Indavara waded over to the feeder channel they had slid down. The steep angle, smooth surface and flowing water made climbing up it a virtual impossibility.

The bald man called out in Aramaic. Recieving no reply, he reached over his shoulder and took an arrow from the quiver.

Cassius and Indavara lowered themselves into the water.

'This drop behind us,' said the bodyguard. 'Drop into what?'

'Probably a cistern – a big tank.'

'Of water?'

'Indavara, we're inside an aqueduct.'

'Deep?'

'Could be.'

The advancing pair were thirty feet away. The man with the lantern opened the shutter wide.

'Got that rope?' asked Indavara.

Cassius pulled the satchel out of the water. Indavara detached the rope and uncoiled it.

'You want to tie us together?'

'If it's deep, you'll have to pull me out of there.'

Cassius hesitated; if the water *was* deep the bodyguard would panic and he stood almost no chance of getting him out. More likely they'd both drown.

The bald man peered along the tunnel towards them. 'I know you're there,' he said in Greek. Holding the bow at an angle to keep it out of the water, he nocked the arrow and drew the string.

'We'll just hold on to it,' said Cassius. 'That's safer.'

The bowstring pinged and arrow flew between them, hitting the water a few yards back.

'It's summer,' said Indavara as they retreated. 'So it shouldn't be that deep, right?'

'Right.' Cassius didn't mention that this was the place where all the water from hundreds of different sources was directed to fill the city's central reservoirs. He passed one end of the rope to Indavara and held the rest in his hand.

'Let's turn round, make sure we go in feet first.'

Cassius heard the bodyguard's breathing accelerate. He could also hear the rumble of falling water not far ahead.

'Just let it take you.'

Indavara said, 'I'll sink.'

'I'm the one wearing the armour – you'll float. Just hold on to the rope.'

'Not a problem.'

'I see you!' yelled the old man.

'Now.' Cassius brought his legs up and was instantly pulled along by the water. 'You there?'

He heard a splutter, then, 'Here!'

They smashed into each other, arms and legs tangling. Cassius went under, felt his feet scrape the bottom, then everything fell away and he was tumbling through the darkness.

There was no splash, no rush of water.

Only a heavy splat as he landed on his back. He put his hands down and felt thick, slimy mud beneath his fingers. The sweet, fetid smell rushed up his nostrils and he almost gagged. Water from the tunnel was cascading down in front of him, splashing his lower half and running in rivulets beneath him. He looked up. Far, far above was a double line of circles admitting a little light.

'Indavara?'

'Here.'

Cassius realised he could see him, a few feet to his right. He could also make out the outline of pillars running along the side of the chamber. Whatever they were in, it was big.

'My Fortuna is watching over us,' said Indavara, almost laughing. 'Mud. Just mud.'

Cassius – still lying on his back – turned to the left. The pillars looked closer on this side and he could make out a horizontal line below them. He also realised he could see no trace of the two dead warriors.

Cassius felt a void form beneath his backside and he dropped several inches into the mud.

Indavara was twisting around. 'Mind you, it might not be easy to—'

'Don't move.'

'What? Oh shit, I think I'm sinking.'

'Spread your arms and legs wide. Stay as still as you can.'

As dread tugged at his throat, Cassius shook the rope off his hand.

'Corbulo, what do we do?'

'Just stay calm. Let go of the rope.'

'What?'

Cassius could feel the mud bubbling around his thighs.

'Let go.'

'I'm sinking!'

347

'Me too, now let go of the rope, you cretin.'

Indavara unravelled it from his wrist and threw it at him. Cassius began coiling it.

'What are you doing?'

Instead of answering, Cassius tied one end of the rope around his belt. He had no idea how long it was. Thirty feet? Forty? Long enough?

He reached down with his left hand and pulled his sword out of the sheath.

'Oh, gods,' wailed Indavara. 'It's coming over my chest. Corbulo!'

Cassius guessed that the bodyguard's fear of mud was probably not all that different to his fear of water. As he tied the other end of the rope around the handle of the sword, he spoke to him as calmly as he could. 'A prayer to Fortuna. Repeat it – she'll get us out of this.'

As the bodyguard stammered something, Cassius tied off the knot. He reckoned he'd worked out where they were. This was a settling basin, a stone tank designed to catch any remaining pollution in the water before it reached baths or a reservoir. The water would flow into and through the mud, leaving foreign bodies and sediment behind. This one was clearly in desperate need of clearing out.

Holding the base of the hilt in his right hand and the blade in his left, he drew his right arm back and threw the sword high into the air. The tremor through the rope told him it had landed.

He pulled it in. The sword caught for a moment but as soon as he yanked on it, it came easily. 'Gods.'

'Corbulo, give me the rope!'

'Stay still. One minute and we'll be out of here.'

Cassius had recovered the sword but his legs were now almost completely submerged. It was difficult to get his right arm out of the mud to prepare for the throw. He looked again; he could see the pillars and – closer – the side of the basin. No more than thirty feet, maybe less.

Come on. This time.

Cassius stretched his arm out wide to get the maximum leverage then launched the sword high. It seemed to be in the air for an impossibly long time. Then came the clatter of metal on stone.

'It's there!'

But he knew it would count for nothing if he couldn't get it to catch on something.

'Corbulo!'

'Just hold on.'

Please, Jupiter. Please.

Three heaves and the rope straightened. The sword was caught.

'Corbulo!' Indavara had somehow got over to him and was pawing at his right arm. 'Is it holding?'

Cassius felt the mud seep over his chest and slide up his neck.

He pulled hard on the rope. It seemed to hold for a moment but then came loose.

'No!' He inhaled half a mouthful of mud. Spitting out what he could, he turned to his right. He could see only Indavara's head and shoulders and now his own legs were sliding under him. He yanked on the rope and felt the sword move. Was there even time for another throw? He pulled on it again but this time it wouldn't move. He heaved with both hands to make sure.

It was stuck.

'It's holding! Come here.' He reached out, grabbed Indavara's arm and pulled him closer.

The bodyguard stretched past him and clutched the rope. 'Well done. Now just hold on to my belt.'

Cassius didn't need much encouragement. He gripped tight with both hands and Indavara was soon hauling their combined weight through the stinking, clinging mud. Gradually the pillars emerged out of the gloom, then the side of the basin. As the sound of the water grew weaker, the bodyguard pulled them to safety.

There were still several yards to go when Cassius finally realised what had saved them. Numerous branches and other bits of refuse had collected by the side of the basin, forming a semi-solid strip several feet thick. Once there, they scrambled up it and threw their hands over the lip of the basin.

While Indavara recovered, Cassius reached down and disentangled the sword. If it hadn't been covered with mud he would have kissed it. 'Glad I insisted we brought that rope.'

'I thought that was the end,' breathed Indavara. 'Really.'

Cassius wiped his sleeve across his mouth, which added to the dirt rather than reducing it. 'Ugh.'

He spat again but the horrid taste remained. 'Submerged beneath a sea of shit – an apt metaphor and a fitting end for these last few years, but I must say I'm rather glad we avoided it.'

'Corbulo, listen. Sorry if I panicked.'

'Think nothing of it. Come on, let's get out of here. There has to be a way up to the surface.'

Cassius was about to pull himself over the lip when he saw flickering light and heard quickly moving footsteps. From nowhere, the bald head of their pursuer appeared, face in shadow with the light behind him. He stepped higher and looked down at them over the lip, tapping the tip of his sword against the stone.

'You two have a nasty habit of getting away,' he rasped. 'But not this time.' He retracted the blade and aimed at Indavara's head. 'Say hello to the ferryman for—'

His whole body went still. The sword dropped between them. The bald man's head snapped upward then shook. He lasted only a few more moments then fell forward over the lip, arms dangling.

Behind him, still holding the lantern, was a wide-eyed fellow with a head of curly black hair. He stared down at the slick, red blade of his dagger and gulped.

'Thanks,' said Indavara. He nabbed the old man's sword then pulled himself up and sat on the lip of the basin, eyeing the interloper. Cassius watched him too and stayed well clear of the blade as he dropped down beside him.

'Who are you?'

The stranger was still looking at the man he had killed. He had struck into the back of his heart; there was a tear in the tunic and a bloody smear.

'I couldn't let him do it,' he said in Greek. 'I have been weak, gone along with them for too long. I should never have got involved.'

'Who are you?' repeated Cassius.

'My name is Kallikres.'

XXXIV

At Cassius's insistence, Kallikres told his tale while they looked for a way out. Even so, a considerable amount of prompting was required to get the sergeant to admit why he'd finally been forced to cooperate with the gang. His main concern now seemed to be getting the boy out of the villa unharmed.

'We will do what we can,' said Cassius. 'Now what are their names, this brother and sister?'

'I don't know. I was never told that. The only names I know are Skiron and Bathyllos. Gods, will we ever get back above ground?'

The way out of the settling basin had been via a staircase at one end of the chamber. They now found themselves in a low, narrow tunnel just below the street. Built into the roof was a series of circular iron gratings, but every one of the eight they had so far passed was bolted from above.

'What if the work crew have warned them?' said Kallikres as he marched along behind Cassius.

Cassius was trying not to consider that possibility. The thought of fumbling around in these accursed tunnels while the architects of the counterfeiting operation got clean away was maddening.

'You're sure nobody saw Cosmas?' he asked.

'Definitely.'

'Then he got away. Which hopefully means he got help and apprehended the crew. We may still have time.'

Indavara ran forward to the next grating. He reached up and gave it a shove. Unlike the others, it moved. Cassius came up beside him with Kallikres' lantern and saw that half of the iron bars had been crushed by a heavy impact from above. Indavara got both hands on it and pushed again. The grating flew up then clanged on to the street.

'Thank the gods,' said Kallikres.

All things considered, Cassius reckoned the sergeant would be wise to consider his own well-being rather than that of his lover. Having colluded with a criminal gang who had sought to exploit the image of the Emperor, he might face the harshest of sanctions.

With some help from the other two, Indavara hauled himself through the opening. He then pulled them up after him.

'Gods, that stench is coming from us,' said Cassius. His clothes and satchel were wet through and every inch of him apart from his face was coated with the malodorous mud.

The trio found themselves at the corner of a small, quiet square. The only lights were coming from an apartment block close by. Cassius looked east and saw that the first rays of sunlight were colouring the clouds above the mountains.

'Know where we are?' asked Indavara.

'Yes,' answered Kallikres.

'Back to the warehouse, then,' said Cassius. 'Quickly.'

'But what about the villa?'

'Listen, I – we – appreciate your late change of heart, believe me. But I have priorities other than your young friend. The sooner we get to the warehouse, the sooner we can get to that villa. Lead on.'

Like Kallikres, they set off at a run.

'Shit on me,' said Indavara. 'What a night.'

The warehouse seemed to be the busiest place in the city. Even before they were let through the gate by Vespilo, Cassius could see Cosmas had done well. There were at least a dozen sergeants there and he found the diminutive Syrian standing in front of nine men lying on the ground, hands tied behind them.

'Jupiter be praised,' said Cosmas when he saw the filthy figures walking towards him. 'It's been hours. What happened?'

'Long story – no time to tell it.'

Noting Cosmas's curious glance at Kallikres, Cassius beckoned him forward and explained why he was with them. Cosmas made little attempt to hide his disdain for the traitor, who was looking warily around at his fellow sergeants.

'Sure you got them all?' asked Indavara, pointing at the men on the ground.

'All that they brought along tonight,' said Cosmas.

'It's all of them,' said Cassius. 'There were only eight named in the ledger plus the supervisor. Get anything out of them?'

'Not yet,' said Cosmas.

'What about Bathyllos?'

'I sent a pair of men to his house with orders to intercept him if he leaves or any message he sends out. I can have him brought in immediately.'

'Do it. We'll question him back at headquarters then head straight out to this villa – hopefully before they find out what's gone on here.'

'And this place?' asked Cosmas, turning towards the factory.

'Lock it up and leave as many men as you can to guard it. Did you find the strongbox?'

Cosmas nodded at the ground; the box was there next to one of the captive's feet. The sergeant then doled out a series of orders to his men.

'I also need a runner to go to the tower and fetch Simo.'

Cosmas called over one of the younger sergeants and Cassius gave him both instructions and directions.

'This way,' said Cosmas, heading off towards the side gate. 'We can use their horses.'

Indavara gave Kallikres a shove and stayed behind him. He already had the sergeant's knife tucked into his belt.

'I'm guessing the tunnel came out there?' said Cassius, pointing at the stables ahead of them.

'Yes,' replied Cosmas. 'I'd only just pulled myself out when those hunters turned up.'

'Hunters?' said Indavara.

'Looked like Itureans to me – from the mountain tribes. No one's ever really been able to conquer that lot. Tough bastards, every one. What happened to them?'

Cassius aimed a thumb at Indavara. 'He did. What about Diadromes?'

'I sent him a message but he might not be able to get away – there was trouble at the forum last night.'

'Gods, what is it this time?'

'They flogged the youths that defaced the statue – did it late last night so no one was around. Only six lashes each but one of the younger lads collapsed after the first stroke and never came round. Even Nemetorius' surgeon couldn't revive him. Somehow word got out.'

'Well, that's not our concern. Apparently this villa's about five miles east of the city. We'll need plenty of men and plenty of horses. I want to be there no later than the second hour.'

As Cassius, Indavara and Kallikres followed Cosmas through the headquarters building, a squad of sergeants jogged past. Every man was equipped with helmet and shield, armed with club and sword. Apparently hundreds of protesters had now congregated outside the forum and the magistrate's residence and every single man had been called in to help.

Gessius was waiting outside the interrogation room. He told them that Bathyllos appeared ready to give up everyone and everything in return for clemency; he was also desperate that his family not learn of his crimes.

Cassius would have preferred to have changed but – until Simo arrived – he was stuck with the filth and the smell.

'Come on.' He opened the door and the four of them filed in.

Bathyllos was sitting on a chair with his bound hands on the table. His hair was unkempt and he was wearing a sleeveless sleeping tunic. He looked away and shook his head when he recognised Cassius.

'I'm going to make this quick. Have you contacted your employers?'

'First you must tell me what I'll recieive in return for coop-eration.'

'I will do what I can but only if you help me now. Time is critical. Have you contacted them? Warned them?'

'But what guarantees—'

Cassius thumped a fist on the table. 'Nothing. And any help you do receive is dependent on my goodwill, so I suggest you start talking.'

Bathyllos took his hands off the table. 'No, I haven't contacted them. I deal only with Skiron.' He looked at Kallikres. 'Him I've never seen before tonight.'

The sergeant had already disclosed that Skiron had called in at Bathyllos' house and instructed him to send the work crew to the factory.

A knock on the door. Gessius entered and whispered to Cosmas then both the sergeants left.

Cassius turned back to Bathyllos. 'If we hadn't intervened how long would it have taken them – to clear out the workshop?'

'Most of the night, I suppose.'

'Kallikres, did they give any indication of how long? Or how they might get word back to the villa?'

'Not that I heard. Sir, please, we must leave.'

Cassius ignored him. 'Bathyllos, I will ask once more – you have not warned them? If I later find out otherwise you can expect the opposite of help from me.'

The Syrian threw up his hands. 'I swear it, upon my wife and children. You must understand, I had no choice – they forced me into it.'

'Sir,' said Kallikres. 'These people are not stupid, they were readying themselves to leave. If they suspect for a moment that something has gone wrong—'

'Don't worry,' said Cassius. 'We're going.'

Outside he found Gessius alone.

'Where's Cosmas?'

'He was called away, sir. As a senior sergeant he must take charge of his squad and lead them out to the governor's residence.'

'Now?'

'Yes, sir. Only a few of us will remain here. He passed on his apologies. There is also a note from Deputy Magistrate Diadromes.'

Cassius took it from him as they set off towards the aid post, where they were to meet Simo.

'Shit.' Once he'd read it, Cassius rolled the scrap of paper into a ball and flung it aside.

'What?' asked Indavara.

'The deputy magistrate also apologises but states that the forum and the residence are virtually surrounded. He informs me that I should use my authority and requisition some legionaries. He seems certain Nemetorius will be too busy dealing with the protesters to even notice.'

'Why not just go alone?' said Indavara as another squad of well-armed sergeants overtook them.

'The gang may already have fled by the time we get there. Three of us? To check all the paths up in those hills and mountains? We need a dozen men at least. Kallikres, how far to the barracks?'

'About a mile.'

'There's Simo,' said Indavara.

The Gaul had waited for the sergeants to rush out. He entered the headquarters clutching a folded blanket.

'In there,' ordered Cassius.

The aid post was empty. Simo dumped the blanket on the table, then unwrapped it. 'Anybody hurt?'

'No,' said Indavara.

'Speak for yourself.' Cassius's shoulder ached so badly that he was convinced the arrow had stuck him, even though he could see the undershirt remained intact. He also had countless bruises and cuts from all that rolling around in the tunnels.

Inside the blanket were one spare tunic for Indavara, a choice of two for Cassius, plus his helmet and the spearhead.

'Simo, some help here.'

Between the two of them they removed the mail shirt, undershirt and mud-encrusted tunic.

Cassius suddenly thought of something. 'Kallikres, how many staff at the villa?'

'At least three maids. Several other male servants and some lads.'

'They have horses, of course.'

357

'I saw a stables, yes.'

Cassius selected the red tunic; his hunch that he might again need to exploit his authority to get the help he needed had proved correct. Once that was on, Simo again assisted him with the armour. He then pulled on his sword belt, which was still filthy.

'Can't believe I lost it.' Indavara was staring glumly down at Skiron's blade, which to Cassius looked a lot more expensive than the bodyguard's old weapon. 'That was a bloody good sword.'

Simo unbuckled the satchel and turned it upside down, emptying muddy water on to the floor.

Cassius stuffed the spearhead inside the bag. 'Simo, you bring my helmet.'

Indavara had also changed and was still tightening his belt as they hurried out of the building. Four guards had been stationed at the gate and dozens of cityfolk – mostly young men – had gathered outside. For now they were simply looking on.

'These your horses?' A sergeant walked over and pointed at the six mounts tied up in the courtyard.

'Some of them,' said Cassius.

When the sergeant noted the colour of his tunic, his manner changed.

'Oh, sorry, sir – are you leaving?'

'We are.'

'It's just that we need to get organised – I think we're in for a long day.'

Cassius was already past him. He, Indavara, Simo and Kallikres untied their horses and mounted up. With the other three men watching the cityfolk, the sergeant opened the gate and waved them through.

Cassius summoned Kallikres to the front. 'The barracks – as fast as you can.'

It was immediately obvious that the sergeant's prediction of a 'long day' wasn't far off the mark. Kallikres did his best to avoid the major avenues but whenever they neared one, it was clear to all that something was wrong. During the first hour it was no surprise to see the city busy, but no one seemed to be working. The men were in groups, either on the move or gathered at temples and statues and other meeting points. And though none seemed to be holding weapons, the anger and determination in their faces was clear. That was, the faces that could be seen; even though the sun was already warming the streets, many were wearing hoods. One group even shouted abuse in Aramaic as Cassius and the others rode past, having spied his red tunic and the crested helmet. There were few women or children around, nor any trace of either sergeants or soldiers – presumably they were all at the forum or the magistrate's residence.

Fortunately, the barracks was some distance from the centre. As he reined in outside the entrance, Cassius offered another prayer to Jupiter. His self-imposed deadline of reaching the villa within the second hour was already looking unlikely.

The sense of unease was not helped by what he saw at the barracks. There was a man in each of the four corner towers and the pair of sentries at the gate were – unusually – inside. Now wearing his helmet, Cassius held up the spearhead.

'Officer Crispian, Imperial Security. I need to commandeer some men. Open up, legionary.'

The nearest soldier came forward. 'Good day, sir. I'm afraid standing orders are to only—'

'Not for an officer with one of those,' said the second sentry, nodding at the spearhead. An older man, he retrieved a large key from a bag hanging from his belt and opened the gate.

Two sides of the parade ground were taken up by barrack blocks – accommodation for the two centuries under Nemetorius' command. Cassius could see only a handful of men; some at the stables and a trio cleaning a stack of shields.

'Who's the duty officer?'

The older legionary steadied Cassius's horse, which didn't seem keen on its new surroundings. 'Guard Officer Papinian, he . . . ah.'

Papinian – identifiable by the single red stripe on his tunic sleeve – was coming down the ladder of the nearest guard tower. He leapt the last three rungs and hurried over. 'Sir?'

'Guard officer, I need some men. How many can you spare?'

Papinian eyed the spearhead. 'Does Chief Centurion Nemetorius know about this, sir?'

'No, but he knows I'm here in Berytus and he will expect you to cooperate. I am on an assignment for Marshal Marcellinus himself.'

Papinian chewed his lip and looked across his parade ground. 'You need them on mounts, sir?'

'Yes.'

'I've got six here that can ride but only four fit horses.'

Cassius muttered a curse. Could the gods really be on the Emperor's side? They didn't seem to be offering much help when it came to capturing these counterfeiters.

'Four will have to do, then. I want them assembled here, armed and ready to leave in five minutes.'

'Yes, sir.'

Pampinian jogged away across the parade ground, his old-fashioned segmented armour jangling.

Cassius turned around. Kallikres was staring out at the street.

'What's the best route? We should try to avoid the centre.'

'We can follow the canal then cut across to the east gate.'

'And about five miles to the villa, you think?'

'Yes.'

Cassius shook his head – probably an hour or more until they got there. At least he'd have enough men to mount some kind of search if the ringleaders had escaped.

'So you don't even know their names, these two?'

'No.' Kallikres looked morosely down at the ground. 'It was always just "Master" or "Mistress".'

He had told Cassius about the fate of the caster Florens and the way they had used both the unfortunate maid and the slave boy to manipulate him.

'What are they like?'

'Clever,' said Kallikres. 'And beautiful, I suppose.'

Cassius raised an eyebrow. 'I'm intrigued.'

XXXV

Though Cassius and the others had not been at the barracks long, Berytus now seemed almost deserted. They had seen only a few gangs of youths, a handful of messenger boys and a mounted squad of sergeants. Kallikres' idea of following the street beside the canal was clearly a good one: with so little trade going on, both it and the waterway were quiet. Away to the left were the high buildings of the centre, from where they could hear the chants of a substantial crowd.

Kallikres was riding alongside Cassius at the front. 'We must cross up here, then turn right.'

The bridge was a squat, single-arch structure. As they approached it, Cassius realised there was a group of men standing in the middle. Then he saw the barrier they had erected; a dense lattice of wooden poles roped between two carts.

'Will they let us through?' he asked as they slowed their horses.

'Who knows?' The sergeant pointed along the canal. 'The next bridge isn't far away but it'll probably be busier.'

Cassius counted eleven men. 'Let's see what they do.'

He was still wearing his helmet. Affecting his most confident manner, he trotted ahead of the others and guided his horse on to the bridge, reining in only a few yards from the protesters. Some of them had quickly raised their hoods, others had pulled on actors' masks just like Ravilla and his men. A few didn't seem concerned about hiding their faces.

'Remove this barrier. I wish to pass.'

'And who are you?' growled one man from behind the folds of his hood. He had a spear strapped to his shoulder and Cassius noted that every last one of his comrades was armed.

'You can see who I am and I'm sure you're well aware of the consequences of disobeying me.'

The Syrian did not reply. He and the other men were looking past Cassius and the others. The avenue behind them ran straight to the forum.

'Something's happened,' said one of them.

Cassius turned and saw scores of men and boys running from the centre. Behind them was a crowd of several hundred.

Some of the horses began to snort and puff.

'Next bridge?' suggested Kallikres.

Cassius looked at the barrier. Even if the men cooperated it would take a while to get through. He glanced back along the avenue; some of the fleeing cityfolk were no more than a hundred yards away and dozens more had joined the flood behind them.

'What's going on?' asked Indavara.

One of the legionaries had his hand over his eyes. 'I think I can see our troops in the square. There must have been a clash with the weavers.'

'We ain't weavers,' spat one of the protesters. 'We're just like them lot and everyone else out on the streets today. All we want is bit of justice in Berytus – not a magistrate who kills boys for the fun of it.'

'Watch your mouth,' warned one of the legionaries.

Cassius held up a calming hand.

The quickest of the crowd were young boys and the moment they arrived they began babbling in Aramaic.

Kallikres translated. 'Some kind of battle. Sounds like the legionaries have used their swords.'

Cassius looked along the canal; there didn't seem to be all that many people near the other bridge.

'On we go,' he ordered. 'Next crossing.'

He guided his horse past Kallikres and Simo, who seemed fixated by the fleeing crowd. Indavara had a more practical problem; his horse was resisting his attempts to turn.

'Pull *down* on the reins,' snapped Cassius.

Three teenage lads had just reached the bridge. Two stopped and bent over, breathing hard. The third fell to his knees in front of Cassius. Tears streaming down his face, he shook his fist and screamed at him in Aramaic.

Cassius guided his mount past them and trotted away towards the next bridge.

Kallikres caught up with him quickly. 'We must hurry; we mustn't get cut off.'

Two hundred yards ahead, more running figures had appeared, converging on the crossing.

'Yah!' Cassius kicked his horse. As they galloped along the street, a pair of skiffs drifted past on the canal, the men inside standing up to see what was going on. Youths in twos and threes appeared from the alleys and side streets to their left, faces wracked with anger and fear.

Cassius looked back over his shoulder. The other six were spread out, with Indavara at the rear, the head of his horse jerking around as he struggled to control it.

'Bloody idiot.'

'Crispian!'

Cassius only just stopped in time to avoid Kallikres, who had abruptly halted. He thumped down on the horse's neck but stayed in the saddle. The sergeant was staring at the bridge, now just fifty yards away. Some of the Syrians were running across it, away from the centre, others were moving in the opposite direction. A group of about twenty had just turned on to the street beside the canal. Several of them were wielding weapons.

'Gods.'

More men ran out from the closest side street, one already shouting at Cassius.

He unbuckled his helmet and pulled it off, wishing he could remove the red tunic too.

'There,' said Kallikres, pointing at a nearby alley.

Cassius waved at the others to follow them but by the time he arrived there, Kallikres was already turning back. Yet more protesters had appeared. Cassius could now see no way out other than a charge, but that risked knocking someone down and further inflaming the crowd. Kallikres was barely maintaining control of his pale grey horse, which was snorting as it backed away from the closest men.

Cassius twisted around. The four legionaries were directly behind him, also struggling with their mounts. He urged his horse backwards and soon found himself next to the low wall that ran alongside the canal.

One man darted forward and tried to grab his reins. The horse lurched away and cracked its knee on the wall. Cassius wrenched the reins back the other way but the protesters had advanced again. He was determined to stay in the saddle but now realised they were trapped; the Syrians had surrounded them.

'Men, dismount.'

Though two of them were shouting at the cityfolk, the legionaries obeyed.

Still holding his helmet in one hand, Cassius kept his horse side on to the crowd. Using the animal as a barrier, he dropped to the ground, let go of the reins and ran the few yards back to the legionaries. They were holding on to their mounts, desperately eyeing the crowd.

'Take your shields and let the horses go,' instructed Cassius.

Kallikres was last to the ground. As soon as he was off the horse, men grabbed the mounts and pulled them all out of the way. Tellingly, no one tried to steal them: once they had been hauled clear, the crowd converged again.

'Get back, you lot,' yelled one of the soldiers, already reaching for his sword.

Cassius smacked his arm. 'Do not draw. Shields up, all of you.'

As the legionaries gripped the handles with both hands, Cassius forced his way behind them and looked back along the street.

Indavara and Simo had been cut off and were now watching helplessly. Though no more than thirty feet away, they could do nothing; the crowd was at least a hundred strong.

Cassius could think of only one man who might be able to help. 'Diadromes! Find Diadromes!'

'What?' Indavara's impaired hearing left him confused but Simo passed on the message. Just as the pair turned their horses around, Cassius felt a hand on his arm.

'Sir, what do we do?' implored the youngest of the legionaries, his face red and clammy beneath his helmet.

They had been pushed so far back that Cassius's calves were scraping the wall. He thought about chucking his helmet in the canal but the crowd knew who he was by now. He squeezed past the soldiers and joined Kallikres, who was pleading with the nearest man in Aramaic.

The noise made it hard to think. The crowd were shouting and jeering; some at the soldiers, some at him, some at each other. He could hear Latin and Greek and Aramaic. They were a mix; fierce-looking working men, fearful boys, even a few women towards the back. He saw spears and swords, farm tools and home-made blades.

At the front of the press was a wild-eyed man wielding a pitchfork, yelling something in Aramaic. His tunic was blotched with wine stains.

Cassius held up his free hand, and was somehow surprised when no one reacted.

'Death to the soldiers of Rome!' shouted someone.

'What are you doing?' Cassius yelled. 'We have done nothing wrong.'

A sturdy fellow holding a bulbous wooden club pushed his way forward. '*You*. You will pay for this.'

'For what?'

'There are dozens of them,' cried another. 'Dozens dead upon the steps of the forum. Nemetorius and Pomponianus care nothing for the people.'

'Take the city,' shouted someone at the back. 'We will take Berytus for ourselves.'

'Sir, get behind us,' said the closest legionary.

Cassius belatedly realised that Kallikres had also withdrawn to the wall and he was two paces ahead of the others. But surely if he retreated – hid behind the legionaries' shields – there was only one way this would end.

'What happened?' he asked the man with the club, trying to keep his voice calm. 'We know nothing of this.'

Some of those close by quietened down to hear the conversation.

'The centurion,' answered the Syrian. 'He ordered the charge. There are women and children bleeding on the ground.'

'Just listen, please! I am not even part of the garrison here. This has nothing to do—'

Something flashed towards him. Pain exploded across his chest and he fell on to his backside. As he struggled for breath he saw half a brick lying between his legs. Then he could see only the legionaries' boots as they shuffled across in front of him.

'Back!' shrieked one of the soldiers. 'Back or we will draw.'

Cassius felt the pain dissipating. He touched his chest; it ached but nothing more – the armour had protected him again. Kallikres got both hands under his arms and helped him to his feet.

One of the legionaries drove his shield at two of the closest men, forcing them back. But the man with the pitchfork lunged at him, the prongs scraping across the top of the shield. The legionary cried out and fell, the shield coming down on top of him. Though they were not battling an enemy army and there were only three of them, the soldiers followed their training and re-formed the line. Cassius looked down and saw blood oozing from two small holes at the base of the soldier's neck; the fork prongs had just cleared the top of his mail shirt. He and Kallikres propped the legionary against the wall. The sergeant reached inside his tunic and pulled out a handkerchief which he held against the wounds.

Cassius spied his helmet lying on the ground close by. He put it on without buckling it then straightened up behind the three soldiers.

'Enough!' he bellowed. 'Whatever has occurred elsewhere today we are not to blame. Harming us does your cause no good.'

'And when does the army ever do us any good?' yelled a woman he couldn't see.

The men with long weapons were jabbing them against the

legionaries' shields. One of the soldiers reached for his sword hilt.

'Do *not* draw!' repeated Cassius, clapping a hand on his shoulder.

'Robbers – that's a better name for you bastards in red,' spat the man with the club. 'You're supposed to protect us but all you do is steal and rape and kill. You're a worse enemy to us than the Persians or the Palmyrans! The lot of you would be better under the ground.'

More men with weapons had arrived at the front. Cassius blinked stinging sweat out of his eyes as blades glinted amid the sea of faces and raging eyes.

He still had the satchel over his shoulder and as it knocked against his side, he remembered the spearhead. He pulled it out and raised it high. 'Please listen.'

The crowd quietened, but only because they were looking at the spearhead.

'Do him! Do them all!'

Something bounced off Cassius's helmet but he continued. 'I am here in Berytus on the orders of Marshal Marcellinus himself. I promise I will pass on your grievances.'

The man with the pitchfork was still jabbing his weapon into the shields. 'If someone doesn't shut that fancy bastard up I'm going to stick him.'

The legionary farthest to the left lowered his shield. By the time Cassius realised his intention, he already had his sword in his hand.

'No!' Cassius smashed the spearhead down into the blade, knocking it out of his hands. An opportunistic lad made a grab for it but Cassius was quicker and threw the sword over his shoulder into the canal. He knew that if the soldiers attacked, all six of them would be dead in moments.

To his utter amazement, the legionary shoved him. 'What in Hades was that?'

Cassius's reaction was instinctive. He smacked the man back-handed across the face. The soldier stared at him, open mouthed.

Cassius jumped up on the wall, took his sword belt off his shoulder and dropped it to the ground. Again, a gesture had more effect than words.

'There need be no more bloodshed,' he shouted. 'In the name of the Emperor, I ask you to lay down your weapons as I have mine. We are all Romans here, let us not see more suffering and death this day.'

'*You* will suffer!' shouted someone.

'It is the will of the gods that we be united under the Emperor, not divided. Please let us go.' Cassius could hear the legionary gurgling below him. 'This man needs help.'

'Look!'

'Look there!'

The crowd turned towards the avenue, where people were still running for the bridge. One man was alone, wandering along beside the wall. In his hands was the limp, battered body of a young boy. Blood was dripping from a gory head wound. The man fell to his knees and screamed at the sky.

Indavara breathed a little easier. Avoiding those fleeing the centre had been difficult and dangerous but now they had a clear run ahead. Simo seemed to know the way to Diadromes's residence so Indavara was simply following him, having finally brought his horse back under control.

Once across another empty street, they emerged into a square where more of the cityfolk had gathered. The Syrians looked up when they heard the hooves clattering on the flagstones but Indavara and Simo were already past them.

On they galloped, briefly nearing the canal for a moment before veering away to the north again. Indavara was concentrating on riding but those glimpses he caught of the city were completely unfamiliar – he had no idea where they were.

Now they passed under a gleaming white arch and emerged on to a porticoed avenue. Simo halted and looked around.

'Where to?'

'I'm not sure,' replied the attendant. 'It's near the statue of Marcus Aurelius. We're close but . . .'

Indavara spotted an old woman sweeping dust away from her door, apparently oblivious to the turmoil elsewhere.

'Hello!' he said in Greek.

The old woman looked up.

'The statue of Marcus Aurelius – where is it?'

She pointed her brush along the avenue. 'That way – second left then up the hill.'

Having made the turn they soon came to a fountain, where a squad of legionaries was being addressed by a senior man. When he spied the horses, the officer marched towards them. 'You two – come here. I'm requisitioning those mounts.'

'No you're not.' Indavara rode on past Simo. 'Come on!'

As one of the legionaries made a grab for him, Indavara guided his horse out of the way. He found the street ahead blocked by a heavily laden cart. The only escape route was to the right. He pressed his mount on and ducked under a low arch as they entered a small sanctuary, scattering dozens of birds. Indavara followed a narrow path under some trees, scraping his back and showering himself with berries.

Fearing he would fall if he looked back he called out. 'Simo?'

'I'm with you. Keep going!'

At the far end of the sanctuary was a steep set of steps leading downward. Indavara tried to slow the horse. Too late.

The animal careered down the steps, hooves sliding on the smooth stone, but somehow staying upright. Indavara clung on until the horse finally stopped, foam streaking from its mouth.

'Good lad. Good lad.'

Simo negotiated the steps far more steadily. Once at the bottom, he pointed to a nearby street leading upward.

'That's the hill. We're almost there.'

◄─8─►

Cassius knew instantly that any chance of extricating himself and the others from the wrath of the mob had gone. While the

Syrians watched the stricken man lower the dead boy to the ground, he looked across the canal.

It wasn't that wide: no more than thirty feet, and they might get across before the pursuers caught up on foot. Better still, there were dwellings on the other side where they might buy themselves some time. He looked at the three legionaries and jutted his jaw at the water, then caught Kallikres' eye. The sergeant got the message and helped the soldier to his feet.

Cassius stuffed the spearhead into his satchel and jumped down off the wall. As he recovered then sheathed his sword and picked up the spare shield, some of the Syrians were already turning.

Hearing the legionaries hit the water one after the other, Cassius raised the shield. Something heavy hit the middle of it and bounced off. He heard a fourth splash, then a fifth. With his peripheral vision picking up shapes closing in from the left and right, he spun around and leapt clean over the wall, hoping no one was directly below.

Water bubbled up his nose. The impact almost tore the shield from his grasp but he held on. The big slab of buoyant wood counteracted the rest of the weight and immediately pulled him back to the surface. Cassius came up under it, still using it for protection as he kicked out with his legs and swam backwards with one arm. His helmet had ended up a few feet away and was already sinking.

The mob were shouting louder than ever.

Something else thudded into the shield. Cassius spat out half a mouthful of foul-tasting water and glanced behind him. Two of the soldiers were swimming hard for the other side. The third legionary was helping Kallikres; they had a hand each and were pulling the injured man along.

Not for the first time in his life, Cassius was grateful for the countless hours his father had spent teaching him to swim. He still had his boots on and was weighed down with sword, satchel and armour but was already halfway across the canal. Forty feet away, an old man in a rowing boat had put down his oars and was watching him.

Cassius spied a rush of movement to his right – the mob was running for the bridge. The first of them would be there in moments.

Still keeping the shield up as best he could, he turned. The first pair of soldiers were approaching a set of steps that led up out of the water between two dwellings.

Cassius had just altered course to follow them when something struck his head. He dipped under, swallowed more water. For a moment he felt as if the weight of all his gear would keep him there but he still had hold of the shield. He came back up spluttering, and saw a knot of wood floating right in front of him. Kicking hard to stay afloat he touched his head where the pain was; there was only a little blood on his fingers.

'Come on, sir!' The quickest legionary had dragged himself up on to the steps and was helping the second man out.

The mail shirt suddenly seemed double the weight and Cassius thanked Jupiter that he'd thought to grab the shield. With no more missiles coming his way, he was now using it as a float pushed out in front of him.

As he caught up with Kallikres and the other two, he glanced again at the bridge. Dozens of the protesters were already across and bolting down the other side, weapons bobbing in the air.

'Legionary, find us somewhere to go.'

The standing soldier wiped his soaking hair from his face and ran.

Cassius pulled himself over some weed-covered rope attached to an iron ring and got his feet on the steps. He let go of the shield and stood there panting, half out of the water, waiting for the injured man to be pulled clear.

'Sir, they're coming!' shouted someone.

'Inside! Anywhere.'

Cassius was last up the steps. The soldiers and Kallikres ran forward along an alley between two houses then funnelled through a narrow doorway into the dwelling on the right. The first of the protesters leaped over a low wall and charged straight towards Cassius as he threw himself through the doorway.

Sword clanking against the wall, he found himself in a cramped, dark kitchen. Crouching in a corner was a woman with two children cowering behind her. She was yelling something in Aramaic.

'Sir, here!'

Cassius followed the others up a set of stairs which turned ninety degrees halfway up. The soldiers piled straight through into the largest of two rooms. Cassius missed the last step and cracked his left knee on the floor. With no time even to curse, he reached the doorway and snatched a backwards glance.

The man previously armed with the pitchfork was first into view. He had replaced his larger weapon with a dagger and as he scrambled up the steps, Cassius took the opportunity to dispense some non-lethal force. He rushed forward and swung a kick at him. His boot struck the Syrian's chin with a bony crack, sending him flying backwards. He landed on the man coming up behind him and the pair of them tumbled downward.

As Cassius ran into the room, the injured man was being lowered to the floor. There was no door, only a curtain, which the legionaries had torn clean off as they came through. The room's only contents were a bed, a set of drawers and four small cages.

Cassius pointed at the doorway. 'Block it. Kallikres, help me here.'

He and the sergeant grabbed the bed. They waited for the soldiers to heave the drawers into place then dumped the bed on top. Cassius moved to the rear of the room and looked out of the window. Several armed men were staring up at him and yelling. Others were flying past straight into the alley and he could hear what sounded like dozens of boots pounding up the stairs.

Something – or more likely someone – smashed into the bed, knocking it several inches in the air. But there was a legionary on either side, holding it in place. A stave punched a hole in one of the planks, then a second blow sent the plank flying.

The timber hit the wall next to Cassius. He saw the press of bodies through the gap in the bed. And a broad-bladed dagger. And a curved sword.

He looked around. The injured legionary was slumped in a corner, hand holding the bloodied handkerchief against his neck, gazing at the door. Kallikres was leaning back against the wall, face twitching.

The legionary whom Cassius had struck was standing beside him, hand on the hilt of his sheathed sword once more. 'Now, sir?'

Hearing a strange noise, Cassius glanced over at the four cages in another corner. They contained dozens of dormice, probably bred to sell as food. As the clamour outside grew, the squeaking rodents scrabbled around, claws scraping the cage.

Cassius looked up. The roof of the dwelling was flat; dried mud brick like the rest of it. With a little time they might have cut through. But they didn't have any time.

Another plank went flying and the drawers were shoved back.

'Sir?' yelled one of the men at the door.

Cassius did not know what else he could have done. 'We kill one of them, the others will kill us all.'

The legionary drew his blade anyway. 'Sorry, sir. Decimus, Laenas – they'll get through. We're better off standing together here.'

The others let go of the bed, took out their swords and stood beside him.

With unblinking eyes, Kallikres stepped forward and slipped his dagger from its sheath.

Cassius saw the dead guard in Arabia, lying on that outhouse floor. The man he had killed.

If he wanted to live he would have to kill again. But these were not enemies of Rome. These were citizens.

He knew what Indavara would say. He gripped the handle and drew his sword. 'Hit the first ones hard. We might just make the others think twice.'

The bed came flying off the drawers and landed in front of them. There were two men in the doorway, one armed with a club, one with a sword. They were being pushed against the drawers, a mass of faces behind them.

'Hold there!' yelled the largest of the pair over his shoulder. 'Do you want us to fall?'

The others stopped pushing.

'Send up the lances.' The big man's tunic was wet through with sweat. Around his neck was a large, cheap amulet of yellow glass.

'You,' said Cassius. 'We can still stop this.'

The big man stared at him with pale, lifeless eyes and thumped his club into his hand.

One of the soldiers stepped forward. 'Vonones, it's me – Cita.' He smiled. 'I went to your wedding.'

The Syrian eyed him for a moment, then spoke over his shoulder. 'The lances – now!'

The men behind him parted.

'Get a bloody move on!'

One of the others tapped Vonones on the shoulder. He turned and watched a tall figure push through the crowd. They had all gone quiet.

Diadromes was panting, chest heaving up and down. He looked into the room, then spoke to Vonones.

'There has been enough killing today. I have been riding across the city talking to all that will listen – I intend to stand for election and replace Pomponianus as magistrate. My first act will be to remove Nemetorius, my second will be to punish all those who have killed without reason; soldiers *and* citizens. The list is already far too long. I have no wish to add to it.'

'You have not done enough,' said Vonones.

'Maybe,' replied Diadromes, eyes locked on the big man. 'But I'm doing something now.'

Vonones glanced around at the others, then slowly lowered his club.

The legionaries muttered curses. Kallikres thanked the gods.

Cassius dropped to his knees, the sword clattering to the floor beside him.

XXXVI

'You must be tired.'

Cassius didn't even have the energy to give Indavara an answer. He was sitting in the kitchen of the dwelling, sipping from a mug of water. Piled up next to him were his sword, satchel, undershirt and mail shirt. Kallikres and the legionaries also had no wish to go outside; the protesters had left the building but there were still dozens gathered in the street. Simo was crouching over the injured legionary, examining his wounds.

Indavara reached down and pulled Cassius to his feet.

'Thanks. Are the horses close?'

'Yes, with the sergeants.'

'I suppose we must go,' said Cassius, though he felt like doing nothing but stripping off, bathing, then lying undisturbed in bed for a week.

'Sir?'

'Stay here and treat him, Simo. Look after my mail shirt. We'll meet you back at the tower. Kallikres.'

The sergeant got up but all sense of urgency had left him. 'We're too late. We're too late now.'

'You don't know that.'

Indavara passed Cassius his sword and satchel and they walked outside into the bright morning light.

'Looks like we got here just in time,' said the bodyguard.

'Thank the gods you found Diadromes. I have had the misfortune to be caught in a mob several times in my life and there is nothing more unpredictable or unpleasant.'

Cassius didn't risk even a glance at the cityfolk, some of whom had been ready to tear him to pieces half an hour earlier. Diadromes – accompanied by several sergeants – was still talking to Vonones and a few others, who thankfully seemed to be listening. The crowd parted as more men arrived on horseback. One of them was Cosmas.

'I'll get the mounts. You can use Simo's.' Indavara ran over to another sergeant, who was watching the horses.

'Why are you still here, sir?' asked Cosmas.

'An unexpected delay. We must get to the villa. Now.'

'I'll go with you.'

'Good. Can you get a spare horse for Kallikres?'

Cosmas spoke to one of the men dismounting.

When Indavara returned, Cassius had to take several long breaths before hauling himself up on to the saddle.

He eyed the sun, now veiled by a thin haze.

'Gods, must be close to the fourth hour.'

As Indavara mounted up, Cosmas and Kallikres rode over. Cassius continued to avoid looking at the protesters even as he guided his horse through them. Once clear of the watching Syrians, he waved Kallikres forward and they set off at a canter.

Other than a brief hold-up at the eastern gate – which was busy with residents trying to leave and a few oblivious traders trying to get in – they made good time. Even beyond the paved section, the road was of smooth, solid earth hardened by the summer heat.

With no protection for his head, Cassius was sweating almost as much as his horse by the time they turned off on to another road that ran up through olive groves and vineyards, past large estates and small farmhouses. They were soon in the foothills of the Lebanon range, whose dark peaks rose up stark and proud in the cloudless sky.

As they neared the villa, Kallikres seemed to acquire a new-found sense of purpose. Unlike Indavara and Cosmas, he was a capable rider and forced the pace, even though Cassius was already pushing his mount as hard as he dared. The sergeant had just announced that there wasn't far to go when he abruptly halted his horse. Cassius stopped next to him.

A whisper of breeze shook the branches of the cedars either side of them. Ahead – where the road bent around to the left – a slow-moving party of people had appeared. At the rear was a small cart being towed by a pair of mules.

'Who are they?' asked Cassius.

The sergeant guided his horse forward.

'Kallikres?'

Cassius and the others followed him until he stopped once more, just in front of the group. There were six of them in all, four women and two men, all dressed in servants' garb. At the front of the cart were some wicker baskets and a few bags. But at the rear were the unmistakable shapes of two bodies, each covered by a blanket.

'Who are they?' repeated Cassius.

'From the villa,' said Kallikres. 'Where is he? Where is Pedrix?'

One of the maids, a pretty, fair-haired girl, answered. 'He is with *them*.'

'Where are they?'

The maid turned and pointed up at the mountains.

'The high trail,' added one of the men.

'What happened?' asked Cassius, transfixed by the bodies.

The man gulped before answering. 'The two stable lads tried to take some gems while loading their horses but they were discovered by Master. Mistress . . . she . . . used his knife on them.'

'Which way on the trail?' asked Kallikres. 'North or south?'

'We don't know.'

'How long ago did they leave?' asked Cassius.

'An hour. No more.'

Kallikres set his horse away and continued up the road.

Cosmas spoke to the servant. 'Wait at the eastern gate. All of you. Someone will be along later.'

The servant nodded solemnly.

Cassius, Indavara and Cosmas rode on. Beyond the bend, the canopy of cedars became more dense, providing welcome relief from the sun. They passed no one but saw three tracks leading off to properties hidden by the trees. Cassius had no idea which one led to the villa.

They eventually caught up with Kallikres two miles later as the trees thinned out again and the road baked under a dazzling heat. The sergeant pointed up and to the south.

'The high trail,' said Cosmas.

The pale path ran along the flank of the mountains, partially visible through the top of the treeline.

'It's more likely they'll head south,' said Kallikres. 'More routes of escape.' He pressed on, oblivious to the protestations of Indavara and Cosmas.

'We must continue,' insisted Cassius, though he felt as if he might slide to the ground and collapse at any moment.

As they neared the high trail, the road began to steepen. The horses had now been pushed hard for an hour and a half and all were struggling. When they reached a small house close to the road, Cosmas offered the resident a coin in return for use of his trough. He, Cassius and Indavara leaned against a gate and drank from the sergeant's flask. The horses slurped noisily, their flesh embroidered with engorged veins. Kallikres took out a good-luck charm and whispered invocations.

'Where does this high trail lead to?' asked Indavara, wiping his brow with his sleeve.

Cosmas said, 'It cuts through a pass at Kaena then enters the Bekaa valley.'

'From there they can pick up any number of roads,' added Cassius.

'You can see the pass from here.' Cosmas backed away from the gate and looked south. 'No more than four or five miles.'

Kallikres had finished his prayers and was dragging his horse away from the trough.

'We have tarried long enough,' said Cassius. 'Let's go.'

The sun grew hotter, the road steeper. But after only half an hour more they finally reached the trail and turned south. Once more on level ground, the mounts rallied a little, as did the riders. The trail was barely wide enough for two horses to pass, allowing the trees to provide much-needed shade. Here and there, bulbous outcrops of rock broke through the ground, many of them coated with bright yellow lichen. Soaring above them were the pale grey slopes of the mountains; below was a carpet of dark green that seemed to stretch for ever, dividing the peaks from the coast. To the west, the sea occasionally sparkled through the summer haze.

They rode on, and twice Cassius had to berate Kallikres for getting too far ahead. Hunched over, face not far from his mount's neck, he wondered what kind of state the four of them would be in if they actually caught up with the fleeing pair. Cursing as Kallikres again disappeared around a bend, Cassius glanced back at the other two. Indavara was a hundred yards behind and slumped back in his saddle, barely holding his reins. Cosmas was beside him and didn't seem to be faring much better. Cassius knew the horses would need water again soon but they hadn't passed a single spring and there were no dwellings this high.

Once around the bend, Cassius saw the sergeant, fifty yards away. Ahead of him were two colossal chunks of rock that had at some point fallen from above. The trail passed the first one to the left then cut down the slope to avoid the second, which was much larger. The sergeant was approaching the first rock when he held up a hand and dismounted.

Cassius looked back again; Indavara and Cosmas had just rounded the bend. He waved to Indavara then held a finger to his mouth. They halted. Cassius dropped gently to the ground and watched Kallikres. The Syrian left his horse and walked carefully forward until he was next to the first rock, close to the point where the trail turned down the slope. His hand drifted to his sword hilt as he walked on, taking care with every step.

'Bloody fool,' breathed Cassius. Kallikres should have waited for them if he thought there was something worth investigating. But could they really have caught up already?

The sergeant reached the edge of the smaller rock and looked around the bend. He then walked swiftly back to his mount. Stroking the animal to keep it calm, he led it back to Cassius.

'What is it?'

'There are two horses tied up, drinking from a pool.'

'Did you see the riders?'

'No. But I heard a woman's voice.'

Once they reached Indavara and Cosmas, Kallikres again described what he'd seen and they led the horses out of sight. While the others tethered them, Cassius walked back to the bend and surveyed the terrain ahead. The weariness had momentarily left him.

'Cosmas, you and Kallikres continue along the trail and get as close as you can. Indavara and I shall come around the right side of the smaller rock and cut them off.'

As the four of them walked along the trail, Cosmas gripped his sword.

'Not yet,' said Cassius. 'Main thing is to get into position, stop them getting to their mounts. We move in when I give the shout, not before.'

Once they reached the smaller rock, Cassius and Indavara edged down the slope. Thankfully, there were few fallen twigs underfoot; it was mainly grass and fern. Cassius kept close to the rock, moving around it until he was only yards from the trail. Conscious of his colourful tunic, he got down on his knees then crawled forward. Positioning himself between two ferns, he examined the ground ahead.

The horses were tied to a low branch on the other side of the trail. One was munching grass, the other was drinking from the pool. Cassius glimpsed something beyond them. He put his head even lower so he could see between the animals' legs.

There they were; standing together in a small clearing. The woman's back was to Cassius, her long hair quite clear. The man was facing her, a shaft of sunlight illuminating his side. Cassius thought they were talking but it was hard to be sure.

Indavara tapped his leg. Cassius withdrew and stood beside him. 'Got them. Man and a woman about forty feet ahead of us. Horses are in the way, though. We'll go round.'

They retreated into the forest, then continued down the slope, staying low and using the trees and the fern for cover. They covered about thirty yards before crossing the trail, where they

380

had a clear view of Kallikres and Cosmas. The two sergeants were standing in the shadow of the larger rock, close to the mounts but well hidden.

Cassius and Indavara continued circling around until they were on the opposite side of the clearing to the horses. The man and the woman were still standing together, talking. Cassius and Indavara darted from tree to tree, the shadows of the canopy shrouding them.

They stopped behind a broad trunk and gently drew their swords.

'He has only the dagger,' whispered Indavara, 'and I see nothing on her. I'll come in from the right and handle him.'

'Got it.'

Keeping his blade behind his body, Indavara moved off. Cassius squatted down and peered around the tree. The woman offered her hands and the man took them. She spoke. They embraced.

Cassius glanced to his right. Indavara was still moving but this opportunity had to be taken. As if hearing his thoughts, the bodyguard turned round and they exchanged a nod.

Cassius stepped out from behind the tree and strode into the clearing.

'Now, Cosmas!'

The pair separated and spun around, eyes darting from one interloper to the other.

'Who are you?' said the man, who was younger than Cassius had expected.

'Imperial Security. I'd like to talk to you about counterfeit coins.'

The man made no attempt to reach for his dagger as Indavara sprang forward and held his arm.

The startled horses whinnied and tugged at their tethers as Cosmas and Kallikres ran around the pool into the clearing. The sergeant gave a cry and for a moment Cassius thought he was about to strike the man but he instead threw his blade aside and embraced him.

'What are you doing?' demanded Indavara, letting go.

Cassius grabbed the woman by the wrist and spun her around. 'Who are you?'

'I am Lyra, sir,' she said, in Latin, with what to Cassius sounded like a German accent. 'I – I – think perhaps you are looking for my master and mistress. They told us to just keep riding but the horses grew tired.'

'Oh no,' said Cosmas.

Kallikres was holding the young man tight, his eyes squeezed shut. Only now did the youth reciprocate, putting his arms around the sergeant.

'Where are they?' Indavara asked the maid. 'Your master and mistress.'

'I don't know,' said the girl. 'They left with the other staff.'

Gritting his teeth, Cassius dug his sword blade into the soil and knelt in front of it. 'The "bodies" under the blanket. They were right there. We had them.'

With a bellow of rage, he stood, pulled the sword out of the ground and heaved it at the nearest tree.

It bounced off and fell into a clump of fern.

XXXVII

'You would like to see her, I suppose – check she's safe?'

'Yes.'

Indavara and Simo were sitting on a low wall next to Diadromes's stables, waiting. A young lad came out of the kitchens, hand covering a taper, and lit the four lanterns in the corners of the courtyard. Indavara glanced up at the purple, pink and yellow that now streaked the darkening sky.

'Anything?' Simo asked the lad, whom they had already consulted twice about progress within. They had seen messengers, clerks and gentlemen coming and going for the past two hours and weren't even sure if Cassius had spoken to Diadromes yet.

'Master's still in his meeting,' replied the lad before returning inside.

Indavara said, 'If he's not out soon, I'm leaving.'

'I'm sure she's all right,' replied Simo. 'The city seems to be getting back to normal.'

'Really? What about that?' Indavara pointed at a distant pall of smoke to the west. Apparently the weavers had set a factory ablaze and the authorities were struggling to bring it under control.

'You should stay – at least see Master Cassius back to the tower. He has enough to worry about.'

'Nobody wins every time.'

'He was so close, though,' said Simo.

'*We* were close. It was me that found the coins, don't forget. If it hadn't been for the stupid bloody magistrate and his centurion mate we would have got to that villa in time.'

'What will happen to the sergeant, do you think?'

'Kallikres? Not our problem. Do you know he cried when he

held that boy in his arms? There were a few of the fighters who went with other men. I've always thought it a bit strange.'

'It is unnatural,' said Simo. 'A terrible sin and an affront to the Lord.'

'Some sins are worse than others, Simo. How many have done violence today?'

'Sometimes there seems to be no end to it.'

'At least some of these folk – the weavers, for example – have a reason to do it.' Indavara kicked his heel into the wall. 'Gods, where is he?'

Cassius was waiting too. As if the trials of the night and morning hadn't been enough, the fruitless pursuit and ensuing frustration had sapped him of any remaining energy. He was sitting on the bench under the pine tree, in the exact position Pomponianus had occupied two days previously. He wondered what the beleaguered magistrate was doing now.

One of Diadromes's clerks had been out to tell him that the deputy would have a few spare minutes soon but that had been an hour ago. The man at least had some other good news: according to latest reports the streets were quieter and further serious incidents had been averted.

Cassius looked down at his scratched, bruised and filthy legs. He could smell himself – horse, probably, or perhaps still the stench of the settling basin. He stuck a finger in his itchy left ear and scraped out more mud – it seemed impossible to get it all out.

A few minutes earlier he had tried drafting his letter to Abascantius and Marcellinus but his addled mind was incapable. He still couldn't believe he had been so easily fooled. If only he'd simply dismounted and lifted those blankets he would have found this sly brother and sister. Still, they had outwitted everyone else too, and if it hadn't been for the delay in Berytus he felt sure they would have been apprehended. In any case, it was too much to think about now; the letter could wait until the morning.

'Crispian!'

Diadromes had at last appeared on the terrace, accompanied by a quartet of assistants.

With a sigh, Cassius dragged himself up and ambled along the path. When he arrived, Diadromes dismissed the men, one of whom pestered him with two final questions before returning inside and pulling a heavy curtain across the doorway.

The deputy magistrate was standing up very straight, as if resisting the forces piling pressure upon him. Below his eyes, the skin was puffy and grey.

Cassius imagined he didn't look much better. 'Long day, eh?'

'The longest.'

'What's the latest?'

'We're talking to Pomponianus' people. He's agreed to hand over control of the sergeants to me for the next week. I'm hopeful he will resign and we can call an early election. Nemetorius is digging his heels in but at least seems to realise he made a mistake at the forum.' Diadromes looked up at the sky. 'More than fifty dead, a dozen soldiers among them.'

'My advice – don't let them out of the barracks for at least a week.'

Diadromes grimaced. 'I need them to keep control of the streets. The governor might send reinforcements but I've already lost dozens to desertion.'

'No offence to your esteemed sergeants but in truth they are little more than a man with a club who takes orders. Why don't you bring in some of the more moderate protesters and appoint them as sergeants? No one who's committed a serious offence, of course – and it would only be temporary – but it might work. All protecting Berytus together; that type of thing.'

'That's actually not a bad idea.'

'It's not original. Some governor did it. Can't remember where.'

Diadromes looked him up and down. 'What about you? No sightings of this accursed pair?'

'No; and the bloody servants all disappeared too, of course. Cosmas plans to search the villa and has men at the harbour and watching the gates but I doubt we'll get anywhere. They're too bright to stick around. They'll be long gone.'

'I apologise. It is our fault you did not reach them in time. Not to mention this traitor Kallikres.'

'At least he made the right decision in the end.'

'Where is he? I don't even know.'

'The cell. Which I imagine is rather full.'

'Actually the sergeants made only a handful of arrests, would you believe? They spent most of their day protecting buildings.'

'And now?'

'All out on patrol. I'm going to ride around the centre, get a look for myself.'

'Well, may I thank you for your timely intervention,' said Cassius. 'They wouldn't have listened to anyone else.'

Diadromes glanced back at the curtain and lowered his voice. 'They all assume I always wanted this. That I was biding my time, waiting for an opportunity. It's not true. Perhaps a few years ago . . .'

'The city needs you.'

'I'm already getting tired of hearing that. What will you do now?'

'Wait and see if Cosmas turns anything up, I suppose. Tomorrow I have several rather difficult letters to write. Then . . . who knows?'

They shook forearms.

'Thank you once again,' said Cassius. 'For a moment there I honestly thought I was going to die in that house.'

'Honestly – for a moment – so did I.'

Cassius drank his wine and gazed out at the city. He could see the collapsed, burnt-out factory and the smoke still rising from the ruin. There were few other obvious signs of what had transpired that day, though they had seen plenty on the way to the tower.

The sergeants were indeed out in force and Diadromes already had work parties attending to the statues that had been attacked and the provocative graffiti that adorned dozens of walls.

386

Members of both the city council and the local assembly were on the streets too, showing their faces to homeowners and merchants whose property had been damaged. Not far from the tower, Cassius and the others had passed a house from which came the anguished shrieks of the bereaved. The men of the family had gathered outside; standing in silence while their women wailed.

Cassius heard feet on the ladder and turned just as Indavara's head appeared.

'Ah, sorry, I thought—'

'No, please,' said Cassius. 'Come up.'

'No, I'll—'

'Indavara, I'd like to speak to you.'

He climbed up through the hatch.

'Wine?'

'No.'

Newly clean, Cassius was clad only in his sleeping tunic. His body craved rest but he knew he wouldn't be able to sleep without some drink to dull the myriad thoughts assailing him. He poured himself some more, his arm aching even with the weight of the jug.

'You seem preoccupied. This girl? What's her name again?'

'Mahalie.'

'Would you like to go and see her?'

'Yes. But . . . it's difficult.'

'You do appreciate that unless Cosmas finds out anything new we will probably have to leave in the next few days.'

Indavara had planted his hands on the stone surround. 'I know.'

'You will have to forget her.'

Cassius looked down at the pink lesions across the back of the bodyguard's calves; a result of their involuntary ride down the water channel. Cassius had the same, all the way up to his backside.

'It is not sensible for us to have attachments, not in our line of work.' He leant against the surround beside Indavara. 'It's not easy for any of us. Don't forget that I haven't seen my family for three years and Simo hasn't seen his father since we were in Antioch. Army life is like this.'

'People like you do not understand what life is like for people like her.'

'Probably true. But this girl is not your responsibility. We are meant for another path.'

'Corbulo, I was powerless for six years. Now I have a place in the world – do not tell me that I cannot use it.'

'I'm not. Nor am I blind to how this is affecting you. Listen, I think . . . perhaps there is something we can do for the girl. But you must promise me that when it is done you will leave with Simo and me. You have taken an oath.'

Indavara turned to him. 'And you need me to protect you.'

'I won't deny it.'

'Just tell me what you can do.'

'I help you and then you run off with her? I don't think so.'

'I am not planning to run off anywhere. They cut her, Corbulo. For nothing. I would sooner kill them than leave her there alone.'

'I don't want to hear talk like that.'

'Then give me another choice.'

Cassius took a long sip of wine. 'Sitting in a locked room at the headquarters are all those amphoras confiscated from the factory. Thousands of denarii. Well, fake denarii. Slaves are expensive, young maids especially, but there is undoubtedly more than enough.'

'To buy her, you mean?'

'I'll have to clear it with Diadromes, of course, but if I tell him the whole story I doubt he'll oppose it. And I'm sure I can make appropriate adjustments to the necessary paperwork. The treasury and my superiors need never know.'

Some of the tension had left Indavara's face. 'We wouldn't even be paying them with proper money.'

'An added bonus. If that fact were to come out – perhaps after we had left Berytus – this master of hers might face a few more problems.'

'How would we do it?'

'I shall go to this man's home and conduct the negotiation.

I'm sure we can find a price agreeable to both parties, payable immediately in cash, of course.'

'How did you . . . what an idea!'

Indavara did not often smile; Cassius had rarely seen him so happy.

'There is a certain elegance to it, I suppose.'

Indavara grabbed his hand and shook it. 'Thank you, Cassius. Thank you.'

The path was so rocky and uneven that they had to walk the last few miles. High above them, the towering peaks were even darker than the sky. The smuggler had only one lantern, making progress even slower. The middle of the night was long past when they finally heard the crying of goats and saw a light up ahead.

'We wait here,' said the smuggler.

Amathea was too tired to complain. Alexon left his horse and walked over to her. As she leant against him, he kissed her head. Despite it all – the tense escape, the exhausting journey – standing there in the dark with her holding on to him felt rather wonderful.

He was the one who had devised the daring, ingenious plan. He was the one that had saved them.

From ahead came the sound of a man quickly descending the trail, his boots sliding, sending grit down the slope. The two locals greeted each other in Aramaic, then the smuggler spoke in Greek.

'We'll bring the horses.' He handed Alexon his lantern. 'You two can go straight up.'

Alexon and Amathea continued on, hand in hand. As they approached the light – which was a lantern hung over the door of a small abode – Alexon glanced up at the sky and stopped for a moment. Only half the moon could be seen but that half seemed unnaturally large; so large that black and grey spots were visible upon the surface.

'Rather beautiful.'

Amathea didn't even look; she continued up the trail, snivelling and wiping her nose.

A woman was waiting at the door. In barely comprehensible Latin she promised them food and hot water and showed them through to their room. Alexon was surprised by the quality of the furniture, though he would have preferred one large bed instead of two small ones. The woman lit a candle, then bustled back into the parlour.

Amathea dropped down on the bed and put her head in her hands.

'We've lost everything. Again.'

'Not true, sister.'

Alexon took off his pack and sat beside her. He unbuckled the pack then took out the bronze box he had been carrying all day. He placed it on her lap, then shut the door. By the time he sat down again, she had already opened it. One half of the box contained a glittering stash of emeralds, sapphires, rubies, pearls and orange carnelian. In the other was the best and most valuable of Amathea's jewellery. She picked up the largest of the emeralds. They had used the fake coins to buy it through a broker in Tyre. It was worth more than a thousand aurei.

'I made a few calculations during the journey,' said Alexon. 'Even with the loss of the workshop, the stock and the slaves, we are still far better off than when we began this venture.' He tapped the pack. 'And we still have the dies.'

Amathea turned to him. 'You have made the most of a bad situation, Alexon. I thank you.'

He put the box on the floor and took her hand in his.

'I thought it was all over,' added Amathea. 'Lying in that horrible cart, hearing their voices.'

'I wish I could have seen this Crispian's face. He must have thought he was so clever, tracking us down.'

'Not as clever as you, brother.'

She glanced down at a tear in her tunic and shook her head. 'But look at us.'

Alexon stroked her hand. 'Try not to think about it. By this time tomorrow we will be safely away from danger.'

Amathea looked around the room. 'My body aches, I've no one to care for me and now I must spend the night in a hovel.'

'No one to care for you?'

Alexon was glad it was just the two of them. All the best moments of his life had been with her. Just her. When he had her all to himself.

She touched his face. 'Sorry, Alexon. I am yours.'

He thought his heart might burst.

He kissed her on the lips. 'And I am yours.'

XXXVIII

Indavara stopped at the corner of the street.

'What is it?' asked Cassius.

'I should tell you. I came here before – waited for them outside the house. I was going to do something but I didn't. They ran off.'

For Cassius, surprise soon gave way to relief. 'Thank the gods you did no more than frighten them. You must stay here. It's probably for the best anyway. Give that to Simo.'

Indavara was carrying a saddlebag containing small cloth bags of the counterfeit denarii, as was Simo. The Gaul turned so that Indavara could hang it on his spare shoulder.

'Wait right here,' said Cassius, pointing at the pavement.

Though he had left his helmet at the tower, he was wearing a fresh red tunic; this was another occasion when emphasising his status might be helpful. Given the situation in Berytus, however, he had taken off his light cloak only upon reaching the street. His sword – newly cleaned and polished by Simo – hung at his side.

'Fifth gate along,' said Indavara.

'Come, Simo.'

They walked up to the house. As the attendant had a considerable load to contend with, Cassius took it upon himself to ring the bell hanging from a chain. While they waited, he looked through the gate. The dwelling was not very large but had one glassed window with an elaborate floral design. He guessed that Mahalie's master might be a middle-ranking city official or a moderately successful merchant.

It was he that came out of the front door, holding the key on a string. The man was, as Indavara had suggested, unremarkable. He approached the gate hesitantly.

'Good day,' said Cassius.

'Good day.' The man's eyes took in the tunic and the sword.

'I'll get straight to the point. I have a proposal for you regarding your slave – I believe she's named Mahalie?'

'Proposal?'

'Yes. I'd like to buy her from you.'

The man scratched his neck with his fingernails. 'She's not for sale.'

'Perhaps we can discuss a price.'

'As I said, she's not for sale. Good day to you.'

Cassius let him get halfway to the door before speaking again. 'I believe you had another visitor the other day. Big fellow with a lot of scars?'

The man stopped and turned.

'He's my bodyguard. He told me what you did to the girl. She will be leaving this house today. We can either do it my way or his. I get the impression that he feels you might deserve a taste of your own medicine and I can assure you that he is more proficient at dispensing pain than you will ever be.'

The man walked back to the gate.

'What's your name?' asked Cassius.

'Fundanus.'

'Open up, Master Fundanus. Swiftly now.'

As he did so, the Syrian cast anxious glances at the street.

Once they were inside, Cassius gestured to the door.

Fundanus stopped just before reaching it. 'I do not appreciate being threatened.'

'Not many people do.'

'What is your name?'

'You don't need to know that. Let's hurry this along.'

They halted inside the atrium, which was tidy and clean, if rather bare. Below the skylight was a circular basin devoid of water.

'Who was that at the . . .' The mistress of the house walked in. Considering her behaviour and the fact that her husband was so exceptionally unexceptional, Cassius had been expecting some sharp-faced bitch, but the wife was actually rather pretty. She frowned at him.

'This man wishes to buy Mahalie,' said Fundanus.

Coins chinked as Simo lowered the saddlebags to the floor.

'How much?' said Cassius.

'Why do you want her?' asked the woman.

'Remember the man on the street?' said Fundanus as he went to stand by his wife. 'The officer's bodyguard. He wants to buy her.'

She absorbed this, then looked at the bags. 'Two thousand.'

'Let's be realistic,' said Cassius. 'I had my man here check the prices at the market this morning. Unless she's literate one thousand two hundred is a fair sum.'

'Two,' said Fundanus.

'One and a half,' said Cassius. The charade would be more convincing if he conducted a proper negotiation.

The wife said, 'One and three-quarters and you can take her right now.'

'Oh, she's coming now, don't worry about that. One thousand six hundred is my final offer. You must also pass on the correct documentation.' He offered his hand to Fundanus, who waited until he got a nod from his wife before shaking it.

'Start counting it out, Simo. Now, where is she?'

The wife walked out of the atrium. Cassius watched Simo retrieve the money bags and place them on a table in rows.

Fundanus said quietly, 'If he wants her for his whore he'll be disappointed. She's no fun at all, that one.'

'Actually I believe he just wants to get her away from you two. You cut her, is that right?'

Fundanus shrugged. 'She is ours.'

'Was.'

The Syrian turned his attention to Simo. 'How much in each bag?'

'One hundred,' said the attendant.

The wife returned, pushing Mahalie ahead of her, one hand on her neck. The girl had a rather plain face and looked very thin but Cassius could see why Indavara found her appealing. She seemed the sort who would never wish harm upon another, who needed protection. They had made a real mess of her hair,

394

and Cassius noted that her tunic was done up to the top, despite the heat.

'Hello, Mahalie,' he said. 'I am a friend of Indavara's. I have just purchased you but I have no intention of keeping you as a slave. It will take a few days to process the appropriate paperwork but you are now, to all intents and purposes, a freedwoman.'

Mahalie stared at him, then her master, then her mistress.

'She's a dopey cow,' said the wife. 'I'm glad to be rid of her.' She shoved Mahalie forward and the girl just stood there, hands resting on the water basin.

Having finished counting out the money, Simo walked over to her. 'What my master says is true. Would you like to get your things?'

'Go on, then,' yelled the wife.

Mahalie ran over to what Cassius assumed to be a cupboard in one corner of the atrium. She pulled back the curtain and he saw that it was in fact a tiny room, complete with a bedroll and a few belongings. She crawled inside and began collecting her things together, then stopped suddenly and began sobbing. Simo hurried over and helped her gather her possessions in a blanket.

'Thank the gods she's leaving,' said the wife. 'I'll never have to listen to that bloody noise again.'

Her husband had been counting the bags. 'It's all there.'

Cassius caught Simo's eye and jutted his jaw towards the door. Mahalie was shaking so much that she couldn't tie the bundle. Simo did it for her and coaxed her out of the atrium.

Fundanus leered at the money bags.

Cassius wished he would be around for the moment when the sergeants arrived. Diadromes had been happy to cooperate. He would wait for Cassius to leave then dispatch Cosmas to the house, acting on a 'tip-off' about counterfeit currency. At a later date Fundanus would be informed that no progress had been made with tracing the man who had posed as an army officer. The confiscated coins would of course have to be melted down.

The husband and wife exchanged a gleeful smile.

'Happy?' said Cassius.

'We visited the temple last night,' said Fundanus. 'We asked for good fortune. I did not expect it to arrive so swiftly.'

'I wouldn't ascribe this to the intervention of the gods,' replied Cassius. 'They seldom heed the good and the noble, so I doubt very much if they would listen to the likes of you.'

'You should leave,' said the wife.

'Fear not, I have no wish to remain in your company a moment longer.'

8

They found a decent tavern several streets away and a well-shaded bench in the courtyard. Corbulo ordered a jug of half and half and Simo poured each of them a mug. Mahalie's belongings were placed on a nearby chair; she seemed unable to take her eyes off them. Indavara had tried to get her to talk but neither he nor Corbulo had made any progress. When the maid came out to take orders, Simo asked what Mahalie wanted and she at least managed to nod when he suggested soup.

Indavara would have liked to reach across and take her hand, tell her everything would be all right, but he had no idea what she would do. It was hard to tell if she was even happy.

'Well,' said Corbulo. 'I suppose we should discuss the future. What would you like to do now, Mahalie?'

She looked at him and chewed her bottom lip.

'You have a sister in Antioch?' said Indavara. 'Isn't that right?'

'Well, that's something,' said Corbulo. 'Although I don't suppose we'll have time to take you up there ourselves.'

Indavara still held out hope for a few weeks in Berytus but he knew that would just make it harder to leave.

'My father could help – perhaps come and get her,' offered Simo.

'Good idea,' said Corbulo. He drank from his mug. 'Mmm. Not bad. Really not bad.'

The bitter wine and water seemed only to make Indavara's throat even drier.

Mahalie looked down at the table; at the holed, grimy timbers.

396

'Is this a dream?'

Now Indavara was the one who couldn't speak. He remembered his first day of freedom; wandering the streets of Pietas Julia wearing only his torn, bloodied tunic. Eventually he'd had to hide from the curious people, most of whom had just witnessed his triumphant escape from the arena. At nightfall he took himself down to the river to clean his wounds then fell asleep under a tree. When he awoke there, he thought he was dreaming. Except that he could see the very place from which he had escaped. And he could touch the soft grass beneath his fingers and hear water flowing close by. It was real.

Simo put a hand on the girl's arm. 'No, Mahalie. This is no dream. You are free.'

She said the word as if it was the first she had ever spoken. 'Free.'

'I wonder where they are now.' Cassius was sitting at the table, resting his head on his hands, watching Simo cook dinner.

'Indavara and Mahalie, sir?'

'No, this brother and sister.'

Having left Indavara to find Mahalie somewhere to stay, Cassius and Simo had called in at headquarters, where Cosmas had reported the results of his initial interviews with the villa staff. Cassius knew he should have conducted them himself but he'd found the prospect too depressing.

'The man was named Alexon, the woman Amathea, the old bastard who Kallikres killed – Skiron. The others were all hired here in Antioch and, despite having lived with them for several months, seem to know precious little about them. I shall pass on the details to Abascantius and the treasury but I don't hold out much hope. And they still have the dies. Marcellinus will not be impressed.'

'Don't be too hard on yourself, sir. You stopped their operation here in Berytus and I'm sure they'd think twice about trying it again.'

'Hopefully. Gods, if Indavara hadn't taken his trip to that dump, I'd still be flailing around in the dark.'

'That letter you were given, sir, was it from Master Quentin?'

'Yes. He'll be here in the morning. Has his own reports to compile, I suppose.'

Cassius looked at Simo's broad back as the attendant tipped some spices into the pot and stirred them into the beef stew. It was one of Cassius's favourites, a Gaulish family recipe with leeks and mushrooms. Simo wasn't humming as he usually did when he cooked; he had been quiet since the morning.

'Quite a moment, wasn't it?'

'Sir?'

'When the poor girl understood that it was really happening.'

'It was, sir.'

'Two years, I pledge it. We will both be free.'

'I do not long for it, sir. My only wish is to lead a good life, whether I am a slave or not.'

'That will be easier if you are free. We both know that.'

Simo smiled then took some more herbs from a little basket and chopped them on a block.

'Do you know I swear I can still smell that settling basin?'

'You smell fine, sir. But perhaps a trip to the baths tomorrow?'

'Oh, certainly.' Cassius put a finger up his nose. Increasingly painful scabs had formed in both nostrils. 'I've definitely caught something. You'll have to find me a treatment, Simo.'

'I will look into it first thing tomorrow, sir.'

'Indavara is fine, of course. Tell me, have you ever known him to be ill? The man has not only the strength of an ox but the constitution.'

'He does seem blessed with good health, sir.'

'I wonder if we'll hear anything from the Service man in Siscia – I would be fascinated to know where Indavara came from. He must have been a warrior, we can assume that at least.'

Simo threw the rest of the herbs into the pot and turned around. 'The woman he remembered after hearing the song, sir – it could have been his mother. He might have an entire family waiting for him somewhere.'

'When the time comes we shall do all we can to help him get home. Agreed?'

'Yes, sir, I think—'

'Gods!'

The knock on the door startled Cassius, even though there had already been two earlier that evening – canvassers wanting to know who the inhabitants would be voting for in the upcoming election. Both visitors had been supporting Diadromes.

'Get rid of them, would you, Simo.'

The Gaul took the spoon out of the stew and laid it beside the griddle.

'But check the spyhole before you open up.'

'Yes, sir.'

Indavara and Mahalie walked out of the inn and on to the street.

He looked back at the place. It was small but orderly and clean, with hanging baskets outside and nice balconies for the rooms. He had rented Mahalie's for a week and paid in advance. It was on the first floor and close to the owner's quarters. They were a middle-aged couple; Indavara wanted a place with a woman and it had taken a while to find one.

'Will you be all right here?'

'It seems very nice.'

He had watched Mahalie place her blanket of belongings on the bed then leave it untouched. Assuming that she didn't want to unpack in front of him, he'd suggested a walk before he left. Corbulo was right; he had to keep his distance. They would be leaving soon.

'Down to the sea?'

'Yes.'

They were less than a hundred yards away and had only to follow the smell of fish and the squawking gulls. This area was west of the main harbour and contained many inns and taverns. Indavara hoped he could find his way back to the tower; it was at least a mile away.

They walked past women lighting lanterns and men returning from work. At the end of the street was a quay where fishermen were unloading their catch. They went to look at the contents of the baskets and saw fish, crabs and lobsters, only a few of which were still moving.

Indavara doubted if Mahalie had said more than ten things all day. He couldn't think of much more to say himself so was almost relieved when a lad carrying a tray of cakes came past. For once he wasn't hungry but he bought two and they ate them sitting on an upturned rowing boat.

'Why did you help me?' she asked when they had finished.

'Just . . . I don't know . . . because I could.'

Because no one helped me.

She wiped crumbs off her mouth. 'You said you were a slave.'

'A fighter. For six years. I won my freedom.'

'I cannot repay you.'

'Seeing you happy will be enough.'

And so she gave him a smile.

'What about before?' she asked. 'Before you were a fighter? Where are you from?'

'The sun is almost down. I must go. May I come and see you tomorrow?'

'Of course,' she said. 'Please. I don't know anyone else.' She pushed her hair out of her eyes and looked out at the sea.

Thank you, my Fortuna. Thank you, thank you, thank you.

Cassius got up and walked over to the door. 'What do you mean, there's no one there?'

Simo moved aside so he could look through the spyhole. Cassius couldn't see much because of the fading light but there indeed seemed to be no one outside the door. He stepped back and exchanged a blank look with Simo.

Then came another knock.

'Who is it?'

'You *are* there, sir.'

Cassius checked the spyhole again. He could see two city sergeants armed with clubs and swords. They were standing too far back for him to see much of their faces.

'Yes. Who are you?'

'We were sent by Master Diadromes, sir. There has been an attack on the barracks – nothing too serious but he wanted to post us here just in case.'

Cassius reached for the top bolt, then hesitated. He looked through the spyhole again. 'Have I met you two?'

'You've met me, sir,' said the second man. 'It's Vespilo.'

Cassius glanced at Simo then let out a sigh of relief. He unbolted the top, Simo did the bottom.

'So what happened at the barracks?'

'Some arrows were shot over the wall. No casualties.' When Vespilo came forward, Cassius recognised his face.

'Good. Any other problems?'

'No, sir. It seems Deputy Diadromes is on top of things. Is your bodyguard around?'

'No, but he'll be back soon. Simo here will bring you out some stew when it's done, how does that sound?'

'Certainly smells good,' said the other sergeant.

'Tastes even better, I assure you.'

Vespilo gave a nod and the pair set off back down the path. Cassius shut the door behind them.

He had no idea what time it was when he awoke. Inside and outside all was dark.

Simo was calling his name. He rolled out of bed and ambled to the top of the stairs. The Gaul was standing by the front door, holding a lamp.

'What is it?'

'Master Cosmas is outside, sir.'

'Well, let him in.'

Clad only in his sleeping tunic, Cassius held on to the wall

401

as he descended the stairs. By the time he reached the bottom, the sergeant was inside.

Cosmas turned and looked back through the doorway. 'Come inside, please. Come on!'

Cassius stood beside Simo as Cosmas pulled Mahalie in, then shut the door behind her.

'What's going on? Where's Indavara?'

Mahalie reached out to Simo and clutched his hand.

'One of our patrols found her wandering the streets.' Cosmas put a hand on her shoulder. 'Come on, girl. You must tell him what you told me.'

'They . . . they took him.'

Cassius felt his entire body shiver. 'What?'

'We were walking back to the inn. They came out of nowhere. Six or seven at least. He fought them, told me to run. By the time I reached the inn and looked back they were gone. He was gone.'

'She said they were all in black,' added Cosmas. 'Hoods. Not one of them said a word.'

Mahalie threw herself into Simo's arms.

'What will I do now?' she wailed. 'What will I do?'

The Gaul just stood there, comforting the girl, staring at his master.

'Sir,' said Cosmas, 'I've got a squad out there now. I've alerted all the sentries at the gates, we will do everything we . . .'

Cassius heard nothing more. He walked away and sat down on the stairs.

They were never after me.

They were after him.

Historical Note

As usual, I thought it appropriate to mention a few of the historical issues featured within the story.

It was indeed the case that after defeating the Palmyrans for a second time in 273 AD, Aurelian turned his attention to his enemies in Egypt. It is thought that the leader of the revolt there was a wealthy merchant named Firmus. The precise nature of the rebellion remains unclear, though we do know that widespread damage was caused in Alexandria and elsewhere. Aurelian dealt with the unrest swiftly before returning to Rome.

Readers of *The Imperial Banner* will recall the first appearance of Marshal Marcellinus. Aurelian did entrust the command of the East to a man of this name, though we know almost nothing about him.

The background to the Emperor's issue of coins was one of debasement and rampant inflation. Although the information about the XX mark is historically accurate (the majority view being that this signified a five per cent silver content), the code actually featured on the *antoninianus* – a coin worth two denarii. These had been in circulation for some time but I used the denarii for the sake of clarity and series consistency.

Aurelian expanded Rome's network of mints, particularly in the East. It is believed that the Tripolis mint was set up to produce coins celebrating the victory over Palmyra and fortify the troops before their Egyptian expedition. Like all emperors, Aurelian also wished to propogate his image and secure the loyalty of his men. The imagery of the solar deity featured on coins from this era exists as described. Readers of the previous book, *The Black Stone*, will recall that although fascinated by the religons of the East, Aurelian was careful not to favour them above the traditional 'great gods' of the Roman pantheon.

Counterfeiting was a widespread problem but generally more prevalent in the West, particularly Britain. Although coin production techniques were relatively simple, they were dependent on precise methods and expert practitioners; high-quality fakes were not easily created.

Berytus (modern day Beirut) was known as the 'most Roman' city in the East. From the third to the sixth centuries, the law schools trained so many officials and issued so many legal texts that it earned the title 'mother of law'.

Although the specific instance of civil unrest described here is an invention of mine, we do know that Berytus's weavers were a significant group and that the presence of Aurelian's army in the eastern provinces brought a variety of pressures. Protest and rioting was a fairly regular feature of Roman life and the use of soldiers to 'keep the peace' often inflamed febrile situations.

Acknowledgements

The Emperor's Silver was completed between February and September 2014.

Sincere thanks to the usual suspects:

My agent David Grossman – for help with everything relating to writing and publishing.

Editor Oliver Johnson – for help making book five as good as possible.

Anne Perry – for being supremely helpful and well organised.

All those historians whose excellent texts I made use of.

And finally my wife Milena – for putting up with my ramblings and the occasional rant.